SLEEPING LIKE THE ~~DEAD~~

Harry Conroy was downstairs listening to three weeks' worth of messages on the answering machine.

Upstairs, Ariadne Conroy unpacked with a vengeance. She emptied her two totes onto the bed and began to sort them into three piles, one for the wash, one for the dry cleaners, one for clothes that might only need ironing . . .

There was a strange smell in the room. Mice? The floral duvet was bunched. Lumpy. Ariadne stretched out a single finger and prodded it. She pulled back her hand instinctively and stepped away from the bed. Goose flesh tingled on her thin, bare, tanned arms.

She backed to the doorway and did not turn her head until she stood in the hall.

"Harry!" she called . . .

Praise for Ann C. Fallon's *Blood Is Thicker*

Books by Ann C. Fallon

Blood Is Thicker
Where Death Lies

Published by POCKET BOOKS

WHERE DEATH LIES

ANN C. FALLON

POCKET BOOKS

New York London Toronto Sydney Tokyo Singapore

This book is a work of fiction. Names, characters, places and incidents are either the product of the author's imagination or are used fictitiously. Any resemblance to actual events or locales or persons, living or dead, is entirely coincidental.

An *Original* Publication of POCKET BOOKS

POCKET BOOKS, a division of Simon & Schuster Inc.
1230 Avenue of the Americas, New York, NY 10020

Copyright © 1991 by Ann C. Fallon

ISBN: 0-671-70624-1

First Pocket Books printing June 1991

10 9 8 7 6 5 4 3 2

POCKET and colophon are registered trademarks of Simon & Schuster Inc.

Cover art by Richard Ross

Printed in the U.S.A.

For Mama

Chapter One

The unheated cab had reached the lights at the top of O'Connell Street before anyone spoke.

"Not bad time from the airport at the peak of the morning rush hour, even if I do say so meself!" The driver broke the silence.

"Thank God," murmured Ariadne to her husband, blowing on her fingertips. "If it takes much longer, I'll die of the cold."

Harry laughed and reached to put an arm around her shoulders, leaning across the soft luggage that was stuffed between them on the seat and that crowded round their feet.

"I don't need you, Harry! I have my luggage to keep me warm."

"For heaven's sake, Ari, it's only that we've been so bloody hot for the last three weeks. After all, it's spring now, not the dead of winter." He glanced through the window at his side, vainly trying to detect signs of a Dublin spring through the rain that coursed down and blurred his vision.

"Been off to one of them Canaries?" inquired the wizened driver, putting the stress on the first syllable.

"What? Oh!" replied Harry, startled into remembering there was another person in the car. "We were in Kenya, on safari," he added proudly, trying out the phrase, as if in practice for telling other and more important listeners.

"Jaysus! Shooting tigers with the darkies," exclaimed the man.

"No, we were on a photo safari. That's when—" But his explanation was lost as the driver took a very sharp and illegal turn that he explained would be a short cut.

Ariadne jabbed her husband. "Don't bother!" she whispered.

From the fashionable address, the amount of designer luggage, and the age of his passengers, the taxi driver, without undue shrewdness, hoped for a good tip. And so he pursued the conversation in a uniformly even tone. "Been gone some time, am I right?"

"Yes, yes," replied Ariadne. "And I must say it will feel good to get to the house. I'm sore all over," she added.

"From the camel rides, I'd expect."

"From your broken suspension, more like."

"Come on, Ari, it's not that bad," Harry addressed her.

"I just want to get home in one piece, if that's not too much to ask. And I'm worried about the house—not that you give a damn. You know I wanted that security system installed before we went. God knows, the place could be stripped bare."

"Look, what good was the holiday if you come back in just the same frame of mind? You know I scheduled to have it in place before we left. And you know they didn't come—"

"Typical!"

"I feel okay about it. I had them hold the mail at the post office. And we had the automatic lighting fixed up."

"You might as well take out an ad. 'Oh, look, the lights in Number 27 come on every night at seven o'clock on the dot.' For heaven's sake, Harry."

"Well, then, if anything had happened, Brona would have

2

contacted us. If the house was robbed, she would have let us know."

"Brona, humph. I doubt that girl would have the sense to notice if the house fell in on top of her."

Harry didn't rise to his wife's taunting. It had been a long, arduous flight from Kenya. After a two-hour delay they had spent six hours on the plane and then had a change at Heathrow. He was mightily glad the luggage had come through. He felt he couldn't have dealt with his wife's escalating irritation.

"Mmm," he answered absentmindedly, slightly worried himself about their home.

"Her name—what does it mean, anyway? After all these years I still don't know."

"Who? Brona? Oh, wind sprite or something like that."

"A bit Irish, isn't it? I mean for a Prod."

"I think her father or uncle or something was an Irish scholar. Anyway, what difference does it make? She's a good tenant."

"I suppose you're right. Even if we did inherit her."

Harry relaxed as his wife's tone eased up a bit. He watched her as she followed the driver's circuitous route, closing her eyes briefly when she saw they were drawing near their destination. The holiday had done her good, he mused. Her lightish brown hair was streaked by the African sun, and her long, lithe limbs were tanned and fit. Even the lines around her eyes and mouth had faded over the three weeks they were away. It had been a good idea, the best present he could have given her for her fortieth birthday. She was taking it so badly. He didn't remember taking it that badly when he hit forty two years before. She certainly hadn't thought he merited even a party, despite the fact that they had been invited to at least seven amongst their intimate circle of friends. He shifted in his seat as the taxi drew up at his front door. He was very glad they had tomorrow to get things into good order before work on Monday.

The driver outdid himself carrying their voluminous luggage up the eight wide granite steps. Ariadne stood clutching her own carrier bag full of souvenirs as Harry located his keys and attempted to open the door. The wind and rain whipped her hair into her eyes and mouth as she groaned audibly.

"I don't bloody know what's wrong with the door, do I?" Harry shouted into the wind.

The door had unlocked easily enough but seemed to be jammed from the inside. He threw his weight at it, conscious of the driver standing on the step beneath him. The door finally gave, but only a little.

"For Jaysus' sake!"

"I knew it!" screeched Ariadne.

"Wait, wait." Harry had squeezed in the narrow opening between the door and the surround only to discover a huge pile of mail. He began to kick it out of the way, pushing the door a bit wider. Inside at last, he bent down to dislodge the letters and papers that were still wedged underneath. Ariadne and the driver with the luggage forced their way into the parquet-floored hall, the April wind blowing the loose papers before them.

"That big brown envelope sticking out of the slot in your door was a dead giveaway. But not to worry," said the driver, watching Harry tug at a newspaper. "Sure you're home, and that's all that matters."

Ariadne had found her purse and was thrusting English pound notes into the driver's open hand. "Right, right, thanks very much," she said as she urged him out the door.

"All the best!" he called, and he smiled to himself as he heard it slam behind him at last.

"My God, the impudence," said Ariadne behind the closed door.

"Of whom? The Post Office?" Harry had straightened up and put the mounds of mail on the hallstand, where the more he stacked it, the more it fell off.

4

"No, you idiot, that driver. He was laughing at us, I tell you."

"So what if he was?" Harry replied, but he had been chagrined nonetheless. "Look. As he said, we're home." He stopped trying to stack the mail and went to embrace her, but she pushed past him.

"Just bring some of the bags upstairs, will you? I want to check the freezer, and then I want to get started unpacking. I daresay everything is wrinkled, and I want to do at least two washes."

Harry managed four of the large canvas and leather totes, two in each hand, and wearily climbed the stairs and landing to their bedroom. He tossed them on the bed, glad that his wife's natural efficiency would look after the unpacking and sorting. They passed each other on the stairs.

"That's bad luck, you know, Ari," he said lightly as she approached. "You should have waited until I came down."

"Your superstitions never cease to amaze me," she called over her shoulder.

"I don't think Africa made the least impression," he mumbled, and he jumped when she called over the bannisters, enquiring what he was doing now.

"Nothing, nothing. I'm just going to play back the tape."

Curious, yet methodical as always, Harry sat down carefully on the Hepplewhite chair beside the hallstand and drew out his Filofax from the pocket of his well-cut safari jacket. He took his pen, pressed re-wind, and leaned back to listen. There were, as he had expected, quite a few messages. One or two silly, jokey calls from his colleagues at the accounting office telling him that they knew that he would have tried the ground rhino horn or even steamed boar's snout, since he was badly in need of an aphrodisiac. Harry grimaced. The next two calls actually pertained to work and reminded even him, a most conscientious manager, of what lay ahead on Monday: a forthcoming audit that he had successfully put out of his mind for two of the three weeks. The remainder of the calls included four invitations.

"Ari, darling, what do you say to drinks tomorrow at Alex's?"

His wife came out to the landing and leaned over the bannister railing, looking down at the top of her husband's head and feeling yet again that slight shock of recognition that his brown hair was thinning.

"What is it?" she said more gently than she'd intended. "You've got heaps of faxes?"

"No, no, not faxes—Alex's—drinks at Alex's?"

"Listen, let me just unpack and I'll think about it." She returned to their bedroom.

By Dublin standards it was a large room. When they'd decided there'd be no children they'd knocked the small front bedroom and the larger back one into a single spacious bed-sitting room. The built-in wardrobes were a joy to Ariadne and had streamlined her homelife, as she told her friends. She unpacked with a vengeance, emptying the first two large totes full of her own clothes. Into one pile went the clothes for the wash, into another the clothes for the dry cleaners, into yet a third clothes that might need only ironing. Monday morning loomed large for her, too. Spurred on by the size of the piles, she turned her attention to her husband's two equally large bags. There was a strange smell in the room. A bad smell. Mice. Surely he hadn't laid traps in the bedroom? But now the smell seemed to be coming from the bags. It couldn't possibly be his socks! She started to pull the nearest bag over. But the bed was lumpy, and what she hadn't noticed before was that the heavy floral duvet she'd recently purchased at Brown Thomas's was bunched in some odd and inconvenient way. She dragged the two unopened bags off the bed and lowered them onto the pale rose wool wall-to-wall carpet.

She hesitated. It was almost as though there was a bag beneath the duvet. She stretched out a single finger and prodded it, and it was hard. She pulled back her hand instinctively and stepped away from the bed. She observed to herself there was something in the bed. Goose flesh tingled on her thin, bare, tanned arms. She backed to the doorway of the room and did not turn her head until she was out on the landing.

"Harry. Harry!" she called, her voice rising, but only slightly.

Harry noted the change at once. He'd heard that tone before. Mice! He cursed to himself. He thought he was finished with them. For all her independent manner Ariadne could not deal with mice. Or the thought of mice. Harry oftened wondered why he, who loathed the little beasts even more, was still called upon to cope with them. Rather a beast in the jungle, he laughed to himself as he climbed the stairs, than a mouse. Yes, he'd have fun telling about this Kenyan trip at the office on Monday.

"I'll get the traps now," he said quickly when he saw his wife's face white beneath her tan.

She touched his arm, also bare. Her fingers were icy cold.

"No, Harry. It's not the wretched mice. I think there's . . . well, just come in and look."

Struck by her tone and demeanor, Harry felt none too brave as he entered their room, his eyes searching each corner and seeing nothing untoward. "What? What?" He seemed to shout in the stillness.

"The bed, damn it. Look at the bed. Didn't you see it when you brought up the bags?"

"See what? No, I didn't see anything." He approached the bed.

"That, do you see that lump?" The bulge seemed to have grown gigantic to Ariadne. "What is it?" she fairly shrieked.

They approached the bed together, and Harry cautiously but firmly lifted the duvet from the top of the overstuffed pillows and drew it down to the footboard in a single slow motion.

"Good God," he whispered hoarsely.

Ariadne, her hand to her mouth, shook her head in horror before turning aside.

Lying on their bed was a naked man, his head cradled in

the valley between their two pillows, for all the world in a deep sleep. Except that he wasn't. And the smell was overpowering.

Harry closed his eyes. He thought he was going to be sick. He exhaled the stench from his nostrils and breathed through his mouth. He opened his eyes. But the body came back. And so did the smell.

"By all that's holy . . ." He turned and stared at his wife's stricken face. "Ari? Ari . . . do you know him? My God, who is it?"

She shook her head slowly, her hand and arm moving stiffly with the motion of her head, as though welded together. He pulled her hand away from her mouth.

"I don't know, God, I don't know. He looks somehow, somehow familiar, but God, I don't know."

Without looking again at the body, Harry pulled the duvet back up over it. Keeping his head averted, he pushed Ariadne backwards out of the room.

"He's dead, isn't he?" Ariadne said, leaning on him.

"Yes, poor bastard," Harry said gruffly. And awkwardly, when Ariadne wasn't watching, he furtively crossed himself.

Chapter Two

About the same time that Harry and Ariadne were changing planes at London's Heathrow Airport, James Fleming, solicitor and owner of the small law firm formerly known as Fitzgeralds, was stoking coal in the light of a very watery dawn.

Stripped to the waist, he shovelled the rough-hewn coal and hurled it with vigour into the furnace of a Beyer Peacock 4-4-0 steam engine, built in 1913, and the prized possession of the Carlow County Railway Preservation Society. And as the fire howled it turned water to a powerful head of steam for what was to be the last run of the day. An eager crowd of twenty men and two women were either busily working at their assorted tasks or posed with cameras at the ready. Mementos of a glorious week.

The weather had been mild and fair for six of the seven days, and the small but energetic band had enjoyed their time spent working on their pride and joy. At night, in their cozy country hotel, there'd been gaiety and swapped stories, albums of photos of other train fests in Ireland and abroad. Friendships were formed or renewed, and amiable disputes had taken place over the varying merits or otherwise of certain steam engines. The drink was mighty, and the gossip, too.

As the train pulled up to the platform for the last time the crowd applauded. James stepped down off the footplate. Sweat still poured off him, and his muscles rippled across his chest. A fellow train enthusiast tossed him a towel, and he was grateful, for the air was chill.

The little group cheered the train driver, who nodded and then called out, "And a round of applause for this morning's stoker!"—much to James's delight. He bowed, laughing, gracious. He had been waiting all week for this opportunity to prove his mettle. Grinning broadly, he clambered back on board for the final run to the housing where they would prepare the train for its rest, storing it safely until the next outing two months off.

James sighed. It had been glorious. Wonderful physical exercise. He felt fit and trim and full of energy. His mind was clear and free from both the pressures and the minutiae of his present life. Hell, it wasn't Peru. He couldn't have done the Peruvian train trip in a week! But it had been great nonetheless.

His latest Citroën ate up the smooth road that led him from Carlow back to Dublin and his flat in fashionable Leeson Park Towers. It felt strange to him to be moving at such enormous speed after a week travelling sedately back and forth on the preserved line of the old steam railway. Ah, a more leisurely age. And thus more civilized. In some ways at least. And he grew nostalgic for a time in his country's past that he had never known. A time without faxes and carphones. But this did not occur to him as he dialled his own telephone number and keyed his answering machine to give him the messages that might have been left. None.

Too good to be true. Indeed, glad as he was not to have had urgent messages from his office, he was slightly disappointed that in one whole week there had been no social calls.

He let himself into the flat, which seemed strangely unfamiliar after so short a period. He was glad he had had the cleaning woman take it in hand while he was away. Perhaps, he laughed aloud to himself, that was why he didn't recognize it.

As he showered and changed into well-cut, wide-wale brown cords and a heather-flecked Aran pullover he debated as to how he would spend his Saturday night. He felt good, ebullient. And he didn't want to lose the mood. And he would, if he spent this evening alone. But there was no special woman in his life now. And there hadn't been since Sarah. He blocked the thought of her quickly. He'd been doing well over that. Pretty well.

He was so fed up with the singles scene. He idly thought of Maggie. Lord, how could he date his own secretary! The office would be buzzing, and . . . no, it would just complicate matters.

His irritability was rising as he found Matt's telephone engaged. It was a bloody long shot anyway. Dorothy would never let him out on a Saturday night. It was probably bath night for their eighteen children. As he slammed the phone down for the third time it rang, startling him so that he looked at it questioningly before he answered.

"Fleming here," he said suavely, recovering his composure on the instant.

"Fleming, ah, Fleming. So glad I reached you. This is Harry Conroy."

"Ah, Conroy . . ." James thought wildly. "Conroy, I'm not sure I—"

"We met a few times, at parties, social things at Kevin's. You know, Kevin Abercrombie, the solicitor. I believe you know him, but he's out of the country at the moment. And well, frankly, I didn't know anyone else to call. Your name came to mind because of that murder thing you were involved in a year or so ago. . . ." The sentence hung in the air as James closed his eyes, a hot flush rising to his neck and face.

"You need a solicitor?" he said, but his voice was very cool.

"Well, this is so damned awkward to explain. Yes, I do, but on sort of an informal basis."

"What do you mean . . . informal?"

"Oh, God, it's just that, you see, there's this body in my house. And the police have been here all day. I hardly know what to say. We just got back from Kenya, and—well, can you help me?"

James heard the anxiety in the man's voice. He tried in vain to recall this Harry person from Kevin's parties. All Kevin's parties were the same, and so were the guests. Boring. One did not stand out from any other in his recollection.

"Listen, Harry, I'd like to help, but—"

The 'but' was lost on Harry as he thanked him profusely and rapidly gave him his address.

"Right," said James wryly. "I'll be round straight away."

After all, it wasn't far, he rationalized. And he was curious. If Harry had just returned from Africa, how had a body managed to be in his house? Given the neighbourhood, the likelihood was that it was a burglar. Not quite what he had pictured for his big night out!

Events had moved very quickly at Harry and Ariadne's house after they had recovered themselves enough to ring for the police. The first to arrive in answer to their rather garbled call was a young policeman assigned to the local area. He saw at once the situation was beyond his scope and phoned for the appropriate assistance. He kept Harry and Ari confined to their own sitting room, where he watched as they poured each other large brandies and held hands in silence on the sofa. Guilty, he mused. Just be the looks of them.

Moments later Harry and Ari's sedate house was invaded by police in plain clothes. Both were startled by this, and at the same time considerably relieved. And they were grateful, too, that they were ignored while men sped past the door and up to their room to take pictures and fingerprints and perform sundry other tasks. They were largely ignored as the medical man went up and remained there for a very long time. But they listened carefully as the original policeman read his notes in the hall to yet another man, superior to him in rank.

After a second brandy they even began to think that their lives would resume a normal pattern. They failed entirely to take note of the air of excitement that gradually filled the house, signalled by increased activity and intense whispered conversations. Out of the blue Ari told Harry that she would never sleep in that room again, or, for that matter, on that floor of the house. Harry grew whiter at this news, and his mind raced ahead to assess the property values as he tried to pin down in his swirling thoughts whether house prices had recently been going up or down.

Then the police inspector entered the sitting room, sat near them on a footstool, and began to ask questions. He seemed to ask them repeatedly the dates they were in Africa, flight times, arrival times, departure times. Harry could sense Ariadne growing angry and impatient, and he asked if he could consult his Filofax still lying beside the phone in the hall. Yet again Harry gave the same information, reading from his diary until his interrogator left to confer with the medical authority in the hall, a grim, tall young man.

A third brandy sustained Ariadne as men arrived and bore the body in a bag of some sort down her hall stairs and past her sitting room door. She rose to close the drapes against the failing afternoon light and averted her eyes from the sight of the body being placed in a police ambulance as a knot of curious on-lookers gathered eagerly at the bottom of her steps.

"Harry! They're all out there staring at the house! I can't

13

bear it." Her voice trembled. Harry heard the anger, but the inspector read it for nerves.

"They'll go soon, I expect, when there's nothing left to see. Anyway, we'll be questioning all your neighbours. This could never be kept under wraps."

"Then while you're at it, why don't you question that silly chit in the garden flat, instead of putting us through this inquisition?"

"Garden flat?" The inspector's voice was sharp.

Ariadne was about to answer when there was further whispering in the hall and a short, slim man, older than the inspector, entered quietly. The younger man nearly snapped to attention.

"Oh, Chief Inspector. I've been attempting to get statements from these two." He waved his pencil in the Conroys' direction.

"Who are?" The Chief Inspector's curiously mild voice held a reproach.

"Pardon me. Chief Inspector Molloy, this is Mr. Harry Conroy and his wife, Ariadne Conroy, the owners of this house, and the people who discovered the body."

"My, my. Most unfortunate, most unfortunate. A shock for you both, I would imagine." His voice was like balm to Harry's troubled mind, and he felt the rigidity leave his muscles. Ariadne remained, however, stiff as a poker.

"May I sit down?" the Chief Inspector smiled benignly at Ariadne. "Mrs. Conroy?"

"Oh, by all means," she replied, but her tone belied her words.

"Listen, my boy," said Molloy to his junior, "you get on with things upstairs. See this is all tidied up. These poor people are tired, as you can see. I'll read your typed notes when I get back to my desk."

Molloy sat down, glancing casually around the room, at his ease. "Pleasant. Very, very pleasant." His small, shrewd bright blue eyes gazed at the mantel. "You've kept the Georgian ambiance without making the room a period piece. A mistake," he said directly to Ari, "to make a house a museum. Common, though, don't you find?"

Nonplussed, Ari didn't answer. She watched as he stood to study more closely the prints near the mantel.

"Fine, very fine. Mezzotints. Inherited?" he said as he removed his coat and sat again, crossing his legs, as though a new but comfortable friend.

"Inherited?" Harry repeated. Stupidly, he realized. "Ah, no, we bought them in London, of all places, although they are of Irish provenance. But you know that. . . ." His voice trailed off as the older man nodded slightly, somehow sagely. Harry couldn't shake the feeling he was looking at some well-bred country priest.

"London. But of course. And what do you do?"

"Do? Oh. Do," said Harry. Ariadne winced at this newly developing habit of repeating everything.

"I'm an accountant, with Price Waterhouse."

"I see."

"What exactly do you see?" Ariadne's voice was edged with sarcasm, and Harry was startled. But Molloy only bent his mild gaze in her direction, easy, calm.

"That your husband is quite successful financially. That it's likely you bought this house and furnished it together. That neither you nor he inherited it or the antiques. That very possibly you also work, perhaps at an equally lucrative profession about which you will in due course tell me. That from the lack of photos or noise or telling signs, you don't have children. Unless you married extremely young and he or she or they are away at college." He smiled, and the gentleness of the smile took the sting out of the observations.

But Ariadne was not impressed as Harry was. She didn't respond.

"And do you?" The mild voice was relentless.

"Do I what?" Ari forced the issue.

"Work, at paid employment?" he qualified the question.

"Yes." She waited.

Molloy then asked if they minded if he smoked. It was, he was afraid, a pipe. But the aroma was mild, and the scent didn't linger. He wasn't apologetic. And Ari agreed. How could she not, with Harry's row of pipes displayed prominently on the now-open rolltop desk in the corner?

They sat in silence. Pale blue smoke curled up from Molloy's pipe as he settled himself in the fireside chair. Ariadne wanted to scream.

"I'll get straight to the point. You've been away in Kenya for three weeks. During that time a man was murdered and placed in your marital bed. Even superficially we can determine he was killed elsewhere, about a week to ten days ago. We will ascertain that you were where you say you were"—he raised his right hand in a mild gesture, gentle but firm—"please, Mrs. Conroy, do not be so quick to fly on the defensive. I am assuming you are telling me the truth. Let us proceed together from that premise, yes?"

Ariadne nodded. Harry nodded, too, feeling foolish and young, like a boy being reprimanded.

"Am I right that you went through the house to see if anything is missing?"

"Yes." Harry was eager to help, eager to answer his interlocutor. "And there isn't."

"Well, we went through the house with your . . . men," Ari added, tilting her head towards the doorway where now all but one of the police team were preparing to leave. "But Harry," she addressed only her husband, "we didn't look in our bedroom."

Harry blushed.

Molloy stood up and courteously waved them ahead of him, and the three slowly proceeded through the now darkening house to the upstairs room. Ari paused at the doorway, revolted, but Molloy gently armed her in.

"I do understand," he said softly, but she shook his arm off. Harry was in a paroxysm of embarrassment at his wife's rudeness but held his tongue. They both moved slowly around the room, each checking individual drawers, belong-

16

ings, jewel cases, valet boxes. Molloy stood unobtrusively by
the door watching them, but never being seen to do so, and
said nothing when Ari whispered to Harry.

"What?"

"My golf trophy," Ari said more distinctly. "It was here
on the mantel." She indicated the narrow white mantel of
an intricately decorative iron bedroom fireplace that had
once been the room's only heat in the early days of this
nineteenth-century house.

Harry glanced wildly around. "You're sure?" he whispered. She nodded and glanced over Harry's shoulder at
Molloy.

"It seems, Mr. Molloy, that a trophy of mine is missing. I
am quite certain it was on this mantel when I left the house
three weeks ago today," she said clearly.

"A plaque, perhaps?" said Molloy without interest.

"No, it was a figure of a female golfer with a driver, I
think, or a putter—no, how silly, a driver, raised as if to
strike—I mean swing. It was fairly standard in style, I
should think."

"A wooden base, perhaps?"

Ari noticed he had put his pipe away. He hadn't been
smoking in her bedroom.

"No. A marble base, oh, p'raps two or three inches high."
She looked at Harry for confirmation, and he nodded at
Molloy, not at her. She grew more furious.

"The figure was perhaps six inches high, and the base was
about three. It was an expensive trophy, and I'm proud of it.
I received it last summer at Palmerston Golf Club. But I
hardly think it was worth anything to a burglar."

"I see. Then shall we go down? Sadly, my men will be
returning to do a complete inventory of the house. Perhaps
at that time you could provide them with a photograph of
the trophy. Possibly your picture was taken with it when it
was awarded to you?" Molloy let the question hang in the air
as he preceded them out of the room.

They returned to their seats in the sitting room. Both

Harry and Ariadne sagged as Molloy explained his men would also be doing extensive tests of items, such as the carpet in the bedroom and on the landing. He explained softly that their room would now be sealed off, and that they would have to sleep in another room, indeed in another place. As long as they let his office know where they could be reached at all times. Molloy's eyes narrowed when Ariadne snapped that they could stay in their own flat below stairs if it weren't for their tenant.

"A sitting tenant, perhaps?" asked Molloy, intrigued at Ariadne's obvious irritation.

"Well, yes, in a manner of speaking." Harry hastened to explain. "When we bought this house about six years ago the garden flat had long been converted, legally I might add, from what would have been the kitchen and maid's room and so forth. It is rather nice, actually. Our tenant was already living there, and we simply kept her on. She's a most respectable young woman who pays her rent and gives us not the slightest trouble." He glanced at Ari as he continued, but she merely shrugged. "She is a graduate student at the College and leads an exceptionally quiet life."

"She keeps cats," said Ariadne.

"A garden flat? Does it have direct access into the main part of the house?"

"That's a yes-and-no answer. There is a door at the top of the stairs, what would have been the communicating door between the ground floor and this floor when the house was all one. It's locked on both sides, her side and ours. I don't think it's ever been opened since we've been here." He looked at Ariadne, and she nodded in agreement.

"This flat, I take it, has a separate entrance?"

"Yes, at the front. There was once a back door, but that has been reconstructed, walled over in fact—also before our time." Harry lifted his hands in defense. "I know, I know, it probably doesn't meet today's building codes, but it was approved then."

Molloy shrugged "That's not my concern," he said,

moving on to question them in detail about their return from Dublin airport and what they did when they arrived home.

"Did you get a good look at the man in your bed?" he asked finally.

"It's hard to say, Chief Inspector. I suppose I looked at him for a few seconds, but the shock was tremendous. And the stench! I was trying to take in the fact that he was not only there, but also dead." Harry sighed and stood up, flexing his legs. Exhaustion showed plainly on his face. "He was naked. It was the corpse of a naked man in our bed."

"And you did not know this man?"

"No."

The phone in the hall rang brightly, and Harry stiffened, reluctant to answer it. Molloy went out and picked up the receiver. He lifted his hand to indicate it was for him, and Harry trailed back to the sofa. The room was dark, and Ariadne was switching on lights and plumping pillows restlessly, vaguely. Molloy returned and sat down again. Her sigh was audible.

"Just one more question, I'm afraid, and then perhaps we'll conclude for today." He paused briefly. "Do either of you know, or know of, an Englishman named Philip Shaw?"

Ariadne's mouth dropped open. "Oh, my God!" she said, staring at Molloy. Harry stared at her.

"You know that name? Is that the name of the man upstairs?" Harry looked wildly from his wife to Molloy and back. "Ari?"

"Do you know the name, Mr. Conroy?"

Harry shook his head and then hesitated. "No, at least I don't think I do."

Ariadne was still standing.

"I thought he looked familiar," she whispered, more to herself than to anyone else.

"And yet just moments ago you said quite firmly you didn't know the man in your bed." Molloy's ironic tone was not lost on Ariadne, and she recovered her composure.

"I didn't. How can I explain? Like Harry, I only looked at his face for a second. It was the fact that he was dead, you see. I was trying to grasp that a man was dead in my . . . room. For a split second it passed through my mind that he was familiar, the way . . . you know." Her voice grew stronger. "I'll tell you. It was as though I knew him, perhaps from the bank. He was familiar the way you might see your bank teller in a pub and think to yourself, oh, I know that face. But you don't know how you recognize it, or where you've last seen it. And yet you might have seen that very face only the day before. But because he wasn't in his usual surroundings—the bank—then you can't place him . . . that sort of thing. . . . " She trailed off.

Harry had listened intently. "And was he the bank teller—from the bank?" he asked Ariadne.

Molloy said nothing as she shook her head impatiently.

"No! I'm using that as an example." She turned to Molloy. "I meet quite a few people in my job—"

"Which is?"

"I produce radio and television ads for one of the big ad agencies. I meet clients, I meet friends of clients, I meet friends of the people I work with. Just going down in the lift I'll meet people from other floors. That's all I'm saying. I see lots of people come through the various studios where we record, other agencies' clients or staff, voice overs."

"Voice overs?"

"The actors who perform the ads. It's slang, I suppose, to refer to them by what they do. It's their voices that are recorded and laid on the sound track—you know, with music, sound effects, and so on."

"But Mr. Shaw was none of those persons you've just listed. Was he?"

"No, of course not."

"How exactly, then, Mrs. Conroy, did you 'know of' Mr. Shaw?" Molloy glanced surreptitiously at Harry and for the first and only time felt sorry for the man.

* * *

"Where is Ariadne now?" said James. It was almost nine o'clock, and he'd just arrived at the Conroys' house. Harry was summarizing the day's events.

"She's in our den, as we call it." He indicated over his head. "There's a room on the top floor we fixed up as a more casual kind of place, to relax. It's got a great view," he added vaguely. "She needed to lie down, felt a migraine coming on."

Pity, thought James. He was sorry he couldn't at least meet Ariadne. He had no real sense of this woman Harry was discussing.

Harry got up to shut the door, to drown out the mini-vac the forensic team was using on the stairs' carpet, monotonously droning over every inch of it, but he lowered his voice nonetheless. "She's had a double shock in a way. To cut a long story short, it seems Ari—Ariadne, that is—once knew this fellow Shaw. She'd started to do a graduate course in media at Preston University, on the west coast of England. A small modern university. After she'd got her bachelor's at Trinity here in Dublin.

"You see, I didn't know her then. We met about ten years ago. Long enough, I guess, but I don't know all the details of her past life. She'd started on this media course, and she took an elective class in the English Department. Shaw taught it. She didn't finish out his class, or the course for that matter. Decided it was too academic, as she told Molloy tonight. She wanted to get real experience and eventually got hired in an ad agency in London, and a couple of years later she returned here. She's still in the same field. She's not English," he said irrelevantly.

James shrugged. It was so late, and he could see Harry was terribly tired. And worried.

"Look," he said at last, "Molloy did not charge your wife. He's gathering information, that's all. It seems more serious than it is right now because of the terrible day you've both had." He nodded in the direction of the hall. "And you're still not being left alone. It's good that you called me. I'd like

21

to speak with Mrs. Conroy tomorrow if possible, or even be present if Molloy wishes to talk with her again." He stood up to leave, hoping that he had been reassuring. "We'll keep it informal, as you said on the phone. There's no need now to retain me."

Harry latched on to the word "now" with panic in his face.

"Harry, get some rest, will you? Take two whiskies and call me in the morning." James slapped him heartily on the back, and Harry managed a weak smile in return.

As James started the Citroën, and it rose on its unique hydropneumatic suspension, he studied the facade of the lovely old house, three floors over a full basement. Beautifully restored, with the brickwork pointed and the paint in perfect order. Money and care had been spent. But with what end in mind, James wondered, and his thoughts ranged over the information he'd just been given.

He sped off down the quiet street, anxious to get to the flat to see if his cleaning woman had tossed out all of his newspapers, hoping against reason that she'd left the relevant ones intact in the untidy pile beneath his desk in the study. Bells had been ringing ever since Harry had mentioned Philip Shaw. The story had broken just before he had left for Carlow. And subsequent events had been a topic of conversation all week.

He thought of Harry and Ari, a laugh coming to his lips at their rhyming names. Mustn't jump to conclusions, very unwise. Mustn't leap to judgment, very unprofessional. But in his gut he felt, like the young policeman, that they were guilty be the looks o' them. It was the how, even more than the why, that fascinated him.

—— *Chapter Three* ——

James appeared on the steps of the National Library promptly at its Sunday opening time of one o'clock. A thorough search of his flat had revealed that his stash of newspapers had been efficiently disposed of in his absence. After a restless night he was further disappointed to discover the newspaper morgues would not allow him in to see their back issues, even though he had proferred money at the door of one of the big dailies.

The day was still young, and the morning glorious. Washed by an early shower, the city of Dublin was looking its best under a canopy of pale, cloudless blue. The brisk April air washed his face, too, and made it tingle, made him glad that he had worn his brown tweed suit. Appropriate, he had thought, for his first, yet still to be arranged, interview with Ariadne Conroy, someone whom he could not but think of as a prospective client for the firm.

The papers of barely two weeks ago were already on microfiche, and James scanned the pages on the screen in front of him. The story was still fresh in his mind—in fact in almost everyone's mind, certainly in Dublin. But he wanted to pin down what hard facts might have been contained in the reports before he met with Harry again.

James had guessed from Harry's demeanor of the night before that he was completely unaware of the story that had been featured in every newspaper in the city during the second and third weeks Harry was in Kenya. Until he clapped eyes on Ariadne he couldn't be so sure of her. Molloy hadn't told them. Clever bastard, thought James admiringly. Wanting to see if they gave themselves away. Would the story have travelled as far away as Kenya? Could the Conroys have picked up Irish or English papers on their "escape-away" trendy sun holiday, far from the cares of their working lives? All questions to be answered, and soon, he hoped.

There. The headlines leapt out of the front page of the first evening paper to carry the story.

"Englishman Missing." This brief report in descending order of heavy type merely stated the first dribble of information. An Englishman had left home from the town of Leston and was en route to Dublin. He had taken the Holyhead-Dublin ferry, boarding at or at least intending to board at Holyhead on the Thursday sailing. His family had not heard from him since he had left his home that morning.

The Saturday morning papers held a few more hard facts. The man had been reported missing by his wife when she didn't receive a phone call telling her of his safe arrival in Dublin. The paper quoted the local English interview with her and showed a blurry photo of a frizzy-haired woman and her teenaged daughter leaning on her shoulder. This interview announced that the missing man, Philip Shaw, had not booked accommodation in Dublin in advance, and, said his wife, "he promised he would let me know where he was staying as soon as he was booked in."

National English papers reported the story briefly and immediately suggested the question of an IRA involvement. But regional English papers of the same dates carried the story at more length, under banner headlines such as

"College Professor Missing." And one scruffier paper ran the headline, in bold, "Find My Father, Teenage Girl Pleads with the Irish Nation." James grimaced.

The following Tuesday the headlines hit again. "Englishman Jumps Overboard," screamed one. "Foul-play Not an Issue," said another. It had come to light that the missing man's overcoat, wallet, and other unnamed items had been discovered on the ferry, albeit a few days later. Explanations would be forthcoming from the authorities.

James considered what he had learned.

In sum, Philip Shaw, married, living in the university town of Leston, and teaching English there, had told his family and colleagues that he was going to Dublin in connection with his work. He was a lecturer in English, and in good standing with his small university. Apparently Shaw had boarded the ferry. His ticket was in his wallet when it was found, and two witnesses had come forward to say they remembered seeing him at the bar, ordering a drink. They had stood near him in the queue.

No one had seen anyone or anything go overboard. The decks had been unusually quiet, according to the staff, on account of the persistent rain.

The authorities in England had accepted the story. James noted a memorial service was held at Shaw's college shortly after the announcement of the suicide. The wife and daughter had refused to comment except to say they were grief-stricken and puzzled.

You're not the only ones, thought James. And he pictured the frizzy-haired wife probably at this minute being told by the local English constabulary that her husband's body had been found. And not floating in the Irish Sea!

The more James thought about it, with the benefit of hindsight, the more he realized the case for Shaw's suicide had been thin. There was no note, no body. On the other hand, the case for a disappearance wasn't so thin.

How many people had just walked off, out of their lives and into others, starting afresh somewhere else? Untraceable, not on account of their amazing cleverness but by the simplicity with which it was done. Men and women walked off weekly, if not daily, never to be heard from again. They might pop up in Canada or Australia years later, married bigamously, happy, working. Those were the details that amazed James. He had encountered two such cases in his career as a solicitor specializing in wills and estates. It was never how they got away. It was what they did when they got there!

Philip Shaw had intended to go to Ireland and had a reason to go there. More than that James could not establish.

He sighed and stretched his arms up and back behind his head, releasing the knot of muscle between his shoulder blades. He took off his new and unfamiliar spectacles and rubbed his eyes. He was still unsure of these glasses. He put them on again and checked his reflection in the dark screen of the machine beside him. But cast back was the outline of a comical bookworm, and he laughed aloud, alone in the small, modern room off the more impressive main reading room.

He returned the microfiche to the attendant at the desk and went down to the basement level, circling down through the small but elegant rotunda, gliding his hands over the magnificent bannisters and his feet on marble worn smooth by generations. He made his call to Harry on the public phone beside the most beautiful men's "tilet" in Dublin, as one of his many ancient teachers in high school had described it. And so it was. Or had been. James didn't stop to find out if it, too, had been "improved."

Harry's voice was tired but keen. They were expecting Chief Inspector Molloy to arrive at four. James said he'd be round at three, and Harry agreed with alacrity. He walked to Harry's house. It was located in that part of the city known to all by its postal designation of Dublin 4, a short phrase that indicated its concentration of prosperity both old and new. Accordingly, James walked up Kildare Street, past the

Natural History Museum and the Dail—the seat of government—to Baggot Street. Passing his favorite pub, Doheny and Nesbits, he continued on to the more residential area, its Georgian architecture standing serene and stately without the workday hurlyburly of traffic.

He paused on Baggot Street Bridge, which spans the canal that circumscribes the inner rim of the city. The canal, full that day of spring rainwater, was sparkling, and he smiled at the ducks and their ducklings practicing their swimming in weekend peace. He followed the canal bank till he reached Percy Street. Here the houses had been either maintained or restored to what they once were, single-family dwellings. A mews ran behind them, with tiny garages that had once been stables, and which now stabled the Volvos and the Audis of the nouveau riche. Few people washed their cars on a Sunday anymore. But James smiled to see men of the older generation engaged in this time-honoured tradition of his youth. Buckets and rags and soap and glowering looks from his mother, James recalled. And his father ritualistically washing down the family car before the de rigueur family drive to the country for some air. Poor father, thought James, and, as was his custom, he shook the memory away.

He straightened his shoulders and his brown slub silk tie and lifted the heavy brass knocker that gleamed on the wine-red door, letting it fall once and heavily. Just a tinge of envy. A good address, an even better house.

"Come in. It's James Fleming, isn't it?" Ariadne opened the door wide and extended her hand to James as he entered. He was slightly bemused, expecting Harry and not this vigorous young woman. She stepped back to close the door, behind which her husband stood wiping his palm on his sleeve before he, too, shook hands with James.

"This way." Ariadne walked ahead of them into the sitting room, which glowed in the pale sunshine. Muted but rich brocade at the windows matched the carefully casual pillows and the paired Queen Anne chairs on either side of the fireplace.

"Drink?" she asked directly, standing near a fully laden trolley of glass and brass. The bottles and Waterford crystal twinkled, and James said he'd take a Cork gin and tonic. Wasn't that the expected, he mused. He accepted the drink, made in the colonial style: warm gin, a very little warm tonic, and a slice of lemon. The first sip brought back fond memories of a great bar in Kuala Lumpur, and he said so.

"Travelled much?" said Harry, ill at ease and gulping down his Ballygowan Bottled Water.

"Mmm, I think most people would say so. Not as much as I'd like, however. I sometimes think my passion for train travel is greatly at odds with my chosen profession. Not enough hours in the day." He directed his small talk at Ariadne but failed to make eye contact.

She sat at last and finally looked up at his face as he stood at ease, his height allowing him to lean an elbow on the mantel. "We're just back from Kenya," she said.

"So I understand from Harry."

"It was a great holiday, pity it's been ruined. Have you been there?" Harry began to unwind.

"Kenya? Yes, years ago now. I daresay it's changed."

James hadn't meant for his remark to sound quite as snobbish as it did, apparently implying to Harry that he'd been to Kenya before it had been discovered by the package-tour operators. He was sorry to note Harry's crestfallen face but said nothing.

"What can we do for you?" Ariadne asked abruptly.

"I think," said James, "it may be a case of what assistance I can render you." He placed his unfinished drink firmly on the coaster that stood at the ready on the low fireside table and sat down, leaning forward, his hands folded loosely between his knees. He studied their faces before he spoke. He had their attention.

"I think you might need a lawyer. I will explain that part later. Right now I want you to be very honest with me. It is crucial always, but especially now, because Molloy is coming here. And I'm afraid he knows a hell of a lot more about this case than you do." He paused as he noticed feverish red spots burning in Ariadne's pale cheeks. She sipped her mineral water and lemon.

"Go on," she said.

"Was either of you aware of this man's—Philip Shaw's —mysterious disappearance nearly two weeks ago?"

They shook their heads in unison.

"Was either of you aware that he had gone missing from the Holyhead to Dun Laoghaire ferry? And that after a few days it was thought that he had committed suicide by jumping overboard?"

"Is that why his body was naked—from being in the sea?" Harry jumped up quickly, as though filled with a sudden energy. James didn't interrupt. "If he killed himself, drowned himself, then—I mean, it's crazy, it's bizarre that his body was here. But it lets us out of the whole mess." He turned, glancing at James. "Right?"

James shrugged.

Ariadne was not as thrilled as her husband. "This is exactly what Harry says it is—bizarre," she remarked.

"Well, let me get back to that. Can you assure me you knew nothing of this incident?" James pressed on.

"Nothing."

"Be careful now. It was splashed all over the papers here and in England. First when Shaw went missing and was reported by his wife. And then again when evidence of his suicide was discovered—"

"Yes, yes, so?" said Harry, sitting down again heavily on the sofa.

"Did you happen to read about it? Or did any of the other people on your tour mention it, even in passing?"

"We were in Africa, for Christ's sake!"

"Then did you phone home?"

"Well, I can honestly say we bought no papers or even magazines when we were away," Ariadne said, easing back into the sofa. "And we didn't even listen to the radio or TV, which really only covered local affairs. You know, Kenyan news."

"You see, James," Harry interrupted, "when Ari and I do this sort of thing, get away like that, we agree together not to read newspapers or listen to radio or whatever. It's great. I recommend it. We've done it for years. Sometimes we take a little place in Connemara just for a week, you know. It's a great cottage. I can let you have details if you . . . well, anyway." He glanced at his wife, who seemed to James to be embarrassed.

But Harry barrelled on. "We spent a week without outside contact, and it was amazing. Connemara felt like another world, another time. It was like culture shock when we got back."

"Not as much of a shock as this, I daresay," said James dryly, and he caught Ariadne's small smile to herself.

"No, of course not."

"Good!" said James. "I needed to clear this issue up at once. I daresay Chief Inspector Molloy will be asking you the very same questions in a few minutes." He glanced at the ormolu clock on the mantel. "Yes. Now, I can stay with you when he arrives, if you want me to. But my presence . . ." James paused. Now he himself was unsure. After all, he mused, he hadn't a great deal of experience in criminal cases.

"Let me be frank. Perhaps my presence might signal to Molloy that you are on the defensive—"

"But on the other hand—" interrupted Ariadne.

"Yes, on the other hand, you did know this man Shaw at some point in your life. Obviously the police are looking for links, connections, something here in Ireland. . . ." He trailed off.

Ariadne looked at Harry and back at James. "I, for one, would like you to stay. I did know Professor Shaw. But that was a long time ago, and I've had no contact with him for eighteen years. But yes—" She stopped, startled by the doorbell, frightened suddenly.

They stood up of one accord, staring at one another as if in a stage play. James looked around for a way to escape, but Ariadne caught his look. "Stay, please," she said, putting her hand very softly on the cloth of his sleeve. He nodded and finally smiled at her. She returned the smile.

——— *Chapter Four* ———

In the end Molloy's dreaded visit had seemed to James to be perfunctory. He had treated James, whom he had not had occasion to meet, as a younger member of the Conroy family. Benign as ever, he spoke frankly in front of him. He asked again, as though he hadn't already been told, if either of the Conroys had known Philip Shaw. And Ariadne explained the circumstances in which she had been his student in England eighteen years earlier. She spoke simply, and James, watching carefully, admired her composure and the clarity of her description. Her story corresponded in every way with what Harry had recounted to James the evening before.

James then related to Molloy that he had told the Conroys about the newspaper reports of Shaw's suicide, and they affirmed that they had had no knowledge of it until then. Molloy seemed satisfied with their veracity. It was all somehow too cordial, too neat, to James's thinking. Molloy he knew by reputation to be a solid investigator, and as sharp as any barrister in his questioning techniques. James sensed Molloy would have more traffic with the Conroys, but he couldn't find a discernible reason for his own suspicion.

"Mr. and Mrs. Conroy," said Molloy as he stood, "I can now return the full use of your home to you. You understand, I'm sure, that we will need to keep for a while the mattress and other smaller items that have been removed."

Ariadne shivered visibly. "Please don't think of returning the mattress," she said with distaste.

"Indeed, I understand. Yes . . . well, that is all for now, Mrs. Conroy. I imagine that we will meet again."

Ariadne merely nodded as James saw Molloy to the front door, closing it with apprehension in his heart. It was time for him to be going also.

"I'll run you home," Ariadne said to him as he stood hesitating in the front hall.

"I'll do that, darling," Harry called from the sitting room, where he was stirring up the fire to a comfortable blaze.

Ariadne put a finger to her lips and glanced at James conspiratorially.

"I'd like the air, really, darling. I feel the drive would revive me," she called.

"Cheerio then, James," said Harry, coming to the door. "Thanks ever so much. I'm glad we kept things informal. I'd say that's the last we'll be hearing from the police."

"Mmm," murmured James, seeming to agree. But he had his doubts.

"Well, for heaven's sake man, what else can they want? We were both in Africa, and since neither of us is Houdini, we can hardly still be suspects. Right?"

"Right!" said James, and he ran down the steps under the protection of Ariadne and her enormous golf umbrella. They rushed along the lane to the mews that housed the Conroy Audi.

James admired the way she drove the car, easily and fast but in full control. "Did you grow up in the country, by any chance?" he said, laughing.

"Why do you ask?" she said, turning briefly to look at him.

"It's been my experience that women who learned to drive in the country tend to drive very fast, but generally very well."

"Point taken. It's true, I'm afraid. And you?"

"Suburban Dublin, born and bred." Very suburban, he thought to himself. "Did you really want the air, or did you have something you wanted to say?" asked James simply. She seemed relieved.

"Yes, actually, I did want to tell you something, and this is to you as my lawyer, for I don't see this as an informal arrangement."

"Go on," said James, his curiosity aroused.

"I didn't want to go into all this in front of Harry. He thinks the whole event is over and done with. And I hope so, too. But I am uneasy. You see . . ." She suddenly pulled the car to the side, along a stretch of pavement lined with early-blooming cherry trees. The wet petals drifted down and stuck to the windscreen, creating a pink-hued haven removed from the outside world.

She spoke. "This is rather difficult. As I said, I did know Philip Shaw when I was his student. But unfortunately I knew him on a personal level as well. I was young, but old enough to know better, I suppose. It's difficult to say now in hindsight. I was very free, very liberal. I thought. It felt great to be on my own, a carefree student in a new place, a different country, although we tend not to think of England as a foreign country.

"Anyway, Philip took a great interest in me and in my work, or so I thought. The media department was impersonal by comparison. I had done Honours English as an undergraduate, and I was flattered Philip thought so highly of my writing. And he was extremely attractive, in that academic way. All tweeds and pipe and beard, a bit scruffy, with wide, sad eyes. He always looked as though he were in

34

pain. Poetic pain, I used to call it. He was married, I knew that. But she wasn't his sort, he used to say. They were in debt—I think they had bought a house. Of course, he didn't earn much money, and I thought that he was terribly noble, being so committed to his teaching, to his poetry and all that. How can I explain? It all sounds so silly now, but I saw him as terribly romantic.

"We took long walks on the campus, and we began to meet at a local café. The whole thing lasted only a matter of weeks. He was giving poetry readings that term, outside of class. On the Romantics, of course, Shelley and Byron and so on. I thought he read so well, so passionately. I tried to drag along some friends from the media course. Few came. It wasn't their scene, but I wanted him to have support. He didn't draw crowds, I can tell you. But when he read he'd look right at me. I believed he was addressing all those golden words directly to me. But any girl would have done, I'm afraid, or should I say any girl as naïve as I was." She sighed and took a breath, the words having come out in a pent-up rush.

"Eventually he told me he needed me. It was just what I wanted to hear. I had digs in a fairly big house with a very disinterested land-lady, and we went to my room there. At the most half a dozen times. I thought it would be glorious, a coming together of two lonely, passionate souls, two hearts, two minds. Oh, Lord, I sound like a romance novel. However, it wasn't anything like that. He'd make love quickly, then he'd turn philosophical and take off. I was very confused. I thought we were beginning a real affair of the heart.

"And then I heard—from various girls who caught on to my feelings and what might be happening—that he was the campus Lothario. At the time it seemed that I was the only stupid girl who didn't know his reputation. Apparently I had fallen for his standard routine. One in a long line of fools. Or that's how I felt. I went to his office and had some dreadful scene—most out of character for me, I might add. I remember he just leaned back in his chair, tilting it on its back legs, and he smiled, or he shrugged. Whatever it was, I went blind with rage and embarrassment. Told him I hated him, that I had trusted him and he had abused my trust, my love. That sort of thing. I think he told me I was a silly Irish schoolgirl! And that the experience had done me a world of good.

"I was young, and it was pretty awful. I felt I couldn't stay in that place a moment longer. Everyone would know what a fool I had been. All my silly fancies. So I quit. I just packed up and left. I doubt now that it made any real difference to my career anyway. I landed an entry-level position at an ad agency in London, and things just moved along from there. But I was bitter and ashamed and embarrassed. I kept the whole story to myself, though. My family didn't question my leaving the course. They were only too glad that I was going to get a job and support myself. The people I knew at the university were new friends, acquaintances really. I didn't keep in touch with any of them. I think I was there maybe nine or ten weeks. A short, painful time leaving behind a painful memory. But up until a few days ago I hadn't thought of Philip Shaw in years. Certainly not since I married Harry. God, it's such ancient history. I don't like it suddenly rearing up now, following me out of the past."

"I need to be very clear about this—you're telling me you've had no contact with Shaw since then."

"Absolutely." She looked at him sharply.

"And you have no idea how he came to be in your bed."

"God, no!"

"And you never told Harry?"

"No, I didn't. I had put the whole affair out of my mind. And I don't want to have to tell Harry now."

"It was a very long time ago, Ariadne," James said softly. "Do you mind if I call you that?" He was distracted from his purpose, watching as she traced with a fingertip the outline of a petal on the glass.

"No," she answered without looking at him. "Please do. Call me Ariadne. I feel, I felt . . ."

"Yes?" he said, his anticipation surprising him.

"I felt that you were on my side—back home just now, with Molloy." Ariadne turned to look at him, her eyes suddenly brimming. She wiped them quickly. "It's the shock, I imagine," she said, her innate sophistication asserting itself.

"No doubt," said James, at a loss for words.

"Since we saw the—the body I have felt such a loneliness, such a sadness . . . it's hard to describe, James. You're not married, are you?"

"No, does it show?" James smiled.

"Frankly, yes. Married people—oh, how can I explain? James, when you're married you can be lonelier than you ever were when you were single. It's as though in sharing yourself, your entire life in marriage, you lose a part of yourself. That's great, grand really . . . but, there are times when for whatever reason the two people grow apart. There are silences that get longer, an awful emptiness. No one's fault. But it can just creep up and then pounce. Oh, dear, I'm afraid I'm rambling. I'm so very tired." She rubbed her face with her long, slim hands before she turned the ignition. "You're around here somewhere, right?"

James quickly gave her directions to his home.

As they pulled up to the kerb she sighed again, looking blankly in front of her.

"Come in, why don't you?" James said on impulse, reluctant to end their conversation.

She smiled wanly. "What, now?"

"Yes. You're cold, you're tired, I know, but perhaps a brief change of scene might help." James hopped out of the car and was around to her door before she answered. But she willingly followed him up to his large and comfortable flat.

He watched her as he stood at the kitchen bar, quickly grinding beans and heating water for their coffee.

She moved slowly around his spacious sitting room,

37

curious. Her unselfconscious sensuality was apparent despite her fatigue. She glanced with interest at the pictures on his walls, lingering over photographs and fingering the tell-tale trivia of someone else's life. He sensed her quick intelligence at work and felt vaguely vulnerable, as though somehow he were revealed too soon. Uneasy for a moment that the lines were blurring between his professional and personal interest, he turned his attention to the task at hand and poured the coffee.

Ariadne stretched out on his sofa, leaning on the corduroy pillows. She studied him as he handed her a cup.

"I shouldn't," she said seriously.

"I know, so I put just a dropeen of brandy in—for the cold, you understand."

"You sound like my granny in Mayo." She laughed a warm laugh rich with fond memories, and her smile made her beautiful.

"Do you visit her?" James said eagerly, longing for detail.

"Ah, no, she's long gone, like so many others. Oh, God . . . I'd better be going." She jumped up quickly from the sofa and snatched her coat.

"Ariadne." James put out his hand to stop her, touching her arm and pulling back quickly.

She looked him in the face.

"Take my card. Here, I'll put my home number on the back. You can ring me . . . any time. I hope you won't have to, I hope there'll be no need, but . . ."

She took the card wordlessly, lightly pressing his hand in farewell.

If she's this attractive under stress, thought James as he slowly closed his door, what must she be like in the good times? As he fixed a small salade Niçoise he pondered his attraction to her. After all, she's older than me, he muttered as he opened a bottle of burgundy and set it aside to breathe, then placed a shepherd's pie in the microwave. He shrugged, ever conscious of his age as time passed him by. And then there was her wit, her brightness. He watched the seconds ticking off on the digital display. And there was her physical grace, a certain knowingness, part of the allure, no doubt. He laid his place at the black glass table. But more than that there was a loneliness that he'd seen in her eyes, one that spoke to his own.

He took up the bottle of burgundy, poured a glass, and lifted it.

"Well," he said to her ghostly presence in his life, "Ariadne . . . are you telling me the truth? And how will I ever know?"

"I don't believe it!" exclaimed Matt as he banged down his pint glass of Guinness and wiped his mouth with the back of his hand. Foam now clung to his salt-and-pepper beard.

"What?" said James, laughing and leaning back in the snug of their favourite city pub, Nesbits. It was just big enough for two, three at a squeeze, and the cracked navy leather seats, and the wooden glass-rail turning white from years of watery rings, and even the scuffed and buckling hardwood flooring were like old, familiar friends. James tapped on the frosted glass serving hatch, twelve inches square, and it opened like magic. A voice emanated from it.

"Whad'll it be?"

"Two pints of stout, when you're ready," ordered James.

"How do these things happen to you? First the Moore case . . ." Matt lowered his voice as James put a finger to his lips and glanced over his shoulder, nervous still after all this time.

Matt went on sotto voce. "First that case all over the papers. High drama and what have you. And now another!" Matt exclaimed again. "Another case splashed all over the papers. I was reading of it only last week. The reporters described the house, the road, what Mr. and Mrs. you-know-who were wearing."

"I know, I know, they'd publish their bank balance if they could. Listen, Matt, the only reason I can discuss this with you at all is that I can keep it just to what the public already knows. She's my client, and the rest is confidential."

"Right, right, but my curiosity is killing me. You like her, I can tell."

James blushed, an unfortunate trait that still hung on from adolescence.

"I feel sorry for the poor English bugger. I take it that what the papers say is true. They don't have any suspect yet in his murder?" Matt asked, changing tack in mid-stream.

"No. No suspects. He was a professor of English. He'd published some good work. I checked it out at the library. Not my field, but it seemed substantial. Lots of literary criticism, that kind of thing, from reputable publishing houses, too. And he was coming over on academic business, you know. Apparently he was expected at the College, according to the newspaper confirmations. Perhaps he was scouting for a new job, but that's something I'll have to check out."

"If they'd made that clear at the time, perhaps the reports wouldn't have jumped to the conclusion of suicide," said Matt seriously. A teacher himself, he felt an empathy with the unknown Englishman. "If he was over here looking to change his job, he'd hardly have been a logical case for suicide."

"Hardly." But James made a mental note. If Shaw was in Dublin seeking a new job, it would answer at least one question.

"So what was the connection with the Conroys?" asked Matt, fishing again.

"Matt, that's not fair! Don't pry. I'm only dying to tell you, but you know I can't and won't. Listen, why don't you tell me about Dorothy. How is she keeping?"

"Grand, grand. Six months along and big as a house. Bigger than our house. I don't know where I'm going to stick another little tax deduction." But pride beamed out of every pore as Matt contemplated his next offspring in drowsy silence.

"Glad to hear it. And my godson, ah . . ."

"Mathew, Mathew! After Matt, your oldest friend. How the hell you can forget his name when he's named after me I'll never know, Fleming. I think it's a Freudian block."

"Either it's a mental block or a Freudian slip," corrected James jovially.

"Oh, so you admit it, then?"

"No, I mean—oh, for God's sake, here's a fiver. Give it to the poor little kid. I feel sorry for him with you for an ignoramus of a father."

" 'Paterfamiliaris' to you, chum. Father to one and all. If only it was really like that at my school. You know, Fleming, it's hard being vice-head. I've got all the work and none of the clout. I know how I could really put the school on the academic map. But I have to tend to the students' 'needs.' The bloody kids at school have me driven crazy with their angst and their moans. Half them drop out, and the other half get nervy over the exams. Spring is the worst. Hormones and homework just don't mix. Can't keep their attention for two minutes together. These damned mixed schools. Give me back the old days, the days of our glorious youth. That was the right way. Where we could be all boys together, all pimply-faced and sweaty, lying through our teeth about kissing girls, and all of us knowing we were only wishing it were true. Now they sit in class ogling each other across two feet of aisle space, pimples of both sexes notwithstanding."

"Matt, please," James groaned.

"What? It's true. Gross, as the Americans say."

"Girls in our day did not have spots."

"No, come to think of it, they didn't. What's happening, the downfall of Irish womanhood? Gone the fair lasses, the colleens of our younger days."

As Matt broke into the chorus of "Oh, the days of the Kerry dances, Oh, gone at last, like my youth too soon," James decided to call it a night.

A bit smushed himself, he drove carefully to Matt's house, where he revived with huge slabs of barm brack and a mug of tea and was treated to a view of Dorothy in her dressing gown, pink and plush, as it swelled over her burgeoning belly. He kissed her goodnight with a pang in his heart. Matt was already fast asleep at the kitchen fire.

Chapter Five

Brona O'Connell dismounted and leaned her heavy black bicycle against the wrought-iron railings that fronted the Conroy's house, Number 27 Percy Street. Extracting a key from the satchel that held her books safe from the evening drizzle, she unlocked the padlock of the gate and swung it wide, out onto the pavement.

As she did so she spotted, in the semi-darkness, a bit of limp white paper twisted around one of the pointed spikes, and she groaned. Carefully she lifted it off and put it into the deep pocket of her long oatmeal-coloured coat.

Tilting the bike at the optimum angle, discovered after years of trial and error, she heaved it down the worn stone steps to the small area at her front door. She unlocked the blue wooden door and pushed it into the hall situated under the flight of granite steps that ran up to the Conroys' front door. At last she shut her door against the cold and the rain.

Brona stepped directly into the large kitchen of her cozy garden flat and switched on the overhead light, then immediately went over and lit the small gas fire. Washing her hands at the sink, she looked at her reflection in the black window, its iron bars framing her small oval face. It had been a good day.

"James! Clarence? Mangan!" she called, and first one, then a second large cat came slowly padding into the kitchen from the dark passage that led off the room to the rest of the flat.

She rubbed their thick fur, one with either hand. "Hello, my little dotes. Where's your brother, then? Out on a skite, is he? Probably half drenched," she murmured on as she opened the tin of cat food. "Ahh, here he comes, the great traitor. James, you only love me for my food. Cupboard love, all of you!" But she smiled maternally as as they ate, neat, quiet, companionable.

Brona removed her coat when she felt the heat from the small gas fire in the wall finally penetrate the cold of rooms that had been unoccupied all day.

"Right, then," she said with renewed energy to the three cats who now sprawled beneath the two glowing red and white bars of the gas fire. "It's time to feed your mistress."

Ten minutes later she sat at one end of the long, smooth, worn wooden table. She took her white damask napkin from its wooden napkin ring and placed it over the folds of her dark blue-flecked heavy skirt and then ate her meal in welcome silence.

The house was quiet and peaceful once again, she reflected gratefully, and she hoped that the Shaw incident upstairs was over and done with. She wanted no more intrusions into her life, into her work, by the police or anyone else. Too much drama and excitement, too much distraction at this crucial time.

Suddenly the phone beneath the rear staircase gave out two shrill rings followed by two more.

"Blast!" Brona exclaimed as she moved quickly to the phone. She lifted the receiver and spoke her number slowly.

"Brona!" The voice was light but shrewish.

"Speaking."

"It's Geraldine, you twit."

"Sorry. I didn't get your voice," Brona sighed.

"And I suppose you didn't get my note asking you to ring me?"

"Note? Oh, was that the bit of paper?"

"Yes, I left it there when I was passing."

"Well, it survived the rain. But I was in such a hurry to get in out of the rain myself I left it in my pocket. Was there something urgent?"

"Of course it's urgent. I'm dying to see you, so you can tell me everything about the murder! The hospital is buzzing with it, but I was discreet, Brona, very discreet. I didn't even tell the other doctors that I'd lived in the Conroy house or that my old flatmate still lives there. But I'm bursting to know the details. I've been on a three-day rotation here, and this is the first moment I've had off. I was going to bring over a bottle of plonk. Or gin, if you prefer. And you're not busy tonight, are you? You're never busy on a weeknight."

Or any other night for that matter, thought Brona before answering. "I had hoped to get a few more pages done tonight."

"Good. They'll keep. You've got scads of time before your deadline. I'll be right over."

Brona smiled wryly as she hung up. Geraldine had the scientist's disdain for what time and effort it took to produce something of literary value or merit. If she had been facing her orals in biochemistry or pharmacology, Geraldine would be sympathetic. But Brona's research had never seemed very real to Ger.

She had barely finished tidying up her tea things before she heard the heavy sound of a car door slamming in the street above her eye level. Seconds later, as the taxi roared off, the bell rang, and Geraldine blew in the door, fresh-faced and vital.

"God, I've forgotten how pokey this flat is!" she exclaimed as she tossed her coat over a kitchen chair and monopolized the fire as she warmed her hands. "Honestly,

Brona, I don't know how you stand it. I don't know how I stood it myself." She laughed gaily.

Geraldine's manner and Geraldine's laugh had allowed her to say outrageous things from the first time she realized that they would get her anything she wanted from her extremely prosperous father. Brona shrugged, long inured to Geraldine's insults and most of her slights.

"So awful you stayed three years?" she said mildly.

"Not so bad, I s'pose. Fag?" She laughed as she offered Brona a French cigarette, her red polished nails catching the light. "No? Then glasses, and lemon and tonic."

Brona looked startled, but Geraldine merely produced the items from her vast black shoulder bag. All but the glasses.

"Brona, Brona. You never change. P'raps that's why I like you. I daren't ask why you like me. P'rhaps because I have such adventures." She lifted her pencil-thin eyebrows theatrically and fell into peals of laughter. "But now you've had an adventure of your own! Come, come, fetch the glasses, and let's get started. I have to be back in the Residents' Hall by eleven. Not even time to turn into a pumpkin. It's worse than when I was an intern."

Brona put out the glasses and the cutting board and watched while Geraldine expertly made their gins.

They settled at the table. Brona admired Geraldine's figure-hugging, red wool knit dress. Her bright red lipstick, finely applied, together with her thin eyebrows and blood-red fingernails, gave her a dramatic Twenties look. And she knew it. Geraldine never followed fashion. She knew what looked good and left it at that, having her clothes made when she couldn't find what she wanted in the better class of second-hand shops.

"Right! Now tell me everything, absolutely everything about the 'murther'!"

It was eight o'clock, and Ariadne Conroy deliberately stretched out on the sofa and laid her head back on the round mauve silk pillow. Her eyes were staring into the flames, unseeing. As stray drops of rain found their way down the chimney the fire hissed and called her back from her waking slumber. She tossed the glossy magazine she had been idly reading onto the fire. The usual trendy article on open marriages and old-fashioned adultery had disturbed her.

Memories of Philip Shaw haunted her thoughts day and night. It was better, though, when she was working, too busy to think except about this extended recording session at the Studios. It was one of the biggest jobs of her career. And she was thoroughly enjoying casting the voices for the radio ad and sitting in on the casting with the London fella who was directing the television commercials. But then suddenly the director's English accent would trigger thoughts of the dead Englishman in her bed. An Englishman she had known so intimately. Revulsion filled her, rising like nausea to her throat. But whether it was revulsion at his death or at his behaviour or at her own, she couldn't distinguish.

Her mind wandered to her present situation. Perhaps closing the room upstairs had not been a good idea after all. Even the closed door was a reminder each time she passed it. Sleeping in the long-unused guest room was bearable, but trying to find her clothes and all the paraphernalia from her dresser, now scattered throughout the other rooms, was intensely annoying. Harry was badly out of sorts. Orderly and habitual in his behaviour, he, too, was distressed by this disruption, but he said nothing, calm as ever. She glanced at the clock. She had been delighted that he had had to entertain one of the firm's big clients. A good heavy meal and a few drinks always made Harry mellow. And he felt free of guilt, felt he wasn't self-indulgent because it was for the firm. Always 'the firm.' His base, his rock, his total security.

"Fortunately his security isn't residing in me," she said aloud to the flickering flames. She sat up and leaned, face in hands, elbows on her knees. No, Harry dear, you never needed me, and I'm so glad . . . because if you had, this whole horrible mess would have destroyed you . . . and us. Her ears picked up the sound of a door slamming. Too early for Harry coming home, responsibly and safely in a taxi after his few drinks. Probably a stray cat come to be fed at that little twit's door downstairs. She walked over to the console television, but before she could turn it on and distract her thoughts, she was startled by a ring at her bell. In the stillness of the house it seemed abnormally loud.

"Who is it?" she called through the closed door, but all she could hear was the wind whipping the rain against the panelling. She turned the lock and opened the door slowly —just a crack—to see a woman sheltering under a huge headscarf.

"Yes?" Ari shouted against the wind.

"Let me in!" the woman replied, her lipstick garish as the light from the hall fell on her face.

"Why should I? Who are you?" she cried, startled by the woman's demanding tone of voice. Ari was uneasy, suspecting that perhaps this odd woman was a particularly persistent reporter.

"Who are you?"

"Someone *you* never met. But someone who has a right to be here," the woman shouted. "I'm Philip Shaw's wife."

Ariadne's first impulse was to laugh in disbelief. Or in admiration of what she still took to be a reporter from one of the English tabloids. She shook her head and moved to force the door shut. Suddenly she felt an equal force as the woman leaned her shoulder against the door. Anger filled her, rage at this intrusion.

"Get out! Get away from here!" she shouted at the woman's face.

"No, I will not. I'm Philip Shaw's wife. I must talk to you, Mrs. Conroy. There are some things we must discuss." The wind was snatching her words away, but Ariadne had heard enough to make her curious. She was glad Harry wasn't home.

* * *

"So you never actually saw the body?" Geraldine pressed Brona for more details. What Brona had already told her was pretty much what she knew from the newspapers.

"God, no. Why would I?" Brona shivered. Geraldine might be used to viewing naked bodies, living or dead, but she wasn't. "You really are too grisly," she admonished her friend.

"Sorry, sorry. Listen, I don't mean to upset you. But it's just so amazing, the whole story. Tell me, did the police come here to talk to you?"

"Oh, yes, that day in fact. The forensic people came in, and they—or the regular police, I don't know—there were about ten men in here." She glanced round the small room. "They tested for fingerprints, particularly on the front door and on this window here and the window at the back—well, you know there are only two. They seemed very thorough.

"I explained how I leave the top of the window open for the cats to leap in and out. One of them was rather impressed with my furries," she added as she stroked Clarence on her lap. "And of course they said I was foolish. But they saw soon enough that the iron bars on the windows were in perfect condition, and that nothing was out of order, front or back. They seemed to conclude that no one could have got in to this flat. Of course, they don't tell you much while they're working."

"And were you questioned, too?" Ger asked eagerly.

"Yes, but not at length. I had been racking my brains from the first minute the policeman had come down to tell me that there was some trouble upstairs. Harry had brought him down to . . . well . . . sort of break the news, I suppose. Poor Harry. He was trembling. But then so was I . . . I couldn't recall any unusual noises during the three weeks they were away in Africa. And I didn't recall seeing anyone near the house or at the door, except the postman. Harry had his mail held, but, typical, one day I saw the postman attempting to deliver. Half the time I get some letters that are meant for upstairs. It's because we're the same house number, but you know all this. Oh, God, I'm just blathering."

"No more gin for you, my girl," said Ger with a quite natural and becoming medical manner. "I'll put on the kettle." She watched as Brona massaged her forehead and eyes with the tips of her delicate fingers, and she was moved with genuine sympathy for her eccentric friend.

"Was it very awful?" she asked softly as she gave her the mug of sweet tea.

"Yes, rather, because all I could think of was this dead body upstairs, over my head. For *days!* That there were men up there doing this horrible thing, and I could have been sound asleep down here, oblivious! Honestly, if the Conroys hadn't decided to stay on here and not go to a hotel, I don't think I could have stayed on either. But . . . well, time passes. I'd succeeded in putting it out of my mind." She looked pointedly at Geraldine, but with no reproof. She knew her old friend too well to find her curiosity surprising. "Perhaps it's helped me to talk about it. I haven't told anyone at College, you see. I'd rather not be associated with all this."

"Any word from upstairs, from Harry or the queen bee?"

"No, not really. You know what they're like."

Geraldine burst into raucous laughter. "I know more than *they* realize, certainly. The stairs! Do you remember how we used to creep up to the top of the stairs and press our ears against the door? Remember we used to hear Harry and old poker face having one of their fights in the front drawing room. I'd nearly forgotten all that."

"I haven't. And you did it, not I. You were dreadful, listening to private quarrels!"

"Oh, are we Miss Priss again?" Geraldine shook a finger at her. "You did it, too, and you had fun doing it."

"Well, we never heard anything from the drawing room. It was only when it spilled out into the front hall . . . I do recall a rip-roaring row about babies!"

"And then they'd go upstairs, remember? And I used to say what they needed was a good roll in the hay, though preferably not with each other!"

"You were always outrageous, Ger. I don't know how I put up with you."

"Because I kept you alive! I don't know who's doing that for you now."

"I like living alone," said Brona neutrally.

"That isn't what I meant, and you know it," said Ger in her lightly teasing tone. "Any men on the horizon—or nearer, for that matter?"

"You mean a boyfriend, I suppose."

"Yes . . . s . . . s . . .?"

"Not anybody special. Well, no one at all. There is a fellow, an American, actually . . ." She looked up shyly.

"I don't believe it! You? You can't stand Yanks, if I remember rightly. Is he black?" she teased.

"For heaven's sake. No! But he is different. He's serious."

"About you!"

"No, about his work. He's here at College as a graduate student. He's not actually a member of College, but he does have special permission to use the research room in the library. It was the librarian who gave him my name. So he came to my carrel one afternoon, about three weeks ago. The librarian knows that I've been doing research on the early nineteenth century. Actually, Bob is rather nice. We had coffee, and he talked very knowledgeably. He asked good questions, too . . . but I haven't seen him since." Brona's voice trailed off as she stroked Clarence and smiled at his throaty purr.

Ger took the hint and attempted to change the subject. "Why didn't you ever get another flatmate after I left?"

"Un-huh . . . I like living alone." Brona smiled. "And I can afford it now, with Daddy's little legacy." Brona's face was sad as she recalled her gentle father, an ineffectual clergyman who had slowly risen to the rank of Canon before his rather untimely death. She missed him, and Geraldine felt a stab of guilt at her forgetting.

"And aren't you getting paid for those dreadful tutorials you do on Saturdays?"

"Yes, not much, but it helps. And they're not dreadful. The freshers are very keen, and they respond to the readings I give them. They all want to do Yeats, of course, but they're willing to look at some of the eighteenth-century people. And I do believe it's because I make it interesting for them," she added quite proudly.

"What's the plan, then? Any chance of a post at the College?"

"None whatsoever. Regardless of how well I do with the doctoral dissertation. But I'm optimistic. Well, I was." She hesitated. "I think I might get something in England. I won't mind, really, I won't."

"Pity," said Ger. "When is the big day? Or the due date, or the viva, or whatever you call these things?"

"The dissertation is due in two weeks, and the oral defense will be set for the following week. That gives them time—you know, the committee—to read the dissertation. And it also allows for the external reader to read it, usually someone in England or up North. Of course, all of them have already seen my proposal and my summary. It's not just a viva, Ger, it can last for hours, and I'm dreading it rather."

"You'll be grand."

Brona resented Ger's easy assumption that she'd be fine. It all looked so simple to medical students, who had suffered numerous vivas and hospital rounds and the fatigue of endless twenty-four-hour duties. But medical students shared a camaraderie that was missing in the humanities departments. They all seemed to Brona to suffer together, whereas she saw herself as pursuing her studies very much alone. "I hope you're right" was all she said, rather hopelessly.

"Wasn't this Shaw an English literature professor?"

"Yes, I read that, and Harry mentioned it, too. Harry's got very nervous, you know."

"I'm not surprised," said Ger. "More tea . . ."

Brona looked pointedly at the kitchen clock, and Ger got the message. "Right, then, I'm off. An early night wouldn't do me any harm. Look, I'm sorry if I was ghoulish. I was just a little worried about you. Not much, mind you." She flung on her coat and glanced through the parting of the curtains. "Sacred Heart, it's not raining! I'll walk back to the hospital —the air will clear my gin-befuddled brain cells." She paused. "Come on, for old times' sake, let's run up the stairs and listen at the door. Come on." Ger giggled like a schoolgirl.

"No." Brona stood up, and Clarence fell to the floor.

"Oh, come on."

"I—I don't think they're home." Brona hesitated.

"Well, if they're not, no harm done. And if they are, who knows what we might learn? After all, the poor man was found dead in their bed. And stark naked at that! I think that's got to have some significance." Ger moved quickly to the hall, her coat swirling around her. She crept up the stairs in the dark, Brona creeping behind her, still reluctant.

"Anyone there?" she whispered, hoping that only silence would greet this endeavour.

"Shush! I can hear voices. It's poker face, I think—no, wait. It's a woman's voice, all right. . . ." Ger closed her eyes to concentrate and then pulled away, her face serious. "It's Ariadne, all right, and a woman. They're shouting or screaming too much, I can't make out the words . . . but they're upset." She tried to see Brona's face in the dark. "I think you're right. Forget this, we're not children anymore."

The two young women moved carefully down the stairs, suddenly aware of every creak and even of the sound of their own breathing. Somehow the mood was changed. Brona walked Ger to the door, and Ger flung it open quickly, stepping out heedlessly into the night. Brona shut it with an audible sigh of relief.

Ariadne, trembling with fear and rage, faced Denise Shaw across her own sitting room. "Get out of this house, I tell you, get out now!"

"I see you use the words 'this house,' not 'my home'!" Denise Shaw responded, ignoring the wet coat and scarf she had thrown on the couch, ignoring the muddied stains her shoes had tracked across the powder-pale carpet. She had taken the room in at a glance. "Not 'our little home,' *this* house! Are you being kept here? Are you a kept woman? Isn't that how you always pursued your career?"

"This is my home." Ari dropped her voice. "Mine and my husband's." She took the woman's wet coat and flung it out into the hall. "Now get out! You have no right to be here."

"I have every right. It was *my* husband who died here. My husband. And that gives me every right to be here. And more than that"—the woman was panting now, trying to recover her breath—"more than that," she said more calmly. "More than that, I want to see where he died."

"That's impossible," snapped Ariadne.

"No, it is not! I'm here, aren't I? Take me to the room where he died."

"No, no, you don't understand. Your husband didn't die here. Go to the police. You must know this anyway. There was no blood, no evidence of a struggle. Honest to God, he didn't die here, he was . . . he was . . . put here." She faltered, and Denise saw her chance.

"How dare you speak of God or of honesty to me? God was never a concern of yours. And honesty certainly never was. You expect me to believe a word out of that mouth that kissed my husband, that made love to him? Lies, yes. Venom and dishonesty and betrayal, adultery, that's all—adultery is all that comes out of your mouth."

Ariadne felt the nausea rising again. Her mouth tasted hot bile.

"Now take me upstairs, take me to the room, show me that bed, *your* bed, where Philip died."

Denise Shaw pushed Ariadne on the shoulder, and Ariadne reacted slowly. She moved as if in a dream state, somehow registering a new noise, a scuffling somewhere in the hall. Mice, she thought wildly. In the distance she heard a door slam with a dull thud. Harry, is it you, Harry? She moved to the hall and placed her foot on the bottom stair. So slowly. Like an old, old woman, she thought. Her body was cold, her mind sluggish. She placed a hand on the baluster and paused. She felt Shaw's wife come up behind, she felt breath hot and sour against her ear.

"Now!" Denise Shaw hissed, pushing her forward. And Ariadne seemed to step into a void.

Chapter Six

On Wednesday night James reluctantly left the conspicuous Citroën in the postage-stamp-sized car park to the right of the warehouse. He picked his footing through the rubble of broken tarmacadam and stood hesitantly at the front of what looked like an abandoned building. But following Ariadne's instructions, he pressed a small bell hidden from general view and was relieved when a dull buzz and click indicated that the heavy door could be opened.

He climbed the bare, steep stairs to the first floor and opened a door into a small square room, entirely carpeted—even the ceiling—in woven purple tweed. A rather sullen and tired-looking girl glanced up at him from behind a small bare desk.

"Good evening," James said formally. "I was told to meet Ms. Ariadne Conroy here. Could you let her know that I've arrived?"

The girl responded by pressing a small buzzer under her desk and flicking her hair and head towards yet another door whose outline James could now detect in the carpeting on the wall. He walked quickly to it and entered a maze of empty corridors in which numerous coaxial and other heavy cables ran like giant snakes, entwined and twisting in and out of the five open doors. He followed the faint sound of human voices to the farthest door and glanced in. He passed through a small lobby, stepping over empty coffee cups and food wrappers and ashtrays overflowing onto the floor. Pushing open a heavy door, he was greeted by the stares of three well-dressed young men who looked up expectantly and then looked away, obviously disappointed. Three other men of various ages, each with sleeves rolled up and days of growth on their chins, lounged on the tubular chairs. The room was filled with blue smoke. They didn't look at James at all. He felt irritated as he asked for Ariadne. One of the men finally nodded towards the glass door above which was a sign in red, lighting the word ON. James paused, wondering how to proceed and wondering, too, if the general staff of the Recording Studios had taken a vow of silence. Impatient now, he pushed open the door to be treated to glares from the technician, and at last by Ariadne, who rose from her padded stool, coming towards him with a lovely smile and a slender ringed finger to her lips. He nodded his understanding and took the stool indicated beside her.

His eyes swept over the enormous console of controls being operated by the sound engineer. As his eyes adjusted to the semi-darkness he perceived through the large glass window in front of them a well-known female ballad singer, looking smaller than he'd imagined. She was approaching the large standing microphone on the bare stage at some twenty feet from the glass.

"Fiona, darling," said Ariadne into the open mike.

James watched as Fiona adjusted her earphones.

"Yes?"

"That last take was the best, but I—"

"I thought you said the third take was the best." The singer's voice was petulant.

"No, that take was really good, darling, it had such depth. Do you think . . . listen, we'll play back the third take. If you could just lift your voice on the word 'home' and keep the rest of the depth. Perhaps just punch the word slightly? Mmm?" Ariadne waited. James could see the tension in the line of her back and in her hand as she tapped her pencil silently against the palm of her other hand. "Fiona, darling, if we get this, and I know we will, the session fellas could get started."

Fiona shrugged.

"And the main thing, of course, is that you could get home." Ariadne's voice was light, coaxing and gentle.

"Right."

The sound man spoke softly into the mike. "Take eleven." And then to Fiona a few endearments. Fiona positioned herself at the mike, her hand to her earphone on her right ear. She watched for the light to signal that the recording had begun. James was astonished as she began to sing the few simple words. She drew her small frame up, closing her eyes, almost hunching her shoulders. Suddenly it was there. Her pure, melodic, powerful voice singing of longing and loneliness and exile: "I'll take you home again . . ." The word "Kathleen" was left off, and the few notes lingered in James's ears.

Ariadne jumped up as the technician hit the communicating button opening the mike. "That's it! That's it! Perfect, Fiona, absolutely perfect!" she said.

The sound man raised his eyebrows at Ariadne in, it seemed to James, a gesture of respect. Fiona gave a thumbs-up through the glass and left the stage. Relief and excitement filled the small room, and James felt it, too. Now very curious, he whispered to Ariadne, "That was marvelous. Tell me, what's the product?"

She looked at him mildly. "Soup," she said simply, and then she smiled—ironically, James thought. But he was never sure with Ariadne.

"Grand, grand," she said aloud. She looked at her watch. "Oh, Mother of God. Three hours behind. Here, I'll tell the session musicians to go on in. Can you just have them lay down a few test tracks? I'll give them the sheet music. I'm going for a break with . . . I'm going for a break. Give me twenty minutes."

"That's all right, take thirty. We'll be here till midnight anyways."

James followed Ariadne and stood by as she sent the musicians on into the studio and graciously, sweetly, and slightly flirtatiously told the three patiently waiting voice-over artists that they were running three hours behind time and perhaps they'd like to call back around half eleven. James was impressed with her tact in dealing with what he had easily seen was a rather temperamental lot. But giving them their due, he was feeling a little temperamental himself with the delays and seeming confusion and the level of tension that was virtually palpable in the studio.

Ariadne sank into the only cushioned chair and kicked off her green Italian leather heels. The soft olive-green jersey skirt and matching loose-fitting cardigan sat well on her and blended with the rich cream of her polo-neck jersey. A single heavy gold chain brightened the outfit, catching and diffusing the unflattering fluorescent light above them.

"Sorry about all this, James. As I mentioned to you, this session is the single biggest I've handled alone. This ad campaign will run in Ireland and in Britain. My agency won out in their creative presentation for this account over two major agencies in London. In other words, this will make or break my particular career, along with a number of others."

"A far cry from writing English essays, then?" James said neutrally.

Ariadne winced. "You're right, of course, to get to the point. And I only have a few minutes. Last night Harry was out at a dinner, a client thing, and I was at home alone. Couldn't settle . . . to get to the point, the doorbell rang—and I can hardly believe it yet! The woman at the door claimed to be Philip Shaw's wife. She virtually forced herself inside and from the start seemed to me to be raving."

"How do you mean?" James said sharply.

"It was a wild night, and she was wind-blown and breathless. She insisted she had a right to see where her husband had died. I must have been mad to allow her in. I can't describe it to you. I was . . . intimidated I guess is the right word. She took me by surprise. And foolishly I allowed her in. Insistent, she was terribly insistent. To the point where she was pushing me, taking my arm and pushing me."

"She used some force, then?"

"Yes, but it was more her, how would you say, menacing attitude. And besides that, she was screeching at me. It seems a blur now, but she was screeching that she had this right.

"In any event"—Ariadne sighed and glanced around as she heard a noise on the far side of the door—"I showed her the room. I didn't go in, but she did, and she stared at the bed. That was the only time she was quiet. She stood for some minutes just staring at the bed. I watched her from the doorway. It was horrible. I felt so ill. I could see what she could only imagine.

"Thank God she asked me no questions then. But as she came towards me when she was leaving the bedroom, she began again. Not quite at such a pitch of hysteria, but still screaming her words."

"Which were?" James prompted.

"That I was responsible, that I had killed her husband. We stood on the landing, and then I backed down the stairs."

"How did you manage to get her to leave?"

"I didn't, really. We came down. I remember telling her she had to go. I don't think I said much. I was trying to appear calm, but I was frightened. She accused me of stealing her husband. I'm afraid I responded to that. I told her I was one of many, at least at that time. She went off on a tangent then, recounting bits of his affairs over the years, naming names I'd never heard of. She told me that between his teaching and his politics and his women she seldom saw him. I wanted to scream then and ask her why she'd stayed with him, since her life was such a misery—"

"Pardon me, but what politics?"

"Well, I'm pretty vague on it now, but he had been a fairly active member of the Socialist Party or some associated political group. God, it was the end of the Sixties, the start of the Seventies. Everybody was something then." James noddod in agreement. "He was prominent in campus politics, but I paid no attention. I was just over from Ireland. It seemed fairly petty. We'd had all that at Trinity. Protests for better food, better wages and conditions of the College cleaning staff. Marx applied by the offspring of the middle class. The issues weren't exactly burning ones."

"But was he sincere?" James wondered how much of her own cynicism obscured her memory, and so he waited.

"Good question," she said at last, "Yes, I believe he was. I remember there had been a racial incident, as they're called. An Indian student was being harassed by some other students. Philip—I mean Shaw—very quickly and quietly organized some rap sessions"—she laughed at the outmoded term—"got groups together to talk openly about racism, its origins, how to dcal with it, weed it out, and so on. I remember thinking he was quite admirable at the time." She stood up suddenly and stretched, glancing at her watch and moving to another chair.

"What worries me, James, is precisely this. Mrs. Shaw swore that Shaw had told her that when he was in Dublin he'd see his Irish girl."

"Are those her exact words?"

"As far as I can remember. She said he was going to see an Irish girl while he was staying in Dublin." She paused. "What's important, or what I think is important, is that she insists she's going to go to the police with this information."

James picked up on her concern and was quiet for a few moments as he watched Ariadne light a cigarette. Yes, she was lovely, attractive, bright, articulate. And strong, he thought. How strong? He was ever wary of being deceived.

"That would bind you to the murder victim even more closely," he said finally. "Have you told Harry?"

Suddenly Ariadne stood up and stubbed out her cigarette. "No, of course not! I'm terribly sorry, James, but I've got to go. It's been more than thirty minutes, and lives are on the line here." She stopped. "How stupid, what a stupid thing to say. Listen, I feel better for having told you." She looked at him expectantly, almost trustfully, as he stood up.

"I'm glad for that, at least," he said, smiling. He wanted to take her hands in his but refrained. "Let me sleep on this." He winced at his own cliché. "Let me give this some thought. We may have to do precisely nothing. I'll have to get back to you." She was moving away quickly but politely towards the studio door.

"Why don't I give you a call, then?" she said, effecting an end to their conversation. James stood for a moment looking at the closed door, and then he wound his way back through the maze whence he had come.

"You've got an invitation today, James," said Maggie enthusiastically as he entered his office premises on Friday morning. "And it's about bloody time. If you don't mind my saying so, you've the dullest social life of any eligible bachelor I know."

"And I imagine you know quite a few," quipped James pleasantly, reluctant to let Maggie see that even he was pleased to get an invite somewhere, anywhere. He opened the envelope.

"Damn," he said. "It's a party tonight, if you must know, Maggie, but I can't go."

"Why not?"

"Because I have a previous engagement."

"With whom, may I ask?"

"Donald," he muttered.

"Oh, a date with your brother? Wow!" Maggie smirked.

She's right, thought James to himself as he entered his own office. He considered that he might go to Ariadne's studio party after all. It was a celebration of the conclusion of her marathon recording session. Surely Donald wouldn't mind his breaking their monthly date. And yet this was exactly why they'd stuck to a regular meeting at the University Club. As a doctor, Donald had a hectic professional and social schedule. Better than mine, thought James ruefully. Yes, it would be nice to see Ariadne relaxing in what he had seen was her own special milieu. He sat down at his desk. Nope, James, he thought, you're getting too close for comfort! He was beginning to realize how much he liked Ariadne, and not merely as a client. He tapped his teeth with his pencil, struggling against the wish to see her again so soon.

He was still holding the invitation when Maggie put Ariadne's call through to him.

"Nice voice," she informed James as she did so.

Getting entirely out of line, is Maggie, thought James.

"Well, can you make it? Tonight?" Ari's voice was genuinely happy. For the first time her rich tones were not tinged with darker, sadder shades.

"Sorry, I would have enjoyed your party, I think."

"I'm not so sure," she replied. "It's a strange crowd, but I thought it might have provided novelty for you, at least."

"No doubt. It's an alien world to me! Unfortunately, I have a long-standing previous engagement."

"Oh, dear. That's a shame. Well, I do realize it was very short notice. I only decided last night, when I knew we'd be wrapping up today. The crews, the technicians, the artists, everybody's been so great. I think it'll be good to let our hair down."

"About the other matter," James said at last, reluctant to disturb her happy mood. "I've decided we will do nothing. If I approach Molloy, it may seem we're running scared. And as you assure me, we are not. You were not this so-called Irish girl Shaw came to see. If we go to Molloy, we'll be protesting too much. Similarly, I've decided that we should not approach Mrs. Shaw. We cannot and should not

feed her fantasies. But be cautious, Ariadne. Avoid being
with her alone, or even in company. If she's come this far,
she may be quite driven, if not deranged."

There was silence, and he sensed she wanted more from
him, but he could think of nothing to add.

"Well, enjoy your party tonight, Ari," he said lamely.
"And thanks for thinking of me."

"Cheerio then, James." Ariadne rang off, but her tone
was not as bright as it had been at the start of their
conversation, and James was very sorry for that.

The small notice reading "Private Party" that was pinned
to the door of the Studio could have been perceived as
misleading, for upstairs the once-empty rooms teemed with
people. A small but very good band was pouring forth a
great mix of Irish traditional and rock music while people
danced or swayed, lounged or stood, drinks in hand. One of
the smaller rooms was filled with the acrid odour of the
cannabis plant as certain partygoers unselfconsciously
puffed away. Ariadne roamed from room to room, glad that
none of the hard stuff was in evidence. She'd asked people to
keep the party clean, and it seemed that both the English
and the Irish guests had kept to the spirit of the occasion.

It was a dual affair; the ad agency and the Studio had
clubbed together. Everyone involved had worked tremen-
dously hard and all were now relaxing just as hard, celebrat-
ing the end of work well done. The atmosphere was great.
Easy. The rooms full of chat, a happy buzz. Ariadne saw
herself as the unofficial host but played her role well.

"Great do," a voice whispered softly in her ear. She
swung around, her usually sophisticated face vulnerably
pleased. Her creative director was leaning against the wall.
His gaunt figure was clothed entirely in very rumpled white
cotton fatigues. He looked like an aging intern.

"Honestly?" she blurted.

"And great work, the best you've done for us. And I

daresay the best you've ever done—to date." In her delight she clasped his cool hands in her own. Although he did not respond with any pressure at all, she felt a thrill, a current of excitement. Sexual excitement, perhaps, running between them. She looked, and he held her eyes, his own unblinking, nearly blank. And they stood, then moved imperceptibly closer. She could feel his breath on her face.

"There you are! Ari! Ari!" Harry's voice came to her as from a great distance. For a second she thought she imagined it, but in that second she dropped John's hands. He drifted away as he had come.

"Harry." Her voice was flat, she hoped. Harry was startled at the tone.

"I've been looking for you," he reprimanded. "It's pretty crowded here."

"That's the idea," she said, and she sighed. Harry caught the sigh.

"Tired?"

"Of course not."

"Sorry." Harry's voice was now edgy. "It's just that I know how hard you've been working. You've hardly slept. And with this other thing . . ."

"What 'other thing'?"

"You know." Harry lowered his voice.

Her shoulders slumped. For the two hours since the party had begun she hadn't thought of that dreadful other thing. She closed her eyes briefly, only to see the distorted face of Mrs. Shaw.

"I do thank you so for reminding me, Harry."

"Sorry! Sorry. Not off to a good start, am I?"

"No," said Ari, about to snap and yet holding her tongue and her anger when she saw the sadness in Harry's eyes, and the fear. A nameless fear, she thought fleetingly.

"Come on, come on. We'll start again." She caught up his hands in hers and kissed him.

He blushed, glancing around. "Ari, not here."

"Oh, for God's sake. This isn't a company meeting, darling." She held herself in check again. "Come on. There are people I want you to meet."

As she led Harry by the hand towards a group of boisterous voice-overs she questioned if this indeed were true. Hitherto she'd kept Harry away from her work, her comrades-in-arms, as she saw them. Their world and some of hers was so alien to Harry. She felt the reluctance in the drag of his arm. Had she made him like this, she wondered.

"Right, you lazy bums. I want you to meet Harry." She introduced the actors and actresses by their first names. Some of them were known to Harry from the many stage plays and musicals he'd attended with Ariadne. The conversation withered, and Ari teased them lightly.

"So much talent all in one room!" she said.

"And so much ego." The group laughed loudly. Harry smiled.

"There's a blooper tape, did you hear?" she asked as silence fell like the final curtain on an unsuccessful play.

"I don't believe it," said one of the older men. "If so, I'm not on it." His tone was deliberately provocative, and a round of vicious gibes followed.

"You're on it, one and all!" she exclaimed.

"If so, then so are you. Let's see. We should hear 'Punch that word, darling, won't you?' and 'More drama, Colum, for God's sake, more drama!' "

Ari blushed, embarrassed yet pleased as they accurately mimicked her voice, her manner, and the key phrases she used in producing the ads, in coaxing (or so she thought) performances. Harry was quiet.

"I never say that," she objected at one point, laughing. "Do I, Harry?" She tried to draw him into the group with her eyes and her voice, but he resisted—sullen, she thought.

"Does she order you about, then?" said one of the English actresses who'd come over specially for the recording.

"I'd say she does," said Harry seriously. The woman paused, quizzical.

"Excuse me. Harry, is it?" broke in Colum. "What line of work are you in?" He was kind, polite. Ari blessed him.

"I'm a manager at Price Waterhouse." Harry's voice was proud and clear.

"You've got a good voice there," commented Patrick Manning.

"What is Price Waterhouse when it's at home?"

Harry looked blank.

"It's an accountancy firm," said Ariadne quickly, nudging Harry. She moved away, smiling archly. "Get ready for the tape! This is very much blackmail material, and the language contained therein is definitely not for those of a nervous disposition."

"For heaven's sake, Ariadne," Harry said loudly.

Ariadne swung around to him. "What? What is it? What have I said now?" She spoke too loudly, and the people near them glanced over. "Let me alone," she hissed, and walked off, leaving Harry to his fate. One he was used to—that of standing, drink in hand, alone in the midst of a crowd.

Ari was impeded at every step, shaking hands, greeting guests, caught up into on-going conversations, laughing, joking, basking in the praise of many. It was an hour before she got a technician to set up the tape. People began to filter in, crowing in merry anticipation of the bloopers. Ari saw Harry in the crowd and moved to his side, contrite again but not admitting it. She squeezed his hand.

The tape played, a matter of ten minutes, filled with mispronounced words, breathless singing, miscues, all liberally interspersed with four-letter words. The more incongruous the blooper, the louder the hoots. Harry stirred uncomfortably as Ari's voice was heard to shout from the speakers.

"I'm sorry," it said in a mid-Atlantic accent. "I'm sorree! But this copywriter needs a bloody brain transplant. No one could read these lines. . . ."

The phrase hung in the air as Ari froze. "The 'bloody

copywriter' is right over here, Ariadne!" the copywriter shouted.

The tape was running. "Maybe the client needs a brain transplant. We're selling soup, not salvation."

At least this was met by roars of appreciation, but Ari felt apprehensive, for she knew the client was present. A few more bloopers rounded off the tape, which was met with cynical applause. Silence fell just in time to allow Harry's voice to carry over the crowd.

". . . so unprofessional! I don't understand you." He stopped. Ari's face was an angry red.

"A drink," said John, like a ghost at her elbow. "You'll have a brainstorm if you don't." She glared at Harry and walked quickly through the thinning crowd.

"Thanks, John," she whispered.

"Forget it. And I mean forget it. Everyone else has. You know these parties."

"I know this business. This will do the rounds. And anyway, I've got a bone to pick with Sean. He was a bastard to put me on the tape like that." Tears filled her eyes and threatened to spill down her flushed cheeks.

John led her to a seat. The crowd was breaking up, clumps of people arranging to go on to favourite pubs, restaurants, and familiar haunts to continue the party into the morning.

"You going on?" He put his arm around her shoulders.

"I don't think so," Ari said sadly, leaning against him.

"Come on." John's voice was low, insistent, alluring.

"Well, maybe. Are you . . ."

She was glancing down, demurely she thought, needily. She saw familiar shoes on the scarred linoleum. She looked up at Harry's stern face.

"I'm going. You coming?" he said succinctly.

John stood up languidly. "See ya." He drifted away like smoke.

"Thanks! Thanks! That was only my boss," she whispered to Harry as she stood. "It's the first time in three years that he paid any personal attention to me."

"Mighty personal, I think. Looks like you spent the whole party at his side."

"That's ridiculous. Why are you taunting me?" Her voice rose. She didn't care. Fatigue, disappointment, irritation, embarrassment churned within her. "I'm not going home with you. Look, everybody's going on somewhere, anywhere! You are so dull!" Tears ran down her face. "You are so dull and stuffy. Look at you in your three-piece suit. You couldn't even dress for this party. You don't know how to relax. Dull, dull, dull."

Harry hushed her as people cutting through the room to the exit glanced over at them. "For God's sake, get a grip on yourself. You're making a spectacle of us both. I'll dress the way I want. You're nothing but a snob yourself, a reverse snob." The veins on Harry's neck stood out like whipcords, but his voice was level. "Get your things. We're going."

"No." Ari's voice was that of a sullen child. Harry pushed her. Shocked, she stood motionless, rigid. "What are you doing?" she asked. "You pushed me. I'm not some stranger."

"Jesus, will you move?" He grasped her upper arm, and they walked stiffly towards the door, through the exit, and down the stairs. Ari grabbed her bag from the secretary who'd been following them, vainly attempting to get Ari's attention. The few guests lingering outside turned to watch them. Their voices could be heard bickering all the way to the car. Angry, tired, and sad, too.

Brona sat at her desk with her thick gray cardigan bunched around her shoulders. Her back ached between her shoulder blades, but she hardly noticed the pain. The interpretation of a single passage of poetry had now held her attention for over two hours.

"And his soul roved out, roved out, and beheld itself, held itself at readiness. . . . Oh, the sidhe, sidhe, come meet me, breathed the soul, and he beheld it, and he held it, as the wind, and the whirl wind, moved the grasses, moved the reeds, moved the leaves of the willow and they brushed him, and they held him, held his soul. . . ."

It was one of her favourite passages in the works of Diarmuid O'Suillebhean, the nineteenth-century, west of Ireland poet who had died of what they now thought to have been tuberculosis at the early age of twenty-four. Brona had pinned a small print of the only picture of him, a daguerreotype, on the wall above her typewriter. Often in the course of the long hours at her desk she would glance up and try to read the expression in the dark and, what she perceived to be, sad eyes. She believed she could read there intimations of mortality, the early knowledge she was sure he had that his life was to be brief, and his lyric gift more precious because of it.

She had successfully linked the language of the passage to the body of nineteenth-century dream poetry that began with the conventional expression "As I roved out," meaning "as I wandered." These dream poems were nearly always set in time and place at dawn in the countryside. But now she was struggling to link the passage successfully, convincingly, with another convention of Irish poetry, one that used the symbolism of the spirits of the wind, spirits thought by the Irish to be found, possibly even seen, in the small winds that turned the leaves in little eddies. Such belief was the predecessor of the more well-known superstition of the banshee, beloved of more modern storytellers.

For now Brona let herself, her inmost self, wed with the words, the tone, the image of the lonely poet, the lonely soul that cried for companionship to the insubstantial wind and the longed-for life that his imagination told him existed behind what was seemingly present, seemingly real. And was what seemed to be real only lies? she mused. Did he long for lies to fade and diminish, to reveal the more substantial and yet intangible truth?

She jumped, startled by the terrific bang of the upstairs front door. Her reverie was broken, and she glanced at the ceiling above her head as it creaked, footsteps pounding across her ceiling, followed by muffled and then more high-pitched shouting, followed by silence, and then by crying.

Brona put her fingers in her ears and wiggled her fingers as hard as she could, the motion drowning out all sound. She continued till her fingers grew tired. And then she stopped, listening. The angry voices and the sorrowful voices had ceased.

"I don't understand you," Ariadne cried angrily, feeling free to shout now that they were safely home. "You know I've told you all about these people, and yet you stood there, stiff as a poker, paralyzing everybody with your . . . with your . . ."

"With what? I hardly spoke."

"That's right. You couldn't maintain a conversation for two minutes together."

"Do you bloody think they cared? Really, Ariadne—"

"I hate it when you call me that. You only ever say my full name when you're being insufferably arrogant."

"Ari, then."

"Oh, does that change anything?" She was sarcastic now.

"I am what I am. What's wrong with that?" Harry tried a slightly mild tone. He had felt the bands of pain tightening across his chest and was frightened at his own anger.

"When I go"—Ari gulped for breath—"when I go to one of your office functions, don't I fit in?"

"Of course."

"And why? I'll tell you why. Because I at least make an effort. I at least ask good questions. I at least lead people out and get them to talk. Am I right?"

"Yes, yes, all true." Harry sat down. "But Ari, let me ask you this." His tone was weary. "Do you, can you say you honestly care what any of those people at my office or any of my clients tell you?" The question hung in the air.

"What do you mean?"

"You know perfectly well what I'm asking you."

"Are you saying I'm some kind of phony?" Ari's voice rose.

"Are you?"

"All right. Okay. I don't always care, often I don't care. But I do it for you. I facilitate *you.* Right?"

"I'm not so sure anymore. I'm not so sure that my friends, my colleagues don't see through you. That false concern. Don't you think they suspect you've forgotten their names by the time you get to the car to go home? And you have, haven't you?"

"So?"

"So it's a facade. Or a charade."

"No, it's just social intercourse. They don't care about me either!"

"Probably not, and they don't pretend to. You pretend."

"You think I'm pretending all the time." Ari felt ill at ease, suddenly cold, frightened at his coldness, the coldness of his tone.

They sat in silence, Ari waiting. She watched as Harry took a deep breath. Then she watched as he filled a pipe and lit it. She shifted restlessly.

He puffed. "You see, even this annoys you. You never say anything."

"No," she said after a pause. "But I hate the smell, and the dirty ashtrays."

"But you can stand all that smoking and filth and dirt at the Recording Studios, for instance?" Harry was derisive.

"It was a party, for pity's sake."

"Answer me this. Do you ever notice these things when you're working with your so-called colleagues? Does it bother you? No, and I'll tell you why. Because it's okay in that life."

"Yes, but it's not 'okay' in this life."

"Two separate lives, then."

"Yes, I suppose so."

"Exactly my point."

"What is, you arrogant creep?" Ari was shaking.

"You pretend. All of the time."

"Oh, and I suppose you pushing me around at the party was okay! If that isn't pretending."

"Oh, I should push you around at home, too?" Harry was equally sarcastic now.

"No . . ."

"Can you ever honestly say I'm not what I am or what I say I am? Your life is a sham. An act. You act the femme fatale at work. I saw you." His voice was strident. "Available. Interested."

"Well, I was."

"Not pretense, not part of the scene, part of the party mood?" Harry's voice trembled slightly on the question.

"No," she answered, defiant.

"Have you been faithful to me?"

"What kind of question is that?"

"A simple one, I would have thought."

"How dare you? Answer me the same."

"Yes."

"In ten years? Then so have I."

"And you never saw Shaw, or spoke to him, or contacted him?"

"Oh, my God, is this what it's all about?"

"No."

"What, then?"

Harry rubbed his face, exhausted. "Nothing. Nothing. Listen, you choose to miss my point. You choose to see why I say you play me and everyone false. I'm going to bed." He looked at her. "Coming?"

She shrugged.

"Suit yourself."

He knocked the pipe into the fire and waited to see the little embers flare and dull. He stood the pipe carefully in the rack. And without looking behind, he left the room.

Brona's mood was dreary now. Her concentration broken by the disruption, she switched off the electric typewriter and began to prepare for bed. Too tired to bathe, she washed just her face and creamed it religiously as always. She pulled down the heavy quilt and climbed into bed, only to get up again and check to see if James and Clarence and Mangan were still at home. She shrugged, discouraged to see the two females peacefully asleep, but missing as usual was James, who was roaming the night, the sly male. Roving out, she thought as she drifted to sleep, roving out to find a soul, a soulmate. She thought briefly of Ariadne in some room upstairs, perhaps crying still.

Ariadne's thoughts did not refer to Brona asleep in the room beneath her. She lay on her back on the sofa in the drawing room and tried to sleep, but sleep would not come. Burning tears slid from between her closed eyes and ran down the sides of her face, at first stinging and then becoming itchy. She rubbed at her nose with the crumpled bit of tissue she'd been clutching in her fist. God, her nose would be a holy red show in the morning. She then thought of her puffy eyes and cried harder, turning on her side to muffle her sobs.

Perhaps it would have been different if there'd been children. She remembered when she was young. Young and single. How she'd envied her friends and workmates as one by one they'd married, and then as one by one they'd had children. Oh, to be sure, she'd not been all that interested in their stories of the babies and of the toddlers. To be sure, she'd stifle her boredom as they recounted small triumphs and larger worries. In time those friendships drifted for lack of interest. Many of her friends had envied, from the security of their marriages and children, her far more glamourous life—a life of challenging work, of exotic vacations, of spare money for shoes and bags, for the latest fashions.

Now as she turned forty she saw they also envied her the lack of physical demands on her personal time. How nice, they'd say, to be able to go home to a clean house, to a cocktail and a good dinner, to have time to oneself, to have time for one's own interests instead of the interests of one's children. She had nothing but time, she thought ruefully. Time marked off on her daily calendar by the hour, by the week, by the month. But she had begun to see that when her friends' children were grown, that time would return to them again. And then there would be grandchildren to look forward to. And what had she? And what had Harry? Their jobs? She sat up. Just their jobs. And this beautiful house, now so completely and effectively decorated there was nothing left to do to it. To whom would they leave it? She was still thinking about them as a couple, a pair.

After tonight she pondered that that might not be the case. And if they parted, what then? Two lonely people, divvying up their belongings.

No! Did he mean it? Her head pounded. She wondered at their anger earlier in the evening. What had inflamed her? What had inflamed him? He had been so unbearably boring, she was embarrassed. It seemed a long time ago. She looked at the clock. After three. Too tired to get her headache medication, she leaned back, now stiff and cold. And he had been so angry over her mild flirtation. Momentary, fleeting. Nonsense, she saw now. But Harry hadn't seen it that way. Hurt. He'd looked hurt, she realized. Hurt flickering across his face, a slight downturn of his mouth and then anger, pomposity, and exertion of his rights over her as his possession. Or so she'd thought. But now he didn't want his possession. Anger welled in her as she remembered how he'd shoved her, pushed her into the car like some recalcitrant child.

Her headache subsided slightly, and she fell into an uncomfortable sleep disturbed by the cries of a cat that rang in her dreams like the sound of an abandoned baby, wailing.

——— *Chapter Seven* ———

The insistent ring on the phone roused James from a dead
sleep. Exhausted after his long weekend trip to Sligo to write
the will of an elderly and cantankerous client, he was
tempted not to answer the phone's summons. He listened
groggily to his own voice as the answering machine picked
up the call. Then an urgent voice, a voice he knew, nearly
cried out over the speaker.

"Fleming, God, Fleming! Are you there? Please pick up
the phone. Are you there?"

"Fleming here. Who is it?"

"Thank God. Fleming, it's Conroy. It's Ariadne. Oh, my
God . . ."

James felt the hairs rise on the back of his neck. "What is
it, man? Get a grip on yourself."

"It's Ari, Ari, oh, God. She's dead. Fleming, she's dead!"

"No. No! Harry, where are you?" James was fully awake,
alert. He saw the time on the digital clock, 1:15 A.M.
Tuesday.

"I'm in the house."

"Where is Ariadne? Does she need help?"

"God, she's dead . . . she's dead."

"Are the police there?" James shouted. He shook his head, making sure he wasn't having a horribly real dream.

"Police. No, I—I—Fleming, what happened? She's dead."

"Harry, you've got to get the police. Are you hurt?" he added as an afterthought.

"No. I wasn't there. I wasn't here." He began to sob, and James despaired of getting him to listen.

"Harry, she might still be alive. Call 999 and ask for an ambulance and for the police. I'm coming over now. Do you hear me? Call 999!"

"I'll call them. Oh, my God. It's all my fault."

James shrieked into the phone as he was reaching for his trousers. "I'm hanging up the phone now. Call 999!" he commanded, and then he slammed down the receiver.

James dressed swiftly, and as he gathered his keys and wallet he played back the tape on his answering machine, which he had listened to inattentively just a couple of hours before. After the messages from Maggie and his mother came the message from Ariadne, her clear, beautifully modulated tones ringing in the room. "James, it's Ariadne. It's Monday, 10:30 A.M. Please ring me at work or at home as soon as you get back. Your office told me you were away but that you'd be back tonight. It's quite urgent—quite, quite urgent. Thanks." Was the voice fearful at the end? Was he reading into it now something he had not heard before? Why hadn't he phoned her back? Because it was too late when he got back. Because he was too tired. Because he hadn't taken the call seriously.

He ran from the flat through the darkness to his car in the small car park at the rear of the townhouse complex. The air was still and the new leaves hanging heavy. The black stillness, the lack of moving air was eerie. James felt sick to his stomach from the shock of the call, and his temples throbbed as he drove, barely slowing at the numerous intersections en route from his neighbourhood to Harry

Conroy's. Like a chant the same words repeated themselves in his mind until he heard himself praying aloud: "Dear God, don't let her be dead, don't let her be dead." Sick, sick at heart, he, too, believed that somehow this was his fault.

A measure of relief flooded his mind as he drew up at the house to see both an ambulance and a police car already there. Light flooded the house, and the door stood open. A young policeman greeted him at the door, and he identified himself. James spotted Chief Inspector Molloy in the hall and was waved through.

"Molloy."

"Fleming."

James looked up the stairs, a question on his face. He looked at Molloy without hope. "Is she dead?"

"I'm afraid so."

Sudden tears stung James's eyes. He blinked them away. Molloy watched him.

"And how is it you're here?" he asked mildly.

"Harry—Mr. Conroy—phoned me."

"As his solicitor?"

"I am here, I was her friend," James said sadly. "Is Harry all right?"

"Yes, Fleming." Harry's voice spoke from the drawing room door. He walked slowly, like a sick, frail man. "I'd like to go up now, Molloy."

The three men went up the stairs to the landing. Harry paused and closed his eyes, touching his fingertips to his eyelids. Molloy and James waited. Harry lifted his head, straightened his back, and stepped forward. Into the room.

Ariadne lay as if asleep in the room and on the bed where Philip Shaw had so recently lain. She had been laid out, perfectly straight, on the bare box spring, her head at rest on a fresh pillow, a plain white sheet drawn up over her figure to her chin. Her arms lay on the outside of the sheet by her sides, her long, slender hands at rest. Her hair was spread on the pillow as if arranged. James swayed and felt for a moment the sensation that Ari was breathing. He could see the sheet rise and fall. He moved forward suddenly, but Molloy grasped his arm, effectively stopping him. Harry stood by the bed, but he didn't touch his wife. He put a hand over his face. The policeman stationed in the room went to the far side and then stood out in the hall.

"This is how you found her?" asked Molloy.

"Yes," Harry whispered.

"And you touched her?"

"Of course I did." Harry turned to face him. "I thought she was sleeping. I thought it was weird. I thought it was weird she didn't answer me, didn't move. So I touched her arm, and it was cold."

"Did you think it strange she lay like this?"

"I thought it was insane that she had gone to bed in this room after all that had happened."

"Did you touch anything else?"

"No." Harry's voice was dead.

"Why not?"

"Why should I? I think when I saw her I knew. I don't know. I came over here to the bed, and I touched her hand. She didn't move. She didn't move, she didn't open her eyes and speak to me. . . ."

James wanted to shout at the man, to ask him hadn't he lifted her into his arms, hadn't he held her, warmed her, brought the colour back into her face? Hadn't he kissed her and cried out her name and called her back from that distant country from which she would not return? Hadn't he kissed those lips one last time? James looked away. From Ari, from Harry. Angry, disgusted.

Suddenly he realized that Molloy had been asking Harry questions. He should have been paying attention.

"What time did you find her?"

"I don't know, I tell you." Harry's voice was shaking.

"Well, what time did you get home? Was she at home?"

Harry was trembling from head to toe, and James moved

to take his arm. Murmurs were heard in the hall, and the team of weary-looking forensic specialists entered the room. Harry turned on them with horror on his face.

"No! Get out, get out!"

James whispered in his ear as Molloy held the men back for a few moments with his upraised hand.

"You won't touch her, will you?" Harry appealed to the men who looked away from his stricken face. James felt the tears in his own eyes. He armed Harry from the room but looked back in farewell at Ariadne.

Molloy could be heard asking questions of the men in the room as James led Harry downstairs. He poured two brandies. The silence was heavy until at last James anxiously conveyed to Harry that he must not mention that he had phoned him before phoning for the police.

Molloy entered the room softly, like a cat, glancing at Harry's face. Harry was gray, his skin like wax. He looked up and on seeing Molloy began to tremble violently.

"I am, as I said, very sorry about your wife, Mr. Conroy. It was only days ago that we were sitting here chatting." He paused. "Let me say that from only a cursory look my men and I cannot find any overt evidence of a forced entry, a struggle, a fight. . . ."

Harry looked up. "I didn't . . . I didn't . . ."

"Go on," said Molloy in his most soothing voice. The voice of the confessional, thought James as he touched Harry's arm in warning.

Harry was oblivious. "Do your men upstairs know if she was"—he hung his head—"molested?"

"Can't say. The medical examiner, of course, will deal with that. He's upstairs now."

Like a horrible repeat of just ten days ago, thought James. As Molloy had said and was now saying again.

"Don't you find it curious that your wife was found in the room where Mr. Shaw was discovered?"

"Curious?" Harry looked up at Molloy.

"Yes. Curious."

"Get out! Get out of my house. Get out and take your men with you." Even Molloy was startled when Harry leapt to his feet.

"I understand how you must feel," he said firmly, recovering himself. "But you must understand also that my men can't leave. In fact, I'd like to ask you come to headquarters and help us with our inquiries."

James now stood up. "Listen, Molloy, he's in no shape. This is a terrible tragedy." James heard his voice shake. "He's just lost his wife. Plus there's been this previous issue of Shaw's death. Conroy's been under a terrific strain. Obviously Ari, Mrs. Conroy, has been murdered—"

"Obviously?" Molloy was curt.

"She's dead. You're here. We are all assuming she's been murdered." James was calm. "Sadly she's been placed in the bed where Shaw was found. This surely is significant. There's a copycat at work. Someone, perhaps insane, certainly diabolical, is out there who's done this. I don't see how Harry can help."

"You are a good solicitor, Mr. Fleming. You've stated the obvious. So will I. This is a domestic matter. A wife is killed in her own home, her husband discovers the body. I've levelled no accusations. Of course Mr. Conroy can help us. He knew her, her movements, her associates and friends, her state of mind. Presumably," he added, staring into Harry's face. "Perhaps you'd like to drive him to the station, Mr. Fleming, but he will be coming. Now."

During the short ride through the empty streets, for the most part trailing Molloy's car, Harry tried to tell James what had happened. He'd been out with a client and hadn't phoned home.

"That's what I can't deal with, Fleming. I didn't talk to her at all today or tonight. It's not as though she were away. Or that I was away. That often happens. No, she was there. At the end of the phone. I could have picked up the phone.

Oh, God." He began to cry. James drove slowly, reluctant to reach the police station until Conroy was under control. And yet he could think of nothing to console Harry. Guilt lay between them. James recalled her voice on his answering machine but did not speak of it to Harry.

"You see"—Harry cleared his throat—"we'd had a terrible argument Friday night. We'd got home late after a party, and it continued." He heaved a sigh from his gut. "When we went to bed that night we weren't speaking."

"Can you tell me"—James braked for a light he hadn't anticipated—"sorry. Go on, Harry."

"It was mutual—the argument, I mean. Our emotions were out of hand. I was angry, but the anger seemed to come from the past as well as the present. It doesn't matter now, does it?"

It was a rhetorical question, and the two men separately held their memories of the woman who had just died. But James felt a definite resentment towards Harry.

"The upshot of this was that we hadn't been speaking for the last few days. We just sort of passed each other in the house. She came and went, and I came and went. You know how it is."

"I'm not married," James said as he parked the car.

Harry went on without heeding. "I just figured it would blow over that first morning. But she didn't speak, and then I didn't. God, it was so childish. And now I can't tell her. . . ." His body heaved in a dry sob, and James despaired of allowing him to go in to be interviewed by Molloy.

"Listen, Harry. Harry? I can only guess what a horror this is for you. But you have to go in now. Listen to me. Molloy suspects you."

Harry's head snapped up, his face white and surprised.

"Yes, Molloy suspects you. Any police officer would. As the husband, as the husband who found the body in his own house. For God's sake, you must see you're the first one they will look at. And then there's this copycat angle." Harry closed his eyes and shuddered. "Harry, I am so sorry. Words are inadequate right now. I just want to cut to the heart of the situation." James felt himself fumbling for words. "I'm giving you advice. As a solicitor. Just be careful, be calm, or try to be calm. You're at your lowest point, and they know it."

James wondered at his own behaviour. Why didn't he just ask Harry directly if he were guilty? Why hesitate, why this reluctance?

"Thanks for coming, James." Harry looked up, his hand on the door handle. James shrugged. "I don't care about Molloy. I loved Ari, and she died thinking I didn't love her. She died thinking that our marriage was a failure." James briefly hated that soft, sad face. "I will have to live with that. I can't tell her now that it's all right. I can't tell her. . . ." He looked out the window into the darkness, forgetting James was there.

"Tell me this before you go. Did anybody see you arguing that night?"

"Oh, God, of course they did. I don't know who they were, but it was at the party in the Studios. There could have been dozens. I didn't care who saw us or who heard us."

James thought of the invitation, and of her happy voice on the phone, and of his dinner with Donald.

"Anyone else?"

"Well, we drove home in my car. She left hers at the Studios—I wonder when she picked it up." He was silent. "We were yelling, I suppose, when we got home. The tenant in the flat might have heard us. I don't even know if she was home. There was no one else that I can think of, no one on the street . . . no taxi driver." Harry saw then the mental picture of the two of them, and the ride from the airport. The taxi driver who had seemed to ridicule him at the door. He rubbed his forehead and his eyes.

"Christ, I've got a headache." He opened the door. "I

hardly know you, Fleming," he said irrelevantly. And then he was gone.

Maggie was surprised to see James already at his desk when she arrived at nine A.M. She didn't question why and wondered privately at his fatigue and preoccupation. He was brusque as he asked her to try to locate a phone number.

"Her first name is Brona." He shrugged. "This isn't helpful, I know. But she lives at Percy Street, in a garden flat at Number 27. The owners of the building are Mr. and Mrs. Conroy. And she's a student."

"Where?"

"Oh, for heaven's sake, I don't know. I drove over there this morning and knocked and rang, but there was no answer. Harry Conroy wasn't at home, and the constable on the door didn't know the tenant's name. Not particularly helpful, in fact." He was irritated at his lack of command of the situation and left Maggie to deal with this trivial but suddenly insurmountable problem.

"Let me get you some coffee."

James smiled at her understanding.

Over coffee and some deliciously fresh currant buns from Bewley's Oriental Café on Grafton Street he felt the adrenaline pump again. He was concerned about the witnesses at the party but felt at least at this stage that a marital tiff at a party with drink taken and in front of any number of interested or disinterested witnesses was less of a threat than a witness to an argument in the privacy of their own home. He wanted to establish that what Harry remembered as a loud argument in fact had not been heard. In that event it could remain a private sadness for Harry but not a real threat. The unknown tenant held the key to this. James sighed. His attitude, he knew, was at this moment hardly objective. In his heart he wanted to know how bad the fight really was. Maggie's buzz broke his train of thought.

"James, a Mr. Conroy on line one."

James blanched. The time for commitment was here.

Harry's voice was tired. "You told me to let you know what happened." James heard the unspoken plea and offered to pick Harry up at a small café near the station.

He was shocked when he saw him, seated hunched over the grubby Formica table, warming his hands on the thick crockery cup of foul coffee. He seemed to have lost ten pounds overnight. Conroy was tucking in his shirt as he stood to greet him.

"You all right?" asked James.

"Grand, grand," Conroy answered in a flat voice. "Let's go."

In the car Harry indicated that Molloy had questioned him closely about Ariadne's movements in the last few days. The issue of the argument at the party and at home did not come up. Because, James thought, Molloy did not yet know. He felt uneasy and wondered if Molloy had discerned the concealment, if concealment it was.

"He seemed to be looking for marital discord, all right." Harry answered James's brief questions. "I'm so tired I can't recall now. He seemed interested in her friends, the trip to Kenya, I don't know. It's such a whirl. He did say there'd be an inquest. I don't think I can deal with . . ." He broke down sobbing, and James was anxious suddenly to get shut of this wreck of a man. He disliked the weakness and the tears, the fatigue and the defeat.

"Jesus, man. Let's get you home and to bed."

When they arrived Harry stretched himself wearily on the sofa. James threw a lap rug over him that he'd found in the hall closet.

"Listen, Conroy. Sleep is what you need now. I'm off. Call me at the office if you decide you require my services."

Harry's eyes were like slits in a rumpled face. "Can't I engage you now?" His formal tone returned. "In fact, I thought we already had." His voice was no longer plaintive.

James was encouraged by this return of self-control. "Yes, I was acting as Ariadne's solicitor, certainly," he agreed.

Harry stuck out a thin white hand from the quilt. "Now it's my turn," he said sadly.

They shook hands, and the handshake was firm.

"Conroy," he remembered to ask as he was leaving, "what's your tenant's surname, the student in the garden flat?"

"You mean Brona, she's Brona O'Connell. Why?"

"Sleep. And let me get to work."

He shut the drawing room door. He paused for a moment to see again the parquet floor, the gilt mirror, the hallstand. To see again as he did that day when he first met Ariadne Conroy. He looked up the stairs, following the polished handrail, seeing for the first time the prints, the framed photographs of what seemed to be family members, relatives, a young girl who looked to be Ariadne at her debs dance. Sixteen, seventeen? He looked at the face, small, happy, expectant. He turned abruptly, very sorry at her death, and very sorry he had ever met Mr. Harry Conroy.

The task that faced James now was inimical to him. By extraordinary circumstances and events he found himself involved in a distasteful situation, distasteful to him. He knew some solicitors and any number of barristers who would be rubbing their hands in anticipation. But Ariadne's voice was still on his tape. Ariadne's appeal was there to be heard. Her appeal to him. An appeal he hadn't answered because he was too tired from listening to the whinings of an old man allocating his earthly possessions. An old fool following the behest of his religion, following the instructions in his Book of Common Prayer to make disposition of his worldly goods before his death. Good provision. He gripped the wheel of the car in irritation, as though it were the man's scrawny neck. Despite his pointed intervention he had failed to persuade him to leave the niece who'd cared for him for thirty years one miserable pound more than he was intending to leave his other and mostly absent nieces and nephews. He felt sorry for that unknown spinster who had laboured in the vineyard in vain. Her reward was not coming in this life, he thought wryly. And if it hadn't been for mean, shrunken Mr. Sullivan of Sullivan and Sons, Fine Leather and Ironmongery, he would have been in Dublin, he would have taken Ari's call. Sullivan! Just one more bit of inherited detritus from Gerald Fitzgerald, James's former boss, now lost in ignominy in the Isle of Man.

Maggie, having had no success on her own, was relieved to obtain Brona's name from James on his return. She located her number in the telephone directory and was impressed when she heard Brona O'Connell's soft, well-spoken voice answer at the other end of the line. And, as she connected Miss O'Connell with James, she wondered with her customary curiosity if Brona might be a new interest in James's recently celibate life.

"Miss O'Connell," said James after he explained who he was, "I'll get straight to the point. Were you at home last night, and are you aware of what happened in the Conroy home?"

"I was and I am," she said simply.

"Have the police questioned you?"

"May I inquire why you are asking?"

"I am a friend and solicitor acting for Mr. Conroy."

"I see. I'm glad to hear it."

"Good." James was taken aback. "Then let me return to the purpose of my call. I need to ask you a few background questions. Your answers may go to help Mr. Conroy."

"Mr. Fleming, the police have questioned me. And I would welcome a chance to help Mr. Conroy. I feel very, very sorry for him."

James heard compassion there and was heartened. This Brona seemingly was older, more mature perhaps than the young student he'd been picturing.

They arranged together to meet that evening in a small, quiet pub known to James, since James was privately reluctant to discuss Harry in what was after all Harry's own house. He gave her directions and set the time. He rang off with a sense of relief. More, he realized, because he'd felt at some disadvantage in speaking with this Miss O'Connell and at the same time admitting to a keen curiosity about what she would be like in person. Her voice was soft, with an accent like Sarah's.

He didn't want reminders of Sarah, including the copy of the *Irish Times* left so blatantly on his desk by none other than Maggie. He glanced down to see the substantial advertisement for Sarah Gallagher's concert the following weekend at the National Concert Hall. He closed his eyes and refolded the paper. Was Maggie right? Who was right? Who could be right? He put all these thoughts from his mind and turned to the next issue at hand—the hiring of a junior who, he hoped, would take the burden off his shoulders of dealing with the irritating likes of Mr. Sullivan. It would leave James's staff of four solicitors and their clerks free of them, too.

The pub and lounge bar that lay along the border that connected the city proper to its nearest suburb was as James remembered. Quiet, sedate, filled with locals who were, for the most part, middle-aged couples. The large fish tank imbedded in the wall was a new addition, out of keeping with the general decor but not unattractive. As he sat nursing his gin and tonic he observed the other patrons over the top of his evening paper. He marvelled, as he always did on these occasions, at the comfortable silence that existed between these assorted couples.

When he was young he used to poke fun at such couples, ever present in the pubs of his youth. He and his companions would gibe one another, swearing they would never end up in such a comatose marital state. Their marriages, if marry they did, would be full of sparkle, wit, flirtation. Silently they criticized these ancient couples of forty-plus, much as they disdained their own parents' social lives, or lack thereof. But now, mused James, he was not so sure, not so quick to ridicule. He hadn't been in such a pub for a while, and he realized that what he once perceived as dull he was beginning to allow might just be comfort.

He sighed. A woman near him caught the sigh and winked. Startled, he blushed and glanced at his paper, repressing the urge to tell her that he didn't often sit alone in pubs, sighing.

Yes, the report was still there. The mysterious death of Mrs. Conroy, the brief description of her home and employment, her connection to the recent and unsolved death of Philip Shaw. Grateful he was that her death had not hit the headlines of the tabloids. World Cup fever had knocked everything off the front pages. People would talk, however. Inevitably there would be an in-depth spread in one of the Sunday papers, no doubt with photographs recent and not so recent. He felt the sweat start up on his forehead, and he loosened his collar. He'd rather have this solved before the gossip-oriented press smelled blood and gallons of printers' ink. He checked his watch again. Brona O'Connell was not late; he had been too early, too anxious. Could this be her?

A young woman of medium height had entered the lounge alone, unwrapping a long black shawl from her head and neck, freeing her shoulder-length brown hair. She glanced almost shyly around the room. Uncertain, he thought. Uncomfortable, too, to be a woman alone looking for someone. Her oval face was pale as she took a pair of glasses from her bag and put them on, glancing again more intently around the room, seeking an empty seat. Her long, full tweed coat brushed the tables as she walked forward with a bit more purpose. He stood and caught her eye and nodded as she looked at him questioningly.

"Brona O'Connell?" She smiled briefly in answer. "I am James Fleming."

They shook hands, hers small, firm, and cold in his. She settled herself as he went to the bar to order. On his return with her Campari and soda he was annoyed to see that their space had been invaded by a jolly group of plump ladies armed with their whiskies and red lemonades and bags of cheese-and-onion-flavoured potato crisps. He squeezed his tall frame between one warm body and Brona's and smiled apologetically.

"It will be all right," she said simply, her voice low but very distinct. "I have gleaned that they are on their way to Bingo." She checked her watch, its face too large for her slim wrist, he thought. "It's half seven now. Perhaps Bingo begins at eight?"

He shrugged and was silent, not knowing how to begin. She sipped her drink, smoothing the skirt of her long black jersey dress. James mentally admired her figure and attempted to guess her age. Although slim, she had an air of composure, an almost commanding demeanor. No, not commanding, he realized. Aloof.

He began. "I'm glad you were willing and able to come."

She nodded. "I like Mr. Conroy," she said at last. "I assume you are trying to help him, and that is why I have come. But I should mention now that I have found this whole series of events very disturbing. To me personally and to my work. I am extremely reluctant to be drawn into a complex situation."

James watched as she methodically shredded the small cocktail napkin in her lap.

"Certainly you are. And understandably so. Violent death, two violent deaths in the house where you make your home can only have been extremely . . . disruptive." He picked his words carefully because her detachment unnerved him.

"Yes, very."

"I understand you are a student, then?"

"From whom do you understand this, Mr. Fleming?" Her voice was quick, sharp. The press of customers had moved them even closer together, and his bony elbow was against her arm. He tried to shift his weight away from her.

"Why, I think it must have been Aria . . . Mrs. Conroy. Or perhaps the police. I'm not sure now. I imagine it came up at the time of Shaw's, ah, death. Is my information correct?" He took a different tack, more professional, less personal. He noted her slight *humph* of distaste.

"I suppose I am a student in the common definition," she said primly. "I am at the present time finishing my doctoral dissertation on Diarmuid O'Suillebhean." She glanced at James quickly but saw no recognition there. "I expect to get my Ph.D. in the very near future. In English," she added, to make the issue at hand more clear.

"At the College?"

"Of course." The pride was apparent in her tone.

"Then you are a very advanced student in your field," James repeated.

"Yes," she said, grateful to be appreciated.

He sensed they were both feeling their way and thought that the way was pleasant. He was looking forward to getting to know Brona O'Connell. He was less interested in what seemed to him her obscure subject matter. But he listened attentively as she reprised her thesis, dealing as it did with the life and work of what he considered to be a very minor Irish poet.

"He is comparable to Keats, I believe, not only in the quality of his work at a parallel age, but also in the fact that his worth was not recognized during his lifetime," she said.

"Ah, but when it was, Keats was hugely influential on English literature and letters. Do you expect your revival of O'Suillebhean to have such an impact on Irish writing today?" James was attempting to acquit himself well and drew on his memory of his own years as an undergraduate in English.

Brona was impressed, as he'd hoped. "Well, yes, it is one of my goals certainly, but an unstated one at the moment. . . . Oh, my goodness, I forgot!"

James turned his eyes in the direction Brona was looking. He watched the tall, striking, black-haired girl stride across the room, tossing aside her scarlet scarf. He watched as the respectable clientele nudged one another and nodded their heads in her direction. Geraldine was out of place just by virtue of her height and her style. James was doubly startled when Brona stood up and waved and sat down again.

"I am sorry, Mr. Fleming." She sounded disappointed. "I was very anxious about our meeting, and I asked a friend to join us. I assure you she's familiar with the situation. It's just that we got so involved in our literary conversation I entirely forgot." With this Geraldine sat down at the tiny table, and James was sure he could detect annoyance in Brona's voice as she introduced Dr. Geraldine Keohane, medical resident at St. Gervase's Hospital in town. He greeted her amicably but was annoyed himself at the unexpected interruption.

Suddenly the barman, who had been unattainable earlier, was at her side. She ordered for all of them as she took off her black kid gloves finger by finger to reveal flaming red nails that matched her lips and set off her gleaming black hair.

"Right, where have we got to—the first or the second murder?"

"Geraldine." Brona's voice was admonishing.

"You're James, if I remember rightly. I recognized the name when Brona told me about your meeting. We met ages ago at one of your brother's parties." She smiled, he thought, with secret knowledge. His brother had been a resident at St. Gervase's, and James wondered uneasily if he'd been discussed.

He nodded noncommittally. Silence fell as each fingered a drink. He was irritated with Brona and had no intention of discussing his personal concerns over Harry with a third party.

"And what's the problem a'tall?" said Geraldine brightly.

Brona did not speak.

"I understood that I had an appointment with Miss O'Connell. We haven't completed our conversation, at least to my satisfaction," said James. He looked at Brona quizzically. "Let me say I didn't expect company." He stressed the last word ever so slightly.

"Oh, for God's sake. You sound just like a solicitor. Picking and choosing your words. And you, Brona, you're as bad." She drank her gin with enthusiasm. "Listen, James." She leaned over conspiratorially. "I've known Brona forever, and I shared digs with her at the Conroys' for too many years." She laughed again, a merry, chiming laugh. James smiled in spite of himself. "I can guess you want a little background. Of course, Brona's actually there, but nothing she tells you is a big secret. I can also give you some background information. I imagine I can read people as well as any solicitor. Perhaps better."

"It's true, Mr. Fleming," said Brona soberly. "I was a bit nervous over meeting you like this. I only had your word that you represented Mr. Conroy. I spoke to him—only at the door, I might add. But by then I'd asked Ger to come along. Perhaps between us we can answer your questions."

"Perhaps, but I am relying on your discretion. I'll get straight to the point. Brona, I need to know if you were home last night when Mrs. Conroy was killed. And if so, did you hear anything?"

"I got back last night at around ten. The police questioned me on this. I listened to some music on the radio for a while, classical music, and I heard nothing at all. Eventually I ran a bath, after which I went to bed and fell into a sound sleep. It sounds so pathetic, really, I know, that on two different occasions when all this violence was taking place directly over my head I was downstairs carrying on with my life. I feel—I felt—almost guilty about it." She looked at Ger for sympathy.

"It's true, James. Brona's the nervy type. I know from our conversations this has been a horror for her."

"Okay, okay. This situation is bizarre."

"Barbarous, really, and yet somehow so civilized."

James looked sharply at Geraldine, wondering exactly how much she knew.

"What I mean is the putting of the bodies in the bed," Geraldine explained. "The absence of violence, this mimicry, this horrible distortion of sleep. I see death fairly regularly."

Her voice was somber, and James felt a growing respect for her insight.

"I see the violence of a deathbed agony, the final struggle. I see death that has crept up on the patient in her sleep. I'm there sometimes when they die. I never get used to it. And I resent that afterwards that same person who had been struggling, fighting perhaps for breath, thrashing, talking even, is now lying there, for all the world peacefully asleep."

After a pause James murmured, "Perhaps they are. In a sense."

"No, I'll tell you what it's like. We've all seen a storm, a violent wind and rain storm—I don't mean on the News at Nine. I mean what we've witnessed ourselves. And then, after some hours or some days, it ceases. And in a very short time there is sunshine, blue sky, beautiful white puffy clouds, a little breeze maybe, a little angel's breath wafting over the fields or roads, touching your cheek." She paused. "Just as though nothing had happened. The wreckage, the suffering—ignored, forgotten! I'll tell you, it's a form of arrogance. On nature's part, I mean." She sat back and sipped her gin.

The jolly group beside them stood up and squeezed past on their way to a pleasant game of Bingo. James ordered a few bags of crisps and resumed his questioning.

"What I also need to know, Brona, concerns Friday night when Harry and Ariadne came home. They had been at a party, and they came in quite late, I believe?"

"What night again?"

"Friday."

"Yes, I'm afraid I do remember."

"Can you tell me—"

"I don't feel I should."

James paused. "I need to know. If the police haven't asked you, they still might. But I need to know what kind of attitude they're going to take with Harry. He has been *helping* the police, as they say, but I suspect that they will move against him."

"Well, then, my evidence won't help him." Brona bristled.

"It will help me."

"For God's sake, Brona, they'll find out soon enough about Harry and Ariadne," said Geraldine.

"What do you mean?" James snapped at her.

"Look, when I was there I knew they didn't have smooth sailing. I heard fights. I'd see them go out in the morning and barely look at each other. I knew when they took separate holidays."

James was taken aback and took some time to ponder this new picture. He didn't like Geraldine's description of the Conroy marriage. It wasn't what he'd observed himself, and it was not how they presented themselves to him. He returned to Brona.

"Apart from this information, did you, Brona, hear them when they came home?"

"Yes, unfortunately, I did hear them. I didn't wish to, I assure you. But the banging of the front door startled me. I was working, and very intent on what I was doing. But the argument distracted me, it broke my concentration. Once I became aware of it I blocked my ears. I think I may have played the wireless."

"Wireless! Brona, where did we get you a'tall?" Geraldine teased, but Brona flared at her.

"The point is, I heard them shouting, I heard angry voices. I don't know what they were saying. I didn't want to eavesdrop. Finally the racket stopped, but I couldn't work any longer, and I went to bed."

"Too bad I wasn't there. I would have listened." Geraldine had been catching James's eye for some few minutes before he realized she was flirting with him. Confused, flattered, he focussed his attention on Brona, who could have told him that Geraldine flirted the way other girls breathed.

"Brona, tell me—had they been fighting recently?"

"Apart from that fight, no. Not since the Shaw"—she hunted for the right word—"death. In fact, it was terribly quiet—rightly so, I suppose. I think they were upset. I know Harry was, anyway." James noted the shift to his Christian name. "I called in to see him one evening."

"When Ari was out, no doubt," Geraldine teased.

Brona glared, and Geraldine smiled back at her.

"Come on, pet," she said kindly. "What's the point? You and I know that you never liked Ariadne Conroy and that you've always had a soft spot for Harry." She glanced at James. "Thought he was hard done by."

"All right, it's true to a degree. I was, I assure you, James, never great friends with the Conroys. I happened to live in the same building as they—that's how I always conducted myself. When they bought the house after dear Mrs. Callahan passed away, they inherited me, I suppose. And shortly thereafter Geraldine joined me. Harry was always pleasant if we met. He'd inquire after my work, though I could tell he understood none of it." She smiled smugly.

"And Mrs. Conroy?" James heard the defensive tone in his voice.

"I always found her quite cold, remote."

"A bit like yourself, me girl." Geraldine signalled for the barman.

"Not in the least, I assure you." Brona flushed. "She struck me as a snob of the worst kind. Her job was shallow, her life was shallow . . . advertising." She gave a little snort.

James spoke. "So the arts, or medicine—these are the worthy professions?" He caught Geraldine's eye again.

"Certainly—isn't it obvious?" Brona stated.

"And the law, perhaps?" James's tone was inscrutable.

"As you say."

"What, what did I say?"

"You said 'perhaps.' "

"Did you ever consider the law yourself?" But James knew his question was rhetorical.

With the arrival of yet another round of drinks the conversation took on a less professional tenor. James watched as Brona rejected her drink and carefully but slowly gathered her scarf and bag and coat into her arms. As he and Geraldine chatted, Geraldine becoming more outrageous with each story she told, he watched Brona take a key from her bag and clench it in her palm.

". . . and so I was at that party your brother Donald threw. Not the famous one, when your parents—your mother, isn't it?—not that one when she was away. Glory be to God, that went down in legend."

James blanched to think of the unknown history of his brother's medical training.

"But you were at the official one Mother gave, when he qualified?" James was struck at this bisecting of their paths.

"Indeed and I was," she said merrily. "Saw the African room and all."

James rolled his eyes. "I don't remember you there," he said simply.

"And I don't remember you. So we're square. Perhaps I was otherwise occupied," she hinted.

"I remember that party." Brona interjected sourly. "That was the party where you broke off with Brendan. Her second engagement," she said pointedly to James.

"Brona, dearest, you are so serious. But that's what I like about you."

"As a doctor, you should take life a little more seriously yourself, Ger," Brona retorted.

"You've never understood, have you, that it's because I take death seriously that I don't take life seriously a'tall, a'tall." And with that she lit her third Gauloise of the evening. The heavy aroma wafted into their faces. Brona stood up. James couldn't tell whether she was reluctant or determined to leave. He stood.

"I must go now," she said severely. "The reading room is open until ten, and I may still get some work done. I've lost too much time over this whole issue."

"I thank you, Brona, for coming here tonight. The meeting didn't go quite as I intended . . ."

"Nor I." Her voice was heavy, bitter.

"But what little you told me unfortunately confirms what Harry had told me. I expect the police may question you again on this very point."

"I see." She didn't offer her hand but fingered her key.

He noticed it. "May I walk you to your car?"

Brona looked up into his face soberly. "Thank you, but I'm on the bike." And with that she strode stiffly, self-consciously towards the door. He sat down and sighed.

"Interested?" asked Geraldine after a brief silence.

"What?" James paused. "Funny you should ask. I thought I was. She—pardon me, Brona—was quite magnificent there, just before you arrived. She was speaking of her work. She was so animated, so intense. So—"

"Full of feeling?"

"Yes, that's it. But, well, I'm not about to gossip. No, I'm not interested. I doubt she would be in me."

"I wouldn't say that, but I'm just fishing to see if the coast is clear."

James looked at her attractive face, the vitality that beamed from her.

"It's clear," he said at last, and they began to arrange to meet the following night. And when he left her at the door of the Residents' Hall, and she kissed him lightly on the nose, he felt a new man. And she hadn't even minded that he did not want to hear Sarah Gallagher, the famous violinist, performing at the Concert Hall on Saturday evening. If she thought him a plebeian for it, it couldn't be helped.

But as he drove carefully home he knew that even a Geraldine could not block out the sun that was Sarah. *And will I keep faith with thee, Cynara.* And he let his thoughts take a literary turn that night.

—— *Chapter Eight* ——

The inquest into Ariadne's death had been quickly convened and as quickly adjourned. James had sat with Harry and then watched as Harry told of discovering the body of his wife on his late return from a professional meeting. The medical examiner gave the cause of death, a profound trauma to the cerebellum, and the approximate time, late in the evening on Monday. When Molloy was called he requested that the inquest be adjourned to a later date pending completion of an active current investigation on a definite line of inquiry. Although Harry was relieved, James guessed it meant only one thing. Molloy was about to make an arrest in the case. He listened as the coroner indicated that Mrs. Conroy's body was now released for burial. The whole episode was over in a matter of minutes.

Harry's spirits had risen, and he immediately told James that he wanted him to make arrangements for Ariadne's funeral as soon as possible and that he'd get back to him. James parted from Harry at his car, puzzled by Harry's profound relief. Puzzled, too, that Harry wished to involve him in the funeral.

When he returned to his office it was to be greeted by Maggie with the news that the junior he had interviewed and had hoped to hire—a fresh-faced, energetic young woman—had called to say she'd gone with another firm. James was crest-fallen. She was the second young solicitor to have rejected him, for that was how he saw it. This train of thought was interrupted by a further buzz from Maggie telling him his mother was on the line and that she, Maggie, had already informed her that James was available.

"How can I thank you, Maggie?" said James sarcastically. "Put her through."

"James, darling, it's your neglected little mother here."

"Not likely."

"Pardon?"

"How sprightly you sound," James recovered.

"Mmm. As I said, you are neglecting me. And Donald."

"Donald? I just saw Donald!"

"Mmm. But he needs an older brother now. He's under great strain. And there are only the two of you."

James had no doubt that Donald was under great strain, having decided to open up his private general practice in their mother's house. There had now been months of applications for planning permission, quotes from builders, disputes with suppliers. But Donald trojaned on. Oblivious. And James could hardly comment. It was his mother's faith—and funds—that had enabled him to buy out Fitzgerald and put the firm in his own hands.

"There's trouble, I take it?"

"Yes, darling, just a little matter of some work the wretched builder did. It's so dreadfully confusing. Some variance at variance with the law. Or perhaps that we just went a tiny bit over the property line. And of course there's Mr. O'Hare next door, who hasn't given up the fight. He's got some unpleasant petition going about the increase in car traffic. Nonsense. Donald can only see one patient at time. That means just one car at a time . . ."

James listened to his mother with but half an ear as he prepared his usual answer.

"No, Mother. I said from the start I would not get involved. Donald has a solicitor."

"But what good is it having a son who's a solicitor if we can't call on him in times of distress?"

He reminded her that she also had her own solicitor and chose not to use the services of her elder son.

"You're so stubborn. Just like your father, I might add."

"Thank you," James said simply. "Now, is there anything else?"

"Yes, James. I want the name of that charming fellow you were at College with, the one in the Planning Office . . ."

"Mother! I have another call. I must go." And indeed this time he did see his second line flashing.

"I'll see you Saturday, then?"

"What? Right. Did we agree on that? Oh, I must go."

With a sigh of relief that was to be replaced by an inward sigh of shock he picked up the line to hear Harry's voice.

"Fleming, I'm on my way." The weak transmission of the car telephone was obvious. "Molloy has called me in. Can you come with me?" His question was full of fear.

"I'll meet you there," said James, and he told Maggie as he ran out through the lobby to re-schedule his morning appointments.

Molloy's demeanor was cordial as ever as Harry and James were shown into his office. But for some moments he did not speak, standing with his back turned, staring out of a rather grimy window into the watery morning light. James had warned Harry before they entered to remain in control, and he was heartened to see that indeed Harry took charge of the dynamics of the situation.

"Inspector Molloy, I assume you've called me here because you have some news. I am quite anxious to know it. I am in the midst of making arrangements for the funeral."

"Oh, indeed, I have news, Mr. Conroy," Molloy said levelly. "A great deal, in fact." He sat in his swivel chair, tapping thin white fingers on the surface of his desk. Finally he opened a deep drawer in his desk and removed an item wrapped in plastic. Silently he placed it before them, glancing from James to Harry.

"Do you, Mr. Conroy, recognize this?"

Harry stood to get a closer look through the shiny surface of the plastic.

"Well"—he hesitated—"it's a golf trophy, obviously. But there are hundreds like it, no doubt."

"Oh, but there is much doubt," said Molloy, his voice caressing, almost lyrical. "There is no other trophy like this one in the whole of Ireland. Look again." He handed Harry a pencil, and Harry used it to prod the trophy, its cheap gilt shining in the light from the window. James shivered.

"It says on the base . . ."

"Yes, go on."

"Ariadne Conroy, Palmerston Golf Club, 1980. When did you last see this trophy, Mr. Conroy?"

Harry sat down heavily. "I haven't the faintest idea. Ari—Ariadne—had quite a few trophies. And I had, too. We'd only keep the current ones out on display."

"Indeed. So you would agree that it isn't like any other in the country?" Molloy waited patiently.

"Of course not, since I see Ariadne's name on it now."

"Well, now, there's a little bit more to it than that. You see, we found this in the attic of your home, Mr. Conroy."

James cleared his throat.

"Mr. Fleming?"

"No, nothing, just a slight cough. Please continue."

"Yes, indeed. Well, now. We found this trophy, you see, and on it we found some fingerprints."

Harry leaned forward anxiously.

"Your wife's fingerprints. And your own."

"Well, naturally," said Harry, almost smiling. "I imagine we'd both handled it at some time."

"I see. Naturally, did you say?" Molloy returned to his stance at the window, rocking on his heels. "Naturally." He turned. "Did you hear, Mr. Fleming?"

But James didn't respond, waiting as he was for the other shoe to drop.

"And so is it natural, too, that this trophy with your fingerprints on it has been determined forensically to be the murder weapon?" He turned to watch the effect of his words on Harry Conroy, but Harry had lowered his head, breathing deeply and loudly.

"Honestly, Molloy," said James crossly, "this is uncalled for. I remind you Mr. Conroy came here of his own free will."

Molloy shushed him like a grandfather. "Fleming, Fleming. I'm merely answering Mr. Conroy's stated and unstated questions. It is a fact that Mrs. Conroy died of one sharp blow to the base of the skull. The medical examiner reports that there was subdural hematoma and very little blood loss. And to answer Mr. Conroy's question of the other day, there was no sign of an assault on her person. Or a struggle, for that matter. Her fingernails weren't even broken. It is clear to me—and no doubt, to you, Fleming—that Mrs. Conroy knew her attacker." He stopped speaking and merely raised his eyebrows. But his expression was not a quizzical one.

Harry opened his eyes and accepted a glass of water James had poured from the jug on the corner table.

"Let me tell you a story, a story which, Mr. Fleming, you will, in the end, admit covers all the facts of this unhappy case." He continued on in his lulling narrative tone.

"One evening, not so very long ago, Mr. and Mrs. Conroy attended a party."

"Light years ago," murmured James.

"And at that party they had quite a heated exchange, indeed an argument. There were plenty of witnesses.

"That argument continued, perhaps in their car on the way home. When they arrived at that home the argument was loud and prolonged.

"Perhaps that argument concerned the recent death of a Philip Shaw. Shaw, who had been, let us say, an intimate friend of Mrs. Conroy—"

"That's ridiculous!" interjected Harry.

"Hearsay!" said James, instantly regretting his mistake.

"Interesting, Mr. Fleming. 'Hearsay.' Now who do you suppose would be in the position to say something that we might want to hear? Mmm? Might it be you, perhaps?" James didn't answer him, but the light of certain knowledge was in Molloy's eye.

Harry looked at James, not following this bit of dialogue. James shook his head, stopping the incipient question on his lips.

"Yes," continued Molloy, resuming his seat. "Perhaps I should explain for Mr. Conroy. Or shall you, Fleming?"

James shook his head again. "Just get on with it, will you?" he said with a control he did not feel.

"Surely. What you don't seem to know, Mr. Conroy, is that Mrs. Shaw has been to see us here."

"Shaw's mother? I mean wife?" Harry was dazed.

"His widow, Mr. Conroy. She came with a very important piece of information. She has confirmed to us that Mr. Shaw was on his way to Dublin to see your wife, Ariadne Conroy."

"That's ridiculous. She hadn't seen the man in twenty years, for God's sake. How would he remember her out of the thousands of students he'd taught? Why, he wouldn't even know her name now that it's Conroy."

"Perhaps, perhaps," murmured Molloy.

"Why do you accept this Shaw woman's lies?" said Harry so quietly the other men were startled.

"Because she was in a position to know. Perhaps your solicitor here can tell you more."

"I have nothing to say at present on this matter," said James. And there's no way Molloy can know what Ariadne told me, he thought to himself. But he felt naked before the man's relentlessly accurate reading of the situation, includ-

ing his assumption that James knew about Shaw's past affair
with Ariadne.

"As I was saying," continued Molloy, "Mr. Conroy and
his wife had a prolonged argument. We can assume it was
over issues connected with the recent death of Shaw.
Perhaps Mr. Conroy was vengeful, perhaps the death of
Shaw was not enough to fulfill his pursuit of natural justice.
Shaw was dead. But the true betrayer, Mrs. Conroy, lived.
Did she taunt him?" The question hung in the air, but Harry
kept his hand over his face.

"Did she threaten to tell the police, to betray him again?
Not with a lover this time, but with some knowledge that
would reveal Mr. Conroy as Shaw's killer?"

"Are you charging my client with the murder of Shaw?"
interjected James.

"I am telling a story, Mr. Fleming. Perhaps there were
other reasons for the Conroys' public argument. Perhaps
one day Mr. Conroy will tell us." His tone was cajoling.

But Harry said nothing.

"We have the murder weapon, as you see." Molloy spoke
directly to James. "It was found in Conroy's house, with his
fingerprints on it. We have evidence of motive: a long and
bitter quarrel spreading over many hours, perhaps days. We
have information from Mrs. Shaw that ties the two victims
together. And the deceased—"

"Mrs. Conroy!" James said sternly.

"And Mrs. Conroy is the sole connection between these
two men—Shaw and her husband. In sum we have, as the
textbooks like to put it, the motive, the means, and, obviously, the opportunity."

Molloy's manner took on that of a lecturer as he turned
his attention to Harry. "Opportunity, Mr. Conroy. The
kind every husband has. You share a house, a flat, a cottage
with a woman, a wife. She comes and goes. Perhaps all is not
as it should be, she thinks. Perhaps we're not getting along,
she thinks. Perhaps there is hatred and betrayal between us,

she thinks. But she comes and she goes; it is, after all, her home. The only haven any of us has in this world. Only a room, or a caravan by the side of the road. No matter. It is our shelter and our safety. But those four walls, whether poor or opulent, can hold danger, can provide—as I said— the ever-present opportunity to the husband, the partner, for violence, for death. Did you kill her when she was sleeping, Mr. Conroy?"

The question galvanized the comatose Harry. He leapt to his feet. "No, by God, I did not."

Molloy paused and then said sadly, "Perhaps, Mr. Conroy, you've yet to experience the truth of the old axiom: Confession is good for the soul." And he hurried on as James began to interrupt. "I charge you, Harry Conroy, with the murder of your wife, Ariadne Conroy."

It had been, for James, a harrowing forty-eight hours during which he felt his inexperience keenly and regretted, for the hundreth time, ever becoming involved with a criminal action. His nights were haunted by dreams of his first criminal case, and throughout them he heard Sarah's voice calling him from a great distance. Sleep brought no rest, and only when bail was set and James negotiated with the bondsman, using Harry's house as surety, did he allow his grip on himself to relax.

He—naïve as he should not have been—was amazed bail was granted at all. It was only the information from a cynical probation officer he had met at the Courts who explained that domestic murder cases routinely got bail "unless it was the wife who done it."

Throughout Harry had insisted that James continue the arrangements for the funeral. James argued to delay it but could not argue against Harry's gothic portrayal of Ariadne's corpse lying alone in the refrigerator of the morgue.

"Is the grave any better?" James had wanted to scream, but on reflection he knew, as did Harry, that it was. The grave would hold some peace for Ariadne, a return of privacy, of dignity, and in time, as for all, of anonymity.

He took Maggie out to dinner.

"You look dreadful," she said as she enjoyed a hearty steak and kidney pudding.

They were seated in an old city hotel along the quays. The dining room was sedate, warm, and decrepit. The service good, the food substantial.

He ate well, enjoying his steak, mashed potatoes, boiled potatoes, and fresh peas.

"Comfort food?"

"Pardon me?"

"Never mind. Have some bread." And she buttered him a doorstep of thick white bread.

"I called your mother yesterday, by the way, and cancelled your date for today."

"Lord, today's Saturday, of course! What'd she say?"

"Not to worry—she'd be in touch."

"No doubt about that," he sighed, replete with food and plonk. "You've been marvelous, Maggie, and this is by way of thanking you. I couldn't have handled Harry's situation and the funeral, too. At least there's a day to rest before that ordeal on Monday. The Pepperpot Church?"

"Yes, very picturesque. I hope you don't get newspaper people."

James groaned at the prospect of what lay ahead. He knew the little church well, having attended Christmas carol concerts there over the years. Because of its unique bell tower it had been dubbed the pepperpot or pepper cannister since the day it opened its doors over a century ago.

"They're Church of Ireland, then?" he mused.

"Mr. Conroy is. Ariadne wasn't very active, like yourself." Maggie's recently found tolerance of non–Catholics beamed from her face. She liked neat distinctions.

"How'd you manage?"

"Harry was very calm. He'd written everything out, and I merely followed his instructions," Maggie said modestly.

ANN C. FALLON

"Her parents are dead. She's one brother in Canada. Harry
had already spoken to him on the phone, and he's not
coming."

"Bastard!"

Maggie shrugged. "It's a long way. On the other hand,
Harry's parents live on the south side, Rathgar, I believe.
And his two sisters and their spouses also live in the burbs.
His mother was very helpful. She liked Ariadne a great
deal." Maggie spun the stem of her wineglass in between her
fingers. "I'm sorry, James."

"So am I," he answered sadly.

James had a thousand questions to ask of Harry, but he
had decided to hold off on all but one until after the funeral.
He dropped Maggie off at her flat and drove to Mountjoy
Prison to pick up Harry. He was surprised to find him more
in control than he had expected. But it didn't last, and
Harry continually reminisced about Ariadne on the drive to
Rathgar.

"Harry, Harry." James's earlier training came to the fore.
"I want to know if Ariadne left a will."

"Not a'tall."

"That was very unwise of her," he said.

"Well, I have one."

"No doubt," mumbled James, swerving to avoid a street
cleaner who'd moved his pushcart too far from the kerb.

"I wanted her to make one when I did. But she is, I
suppose she was, superstitious."

"As are so many Irish people," added James, knowing
only too well the opposite side of the coin of his particular
realm.

"And then, well, we had no children. She didn't see the
need. She'd just say that I'd get everything, and that I
deserved it."

"Well, what is everything?" James prodded.

"Nothing, actually. Everything was held jointly. She
didn't have anything to leave . . . behind. . . ."

108

And in especial, no children, mused James, but he would have to wait to learn more.

He was very glad of Geraldine's company as he drove to the funeral on Monday morning through a downpour. The weather had turned cold, and the wind was sharp. Typical, Geraldine had observed, of all the funerals she'd attended. But she hadn't attended as many as James, and he recalled two in particular. Both on beautiful sunny mornings, when petals from cherry tress had blown in the wind and large brilliant drops of rain had fallen from blue sky. Jack Moore's funeral in Wexford, with but five people at the graveside. And his own father's funeral. James saw not for the first time the callow youth he had been as he stood, the first of many to lift the small trowel and fling the earth that fell with a thud on his father's coffin.

"James. James!" He heard Geraldine's voice from afar telling him she'd spotted a space to park the car.

The small church was filled to capacity, with many of the mourners forced to stand at the back and in the aisles. James carried the wreath marked with his own name and the wreath Maggie had ordered from the firm up the centre aisle and laid them on the steps of the altar. He paused for a moment in prayer and glanced at the gleaming pale wood coffin. Wreaths and sprays almost covered it and lay in profusion at the feet of the metal trolley and along the three red-carpeted steps. He moved aside as a couple came up behind him, bearing their wreaths. As he turned he caught Harry's eye, sad and red in an ashen face. He saw his mother's hand on his arm, rhythmically patting it as one would do with a child, for her child he was.

As James returned to his seat he scanned the congregation but recognized no-one. He hoped Molloy had had the grace to stay away himself, to send someone anonymous to spy on Harry.

He felt again, as he had on occasion before, that he was at the funeral service of a stranger. He tried to picture Ariadne in the coffin that lay before them but could not. Or would not. He heard only snatches of the familiar psalms, and then the mellow voice of the clergyman, a friend it seemed of Harry's family. He wondered at Ariadne's religious beliefs; had she any, and were her questions answered now? So young, so lovely. He watched Harry following the coffin up the aisle, leaning on his mother and father, dry-eyed and broken. What suspicions James had were temporarily allayed. No one could doubt Harry's grief during this last week. But why had he not called the police? The question nagged James at the most unlikely times. But all these thoughts were swamped in the swell of grief he felt as he heard the heart-rending strains, the beautiful solo voice lifted in the moving hymn "Abide with Me." James shed his tears and was not ashamed to be seen to do so.

"Did you see Brona?" was Geraldine's first question as they ran to his car through the now-drenching mist. James idled the motor as he waited for the signal to join the lengthy queue of cars composing the funeral procession.

"Did you?" Geraldine repeated when she had his attention. It would be a long ride to the cemetery in Wicklow.

"Brona? No, I'm afraid I didn't."

"Nor I. I was just wondering if she made it. I asked her to join us, you know," she said off-handedly as she smoothed the skirt of her two-piece black suit. James glanced at her and wondered if it was a Chanel. She lifted the black veil of her small black cloche in order to light her cigarette.

"Must you?" he said, slightly irritated.

"No, I choose to," she said, "but I won't now."

"It's the car, you see."

"Pristine, yes, I had noticed." She laughed. "It's okay, James, just a reflex action on my part. Dead bodies cause me to smoke. Now, about Brona—"

"You asked her to come along with us?"

"Mmm. But she said she'd make her own way."

"On her bike? It's a long way to Wicklow."

"No, she could have walked to the church, obviously. I just wondered with whom she would go to the grave, if she does."

"We shall see." And they drove in silence, a silence he hadn't realized he'd imposed himself.

"I shouldn't have worn these shoes," said Geraldine, apropos of nothing.

"Why not?" He glanced down. "They seem quite nice."

"They are nice, and they're new. I forgot, you see."

"Forgot?"

"It's bad luck to wear new shoes to a funeral."

James was heartened to see the substantial numbers of mourners who had come to the graveside. They picked their way carefully down the narrow paths, squeezing between the tall, thin, lichen-covered stones. High heels sank in the mud, and black umbrellas of every size sprang up like mushrooms in the now-heavy downpour. Irish mourners were used to rain in cemeteries, thought James glumly. Perhaps that was why they claimed it was good luck. So many superstitions, he thought. The Irish are always hedging against the great unknown, of which they seemed to be so acutely, mystically aware.

Geraldine huddled under his umbrella, pressing against him. They were barely able to hear the prayers, stationed as they were at the back of the crowd. James had a sense of unreality, common at these occasions, but more so, he thought, on this particular day. He half-heartedly glanced through the crowd only to spot Molloy, soberly dressed in a well-cut gray coat, the rain falling on his thick head of silver hair. Typical country policeman, thought James bitterly. Yet why so bitter? It was entirely possible—and James had almost admitted it to himself a number of times—that Harry was guilty.

Everything Molloy had postulated could be true. James shivered as a gust of wind caught them from the west.

Umbrellas turned inside out, and the clergyman's long cassock wrapped itself around his legs. Molloy stood impassive, unaware of James's stare. Yes, Harry could have done it, thought James. But could he have feigned such devastating grief, such weakness and incapacity? But then, what did James know of Harry? He told Molloy he was a friend, but that wasn't the truth. He'd claimed Ariadne in his heart as a friend, and yet she, too, was an unknown to him. But he'd liked her, and she was gone.

Gone, soon to be gone from sight, under the earth, covered with grass that would grow in time, covered by sprays of flowers. And what would the headstone read? No, he didn't want to accept that the man she'd lived with, loved, married, could have taken her life. In such a heinous way, vindictive, violent. Harry hadn't known that she and Shaw had been lovers once. She'd never told him.

Or had she? In the last few days? Is that what she had wanted to tell him on the phone? That she'd told Harry, and that he was angry? Harry did not have cause to murder Shaw, a complete stranger. Unless he'd known of her relationship with him, had found out unbeknownst to her. Had Philip Shaw's wife told him? When and why? Had Harry also feigned surprise at Shaw's death? Could he be such a consummate actor? He was not acting now as he wept at her grave, but this could be real sadness for what had once been.

The crowd broke into smaller groups, some talking, most hurrying back towards their cars. James shook hands with Harry and gently refused his invitation to return to his mother's home for drinks and sandwiches. Harry nodded absently to Geraldine and also to Brona, who had come up behind them. James waited as she expressed her sympathy, warm and sincere. Harry's face softened a little as she urged him to be strong in the face of adversity. She murmured some quote—biblical, literary. James couldn't place it.

"It's shocking, really," Brona said soberly as they walked away.

112

Geraldine nodded and nudged James to speak. "Brona, would you like a lift back to town?"

"Yes, thanks. I hitched a lift with some advertising type, but I think she's gone off now." Brona's wiftiness, her lack of concern as to what she was doing and how, intrigued James.

"Well, shall we go?"

They left Harry standing, still receiving condolences. His parents had gone on, no doubt to prepare the way and receive the visitors at home.

In the car Geraldine asked if there had been a receiving of the remains at the church the night before.

"No, I'm sure there wasn't," snapped Brona.

"For God's sake, Brona," said Geraldine, lighting up her cigarette. This time James said nothing. "Why not? I don't see why we do and you lot don't."

"Unnecessary, entirely unnecessary," replied Brona.

"I don't know about that. I think it's rather nice," said James, musing as they drove through the rain.

"The service, Brona, is an old one."

Geraldine explained pointedly to Brona that the parish priest would greet the arrival of the deceased person at dusk, at the door of his church. There he would pray for the soul of the faithful departed, and the family would pray with him. The coffin would stand on a trestle in a side chapel, with the grillwork doors closed over, and would rest there through the night, candles lit, someone keeping watch.

"I agree, Ger," said James. "It's a warm, almost welcoming service. The Catholic Church has a more human, more sheltering aspect to it that appeals at least to me. Perhaps, Brona, the Church of Ireland could use a little more of that nurturing, comforting approach."

Brona merely snapped, "And perhaps you are misled, James, into confusing sentimentalism with true solace."

After a few minutes of continued gloom Geraldine commented that she was glad Brona had decided to attend the service.

"Why did you think I wouldn't? I might have disliked

113

Ariadne," she added, "but I'm not disrespectful. And besides, I wanted to show my support for Harry. He looked dreadful, don't you think?"

"Dreadful!" Geraldine echoed.

In time they reached the outskirts of Dublin. Brona's flat was en route, and James headed straight for it. The house was silent, empty, dead from the outside. Even the constable had been released back to active duty. No reporters, James was relieved to see. The rain had kept them from the cemetery and from the street.

"Would you like to come in, Ger? James?" Brona said in a less defiant voice.

"Sorry, pet, but I've got to get back. Padraig's only covering my wards for the length of the service. He'll be in a foul humour as it is. The tail end of one of his forty-eight-hour stints. My turn next. Aaggh!"

When Brona didn't respond James suggested he drive Geraldine to the hospital and return to Brona's flat. And when Brona agreed readily to go along for the ride he realized how reluctant she was to go home. He seized his chance.

They were back in front of the house in a matter of minutes, but their mood was glum without Geraldine's ebullience, her constant challenging. James got out and came around to open Brona's door. He handed her out, and she seemed to him then like a small fluttering bird, light-boned, and he imagined her heart beating at some rapid rate, like a bird's.

"Do come in," she said formally, and he followed her, ducking his head in time to avoid the low lintel.

James liked the flat immediately. The kitchen, with its large table and weathered sideboard and press, reminded him of his great-aunt's kitchen when he used to spend his childhood summers down the country. It was welcoming after the rain. Brona moved efficiently but almost surreptitiously, lighting up the gas fire, setting out a tray, putting the electric kettle on to boil. It was a routine, James realized, come of long usage. Economical—that was the word for her. Economy of movement, often of words. Somehow it appealed to him, lulled him, made him feel secure.

The orderliness of the room was complete, down to the tea towels drying on the little rods that folded out from the counter. Although the room was the least modern of the many flats he'd visited in recent years, it was more attractive. Before he'd finished his survey of its little nooks and crannies the tray was laid, and he took it from her and followed her past the stairs in the hallway and past the telephone table and into a minute study. He set the tray down on a small wood and rush-woven stool, once common to every house in Ireland.

"I noticed," he said conversationally, "that many of these items—attractive, I might add—date from my childhood and beyond. Were they here when you took the flat?"

"The table was, and the big press. But all the rest of the things you see are mine own. From my childhood, things from Daddy's—I mean Father's—rectory."

"Your father's a clergyman?" James blurted.

"Was. He passed away some years ago."

"I'm sorry."

She shrugged, pouring the tea expertly.

"I'm just surprised you seem to know so little about the Catholic services. I would have thought you'd be familiar with the 'other side'."

"It holds no appeal for me. Too much emotion."

"But surely it's a hugely important factor in your studies of nineteenth-century Irish literature." He sat back and sipped his tea, hot and very sweet, the way he liked it. He took the Home Wheat biscuits she offered politely, formally.

They sat in silence, companionable he wasn't sure. The room was small and square. A servant's room in the old house, he concluded. The walls were painted white, like white-wash, and the two chocolate-brown overstuffed chairs, the small oak table with the radio, the prie dieux at an angle in the corner seemed made for it. A lectern of pure, clean lines held not a prayer book, but an English-Irish dictionary.

"An bhfuil Gaeilge agat?" he asked.

Her response in Irish was lengthy, and he was chagrined.

"I apologize for teasing."

"Is that what you were doing? I take it then you don't have the Irish."

"If I ever did, it was schoolboy Irish."

"Like most of you. I thought when you spoke you already knew about my uncle, Sean O'Connell."

"He's your uncle?" James was startled again. This man was regularly in the media, a foremost expert in the Irish language. A big, robust man, full-bearded and articulate, a regular guest on talk shows and a convincing proponent of the language. His scholarship sat easily on him. Brona was well connected after all. "A great man" was what he said aloud.

"Indeed."

"Your flat has a cottage feel to it. The white-washed look, the dark furniture. You've lovely taste."

"Thank you."

As she poured his second cup an enormous cat strolled in, taking account of the room and its latest visitor. He or she decided to ignore James and instead strode magnificently over to Brona, waiting until her hands were free. With the coiled spring of the cat family, Mangan, for it was she, sprang into Brona's lap. James liked cats and was impressed with the animal, whose purr sounded like a well-tuned motor.

"This is Mangan," said Brona as she stroked the fur. With that remark the other two cats appeared, one circling her black-clad legs, the other moving slowly across the top of the chair to settle on James's knee.

"You should be flattered."

"I am."

"That's James, and this is Clarence."

James hooted with laughter. "James Clarence Mangan. The nineteenth-century Irish poet. I love it," he said, and Brona smiled a genuine smile at his appreciation.

"Is this where you work?" he said, leading the witness.

"No, actually, although I do read in here. My bedroom (did she blush, thought James) is quite capacious. A boudoir, really."

"You hardly are the sulking type," said James.

Brona paused and then answered, "Your French is better than your Irish, certainly. No, it is not my sulking room, as the word implies. I should have said it was a bed-sitting room," she added precisely.

James nodded, feeling he'd scored a point.

"Get more practice. I'm sorry—you were saying . . ."

"I have a large work space—for the electric typewriter, my files, my bookcase, and so on. This room I keep free for leisure reading, or music, or visitors."

Such demarcations. Each room with a purpose. Everything in its place.

She read his mind. "I live a life of the mind, James. I need to have order. It reflects my mental habits as well. If I can prepare a good meal quickly, then it frees me to work. If I tidy up after that meal, it means I don't have dirty dishes to face the next morning. If I have everything in its place, to hand, then I save time and valuable energy I can expend on my work. I learned young the value of time and orderly habits."

James wondered at this life of the mind. Was it as rigid as her life-style, her housekeeping? Surely there would be room for emotion, for the accidental occurrences that made life unpredictable and, consequently, interesting. And he said as much.

"I hardly crave excitement. I find the literature exciting. You think I live through or in my work. Perhaps I do. I don't see why people find that strange. It's merely a different form of excitement to theirs."

"And better?"

"Perhaps." The cat left her, and she brushed the long hairs from her green wool skirt. The high-necked, bottle-green sweater suited her. Her small face was like a cameo, white, framed by her brown hair, serene. He envied her her serenity. Her confidence.

"And so I imagine you dislike interruption from the outside."

"Naturally."

"Such as the Conroys upstairs."

"Exactly." She was heated. "Mrs. Conroy never in all these years showed me any consideration. Oh, I know I should not speak ill of the dead, but this is the truth. I needed, still need, the peace to which I am entitled.

"The parties were the worst. A few years ago they must have decided to widen their social circle, I don't know. But at least twice a month—no, every weekend—late parties, drinks parties, afternoon teas. The cars coming and going. The thump of music. It was very bad, but things died down eventually. And do you know, then and since, she never invited me to a single party?" Brona stood up abruptly and started to load the tray.

"To be fair, Harry did. In fact, I had drinks once with Harry 'upstairs!' " Her voice was heavy with sarcasm. "Looking back, I suppose that's when I began to see that marriage for what it was. Poor Harry. She was very dismissive."

They moved into the kitchen. "How so?"

"Very belittling—of his job in particular. And really, of him. I don't know why he put up with it for so long."

"Love?" said James quietly, but Brona merely sniffed. He added: "Would you say then Harry might have had a pretty strong motive?"

"No, I wouldn't say that. I'm surprised you asked. I thought you said he was a friend of yours. Seems to me a friend would have more faith."

"I'm a lawyer, Brona."

"'Tis a strange friendship, then." She poured boiling

118

water from the kettle into the basin and began to rinse off the tea things. "Harry is a nice man. He didn't deserve her derogatory behaviour, her lack of respect for him. But I do not believe that he killed her. He always struck me as rather weak."

James took up the linen tea towel and carefully dried as she washed, careful, too, of his smartly cut Irish merino wool tweed suit, which he had only recently purchased.

"He's a weak man, a passive man. Like most men. Easily led, lacking imagination," she continued conversationally.

"Most men?" James began to bridle.

"Indeed. Perhaps I should qualify it, then, for the law." She smiled to herself. "Most men in Ireland, most men I've known. Is that specific enough?"

He wondered how many men she'd known. "Yes," he said.

"In fact, most people lack imagination, don't you find?"

"You value this highly, then?"

"Certainly. It is among the highest attributes. Imagination. Creativity. Knowledge."

"For its own sake?"

"Certainly."

"Without application?"

"Possibly. I suppose you are going to bring up that old argument. Mr. Fleming, I've heard anything you might say more than once." Her tone was dismissive. "You don't get this far in an academic career without being challenged by the ignorant."

"But surely you personally would feel more justified, more validated, if you were making a contribution to scholarship in the field of—well, let's say, Yeatsian studies."

"Or medicine?"

"No, obviously your field is your field. You've chosen it, your talents have led you there. But surely you would rather that many people read your dissertation, not just a few other experts in the field. Will your years of effort and work and

119

sacrifice make a jot of difference to anyone's life?" James was sharp, irritated.

"Who imposes that standard on me? You?"

"Society, I suppose."

She turned to face him, drying her hands on a towel. "I'll tell you," she said levelly. "It makes a difference in *my* life. O'Suillebhean's poetry speaks to *my* soul! Is one person enough? It will make a difference because by means of his work, his life, I will obtain the highest degree awarded within the university. A good degree. And with that doctorate I will carve out my life. I will teach. What do you think—won't my teaching reach hundreds of students over the years, and won't I change people, not leave them as I find them? Do I have to use a scalpel or plead in a court to change lives?" She paused to draw breath. "I think not."

She carefully folded her hand towel and began to put away the crockery in the press and the foodstuffs in the tall cupboard.

"We don't agree, I take it," she said at last, pleasantly, almost apologetically.

"I agree you may change lives when you teach. I think you've evaded the issue when I claimed, with all due respect, that your poet, and your exposition of this poet, can have no real impact on anyone else."

"And you won't take my point that it does not need to!"

"I accept, however," James went on, ignoring her interruption, "that you are extremely selfless, that only literature seems to fire you. You are one of the least materialistic people I've met." She blushed a deep red. He wondered. Was it embarrassment or anger? He went on. "I imagine that comes through to you from your father."

She didn't answer.

He felt suddenly tired. "I must get back to work."

"As must I."

"But of course." He felt her disdain and didn't like it. He hadn't wanted to alienate her. What she said or didn't say about Harry and Ariadne could have a real impact on the case for the defense. If she were a witness, he didn't want her hostile.

She watched him and then spoke, indefatigably courteous. "What do you do exactly, Mr. Fleming?"

"Wills, mostly."

"Lot of impact on the living, then?"

"You'd be surprised."

She shut the door with a polite farewell.

James sat in the easy chair in his office and sighed. He was tired, tired from the strain of the funeral, tired from sparring with Brona. He reviewed what information he had garnered and jotted a few notes on the pad on his lap. It was atrociously little. He had merely confirmed that Brona was friendly towards Harry and his defense, yet at the same time that she could testify that Harry and Ariadne had quarrelled that night.

He closed his eyes to see again the mourners at the graveside. For that was what Molloy had been doing there—observing, not Harry, but the others. Was he looking for somebody in particular? James leapt to his feet. Mrs. Shaw! Molloy had said she had come to him, spoken to him. Could she still be in Dublin? Fool, fool. He'd lost four days, distracted by Harry and by the funeral. He phoned Molloy directly and bluntly asked him if Mrs. Shaw was still in Dublin.

"Bit late in the day, Fleming," said the mild Molloy. "She left last week."

"So she told you about Mrs. Conroy's alleged behaviour with her husband. When?" James was suspicious.

"Two weeks ago, when she came over to take charge of the arrangements for getting Shaw's body back to England. When she was here at headquarters dealing with all the paperwork, of course, I questioned her. That information came out in the course of our conversations."

"How did she seem to you, Molloy?"

"What do you mean?" Now it was Molloy's turn to be suspicious.

James was careful. "Was she upset? Do you think perhaps she was tired and emotional, as they say?"

"No comment."

"When exactly did she leave the country?"

"No comment."

James rang off. He was exasperated. It would take him time to verify the exact date of Mrs. Shaw's departure.

"Maggie," he said as he walked tiredly to her desk, "I'm handing over my caseload to Bill."

"Well, whatever you say, but Mr. Carey is up to his eyes with the McCarthy family trying to break the mother's will. How about Mr. Webster?"

"No, Carey can handle it. I'll only be gone a couple of days, and Webster's going on his holidays, lucky bastard." Maggie was startled.

"Sorry. Listen, I've got to go over to England. Tomorrow if possible. Book my flight, and I guess I'll need a car—no, wait. If I'm going to do this, I might as well do it right. I'll aim for the evening ferry from Dun Laoghaire. Try for a ticket, will you?"

He spoke with Bill Carey and then drove wearily to Harry's house. The drive had become too familiar in just a few days, too onerous.

He sat for a few moments and rested his forehead on the steering wheel, dreading the interview to come. He could see a light in the sitting room and tried to picture Harry's loneliness on the night of his wife's funeral. There was nothing for it. He would have to talk to Harry, tell him what he intended to do—in a sense he could hardly do it without Harry's permission. And to get that permission he'd have to tell Harry the truth. Armed with this incentive, he rang the doorbell. Harry called through the locked door.

"It's all right, Conroy. It's James Fleming."

Harry opened the door. He was dressed more casually

than James had seen him. Cord trousers, a light jersey, and a comfortable but evidently new cardigan. He grasped James's outstretched hand firmly. James was surprised.

"Drink?"

"Well, all right, if you're having one."

"Indeed I am. Banishes the chill. That rain got into my bones. How about you?"

"No, I—I'm just a bit tired." More tired than you, Conroy, it seems. James was irrationally annoyed. "I'm sorry, Harry."

"I know. Thank you. It was a bitch of a day." He looked soberly into the grate where now no merry fire danced. "There was a good crowd, don't you think?"

"Yes, very heartening."

"A good crowd at my mother's place, too. She'd brought in caterers. Hadn't told me. I guess it's the done thing."

"Yes, it's quite fashionable nowadays," said James.

"You seem to know a lot about funerals, then," Harry looked at James, puzzled, and James realized how little they knew of each other's lives.

"It's my line of work." He smiled. "Mostly wills and estates. So I'm often invited or need to attend in a professional capacity. And, of course, I make arrangements, or my office does."

"You've been marvelous, old chap. I should have said it before. Mother said that your secretary was brilliant. They got on well. . . ." His voice trailed off.

James said nothing.

"It's the silence. I mean, there were many nights Ari wasn't here. Nights she was working or even away—in London, mostly—on those bloody recordings. Or talking to jingle writers. Can you imagine, there are people who make a good living writing those bloody things? Stick in your mind till you can't get rid of them, end up singing the damn things."

"I think that's the point," James said dryly.

"Mmmph. Oh, yes, of course . . ."

James didn't know how to begin. And they sat in silence.

"You see, you see what I mean. It's not like before. The house was never quiet like this when I would be here—before. God, it's a horrible nightmare. I can't believe she's gone."

James didn't know which he disliked more—a distraught Harry or the calm man who met him at the door. He was forced to speak.

"Harry, this may not appear to be the right time, but it can't be helped. You're out on bail. We've got to use every minute we have to prepare for your defense. I'd like your permission to bring in and brief a barrister. I have a man in mind."

"What? Now? Right away?"

"I'm afraid so. There are things that must be done. There's information I have to collect. I want to keep one step ahead of Molloy. You are vital to your own defense, Harry. And I'll be asking some hard questions over the coming weeks. But I wanted to get the wheels in motion."

"All right, I suppose. Well, who is this barrister, then? Anyone I'd know?"

"His name's Madigan. I've worked with him occasionally. He's a fine man and a good barrister. We'll be lucky to get him. I'd like to ring him tomorrow."

"Whatever you say."

"There's another thing. After I discuss your case with Madigan I think it likely that I'll have to go over to England. I'll be gone a few days."

"Is this relevant to my case?" Harry seemed genuinely puzzled.

"Yes. Because I'm going to attempt to see Mrs. Shaw. Philip Shaw's widow."

"What?" Harry exploded. "What for? Wait—Molloy said she'd talked to him. That crazy idea about Ari and Shaw! Listen. Ari told me she knew him. He'd been a teacher at that college she was at for a while. I don't think she knew Mrs. Shaw. In fact, I don't understand why Molloy wants to tie the two deaths together. He'd be better served trying to find my wife's murderer!" Harry was standing, pacing, purple in the face.

"He thinks he already has, Harry," James said softly.

"God, oh, God."

"Listen, Harry. There's a couple of things I have to tell you. Get yourself a drink, and one for me, if you please."

Harry stared at him.

"Harry! Ariadne confided some things to me, as her lawyer. Both will be upsetting to you, for different reasons. Firstly, you should know that Mrs. Shaw was here in Dublin. She came here to your house one evening, when you were having dinner with a client. Ariadne was alone, and according to her Mrs. Shaw pretty much forced her way in. She wanted to see where her husband had died. Ari allowed that, but the woman was, let's say, very distraught. Very angry."

"This is preposterous," Harry was blustering. "First this crazy woman coming here. And then Ari letting her in. She must have been mad. And then she doesn't tell me. Christ, that must have been only last week, wasn't it?" Harry ran his hands through his short, thick hair.

James was not encouraged, and he hesitated to hit Harry with the second piece of news, more grave in its implications and its nature.

"Please calm down, Harry. All that is irrelevant now. What I'm working on is the theory that Mrs. Shaw might have been deranged, or animated by some motive of revenge or jealousy against Ariadne. All that was evident that night. But unfortunately we have no witness to her visit here, or her behaviour towards Ariadne. And she's covered herself, apparently, in my opinion, by going to the police with her own theory. I'm thinking that—"

"Thinking that this woman might have killed Ariadne? But why, for God's sake, man? Why?"

"That's—that's the rest of what I need to tell you. It's true that Ariadne knew Shaw in England eighteen years ago. It's true she hadn't seen him since then, until he turned up dead. But there was something she hadn't told you, which she did tell me, because at the time she thought she might be charged with murdering Shaw."

"Get to the point, Fleming."

"She mentioned to me that she had—well, that she had been taken advantage of by Shaw."

"Pardon me?"

"She and Shaw were lovers—for a very short time— when she was at the university in England. It was brief, very brief." He watched Harry's face deepen to a crimson. His eyes were staring.

"And?"

"There's no 'and.' It was over in a matter of weeks. She felt embarrassed and hurt and perhaps bitter. She left and went to London and—well, I assume you know the rest."

"So she told you, Fleming, and not me. Both these things. She must have liked you."

"I hope so. I liked her, Harry," James said simply.

"Liked, Fleming?" Harry was enraged. "Are you sure it wasn't more than that? Perhaps she knew you, too, somewhere in the not-so-distant past."

James let the remark go by. "The affair with Shaw, Harry, was a very long time ago. You know that. College days. It was just a matter of weeks, if that. We all go through that stage, Harry. I know there were things I did in my college days that I only came to regret as I matured. Surely you, too—"

"Don't include me in this sweeping generalization. No, I did not sow wild oats, as people like to say. Is that—is sowing wild oats some kind of defense?" Harry's voice rose, and he stood up and began to pace.

"Look, man, what happened occurred a very long time ago, years before you and Ariadne met. Don't be angry with her for something so far in the past, especially now."

"Don't tell me what I can or cannot do!" shouted Harry.

James was startled at the sudden violence of his manner. He was a man transformed. By jealousy, it seemed.

"He wasn't the first, and he wasn't the last. I'll tell you something, Fleming." Harry stood and stared down into James's face. "He was one of many, I tell you. Many."

"I don't really want to hear this, Conroy."

"Why not? Tarnish your image of her a bit?"

"No, I believe it's disrespectful. You just buried her this morning."

"Perhaps she was dead to me long ago. Oh, she never flaunted these things in my face. Everything was discreet."

"I find this hard to believe. And if it's true, then why would she stay married to you?"

"Why, because this is Ireland. You of all people should know the law. There's no divorce for the likes of us."

"You're upset, Harry, and you're bitter. But I'm not so sure you've grounds for these accusations against your wife." Especially when she's not here to defend herself, he thought bitterly.

"What do you think the fight was over, Fleming? The fight you're all so keen to know about. Anyone at that party could tell you. She was flirting with her bloody boss, and I caught her."

"It was her party, Harry." James's voice was sad, tired.

"And I'll tell you something else, Fleming! There were a lot of men before we got married. So why would she have stopped afterwards?"

"Just because you were married. She chose *you*, Conroy. You should see it from that point of view."

"I'll tell you how I see it, Fleming. That my wife is dead and I'm sitting here alone in the world. I have no children. Where are my children, now that she is gone? Children to comfort me, to remind me of my wife, to go on into the future when I, too, am gone. Under the ground." Harry's voice broke, and James was momentarily relieved. But Harry flared once again.

"I don't have children because of her bloody affairs! Don't you think we tried? At first we hadn't wanted children, too early in the marriage. But then we tried casually, and later with more desperation. And then we went for tests. I was thankful it wasn't me then. But now I wish it had been my 'fault,' as they say. Because it surely was hers—"

"Harry, stop at once!" James leapt to his feet. "Stop, do you hear me? On this night of all nights. She's dead. Let those memories go. Hold on to the good ones. She loved you, she married you. God, have some respect."

"Memories? Are you mad? Fleming"—he pointed to the ceiling—"memories of that man Shaw in my bed. Memories of her in my bed. You come here tonight and tell me they were once lovers. Don't you think it's more than bloody coincidence that he was dead in her bed? You go along now, Fleming!" Harry was shouting, raving. "You go along now, and leave me with those wonderful memories. Great solace they'll be . . . I'm telling you . . ."

James walked out.

Madigan's voice on the phone immediately soothed James's raw nerves. He liked this smooth, sophisticated, and very successful barrister and was relieved when he agreed to take on the Conroy case. His confident tone buoyed James.

"So you're off to England in the A.M., then, James?"

"Yes, I really believe I can establish Shaw's wife as a viable suspect in Mrs. Conroy's death."

"And in Shaw's?" Madigan was serious.

"Possibly. A murderous jealousy, perhaps, as the motive." James closed his eyes against the mental picture of Harry's own jealous rage.

"So, James, you're following your usual pattern, are you?" His voice now was lighter but not mocking.

"How so?" James replied anxiously.

"Oh, delving into character, into the personalities of the various people involved. It was my experience of you in our last case together that it was human psychology that drew you in. Is that not a fair observation?"

James paused, reflecting. "I never saw it that clearly before, but surely in that way I learn the key to the murderer's thinking."

"Indeed, but I just caution you, James, to continue to take note of the physical evidence. It worked for you, for us, before, and successfully."

"True," James said slowly. "I'll keep it in mind, surely." But he felt chagrined, nervous that Madigan had found him wanting.

"It's not a criticism, James. Indeed, it's your strength. At least in this area of endeavour." The urbane voice was reassuring. "Carry on. We'll speak on your return. And in the meanwhile I'll get a few people of my own to ask some questions. Background on Mrs. Conroy's recent life in particular. Agreed?"

"Madigan, I can't thank you enough."

James replaced the receiver and began to pack for the morrow, ruminating on Madigan's words. What he hadn't liked to admit to the insightful barrister was that the hard evidence had him baffled. The murder weapons, the bodies in the bed . . . no, somehow it gave him a sense of productive action to get at the people involved in this bizarre situation. He just hoped this trip to England was not going to prove to be a wild goose chase.

Chapter Nine

The ferry from Dun Laoghaire left port bound for Holyhead on the Welsh coast on a clear and cloudless evening. James stood a long time at the railing, watching as the twin piers fell away, watching as the horizon seemed to sink into the sea, the two church spires the very last to disappear. The wind became brisk by that point, and he shivered with cold. He was always nostalgic, as were many of his fellow travellers, when he took the ferry. Inevitably it would remind people of their younger days or their student days, when they would set off to England by the cheapest possible means, before the years brought prosperity and air travel.

But it was more than that. Every passenger recalled somewhere in his or her heart the memory of the thousands who had left Ireland by sea, for England, America, Australia —never to return. Driven away by poverty, oppression, lack of opportunity. The country already decimated by the great famines of the nineteenth century was decimated too by the inevitable emigration of so many who had barely survived. James was somber as he looked into the water, hypnotized by the rhythmic swathe of waves, the flowing wake at the side of the ship. Many tears had been shed into this part of the Irish Sea that separated Ireland from its nearest neighbour and long-time enemy. Like members of the same family tied together by hatred, grieving over the fact that proximity only exacerbated what lay wrong between them.

James wandered the deck before the cold and the falling night drove him inside. He was impressed by the new ship, a far cry in its comforts and decor from the more spartan boats of his youth. Good lighting, handrails, prompt service for the most part.

He went below and waited as the crowd at the bar eventually thinned. He bought a pint of lager but regretted it as the ship suddenly lurched. Glasswear and people went skittering to the port side. Eye caught eye, knowing look met despairing nod; they were in for a heavy crossing. Anticipation weighed heavy as everyone waited for the next lurch, but the ship unexpectedly settled, and life continued as before. James thought better of his drink, however, and put it down.

Casually he approached one of the uniformed stewards and asked if he knew anything about the recent suicide of Philip Shaw. The young man's face lit up.

"Indeed." He beamed. "It was a mighty bit of crack, I can tell you, sur." His voice was heavy with a west of Ireland accent.

James smiled encouragingly.

"Are you a reporter?" the youth asked quickly.

"Ah, no, I'm not, but I am writing a report on it." The man was satisfied with this, only too happy to talk.

"I was on duty that night. Thing is, we never seen the fella jump."

"And that was because he hadn't, right?"

"Right," the young man said enthusiastically. "O' course we didn't know that then. I was kinda, y'know like, excited. I've never seen a jumper. That's what we call them here on board."

ANN C. FALLON

"Then how did you know something was amiss? I didn't see all the news reports at that time," James lied.

"Well, we only knew that something was—amiss—after the authorities got in touch. The captain told the head-steward, and of course he told the rest of us to be on the look-out for a letter, a note, an unclaimed possession or suitcase."

"So it wasn't obvious, like his coat or whatever, left on the deck, maybe with a note, left at the point where he might have gone over?"

"Not a'tall. That happened, though, 'bout two year ago. Before I was on board. This fella left his stuff on deck, but someone saw him go over. He was too far away to help. By the time the ship could slow and turn it was hopeless. It was dark. It was the night crossing. He was gone anyway, y'know. That water's mighty cold."

James nodded. "What happened, I mean after the head steward spoke to you all?"

"Well, I'll tell you now. None of us went out our way huntin' like, but just kept a sharp eye out when we were cleaning or making up bunks, or what have you. The cabin attendants, now, they were in a good spot to be looking. Here, come on and I'll bring ye to Mike. He can tell you the whole story."

James followed and soon was introduced to a much older man enjoying his mug of tea and break. He, too, was willing to talk of the recent excitement.

"Och, indeed. It was meself that found the por man's wallet and his por bits and pieces. Y'know the likes of the wee things you be keepin' in your pockets. There was the wallet, with his money. There was English and Irish money there. And a few of them pound coins they have beyont in England. Useless yokes they are, I do believe, and I hope they don't be planning to bring them in over here. Now, where was I?"

"The coins," the young steward prompted, joining him in a mug of tea.

"Righteo. There was a nose rag—I beg your pardon—a

132

handkerchief. And then there was keys. A few bits of folded paper with scribbling on them. A nail clipper. I remember that now. Very handy."

"That's it?"

"Yes, sir."

"Tell him where, for heaven's sakes," said the younger man.

"Ah, right. This was the strange part. I found them hidden under a mattress. Like he'd hidden them there while he went off for a stroll."

"It was in one of the cabins, you know, one of the lower cabins. The stuff was under the mattress." The boy clarified the story.

"But that's not strange," the old man added. "What's strange is the fact the polis knew what cabin he'd been in, from the booking office. And this wasn't it."

"What do you make of it?" asked James.

"I don't know," they answered simply, in unison.

They were not suspicious by nature—James liked that. He sometimes grew tired of his own suspicious mind. He had quickly concluded the items had been planted, deliberately left and possibly after Shaw's death. Planted to make the disappearance seem a suicide.

"When were they found?"

"Well, we didn't know it then, o' course, but I found them after the poor soul would have been already dead, kilt dead." The old man blessed himself. "'Course, as I said, we couldn't know that. The man had gone missing, and when I found them items the captain and head steward went crazy. We were hunting all over the show for bits of evidence. When I found the wallet the first thing everybody thought of was suicide. Not that uncommon on these crossings, sad to say."

"That's right, sir. Mike, now, he's been on this crossing for donkey's years. Been more than twenty in his time." The young man's voice was filled with awe, but the old man merely shook his head sadly.

"I'm just sorry yer man Crossan isn't aboard. He was the one who found the other stuff. He's on rotation, off this trip, you see."

"Can you tell me his story?" James said pleasantly, finally taking a mug of tea.

"It was he who found the cardigan and the raincoat. Now you'd think, says he—he'd tell you this himself if he was here—you'd think he'd 'a' left these on the deck when he jumped. But no, he did not."

"Who's to know what's in their minds?" old Mike murmured.

"That's true, Mikey, but jes' remember this one wasn't a jumper."

James cringed at the callousness of youth. "Crossan found the raincoat and the sweater where?" he asked.

"They were rolled up in a ball and stuffed between some ropes on deck, in the stern. Anyone can walk or crawl around there, but I tell you, the passengers don't. There is just a pile of coiled rope." James made a mental note to see this spot.

"And like them things I found, Crossan found them on the same trip."

"Which was?"

"The evening return from Holyhead."

"The strange thing is this, sir. This ship and all the others are constantly being cleaned. Bed linen changed, bunks made up. There's no way any of these things would have been aboard and not found for two whole days. The crew would have been checking them ropes, and me and the likes o' me doing the clean-up. If you asks me, someone on that return trip from Holyhead put them there."

"You'd make a fine detective, Mike," said James, and he gave the two men a generous tip for their time before leaving to locate his own small cabin. It was too dark to search the stern. But there'd be no clues there, he believed.

James lay back on his narrow bunk, not bothering to climb beneath the rough wool blanket. He closed his eyes and reviewed what he had learned. It would, he decided, be fairly simple for someone to board the Dublin ferry at the port of Holyhead, plant the items, and return to Holyhead. Many day-trippers enjoyed an outing on the ferry, making the crossing over and back in a single day. Of course, the person who did that had to know the name of the ferry, but that was simple also. The names and schedules were readily available in both countries. Perhaps the delay of two days meant that person had to wait until Shaw's ferry was in port.

And who was to say that Shaw had had with him those exact items? Perhaps he'd worn an overcoat, had a second or even third sweater. And who would know that better than his wife? James was pleased with fitting this piece into the puzzle. This new theory explained at least these few facts.

But the wallet. Did many men have more than one? Perhaps an old one, thrown in the bottom of a sock drawer. A spare set of keys and a few coins to complete the picture. If that wallet had nothing irreplaceable in it, nothing that Shaw would have wanted to carry on him, this would verify his theory. He could do nothing about that until he checked back with the police in Dublin. But Mrs. Shaw—he could question her on these points.

He smiled to himself. It was possible to cross over to Holyhead from Dublin and return in a single day. Mrs. Shaw could have accomplished the task from either side. Perhaps he would finally get a break in this case.

He recalled Madigan's response of the previous night and wondered at his own persistence. He had weighed up resigning from the case and advising Harry to seek another solicitor. It was not loyalty to Harry that finally tipped the balance, but a genuine desire to find the murderer of Ariadne Conroy. He remembered for the hundredth time her voice on the tape. "Urgent," she had said, and he hadn't answered her call for help. Perhaps by bringing her killer to justice he could finally put her and her appeal from his mind and his heart.

James rolled onto his side, vaguely aware of someone

coming in, crawling into the bunk above him. But nothing, not even another man's snores, could interfere with his now inevitable descent into slumber.

Mrs. Philip Shaw was at home, James determined, noting with relief the open front door as well as the open windows in the second storey of the small post-war terraced house. James had driven around the small university town for more than an hour, attempting to get a sense of the place. From what he could observe, the university certainly seemed to be the single economic factor in a town surrounded by green suburbs and some small farm lands and forests. It was a pretty area and featured a small port, but it lacked the splendour and rolling countryside of other English towns he'd visited.

The university dated from the Fifties, he determined by its red-brick architecture, one of a number built in a national scheme to bring higher education within the means and locale of the population. The town had responded to its new neighbour by providing the usual cafés, student pubs, a small commercial theatre. James had eaten lunch in one café—bangers and mash. He laughed to see that sausages and potato were still favourite student fare. There were clothing shops, well-stocked but unexciting bookstores—almost everything provided on the long main street and the few side streets that ran off it and on into the immediate suburbs. Safe. Dull. These were the words that sprang to mind. Perhaps charmless.

Mrs. Shaw showed little surprise as he introduced himself on the step. She waved him into the house, and he picked his way through cartons and boxes in the hall and sitting room. She sat down wearily and asked him to sit also.

"First allow me to offer my condolences on the death of your husband, Mrs. Shaw. And let me say it is very kind of you to see me like this, with no warning," he said affably as he took note of her unflattering dress and the fatigue lines in her face. He guessed her age at around fifty, but she seemed older.

"I'm not surprised you're here," she said, her accent clipped and precise. "After all, as far as I can see, absolutely nothing's been done so far about Philip's murder. Perhaps the trial of this man Conroy will lead to something."

"You think there's a connection, then—between your husband's death and Mrs. Conroy's?"

"It's perfectly obvious to me. It must be to you." She stared into his eyes, angry, intent. "Two people killed within a matter of days, in the same house, in the same bed! Of course there's a connection. And the main one is that Philip had gone to Dublin to see that Conroy woman despite all his talk of having business there. I have some questions as to why Molloy didn't do something about her sooner."

"You spoke to Molloy, I understand. Could you tell me what you told him—exactly?"

"I told him Philip had gone to see her in Dublin."

"Why?"

"Because she was his fancy bit on the side—or didn't you know that either?" Her voice was bitter.

"Pardon my asking at a time like this, but did your husband tell you that?"

"He told me that years ago. After his flings he'd tell me, even their names. I remember all of them. She was Ariadne Cullinane then."

"But when these flings were over wouldn't he lose touch with the girls involved?"

"Of course. And he'd be all right for a while. Sometimes a year or more would go by, then another naïve one would fall in love with him, and it would start all over again."

"Then surely he'd have forgotten Mrs. Conroy—wouldn't even know her married name, in fact, after all this time."

"Oh, that's puzzling you, too, is it?"

"Yes. Had they been in touch, then, in recent years? Corresponded, something of that nature?"

"That's possible, but I have no way of knowing that. He led a separate life at the College, always had. He had his departmental mail box there. Nothing much ever came for him here."

"Then how did you determine he knew her in later years?"

"When he died the secretary cleaned out his office and sent these boxes to me. They're still here. I'm not sure what to do with them. My daughter won't let me discard them, but she won't deal with them herself. I looked through them, mostly books, textbooks, notes, hundreds of lecture notes. He taught for more than twenty years, you know." Pride crept into her voice.

"A fine career," James said through his teeth. "Was there anything else?" He prodded her back on track.

"Yes. There were lots of scrapbooks. It seemed he kept them for years. Here, this is an example." She handed him a simple large book of now browned pages. As he turned them bits of the edges of the leaves fell away, brown and dry in his fingers. It seemed this album contained clippings and mementos from the early Seventies. These were letters of praise from students, articles from the student papers in which Shaw had been mentioned. Articles, notices of campus events in which presumably he'd taken part. He took up another scrapbook, from 1974. This was thicker, crammed with newspaper articles, some from the national and local press, where Shaw was mentioned. He was a rabble-rouser in some opinions, a leader in others. He'd taken a very strong stand on police brutality. Had led a group from the College to march at Downing Street over proposed budget cuts in education spending.

James scanned them quickly—it had been a political year, perhaps just one of many. He recalled that newspaper reports of the death had implied that it might have had political overtones, but his politics did not seem that ambitious, that threatening, or that bizarre. Mrs. Shaw confirmed this for him.

"I don't think I understand, Mrs. Shaw, how these albums could be connected with Ariadne Cullinane." He was uncomfortable, uncertain of the person with whom he was dealing. He had expected hysteria, vituperation, not this calm acceptance, this objectivity!

"Oh, here. This particular album will enlighten you."

This album, James noticed, was less crowded with notes of Shaw's political and campus life, although they were still represented. There were more clippings about publications of books, reviews and notices of books, poems clipped from magazines and dated, the occasional personal letter. James scanned the letters. All of them were from former students, all of them women, telling Shaw what they'd done or been doing since they'd left—him? James began to understand. He continued to scan the clippings and saw that the names had been underlined. He put his finger on one and looked up questioningly.

"It is as you think. It took me a little while to figure it out, too. All those clippings refer to his former students. I'm not sure if he cut out all of these items himself. Perhaps some of them were sent to him."

"But he kept them all, it seems."

"Well, if there were more than these, I . . ." She turned her head in momentary disgust.

He'd lived through these students, thought James, filling his life with other people's lives, taking credit at least in his own mind for their achievements, their accomplishments. But was that such a bad thing for a teacher who might have craved more fame, more recognition in his own field and hadn't found it? After all, if he hadn't been murdered, would anyone but Shaw himself ever have seen these albums, bolstering as they did his own ego. He said as much.

"That's a kind way of interpreting the facts, Mr. Fleming. To me it seems as though he couldn't let any of them go. As though their liaisons with him would have radically changed their lives, caused them to achieve success. If you look closely—and believe me, I have—you will see that virtually every one of those clippings not referring to Philip himself refers to a female. And you will see there's a clipping here"—she flipped through the album—"here, this one has to do with Ariadne Cullinane."

There it was, a small notice from a column, a TV column perhaps, in which Ariadne had been mentioned among others as having worked on an ad campaign that had won third prize in the humour category. It was so small he couldn't imagine that Shaw had scoured the papers daily! Had Ari sent it to him? Perhaps he'd seen it by accident, reading the TV page quite casually.

The second item Mrs. Shaw pointed out was from an Irish magazine, a business magazine, from just a few years back. It showed a black and white head shot of Ariadne, listing her maiden and married names and announcing her appointment as a member of the board of one of the smaller ad agencies in Dublin. Again James was puzzled. Did Shaw read Irish business magazines? And if so, why? He found it hard to believe he was scouring them for word of former Irish students. He handed back the book in silence. One question answered had raised so many more imponderables.

"Did your husband go to Dublin often, Mrs. Shaw?"

"Often, no. He'd go over every few years. It always depended on whether he'd been invited to be a reader. No, it wasn't a regular thing." He saw a question form on her face, but she didn't share it.

"Can you tell me what your husband was wearing when he left home?"

She was surprised at the sudden shift in the questioning. "Yes," she said, and she described the items that had already been found on the ferry.

This solved nothing for James.

"And none of these have been returned to you?"

"No. In fact, nothing's been returned to me—except his naked body! Molloy said they'd need to keep everything in the event of a trial."

James was stymied. He'd assumed this woman would be hostile to him; he'd assumed he could use her anger, her hysteria to his advantage, gleaning from her tirades some sense of whether she could be a cold-blooded killer. It was hard for him now to picture her following Shaw to Dublin, plotting to kill him, and killing him at Ariadne's house. But it wasn't impossible.

"Can you account for your movements on the day and night of your husband's death?"

She laughed harshly. "Are you serious? Do you think I killed my husband? You surprise me. You must be desperate to clear your client's name."

"Well, can you?" James realized he was on rocky ground now.

"I think you'd better leave, Mr. Fleming." And Mrs. Shaw stood up and walked briskly to the still-open front door. James had little choice but to follow her.

Discouraged, he returned to his rental car and sat for a while. He was uncertain what he had accomplished. His hunch that Mrs. Shaw had killed Ariadne was no more than that—a hunch. But if she had killed Shaw, and if she had planned to kill Ariadne, why had she revealed her hand to Ariadne? Why let her know in advance that she was in Dublin? Why the dramatic visit to the house? Had it been the murderer's desire to return to the scene of the crime? But that was fiction, not fact. Had it been that she wanted to make sure that Ariadne knew she, Shaw's wife, was out for her revenge? But then why had she gone to Molloy, why had she attempted to incriminate Ariadne in Shaw's death?

That was simple, it struck him suddenly. Mrs. Shaw's ploy had worked! Molloy had seen the connection, and the connection was Harry, not Denise Shaw. He was excited now, and anxious to discuss with Madigan this new idea that Mrs. Shaw had set Harry up.

Encouraged by this insight, he started the car and returned to the university. There were still more questions to be answered. He was surprised that the campus was so quiet until he realized from the various notice boards he passed that the exam period was in session. He went into the library, a large, bright modern structure, and saw every available desk and chair occupied by intent students. He asked directions to the English Department from the woman at the information desk and quickly found the office in an adjoining building. A pleasant secretary greeted him and told him that he was in luck. The chairman, Professor Hart, was in his office and would speak with him.

"Mr. Fleming, how can I help you?" A rather ordinary man in a blue serge suit and black eyeglasses stood up from an extremely tidy desk. He was young for his post, perhaps fifty, and pompous in his manner.

James quickly summarized who he was and why he'd come.

"We were deeply shocked," said Professor Hart. He straightened the already neat stacks of papers on his desk and flicked invisible dust from their surface. He tapped them with his fingers. "Exam papers, you see. Must be very careful."

"The fact he was missing must have been difficult for your department," said James, sensing that this approach would be more productive.

"It was awkward. But he only missed one class, and we covered that. You see, his wife telephoned this office when she hadn't heard from her husband on his arrival in Dublin. And then, of course, we were kept abreast of things when the local police came to make their enquiries, and thereafter from the newspapers."

"Do you recall what Mrs. Shaw said when she telephoned you?"

"Yes. She had hoped that perhaps he'd contacted us, but . . ."

The man's pedantic manner of speech was irritating, and James wondered how his classes survived. But he pushed on.

"Do you know Mrs. Shaw?"

"Oh, dear, no. We didn't know her at all. Most surprised when she phoned here."

His manner is insufferable, thought James.

"Could you tell me about Professor Shaw, then?"

"Only a little. You see, I only came here as chairman two years ago. I wasn't a popular choice, but the politics of the situation would bore you. It was a bit difficult at first, especially with the older members of the department. Set in their ways. Dead wood in some cases."

"Shaw was dead wood?" This somehow didn't fit James's mental picture of the murdered man.

"No, not exactly. He was—let me put it this way: He was what I like to call a dinosaur."

"Pardon?"

"A dinosaur. A leftover, someone with no place in our world. He was older than I. Not much, but we seemed to come from different eras. However, I must say I didn't detect any animosity in him. I think he might have wanted this post, but of course that wouldn't have been realistic thinking on his part. He was political in an outmoded sense. He seemed to me still stuck in the Seventies—he hadn't moved on. We weren't friends, of course. Actually, now that you've asked me, I can't say I knew the man."

"But was he effective as a teacher?"

"Apparently. Popular with the female students, I heard. The thing is, he published regularly. He was prodigious, actually, with his articles, poems, monographs, interviews, reviews—not all in his field. He often picked up on obscure or neglected material and could rather quickly work it up, find a venue for it, and publish it. He had quite a knack. His bibliography is lengthy." Hart blew some more invisible dust from the surface of his desk.

"His work was his life, then?"

"I wouldn't say that. He seemed more to have a drive to see his name in print. I never really knew the depth of his

sincerity in his work. After thirty years people burn out, as
the Americans say. Consequently the dead wood I spoke
of."

James was confused. "Surely his publications are evidence of his commitment?"

"I really can't say, as I haven't read his work, I only know
of it."

"How about campus activities? I understand he was a
Leftist of some sort."

"Political life doesn't exist here, Mr. Fleming." Hart sat
back at his ease, examining his fingertips.

"Can you tell me why he went to Dublin?"

"No."

"But I understand that he'd been there before."

"Yes, that's true. He was a reader, an extern reader.
Occasionally he was asked to read a thesis from another
department and evaluate it, offering written comments.
Depending on the structure in use by a particular department, he might be invited to sit in on the oral defense of the
thesis, if one was required. I do believe it was all part of the
ceaseless activity of which I just spoke."

"And . . ." James couldn't understand how the man
would so abruptly stop. Perhaps it was his lecture style,
allowing the students time to write down his every word.

"And so he would do it whenever opportunity arose. But
because the colleges involved deal directly with the professor, we have no details. You would have to speak with the
individual departments."

"So you've no certain idea what he was intending to do in
Dublin on this particular trip?"

"No."

"Could he have been going for an interview?"

Professor Hart was visibly startled. "It's possible," he
said slowly. "Perhaps he'd seen an advertisement. Perhaps
he could have been going for that."

"You seem to hesitate."

"Professor Shaw was here for a very long time. He didn't

seem dissatisfied. I don't know what would appeal to him in uprooting himself and his family and moving to Ireland." He stopped, embarrassed to let his prejudice slip. "I had no sense that he was actively looking to move," he finished succinctly.

"But you didn't know him well."

"As I said, no."

"So it's possible you wouldn't know?"

"Of course."

James took his leave, a little wiser and with a new agenda. He wanted to ascertain just exactly why Shaw was in Dublin. Hart's mention of Mrs. Shaw's call disturbed him, however. Had she thought her plan out in such infinite detail that she would have included a concerned call to Shaw's department? It was so convincing. It seemed to James to ring true. And yet that would have been exactly the desired result.

James had just time to return the rental car and make his way to the local train station. He stood on the small concrete platform and allowed himself to relax. He had done what he'd intended. How effectively he was not sure. But now was the time to indulge his avocation. He sat on the small, neat green bench and let his eyes wander. There were only two other travellers, standing further down the short platform. Lining the two far ends of the platform were large, round wooden tubs filled with an array of early-blooming variegated petunias. The tubs were painted white and red, as was the wooden picket fence that surrounded the small station. The waiting room he had passed through was spotless, as had been the men's rest room where he had washed away fourteen hours of travel time.

He smiled at how the reality matched the stereotype. The English were famous for maintaining their railway stations. Much, of course, depended on the stationmaster, but there was for the most part universal pride and interest, care and attention evident. He thought how simple it was, really.

Everything cleaned, the platform swept, graffiti erased, flowers tended. He listened to the sound of birds tweeting in the nearby trees, the lazy hum of some busy insect. A gentle breeze stirred his hair. Peace settled on him.

And then the thrill. He sensed, felt, that initial hum on the tracks long before the sound or sight of the train became apparent. He watched the lights change, the signals switching into action slowly, mechanically. He watched as the stationmaster came to the platform, adjusted his cap, took out his pocket watch, and checked the time. He saw him methodically check it against the platform clock, as he must have done a thousand times before. He watched him as he walked to the end of the platform and stood complacently, waiting for sight of the train. He returned his watch to his navy waistcoat pocket. At that moment James would gladly have changed places with the man, whose life was as ordered and regular as the trains he obviously loved: peaceful, contained, and yet eminently useful.

The train approached, and James noted in the small book he kept for the purpose the time, date, type, and location. He boarded and took his seat, delighted it was one of the older compartment trains. He walked the length of the car before he selected an empty compartment. He slid the door closed behind him and took his seat at the window. He regretted now deciding to spend only one full day in England. It had meant two nights without sleeping in a bed. The clickedy-clack of the train's wheels was working its hypnotic magic. Pleased it was not a continuous rail, he felt lulled by the rhythm. And he watched the green countryside slip past, sometimes looking into the rear yards of houses clustered in small villages, sometimes looking onto green fields, occasionally passing through a small industrial area. He felt his eyelids grow heavy, a contentment seeping into his limbs, a warmth, a coziness. It was just as well the train's terminus was the ferry port, where the jolt of the change of points awakened him. As he shook himself and straightened the comfortable brown tweed suit he kept for travelling he wished that instead he would have woken in a small village, strolling out to find a pleasant B&B, as he had used to in his college days. He sighed and joined the long, snaking queue that led through the port authority buildings to the pier where he eventually boarded the ferry

There was no nostalgia now as the ship pulled out to sea. Much as he liked England and its wonderful trains and stations he was glad to be returning to Ireland, to its shabby genteelness and its honesty.

During the rough crossing he kept his mind off his lurching stomach by making voluminous notes for his long-postponed trip to Peru. But for the first time he wished he wouldn't be travelling alone. It would be nice to share his excitement with a fellow enthusiast, for this trip was not for the faint-hearted. Thoughts of Harry and Ari crept into his consciousness. As a couple they had shared a lot, he mused, even the trip to Kenya at the end. Loneliness swept over him. He tried to shake it off, but physical fatigue fanned the flames of his melancholy. He was tired, so tired of the emotional roller coaster he'd been on. How nice to be settled, he thought. And an image of Matt floated into the mix. Matt, whom he hadn't seen for weeks—his fault, no doubt. That was it. Matt, with his wisdom and his common sense, would be the antidote to his strange mood, weary as he was of other men's unhappy marriages, other men's chaotic lives, other men's worldly possessions.

He dozed over his writing, his body slumping in the form-fitting, molded heavy polymer chair bolted to the floor. And he swayed with the rhythm of the ship, as did the other sleeping passengers around him, vulnerable to the wide, rough sea and the empty night.

─── *Chapter Ten* ───

On the same day that James was visiting Leston a scruffy, unshaven itinerant stumbled into a pub on Tara Street. The publican looked at him with distaste and not a little apprehension. The few late-morning patrons turned their backs, avoiding the man altogether.

"I'll have no trouble here, you!" said the publican as the man leaned on the bar. "We don't favour the likes o' you in here a'tall."

"Me money's as good as the next one's," snapped the man, showing his yellowed and broken teeth, a prominent gap where his two front teeth should have been.

"I daresay and it isn't," said the publican as he ran his hand through thinning gray strands that lay plastered across his skull.

"And what do you be meaning by that?"

"I mean you don't get it the way the rest of us do—by bloody workin' for it. Makin' your money off your women, sending them out to beg, and with your children, too!"

"I have the right to be served, and well you know it," growled the man.

"Ach! You lot always know a deal about your rights. What'll it be, then?" The publican knew that the man indeed had a right, honoured by time and custom, and to some degree by law, to be served at least water, and to be allowed to sit down in this public house. He shrugged and served the man his whiskey with ill grace, making a point, before putting the coins in the till, of rubbing them clean on his trousers.

The publican paid little heed to the man as he drank in a dark corner and eventually dozed off, head sunk on his chest. As the time of holy hour approached the publican urged the customers to drink up and get on with it. He was tired from working hard the night before, serving the crowd as had come in after a local football match. He wearily lifted up the heavy wooden shutters and hooked them into the existing hinges, lowering them and snapping each into place. Only three windows at the front, thank God. His arms were heavy. A lot of work, he thought, for an hour's respite and a few minutes shuteye in the cold room with the barrels. It was only then he realized he was not yet quite alone.

"Glory be to God," said the publican as the itinerant came up behind him, his red, straw-textured hair standing out from his head.

"Get me a drink," he said menancingly. The publican saw the empty bottle of fermented cider in his hand. He knew from of old how intoxicated the travelling people, or itinerants, became—as indeed anyone would—on this lethal cheap alcohol. He saw his disadvantage.

"I'll give you a ball of malt, if you want, but that's it," he said in his usual tone. The itinerant responded, as he had hoped, to the familiar tones of scorn and disrespect by sinking back heavily into his seat.

He brought over the drink and turned to go but made the mistake of not asking payment.

"Another," he said gruffly.

"'Tis the holy hour, and well you know it. D'you want me to lose my license?" The tone was reasonable.

"Do I feckin' care about your bloody license?"

The publican returned to the bar and debated, as he poured a double, at the chance he was taking. The phone was in plain sight, and the doors and windows were now very effectively barred by his own hand against him. He decided to go through the rear door to the street, leaving his valuable stock at the mercy of this drunken wretch. Perhaps, after all, he could stick it out until opening time, now less than half an hour away. So much for his forty winks, he thought ruefully.

The itinerant banged the empty glass on the table. God, he thought, three full measures of whiskey in the last fifteen minutes alone, and the man's still standing!

"Look here, don't you think you've had enough?" His intention was kindly, but it threw the man into a rage. He pulled from the pocket of his coat—a decent coat, the publican noticed suddenly—a broken rosary, and he held it high over his head. In a mix of old Gaelic and English and—the publican hoped—some weird gobbledygook, he roared out the beginnings of a curse, calling on God and the saints. The publican heard no more. Terror struck through him as no physical fear would have.

"Jesus, Mary and Joseph," he called out, and he blessed himself as he ran for the rear door, through the cold room. His fingers fumbled as he unbolted the door, but he heard only the loud ranting. No footsteps followed him. He threw open the door and stumbled into the deserted alley. He ran to the corner and was relieved to see two young Gardai on the beat, standing amiably in the bright light of day. The terror left him as he called for their help.

It was on account of the tweed jacket, of fine make, that they brought the man to the station.

James phoned Maggie and was relieved there was nothing pressing for him to deal with. His intentions that morning were various and had taken on an urgency of their own.

His first stop was Molloy's office. Refreshed after a shower and change of clothes at his flat, he sped in the Citroën into the centre of town. He was surprised at Molloy's pleasant greeting, remembering vividly their last encounter.

"Been to England, I understand," he said as he ordered tea to be brought in.

"I won't even ask how you know that, Molloy," said James, covering his surprise.

"Learn anything we don't already know?" Molloy smiled, but without sarcasm. He proffered the plate of biscuits, but James waved it aside.

"Let me say it led me to form a few questions to which I believe only you have the answers."

"Fire away."

"I want to know what you make of the items being found on the ferry on a date subsequent to Shaw's death."

"Ah, Shaw, is it?" His tone implied how far off track James's sleuthing had gone.

"Yes. Shaw," James said patiently.

"Surely you are working on the wrong murder."

"Don't palm me off, Molloy. I want to know if you agree that the items on the ferry can implicate Mrs. Shaw."

"It's interesting you should ask that." He peered at James out of pale blue eyes. "Just now."

"Well, if you must know, it occurred to me in England that Mrs. Shaw could as easily be a suspect in Shaw's murder as you have implied both Ariadne and Harry are, and were. Mrs. Shaw's statement to you concerning her husband's remark about going to see an Irish girl here in Dublin has thrown you off the track. She planted that story on you, Molloy, just as she planted old personal belongings of her husband on that ferry." James paused for breath, surprised at his own outburst.

"I see."

"What do you see?"

Molloy shushed him. "No need to be hostile, Fleming. I am going to share something with you. Make of it what you will. But as to your larger questions, I am hardly going to make out a case for the defense of Harry Conroy. Mrs. Shaw's remarks to me were only a small part of the larger overall evidence against him."

James sighed with exasperation. "All right, Molloy. What is this news?"

"Yesterday two constables brought in a traveller. Seems he'd been a bit menacing in a pub on Tara Street. Hadn't done anything physical, mind you. And we normally would have let him sleep it off somewhere, but for the jacket. Good cut, good cloth, and clean. Too good to have come from the Vincent de Paul, they thought. A sharp-eyed pair."

"What are you saying?" James was on the edge of his seat.

"To cut a long story short, the jacket matched a description of Shaw's, given to us by the wife. There was a label, and the lab people verified its origins, a local shop in Leston. There had been some slight alterations done at the time of purchase—not so long ago—and the tailor thinks he might know it from the description over the phone. Our man's gone over with it, so the tailor and Mrs. Shaw can make a final ID. But—"

"Shaw's jacket! On an itinerant. Do you think a traveller killed Shaw?" James was enthusiastic.

"No, I don't think he did it."

"But surely it takes some pressure off Conroy."

"Not really. He's charged with his wife's death, and I think I made my case very plain to you. Unlike yourself, I don't believe Ariadne Conroy's death was a copycat murder designed to throw us off. I think Conroy was tied to Shaw's death—that he killed his wife, and that perhaps he thought he was being a clever bastard, using the bed the second the time to leave the body, and to feign the discovery. Ach!" Molloy sounded disgusted.

Not wishing to antagonize Molloy further, James dropped the rest of his questions. But he felt compelled to clear up one issue.

"Surely it's significant that there was absolutely nothing

of Shaw's found in the house, except the body. That every item belonging to Shaw was gone."

"Fleming," said Molloy, having regained his patience, "Shaw was most definitely killed somewhere other than at the house. There is, in fact, very little forensic or physical evidence—little blood, few fibers, and so on. Bruises on the body are consistent with its being moved after death. Wherever he was killed, we can assume that that is where his clothing and belongings were taken from him."

"I'm glad to hear it. It certainly widens the scope, doesn't it? If you had looked at a wider field and not latched on to Ariadne Conroy, Shaw's murderer might already be in custody."

"He is," said Molloy, smirking.

James realized he was getting nowhere. "Right, then, what about this jacket? Is the man in custody?"

"Not a'tall. He lives at the big site out beyond Finglas. Twenty, thirty caravans there. Got no sense out of him, nor out of them. He claimed he found it. We had nothing to charge him with. No blood on the jacket. No motive. So no, he's not in custody." Molloy looked at his watch. "That's it, Fleming. I've to be in court in a few minutes. Hate testifying, I can tell you. Worst part of this job."

"And the best?" Jame murmured, half to himself.

"The same," said Molloy.

"The same what?"

"The same as yourself, Fleming, and don't deny it. It's the puzzle, man, the puzzle!"

James stepped out into an autumn day. The warm spring day he'd left outside moments earlier had now blown away in a gale of wind and water. He ran for his car, his navy summer-wool three-piece suit soaked in the downpour. He cursed his bad luck and turned the car for home.

As he changed he pondered his next step. The more he teased the threads of this puzzle, as Molloy had called it, the more they seemed to unwind, to fray at the ends and separate into ever smaller strands. He glanced at the art deco clock, one of his more prized possessions, and realized with a shock it was after three. He sat heavily on his bed. He had thought the day was still before him. Too late now to visit the College and parry and thrust with yet more professors. Too late now, to his liking, to follow up Molloy's gift of a clue about the jacket.

He threw himself back on the pillows with a sense of relief and freedom he hadn't felt since the day Harry Conroy had phoned him. A need to refresh his mind, his spirit, and indeed his thirst came upon him. He lifted the phone with anticipation.

"Yuppies. That's it, yuppies one and all," exclaimed Matt as he banged his pint glass on the small table against which their knees were jammed.

"Matt, will you keep your voice down?" pleaded James.

"And why, may I ask?" said Matt pleasantly. "Aren't we sitting alone in this tidy little snug? And who's to hear us?"

"There's people standing just outside the door."

"Above this roar? Couldn't hear themselves talk, let alone meself. Fleming, you are getting worse. This soliciting has turned your brain."

James laughed heartily. "I'm inclined to agree with you."

"Do you—now take my point here—aha, not my pint—"

"Oh, God, now we have humour," James broke in.

Matt went on, unheeding. "Out of the last six times we've gone for a pint, six of those times we've been in snugs in various pubs around the city."

"You exaggerate."

"I do not. This cloak-and-dagger stuff has got to stop. Ever since—"

James put up his hand.

"Sorry. Won't mention it. Forgot."

"S'all right. Another?"

"It's my twist."

"No, the night's on me."

"I'll get you next time," said Matt, appreciating James's unspoken generosity. "Will you come back to the house after?"

"Just for a minute. I don't want any supper," said James.

"Good. Dorothy will be relieved."

James tapped on the small pane of glass in the front snug of Ryan's of Parkgate Street. Ever since Matt's move to a slightly bigger house in this neighbourhood, to accommodate his ever-burgeoning family, they'd met at Ryan's. "How is the house?"

"Better, better, two kids per bedroom. Must be heaven, right?" But Matt laughed. "O' course, it's added twenty minutes to my morning drive to school, but not to worry."

James smiled. His friend's tolerance of the vagaries of life was what he had been missing.

"You're a breath of fresh air, Matt," he said, embarrassing himself and Matt immediately.

"I wouldn't wonder, considering what pollution you've been inhaling. Yuppies, I tell you. Some of the parents at school are yuppies. Can't abide 'em."

James laughed again.

"I'm surprised to hear you using this Americanism, and you a Gaelgoir."

An unattached hand pushed open the small glass door with two pints and balanced them on the narrow sill. James removed the dripping glasses and gave into the hand exact change. The experienced hand closed around it, knocking once on the tiny counter to acknowledge payment.

Matt and James contemplated the dripping glasses of black nectar with a sense of anticipated satisfaction.

"Why, it's a good word. Yuppies. Says it all."

"Such as . . ."

"Such as, you'd never find a yuppie sitting in here and looking at wet glasses that are about to drop large blobs of brown foam all over their knees. Nor would they wipe their mouths with the backs of their hands." He took up his glass and demonstrated. James was amused to follow suit.

"This is true."

"Fleming, you've got to get back to the people. This traveller, now . . ."

"Oh, he's people, I suppose. And you'd spend an evening with him, is that it?"

Matt paused.

"Listen," said James. "I know when I summarize these stories for you I get across neither the pain nor the feeling involved."

"No, possibly it's obscured by the kind of house you're describing, and the trips, and the cars, and the jobs, a picture of a life and a love of appearance without substance."

"Come on." James's tone was sad. "I'm not getting across to you—"

"What? What? That those two lived just for themselves? That they had damn good jobs and money I'll never see? And what did they do with it, the fine house, the money? For God's sake, Fleming. Look how hollow it all is, or was."

"Hollow? How can we pass judgment? My life's mighty hollow, come to think of it. If we're judging according to your rules."

"Oh, and is this it, then? Is this what's at the bottom of all this palaver? Another woman—or lack of one?"

"No, not this time, Matt. But there's something in what you say. Perhaps it is the—"

"Hollowness."

"No! Let me get the word . . . perhaps it's the lack of centre. The lack of, well, something to be going on with."

Matt was serious, as he often could be. "I'm listening."

James stared into his pint of Guinness as though watching some scene enacted there. "Your word 'hollow' frightens me, Matt. As I just said, my life could so easily be perceived that way. The job, the car, the clothes, the holidays—when I used to be able to take any! No ties or commitments. No doubt that's how many people would view me. I hope it's the ones who don't know me."

"Mmm."

"But I always, or almost always, have a sense that there's more, there will be more. I think to myself there will be a woman some day, someone to love who will love me."

"You had that."

"Please, Matt, not Sarah."

"Right, sorry. Closed book. Go on."

"That there would be someone, and there'd be marriage, and of course children. I always take it for granted—you know, that I'll have that. So although I don't now, I allow for it. Let's say there is the potential, there is—well, there is the future," James finished lamely.

"Ahh." Matt sipped his pint. "I think I understand you."

"But you've got all that, Matt. You've got Dorothy, you've got the three—"

"Four, Fleming, four."

"Four kids. You've got your centre, your focus, your future. Surely Dorothy and the children make it so."

"No doubt. The children make a difference. I have no sense of what life would be like without them. There's always my job, of course. Despite that I groan and complain, I still love the teaching. But yes, it's the children, my children. There is just so much to do—physically I mean—with the four of them. School, sports, friends, one of them or the other is invariably sick. You can get caught up in the day-to-day grind. It's like never lifting your head up to look ahead a year, a month, or even a week. It takes all your energy to get through each day. You become short-sighted. But then . . ."

"Then?"

"Then suddenly, when you least expect it, you think— What if I don't survive? You see something in the paper, or on the news. Or you hear of someone you went to school with who has died. It strikes fear into your very heart, your very soul. You take so much for granted. You think to yourself, oh, I'll be there for David, for James, for all of them. And suddenly you think: What if I die? It isn't the fear of death. No, it's trying to imagine your own absence from their lives. Who would they talk to? Who would advise them?" Matt's voice got thick.

"Is there anything you're not telling me?" James was alarmed at this sign of emotion.

"No, no, I'm getting to be a sentimental fool. Maybe it's that I'm headin' for the big four-oh! What I meant to say was, without children in a marriage, I wonder what there is to keep it together."

"Matt, I am amazed. You and Dorothy, I mean—"

"Oh, we're fine. It's just that that love you feel when you're courtin', in the early days. How does that grow? I don't know how we would be with one another if we didn't see each other as parents, as sharing in this job, as partners raising the children up to health and strength, giving them some values, some wisdom. I tell you, Fleming, raising these kids is the hardest thing I've ever done in my life."

The two friends were silent, but it was a comfortable silence. James felt in some way heartened by Matt's confidences. He felt as he had at the start, that all of this great mystery—of marriage, of children—was still there for the taking, still ahead of him, still a potential. But as he sat he began to fear that perhaps this was mere adolescent faith. What grounds, after all, did he have for such optimism? He wasn't about to marry. But he had loved. Twice. Heart-felt, deep, real. But had it been real, he wondered. Teresa married with children, Sarah unattainable. Was he merely waiting for something to happen, someone to happen along?

"Well, does all this talk of marriage put you in mind of it?" Matt broke into his thoughts, handing him a fresh pint he'd ordered as James had sat dreaming.

158

"I'm always in mind of it, Matt."

"Any new woman on the scene, then?" Matt was enthusiastic.

"Indeed and there is. A medical student, a resident actually. Very attractive, very—well, lively. She interests me a lot. I like her outlook on life."

"Sounds promising, I think. But I'm not hearing lust here."

"Matt!"

"Well, it's always a starting point." Matt roared. "It's a damn good thing you have me to bring you back to earth, Fleming. Much too idealistic. Your Anglo-Irish Prod blood is getting too thin. I've got to beef you up."

"I'd point out your background's much the same as my own!"

"There, so I know whereof I speak. You want a nice, plump, young, strong country girl—bear you ten children and idolize you for your looks and your money."

"I'm not buying a heifer."

"Right, right. How did we get off the track? I want to hear more about these yuppies, and don't deny that's what they are."

"I do. We cannot know what goes on in the hearts of other people. I am learning that, at least. And we can't judge by appearances. I thought that this was a truly solid marriage. They were both thirty when they married. They had shared interests and so on. And now I'm learning bits and pieces about that marriage, about Conroy's fears about his wife's infidelity. He hasn't a shred of evidence for that. But there is this terrible suspicion in his heart."

"A knotty problem, James?" Matt asked after James's prolonged silence.

"A woolly brain, more like. I'm not sure if I'm such a good judge of character. I don't have much of a track record," he said ruefully.

As he'd hoped, Matt pointed out that he'd the sense to be

a friend of his, and this said much for his sound common sense.

"All of this is in confidence, Matt, obviously. It's just that although I am committed to a particular person's innocence, I've begun to see that that person might have the capacity for, let's say, vindictiveness. A streak of anger in this person that could lead on to violence."

"But for God's sake, man, you could say that of all of us. We all have a capacity for evil, given certain conditions—sort of like an experiment in chemistry. Certain climate, temperature, chemicals, introduce a catalyst and—boom!"

"No, I can't agree—there are people who would be immune to even that. The ones you know whose souls are true."

"And you're now not sure of this soul. Male or female?"

James was startled. He was so concentrated on Harry that he assumed Matt must know. He was right! He had reminded James of his primary suspect—Mrs. Shaw. From Ariadne's description she seemed to be a woman capable of frenzy, rage, jealousy. She was obviously driven to visit Ari's house. And capable of violence, too. But why had he not detected that in her during their interview in England? It was as if his ideas of Mrs. Shaw and Harry had subtly changed places. Physical evidence—that was what he needed, that was what would orient his case.

He drove Matt, considerably the worse for wear, home. Dorothy greeted them frostily but treated James to the sight of her four sleeping urchins. Mouths open or jammed with chubby fingers, depending on their ages. Blond hair, red hair, chestnut curls, tousled and sticking to warm foreheads, rosy cheeks. The youngest, a big plump baby of about two years, lay asleep in her well-worn cot, her round bottom, fatter because of the nappy under her sleeping suit, stuck up, knees bent under her. She murmured in her sleep. James wanted to take her home and said as much.

"Ah, sure you say that now," whispered Dorothy. "But it

would be different at four in the morning when she's crying for her bottle or perhaps has the longing to go on out the back and have a swing on the swing set."

James smiled. It sounded very appealing to him. Who could mind, and he knew Dorothy didn't, being awakened by that sweet voice, that warm, flushed face? Who could mind when she put her chubby arms around your neck and whispered "Dada" or "up"? Not he, not he. And he bade his friends a very abrupt good-bye.

"Who would think it?" said Dorothy as she poured out a huge mug of tea for Matt, to sober him up and settle him down, she said.

"Think what?" he said blearily.

"That even fellas can get broody."

"Broody, how can you be broody when you are already expectin'?"

"Hush up," she said. "And drink your tea."

The years fell away as James passed through the front gate of the ancient College where he had been a student. He paused for a moment to glance, as any tourist, at the pair of statues set on the small grass lawns—smooth as a billiard table—on either side of the great wooden door that filled the ancient archway. Oliver Goldsmith and Edmund Burke, great writers and thinkers of their day, graduates of this place of learning. Known not as Irish writers, but as British writers. What did it matter, mused James, that their Protestantism bound their reputations to England? England had honoured them, claimed them. And after all, he observed, the College itself had been founded by Queen Elizabeth the First, completing the glorious trinity of Oxford and Cambridge.

As he stood inside the small rotunda the porter looked at him cannily and then came to the little window of the gate lodge.

"Bless my soul and body, I say you look a lot like a skinny

fella that once did plague me about his bicycle, or want of one."

James laughed. "Indeed, that was myself. But I wasn't alone."

"No, but by my stars and garters you've not changed much."

"No, nor you, nor your little nest in there that I often envied on a wet and windy night."

"Home to me anyways, sir."

"Tell me, Lambert, is term over?"

"Just this week. Lectures are finished. The third years are gone, o' course. But the rest are here. The library is jammed, they tell me."

"And the staff?"

"Oh, widely dispersed, sir, widely dispersed. You'll do as well to check for yourself."

"Right you are." James ambled on, reminiscing, reading the notice boards, the schedule of exams posted behind the glass display windows put there for that purpose so many years before. He examined the smallest notice board, no bigger than a manila folder, crammed as always with lists of books for sale, pleas for rides to every part of the four provinces of Ireland. Bikes for sale, pleas for bikes to be returned. A few folded notes with names on them, their contents romantic in nature, no doubt. Assignations. The best part of finding a scrap of paper with one's own name on it pinned on the board. Oh, it had been fun, he thought, such fun.

He passed into Front Square, lifting his eyes to the Campanile straight ahead, turning to check behind him that the great blue-faced clock kept good time around its gold Roman numerals, checking its partner on the front of the gray edifice known as the Dining Hall. He glanced to his right to see a small group of higher graduates emerging, sheltering briefly in the colonnade of the porch of the magnificent Exam Hall. How many times had he sat within, nervously filling up blue book after blue book, watched over by the gigantic portraits of the early provosts of the College? The graduates adjusted their hoods—some of ermine, some of scarlet, some of black. He wondered what degree-granting was taking place and looked enviously at the happy clusters of friends and family. Nothing changes, he saw, and he was glad.

The wooden floors of the English Department echoed with his footsteps and told him how empty the offices were. The rooms on the top two floors, however, still showed signs of life. The breeze sucked net curtains through open windows, and glass milk bottles here and there kept cool on the sills. He found the secretary of the English Department barricaded behind her large desk in a very small and crooked room. It was a very old building.

"Gone, I'm afraid, Mr. Fleming," she answered when he explained his errand. "But actually"——her clipped tones belied the soft, faded face—"if you have general questions of procedure, I am equipped to help you." Intimidating as ever, she did not remember him, but he remembered her.

He explained, and she repeated what he already knew.

"I can tell you from our records that Professor Shaw was, had been, an extern reader for this department since they started using this particular system. In other words, for a number of years. What I cannot tell you is if he was to be an extern reader for this current term."

"Why not?" James bristled.

"Because it is confidential. I'll explain, shall I? The date and time for a defense is posted publicly in the College. Such a defense is open to the academic community and, in fact, to the public, although outsiders rarely come. The professors sitting on the panel are mentioned by name, including the extern reader. Extern readers hand in their written comments to the advisor before this date. It is a matter between the committee and the candidate. I can't tell you until the notice is posted publicly."

James argued briefly, fruitlessly. The woman would have been happy to have lived in Goldsmith's day, he fumed as he left the hallowed halls of learning, not very much the wiser.

He strolled back towards his office on Merrion Square, a stone's throw from the back gate of the College, pausing to watch some white-clad cricketers on the wide green expanse of the College cricket field. And he thought idly of how he'd like to take it up again, if time allowed. But cricket schedules wouldn't permit him his freedom to pursue his trains across the face of the globe.

The campsite Molloy had mentioned was a blot on the landscape of North County Dublin but was called home by at least thirty families of what the general Irish populace still referred to as tinkers or itinerants. They preferred to be known as the travelling people. Their caravans were of an amazing assortment, and James studied them from the relative safety of his car.

There were on the fringes of the camp some of the colourful, traditional horse-drawn wooden caravans that mimicked what the early generations of travelling people had used. Two, he could see from where he sat, were in fairly good shape. Others, with broken shafts and peeling paint, seemed to be store houses for God knew what, and He wasn't telling.

About a dozen piebald horses and a donkey grazed lethargically on already-cropped grass, none of them tethered, but none of them wandering either.

The majority of the caravans were mobile homes of the type popular in the fifties, small with rounded roofs—easy enough to tow if you had a decent car. There was barely a decent car among the six or so scattered about, parked along the side of the access road.

James took note of the fact that this campground was not one of the official stopping sites allowed the tinkers by the government. They tended to eschew the sites that had water laid on cold from standing taps, and sometimes electricity. To use one of these sites would have been capitulation, the same as settling into government housing. James recalled his clergyman friend, an earnest member of the committee working to help the travelling people. He gave many instances of why settling them in the small, neat bungalows had failed. For a start, they had stored their coal in the bathtubs. They had also chosen to house their various livestock with them in the bungalows.

"Ignorant," James had concluded, but he was chided by his friend.

"It'd be hard tellin'," he'd say. "Shrewd, they are. Subtle. Were they telling us to take their needs into account when designing the homes they were to settle in, the homes they were to give up the life of the open road for?" James reflected that he'd altered some of his prejudices since then, but the last one remained. He was nervous of these people.

With that he manfully got out of his very French, very attractive car and ambled, or so he hoped, towards the site. A horse near him whinnied, like a guard dog warning of an approach by strangers. James had ridden horses all his life and felt assured he'd win this one over, but his gestures, his intentions were read clearly by the horse. It reared up his thick head on his short, powerful neck, and the others, all piebald and rough-coated, moved restlessly, grouping together. James walked towards them, and they shied off. Hardly in bloody fright, thought James, knowing full well what such horses endured in the course of an ordinary day.

A breeze rustled the new leaves on the sparsely planted tress on this former construction site. The whole area was flat, abandoned, dry and rocky. No matter. The horses lifted their heads with that early spring breeze like the most beloved colts and foals of the lush fields of Kildare. They started to trot and, as of one mind, broke into a gallop, shifting to the left and to the right, turning as if moving to a music only they could hear.

James stood transfixed until suddenly they galloped off towards the road. And shouts, rough, coarse, and meant for him, followed.

"Hi, hi hi, yaa!" A war whoop preceded a short, thick-set man with a stick in his hand.

"You bleedin' eejit, you friggin' git, what the hell are ya playin' at?" he managed to shout at James as he sped past him, running flat out, calling to the horses as he passed on down the fortunately quiet roadway.

The donkey remained, staring at James as though he recognized a certain kinship.

Surprisingly, few of the camp's inhabitants had come out to view the commotion. A certain silence held sway as James walked on towards the caravans, set out, he observed now that he was among them, in rough rows of about six or seven, with wide paths between them.

He smiled, kindly he hoped, at the children of school age and younger who appeared between the mobile homes, climbing over the tow bars, swinging their bare, thin legs. They stared warily. He wondered if he'd encountered these same faces on O'Connell Bridge, on Nassau Street, begging, alone, cardboard box in hand. Were these children the babies he'd seen over the years in their mothers' arms, in the cold, driving rain of December, when the itinerants left the countryside and came back towards Dublin, like people on a cold day moving ever closer towards the fire to get warm?

Oh, the readers of the newspapers were well told that those babies in the arms of the young mothers, painful portrayals of the Madonna and Child which cut to the quick of every Irish soul, weren't always the birth children of those women. Oh, no, the papers told them and told them truly. The prettiest of the women and the prettiest of the babes were paired and sent off to beg and bring back their earnings to the men of the camp. And such babies they were, round-eyed and accusing, or asleep and even more guilt-provoking. But they grew, and there was an indeterminate age when they lost their appeal to the giving public—no longer infants in arms—and before they could go out and beg for themselves. An unappealing age, apparently—the age of the children that now crept out in ragged dresses and trousers and peered at him, curious, but only as to why he was there. They put their babyhood training quickly into practice, and suddenly he was surrounded.

"Please, sur, a penny, a penny for me ma. She's terrible sick, sur." The boldest of the boys had stymied him. He looked down at the boy, a dirty face, mud obscuring the characteristic spray of freckles across his nose and cheeks. Blue eyes looked out from a wide-boned face, a thick line of brow, all capped by thick, coarse red hair.

James admired the cheekiness of the child until suddenly ten others were tugging at his coat, his hands, his legs. He gave out a handful of change in some faint recollection of Hallowe'en. And they blessed him, his soul, and the mother who bore him. And then they were gone, back to their hidey holes, their childish games, and a knowledge of life that he had yet to acquire.

He walked on, uncertain of how to get somebody's attention yet primed with his story, primed by Maggie and half of his office staff. In the door of one caravan, cleaner, newer than many, sat a woman of perhaps fifty but with a much older face. She caught his eye and lifted her chin in an an unspoken question.

"I beg your pardon," said James as he approached. "I'd like to have my fortune told."

"Then it's me daughter y'd be wantin'. I've retired."

"Then could I see her, if she's not busy?"

"Indeed you could see her if she was here. I can't say if she's busy."

"Perhaps you could find out."

"I would if she were here."

"Is she not here, then?" James saw the cat-and-mouse game eventually.

"She may be. Or she may not be. I could tell her who is askin' after her."

"James, my name is James."

"You've come a long way, James, and we wouldn't want to disappoint you, now, would we?" She gestured him in.

James was surprised at the cleanliness, the order, the prosperity he saw inside. As clean as any suburban home. Plastic flowers adorned the windows in merry little vases, dishes neatly displayed, glassware and mugs hanging from hooks. There was care, and choice, and taste—not his, but a sense of propriety, a sense of—yes, of home. He relaxed slightly.

"Sit down here at the table. I'll tell you, you're in luck. I taught my daughter everything she knows, and she's good, mind you. Clever like. Can read people. But she's not got the gift. I do," she added simply. And James believed her.

"It's very quiet here," he said by way of making conversation, but he was curious. There was an eerie silence.

"Sure, they're all at the horse fair in Blessington. The men now, they drove the horses there on the weekend. It's a good fair, better than Thurles even. They'll do well this year, the horses are good, good spring grazing, they're fat and there's a lovely sheen on them."

"Blessington. I thought the races were on at Punchestown or Fairyhouse this week."

"Fair, not races. They'll be trading the beasts. And a good price they'll get. We're known—this site, I mean—for our horses. Strange, I would'a said you were a man of horses, now. You ride. You've been riding for years."

James was horrified as he felt a blush rise up his face. "I like to ride, surely. But I'm a weekend horseman."

"Well, now, these horses are going to the farms and such. Not your breed. The fair is where we trade. Money, but goods, too. They get good horses. The settled people know this."

A far cry from mending tin pots, thought James, from which old occupation they derived their name in famine times.

"Cross me palm," she said abruptly, not liking his silence.

He took a pound note, having given up his change, and crossed her palm. She smiled as she lay it to one side on the tiny round table.

"Cards or palm? It will cost you more for the cards."

"Palm, then," said James, anxious to get on with it, fearful of the mysterious Tarot cards and of this woman who seemed older by the minute.

She was silent for some time as she held his hand in her calloused one. At last she spoke.

"I'll tell you now, there's more here than I expected. Your life line, now, that's long." She traced it with a painted fingernail till it tickled. "And here, there's a lot of . . . trouble . . . love life. A very turbulent love life, three—no, four affairs of the heart. Some are behind you." She glanced quickly at his face. "One, even two, not yet over." She pondered his hand, and he studied it, too, to see what she read there.

"Your father, he's dead," she said abruptly. "You've one brother and a sister. No, a sister that's dead."

James shook his head.

"Believe me, so. There was a sister, and now she's gone."

"Go on, please."

"This worries me," she murmured. "Wait, you travel over water—no, you travel all the time, there's water, but wheels, lots of wheels. Cars, trains, land rovers, perhaps." She looked up, a glint in her eye, but she never smiled.

James laughed. She'd pinpointed his suburban aspirations and avocations as soon as she saw him walking down the path to her caravan.

"Please," he said more genuinely, intrigued by both her insight and by her gift of second sight.

"I don't like saying this, sir, but I'm not convinced you've come for this or want to hear it. It's different when people come who really want to know. I'm asking you now before I go on, do you want to know the rest?"

"By all means," he replied, but his formal words cloaked a fear.

169

"There's death around you. I'm not reading it here. The palm, ach!" she said dismissively, "it tells you mostly the past, and a bit about the future. Your length of life, which is long. And the affairs of the heart. Family. But I'm sensing more. Let me do the cards for you—no charge."

She let him think for a minute. Curiosity overpowered him, and suddenly his skepticism of long standing and long training was gone, as it was always gone when you scratched an Irish man's skin.

"In for a penny, in for a pound," he said at last.

"More like hung for a sheep as a lamb."

She took out the cards, he cut them, and she dealt. He was sorry when she finished. His memory of it would always be confused. There had been death, death in the past, in the present, in the future. There was danger, travelling over water. The Fool seemed to be prominent. He was to come into money, pots of money. Wills and bequests were mentioned. Words, words, and more words. So much so that she insisted that he was a writer.

And there were babies. Or one baby. She couldn't be sure. He shook his head—no babies, anyway. She was adamant. Too used to counselling young women desperate to marry, desperate for families, so desperate they sought divine as well as occult help.

And there was a woman. Alone. Speaking without words. She rubbed her forehead and closed her eyes. She lay out the cards again, but the same pattern emerged. Cold, dead, white, calling. But wait, perhaps it was more than one woman. Two, perhaps three. Circling around him, encircling.

James stood up. He'd had enough.

"Why did you come?" the old gypsy asked him harshly.

"I'm sorry. I should have been straight with you. I pretend to be a sleuth, an ineffective one apparently."

"I wouldn't—the cards wouldn't—agree. Go on." The woman whose name he'd never know put the kettle on to boil over the primus stove in the corner of her kitchen.

"I'm checking up on—"

"You're never the polis!"

"No, I'm not the police."

"I didn't think so. They've already been, sniffing around," she said disdainfully.

"I'm checking on some clothing and other items which have turned up at this camp. A . . . fella . . . wearing a good plaid tweed jacket, good cut, English, came to the attention of the police. I need to know. I need to know where he might have got it."

"Our boys don't do no murdering." The tone had lifted.

"No, I didn't think so. But it's very important that I know where he got it."

"Where did he say he got it, then?" she said archly.

"He said he found it. He stuck to the story, apparently. Found it in a dumpster or a pile of rubbish near the camp. This camp." James turned and looked at the shrivelled woman with the scrawny skin on her forearms, at the hands that so lately had held his own. "Would you know anything about it?"

"I might," she said.

"Is it money, then?"

"No, sur. Don't be insultin' me. No amount of money would cause me tell you if I didn't want to. I've taken a likin' to you. Not sure why. Might be I feel sorry for you. Be the looks of them cards you're in need of help, of all kinds. And don't turn your head away. The cards don't lie. Divine help shouldn't be neglected neither."

"I'm listening," James said, sitting down on the small stool.

"I know a bit of the story. One day, just a while ago now, a woman came here. Not as far into the camp as you did. And she didn't have that kind of flash car you have—I'd keep an eye on that if I were you," she added. "She came a ways into the camp carrying a bag."

"A woman. Can you describe her?" His voice was anxious.

"I watched her from here, from the step. Some o' the young wans went out to her. She was thin and dark, not too dark. Of middlin' age. I'm sorry now I didn't have her in for the cards. I can read a person well, you know."

"I believe it."

"The young wans—they spoke of her when she left. On foot, as I said. She'd talked nice, they said, sweet like. The young wans, they don't like that, you see. They know when it's false. She's a false wan, they said."

"What did she want?"

"I wish I knew. We, the women, stayed back, you see. We don't want truck with social workers. Forever coming around to help us, you know. We don't mind the visitin' nurse, now. She's a grand help when the babies are . . ."

"Please, go on."

"Well, she wasn't the district nurse. The little wans thought she must be from a church. They're the other ones who come round. Forever helping. With other peoples' clothes, as though we'd none of our own."

Her pride was to the fore now, thought James.

"She took out the jacket you're talkin' about. And some shirts, I think. The kids took them off her and played with them a bit. They left them down, and after a while some of the women took hold of them. That's how Mike would have got it. From his missus. No mystery in that. She took it up and dusted it off. She said it was fine cloth, and new, too."

"So what do you think?"

"A do-gooder. She'd fine leather shoes, little Mary told me after. And good stockin's. They notice these things. It's from always seein' shoes and feet and boots when they're sittin' on the pavement beggin'."

James closed his eyes at the image, but only briefly. "A well-heeled type," he said, and then he bit his tongue.

"You have it there, a well-heeled type from a fine house, and with something on her conscience. Salvin' it by workin' for the church or the mother's union. Do-gooder out makin' herself feel good."

James stood up to leave. The light was fading, and she warned him to take care with his car. He left a ten-pound note on her table, under the sugar bowl, and she didn't say nay, merely closing the door behind him. He walked in the eerie silence to his car, not knowing whether he imagined or felt the curious concealed eyes watching him leave.

The sight of the circles of soap all over the paintwork of his car gave him pause, pause to be thankful it wasn't scratches from the myriad sharp stones that lay around on the arid soil.

From nowhere a little band of bedraggled boys appeared beside him.

"Ah, sure now, aren't we very good, sur? And us just after washing down your beeyouteeful motor." Their eyes were laughing, but their childish mouths sincere. He was nonplussed.

"Good?" He said stupidly.

"Yes, sur, so good as we did wash it and not take it into our heads to do somethin' else." The tiny leader of the group stepped forward, hand outstretched. "A valuable job done, now wouldn't you say, sur?"

James paid into the small hand his last few single notes and felt it was cheap at the price. As he drove away he knew that he and his pride had been mercifully spared by an urchin a quarter of his age.

Crawling across the city of Dublin from the north side to the south at rush hour, he had ample time to analyze his adventure.

Ariadne? His heart sank. Well-heeled, middle age, brown hair. Ill at ease, a fish out of water with those people. As he had been. Afraid. Afraid to venture too far into the camp, but driven there to dispose of the items belonging to Shaw. Afraid to put them in the trash at her own house. Unable to destroy them. She'd planned ahead. His mind swam as he sat for twenty minutes on O'Connell Street in a jam behind a bus that had broken down. Planned ahead. Had left her car far enough away so that it hadn't been noticed. And why

would they look to see her car? Used as they were to
timid—what had she said?—do-gooders.

He smiled now at the children's accurate description.
Good shoes. Oh, Ariadne. He attempted to concentrate as
he squeezed past the bus, his tires scraping the kerb on his
right side.

What else had she said? A woman calling with no words.
That had to be her voice on his answering machine!
Ariadne's last message to him. And then these other women
around him. Sarah, no doubt. And Geraldine. He realized
with a jolt that he hadn't phoned Geraldine, hadn't let her
know how busy he had been. And this baby. Ridiculous. No
babies in his life. And him a writer. More nonsense. Just
showed how much of it was guesswork. He tried to put her
reading of the cards from his mind and hold on to the facts.

But he didn't want to hold on to this new fact, the fact
that a woman answering Ariadne's general description was
known to have visited the campsite with Shaw's jacket. He
sighed as he climbed out of the car, stiff from cramped
quarters. In the caravan. In the car. He put his key in the
lock of the door to his flat. Death was a fact. And she'd said
death all around him. But that was true. For God's sake, all
he ever dealt with were wills and last testaments. Death all
around him, he thought as he chopped onions and put a
good frying steak onto the pan to sear it. Death, he thought,
all around him, as he poured out a bottle of Châteauneuf du
Pape. But not threatening him.

And these women that she also saw around him. Two or
three women. Ariadne, of course. And Geraldine a doctor.
The woman calling—that had to be Ariadne. Calling for
help. As she had wanted to when Mrs. Shaw had forced her
way into her house. Mrs. Shaw.

Of course, *she* was the second woman. A woman linked to
death—of her husband or Ariadne? Mrs. Shaw, who as a
suburban matron could easily meet the gypsy's description.
A shrewd woman, yes. Was it part of her larger plan to

confuse the police, as the murder itself had, as the placement of the body had?

He felt a new energy surge through him. This fact would fit his initial theory. She could have killed Shaw, and—as Molloy insisted—whoever had killed Shaw had killed Ariadne. Or rather, whoever had killed Ariadne had previously killed Shaw. Ariadne hadn't killed Shaw, nor had Harry. And Harry hadn't killed his wife. James's head swam. But as he ate he realized he held one very crucial card that Molloy did not have. Molloy did not know about the woman who'd brought the jacket.

But by the time he'd finished his wine the picture did not look as encouraging. He moved to his desk and jotted down the larger questions that were forming in his mind:

If Mrs. Shaw murdered Shaw, it meant she'd followed him from England, killed him in as yet an unknown place, conveyed the body to the house, and placed it in the bed. It meant that she had contacted the police in Dublin, pretending she was in England, dispersed the clothing around Dublin, and returned on the ferry, placing the remaining clues to throw off the police and indicate suicide. And was still available to greet the tabloid press. It would have to have been a daring, masterful plan that had required strategy, advance information, and nerve. James shook his head. It didn't seem to him as though a woman could have done it, or not a woman on her own. James stopped short.

Was this the connection between the two murders he'd been seeking? Had she had an accomplice? But who? Who would help a wife so crazed by jealousy and revenge? No, this was a domestic situation. And all of this depended on the one fact that they could not verify—that Mrs. Shaw and only Mrs. Shaw claimed to be true—that Shaw and Ariadne were still lovers.

James paused. If the line of his thinking was on target, it would indicate that Mrs. Shaw had an accomplice. Who that was he had yet to consider. But if it meant more than one person was involved, then it followed that the motive was more complicated. He knew, too, that once more than one person was involved in a crime they were more likely to be discovered.

James grew even more serious. What had anyone else to gain in helping Mrs. Shaw murder her husband? Who could have hated him as much as did his wife? There was only one person James could think of—a wildly jealous and vindictive man who believed, as Mrs. Shaw did, that Ariadne and Shaw were lovers. Harry Conroy.

Mrs. Shaw's unfaithful husband was dead.

Harry Conroy's unfaithful wife was dead.

The awful parallel was there. The connection that Molloy had insisted existed between the two murders, that James would have seen except for his faith in Harry and his faith in Ariadne. It didn't seem to matter that it was only the word of these two people that accused their spouses, now dead and silent in their own defense. The accusation was there: They had been unfaithful. And there was no one to deny it.

James felt his flesh creep. He thought of Harry at this moment, no doubt enjoying a brandy in front of the fire in his beautiful Georgian home. Alone. Harry—his client.

Mrs. Shaw and Harry. Ariadne and Shaw. A shared knowledge, a shared grievance, a shared motive, a shared gain. And a shared guilt.

Was the reason that Harry seemed to believe so strenuously that his wife had been unfaithful, even after her marriage, derived from his converse with Mrs. Shaw? It would explain a lot.

James considered the prosperous, respectable, established accountant and the tired, drained, and driven English housewife.

He was glad for the moment that Molloy did not know about the woman at the campsite. Not because for a while he'd believed that woman to have been Ariadne. That had saddened James: for her to be both dead and guilty of such a heinous act.

No, he was glad because this discovery, his own, served to point out a startling new train of thought, the possible involvement of Mrs. Shaw with Harry. And it exonerated Ariadne. But that was worse! James shook himself. For him to believe that his client was guilty would be a terrible burden. There was no turning back. Or was there? He glanced at his phone with a longing to call Madigan. He could almost hear Madigan's soothing, perfect tones reassuring him—as he had in the Moore case—that he'd get used to it! He didn't pick up the phone. Instead he shoved his notes into his briefcase and locked it.

James did not sleep well that night. Nor for many nights to come.

—— *Chapter Eleven* ——

Brona lowered the phone back into its cradle and then glared at it. She stood in the continual twilight that filled the hall that ran alongside the staircase to the floor above. She waited, but it didn't ring again. She wasn't sure that she had kept the irritation out of her voice as Geraldine had rattled on about James Fleming and the great night they'd had at the Gate Theatre. She'd wanted to slam the phone down and erase from her memory the sound of that confident, happy voice.

It wasn't fair, she fumed as she went into the kitchen and switched on the overhead light. Geraldine was a flirt. She always had been. All the years that they'd shared the flat. She wondered now as she looked around how the two of them had managed. Of course, then she hadn't needed all the space in their bedroom for her research, her manuscripts, her collection of books. She leaned on the door jamb of the bedroom as she waited for the kettle to boil. And she recalled the second small bed, the clothes strewn everywhere, the makeup case that used to lie on the floor in the corner. It hadn't been easy, she remembered now. It was only that she herself was so orderly in her habits, and of course her wardrobe was never as extensive as Ger's.

It was better this way. Her own personality was evident everywhere in the small flat. She was admiring yet again her two Jack Yeats prints, inherited from her father, which brought such pleasure into her life. The kettle whistled, calling her back to the kitchen. She looked longingly at Mangan curled in the centre of her cozy bed, its down quilt full of little warm hills and valleys. Lord! What was she going to do with all her things *and* the cats if she had to move to England to take up a post? The mail this week had been dismal. Two letters of polite rejection of her applications for junior lecturing posts. There was still the interview up North, pending the outcome of her degree. She thought of the Irish Institute, just a stone's throw from where she stood. She pictured the scholars there, working in such security, such serenity, their stipends assured. She pictured them chatting over their beloved Irish literature and language—her aged, respected uncle among them. Perhaps she should approach him. Her father would have advised that, she was sure. But that offer to teach a summer session to a class of ignorant foreigners had been an insult she couldn't forgive.

She wandered, disconsolate, back into her pleasant kitchen. Tea held no attraction now she was no longer in a good mood. Geraldine had disturbed that. Yet again.

She saw the half-full bottle of red wine she'd bought for herself on Saturday and took it and one of her two wineglasses into the tiny study. Geraldine was like a flame, and men—silly, foolish men—like the proverbial moths. She had waited all those years, living vicariously through Geraldine's many affairs of the heart. Not one had seen through her. Only herself. Only as a woman would see through another as through a pane of glass. She was never serious. And the two broken engagements. She'd felt so sorry for those young fellas. How hurt she would have been if she had been they. She mused as she sipped her wine, relaxing ever so slightly. She wouldn't drink too much. She had too much work to complete this day.

She shifted her chair in order to look out the large window that gave onto the garden. James and Clarence frolicked about like the kittens they had been long ago. Spring had aroused their blood, and they played with each other, chasing their own tails, the quivering grass, the odd butterfly. The white wrought-iron lawn furniture provided platforms for their play. But nonetheless it stood forlorn, lonely, waiting for Ariadne to carry out her coffee, to sip and to look at the grass that had once been like a lawn. The tulips along the long left wall were overblown, their petals fallen into the borders and rotting. The wind stirred the bank of Michaelmas daisies that ran along the right-hand side. They had grown stalky and bushy. Few of them would bloom this year, thought Brona. But the daffodils that had been naturalized throughout the lawn bravely raised their trumpets above the tall, increasingly weedy grass.

At this rate the garden would be full of hay, she speculated. It had been pleasant to look out on all these years. It was possibly Ariadne's one saving grace, she observed reluctantly—her love of the garden. She'd kept it simple. And in doing so had followed on old Mrs. Callahan's plans. But Ariadne had had the walls re-painted, and she'd restored the stable at the end of the garden into a pretty little house for their cars. She'd pruned the old gnarled apple trees and the two Victoria plum trees. The weeping birch had been a mistake, though, thought Brona, recalling the Sunday afternoon when Ari and Harry had planted it. She could have told them it would grow far too tall to fit in with the miniature style of this walled garden. Most Sundays they'd worked there. Mostly in silence, she remembered now, Harry following Ari's instructions. It had reminded her faintly of her own parents as they'd pottered in the much more extensive garden that surrounded the old rectory in Monaghan. Oh, they'd had apples then, hadn't they? And she'd made apple tarts with her mother in the big old kitchen. They'd had black currants, too. She'd hated picking them and cleaning them with their tiny tough stalks. Her little fingers would ache, but when they made their jam . . . she had loved the jam, its smell filling the old house when she'd come in from school.

A pity, she thought, her parents had married so late in life. And so they'd died and left her entirely alone, the only child of a late marriage. But she hadn't minded then that she had no brother, no sisters. And now they were gone she had grown accustomed to being alone. It didn't matter, really, that they'd not be there to see her at the commencement ceremony, robed for the great presentation. No one to stand beside her as photographs were taken of proud parents and successful candidates on the steps of the great Exam Hall. She'd gotten used to all that. Everything was fine as long as she didn't let herself remember the big old house, the ancient garden with its fruitful trees, the hidden places where she'd played with her dolls and then, as she grew, read her books and lay dreaming, wrapped in her father's old cardigan, staring up through the branches of the trees at the sky beyond, her imagination peopled with all the characters from her reading. No, she hadn't been lonely then. And she wasn't lonely now. But the sight of the overgrown garden troubled her.

What did it matter if Geraldine had captured James Fleming? Brona hadn't really had any interest in him, except at the very beginning. He seemed a serious sort, and literate, too. Interested in her work. It might have been interesting to get to know him—if Geraldine hadn't come along. And she'd done that herself. Wanting reinforcements, as though her meeting had been a blind date. She'd given up on those a long time ago.

She finished her glass of wine and stood up, moving restlessly, envious of her cats, gamboling like lambs in the grass. It really was a pity.

And moved by this thought she left the flat and climbed the high granite-clad steps that led to the Conroys' front door.

"Brona, I'm . . . do come in." Harry stood, huddled in a long blue pullover, holding a whiskey glass. Brona entered and walked ahead of him into the sitting room. She did not sit, and he did not ask her to. They stood in silence for a few moments, Harry seemingly at a loss for something to say.

"Harry? Could you come with me, please?" Brona walked through into the dining room. It was not as Ariadne would have left it. The beautiful mahogany table was littered with papers, letters, printed cards, cards of condolence, legal-sized paper, torn envelopes. Harry's briefcase stood where once a bowl of flowers would have adorned the room. The sideboard, too, was obscured by more papers, dirty glasses, some still full, just left there. And the room was stuffy, a smell of pipe tobacco lingering from the pipes and ashtrays that also lay on the table.

"Sorry," said Harry perfunctorily, "I've been working." But it was clear he had been neither working nor sleeping. His formerly square face was drawn, haggard, the cheeks hollow. His habitually well-groomed brown hair now hung limp. His eyes seemed to stare, and as if he'd noticed her appraising glance he took out his reading glasses and put them on.

"Harry. It's a very beautiful spring day."

"Is it?" He said in a dead voice.

"Yes, come. Come here and look out." The glass behind the long white lace curtains was filmed with smoke. "Here, look at the garden. James and Mangan are having a ball."

"Or a feast. You know I never liked them killing the birds here, especially in the spring." His voice was glum.

Brona retorted rather sharply in defense of her cats. "It's their nature, Harry. You can't go against nature like that. It's not malicious. They don't do it for pleasure."

"Of course they do. It's obvious. They enjoy the hunt, they enjoy the kill."

"Well, as much can be said of people riding to hounds," she said defiantly.

"Haven't done it in years now. And you?"

"Not since—not since I left the rectory. Here, look out. Forget the cats."

He moved reluctantly to the window.

"It's a beautiful garden, Harry. Or it was," she said significantly.

"Mmmm. Ariadne loved it, didn't she?" Harry answered sadly.

"Well." Brona was brusque. "I imagine she did. The point is, you do, too. I know you've put a lot of work into it."

"Never cared for it myself. Weekend gardening and mowing."

Brona grew vexed. "Harry, it is a great garden. It represents a lot of your work. It represents an investment." This last point, at least, she thought, would move him.

"What difference does it make now?"

"It means that you should, could"—she modified it—"could get out there. You could get some fresh air, exercise, clear your mind. You could get the garden back into shape. Everything is growing, Harry. Look, look at the grass." She flicked the curtain impatiently.

"I can't think about the garden, Brona. I've too much on my mind. You see"—he paused, unused to forming the words—"my firm has asked me to take a leave of absence. Oh, it's not the money. They're paying me my salary. But . . ." His voice trailed off as he shrugged like a cranky child.

"Oh, Harry, I am sorry. They surely don't think that you had anything to do with—with all of this." Brona waved her long, slim hands in some vague gesture.

"God, I don't know what to think." Harry leaned on the frame of the window, fiddling with the round knob of the internal shutter. "Of course, they were terribly polite. They said they felt I needed time and rest. Time to prepare my defense, as one of the senior partners put it."

"But *you* are one of the senior partners!"

"True. I couldn't be fired without trouble, but they made their case plain." He sighed and looked unseeing into the garden.

"What case?"

"That it was for the greater good of the firm, that some of the clients had made polite enquiries as to my status—you know, that kind of thing. It's bad publicity. I can see that. It's just with this enforced idleness I'll go mad. My job is everything to me. The days are so long and empty now."

Brona looked at him as he stood unaware of her scrutiny.

"I see," she said mildly. "Well, then," she added more directly, "this is a perfect opportunity. The time is obviously heavy on your hands. And the garden awaits."

She looked at him expectantly, but he ignored her, returning to the cluttered drinks trolley and refilling his rather dirty glass. She spoke again, but it was apparent he wasn't listening.

"If anything, I suppose I could get in some golf," he said abstractedly. "But it's a bit early in the year." He sat heavily on one of the wing chairs.

She stared at him and his posture. The room was exactly as it would have been except for the clutter and the glasses. All the items in place, the lovely decorations and ornaments that made the room a home to Ariadne, that she had, sometimes with Harry, so lovingly and carefully selected. All was still there, her taste evident in the lightness and brightness of the room. Brona looked at Harry with disgust, ashamed for him, when he had not the sense to see it in her face. His lethargy and selfishness appalled her.

"Harry. I do believe if you don't have the time or inclination . . . to tend to the garden . . . that you might call in one of the gardener's jobbers to do a quick whip round. It would only take a man like that a day or less."

"We'll see."

"And there's another reason I've come." She strode towards the door leading to the hall and stood waiting until he looked at her.

"Yes. What is it, for God's sake, Brona?"

His stinging tone did not affect her now.

"I just wanted to give you notice, in ample time. You've a right to that."

"What? You're leaving?" He was as shocked as if removal men had just arrived to repossess the furnishings of his house. "Is it because . . . you know? I'm sorry about the police and all that. It was just your proximity to all this business in the past month. They interviewed the neighbours, you know. You've been here, well, since we moved in—what, six years ago?"

"Longer, Harry. I was here when Mr. Callahan was alive. No, it isn't on account of recent events." She drew herself up, unconsciously, to her full stature. "You may not be aware, but I will shortly receive my doctorate. Of course, I will be moving on." She saw his face lose its concentration. "I'll be moving on," she repeated, "to a teaching post, possibly in England or in the North. Or less likely—but one never knows—here in Ireland. Even if it's in Dublin"—she punched her words at him, trying to break through his indifference—"even if I get a post in Dublin I would be moving into more . . . appropriate quarters." She hoped he was hurt by her last remark. She couldn't tell, because the doorbell pealed loudly. His eyes flickered briefly.

"Get that, Brona, on your way out. No, wait." He got up quickly. "I don't want any reporters here." He pushed past her and opened the door as she hung back.

"Fleming, it's you!" said Harry. "Here, come in, come in. What news?"

James caught Brona's eyes watching him, wide and impassive, and he nodded to her as he was led forcefully into the room. Harry never acknowledged her leaving.

The door shut, and Harry sighed. "Silly twit. She's up here twittering to me about the garden, for God's sake.

These old maids, you wonder what their function in this world is. Bloody bookworm. Ariadne was right about her."

Without waiting for a reply he asked James to have a drink, and for a fleeting moment James felt guilty at not rising to Brona's defense. But thoughts of her faded as he braced himself to examine his client and to find therein some cause to believe in his innocence. But a close look at Harry and the state of the room inspired him to a different tactic.

James placed his glass of whiskey back on the tray. "Right, Harry. Let's go, let's get out of this, let's get out of the house." James suddenly wanted a fresh sea breeze to blow the cobwebs away and bring some colour into Harry's ashen face.

"I'd rather not, Fleming. Thanks." He went to fill his glass again, but James closed his hand around his wrist.

"No, I'm serious, we're going out—just for a short while. It'll do you good. And me." James coaxed the reluctant Harry out to the car. Brona was coming up from her flat hauling her bike with her, and James was glad to repair the slight of their earlier meeting.

"Brona?" he said heartily. "Let me help you with that. Off to enjoy this glorious weather?" He lifted the bicycle from her hands.

"Hardly, Mr. Fleming. I'm off, as you say, to the Long Room to complete some research on my bibliography on the O'Suillebhean manuscripts there. Good day to you." She walked off briskly, and James was puzzled at the severity of her snub.

"Bookworm!" murmured Harry as he buckled himself into the bucket seat of James's car and waited as the Citroën rose up.

James roared off at the maximum speed for the city limits and waited for Harry to speak.

"Where are we going?" he said at last, rousing himself briefly.

"Howth, I thought. Walk on the pier might do us both a power of good."

"Howth. I remember Howth." He said it as if it were in a distant country. "Ariadne and I went there once, years now, went to see the rhododendrons."

"Rather like Bloom and Molly."

"What?"

"Forget it," James said, and he shrugged. They drove in silence north of the city, passing eventually to the north side of Dublin Harbour and along the strand at Clontarf. Harry seemed to come to life as they saw the blue water sparkling beyond the trees and the wall. James broached his subject.

"Harry, I've got to ask you some tough questions this afternoon. I want you to bear with me, okay?"

"A drink would have helped," said Harry petulantly.

"Well, perhaps later, all right?" James sighed. "I want to remind you that Molloy is operating on the theory that whoever killed Ariadne also killed Shaw. And conversely, that whoever killed Shaw killed Ari. You can see his logic, I expect. The thing is," he said, not waiting for a response, "there is an apparent connection. Shaw's connection with Ari, Ari's with Shaw, and yours with Ari, obviously."

"What are you getting at?"

"I'd like some background on this, Harry. Madigan's going to want to know, so there are no surprises when—if—we go to trial."

"Ask away." Harry's voice was dull.

"Listen, you mentioned in the heat of the moment that Ariadne was rather 'experienced,' let's say. Perhaps you were just letting off steam. Do you know, actually know, that she had any attachments during your marriage?"

The silence James dreaded filled the car.

"If you want evidence, I don't have evidence." Harry's voice was bitter. "I never caught her with anybody, if that's what you want."

"It's not what I want!" James almost shouted. "I need, and Madigan needs, to know how the prosecution will paint their picture. Look, Harry, you're charged with her murder. They're going to want to establish a powerful motive. Jealousy is always a hefty motive, as is revenge."

"What are you asking? You're asking two different things. Yes, I was jealous. Yes, I think I had cause to be. Ariadne was very attractive, was she not?"

"Indeed."

"You see, that's the way it was."

"No, I don't see." James screeched to a halt at a pedestrian crosswalk. He quelled his anger so that he could concentrate on his driving. The man was so exasperating.

"All kinds of men found her attractive. I could see it in their eyes. My colleagues, my friends, my clients. And of course her clients, her workmates." His tone was dismissive. "And she flirted, sometimes outrageously."

James thought briefly of Geraldine and wondered. "But was that it?" He was hopeful.

"I don't think there's smoke without fire. She flirted a lot, not all the time, but she flirted, and men were drawn to her. It went on for years."

"Okay, I have to accept that she did this, but—"

"She did it with you, Fleming!"

"She did not." James's voice rose in rapid anger. "Don't say it again. Don't impugn my professional integrity," he said more calmly.

"Yeah, well, I think there was some question of your integrity over that Moore case."

James saw ahead a familiar turn-off and made a sharp left off the main road. His abrupt manoeuvre silenced Harry, which was precisely James's intention. His main goal was to get back to his basic question. He drove on down an old track and, pulling off, parked on the edge of a flat field. He gazed out the windscreen for a few moments before he took out his recently acquired Donegal tweed cap and pulled it on. "Come on, Conroy."

The two men walked across the field, James careful of his leather boots against the numerous low brambles. They headed for what seemed to be a very large shed.

"Fleming, what are we doing here?" said Conroy in a more natural tone of voice.

"Since we were out here in Sutton, I wanted to check on this shed. It's the last standing wooden tram shed in the country, or at least the last one in good condition. See?" He kicked aside the grass here and there and showed Harry where tracks had once lain. All that was left of what had once been a bustling rural station, a terminus for the old Dublin tramway, was the enormous shed in front of them.

"You might remember, oh fifteen years ago now, this shed was going to be demolished by the erstwhile owner. Some demolition outfit wanted to take it down to get the lead out of the roof and to get its hands on the magnificent wooden beamwork."

Harry shrugged.

"Well, I mention it because it was one of the highlights of my career—well, my avocation. A group of us from the train preservation society were tipped off by one of the labourers on the site here. We all piled out and stood in front of the workers, who really didn't give a hoot one way or the other. We successfully got an injunction, and they lay around in the grass for three days before the case was resolved. But there was one little bastard who'd sneak back at night for the lead. He was selling it on the sly. His boss didn't even know it. I had the night watch. It was fun. My picture was in the *Evening Herald*."

"Sorry I missed it," Harry murmured.

"Right. Well, I've checked it out. All is as it should be. You know, someday we're going to restore it and open it to the public," he said, heading back to his car, "but that's a long way off. Harry?"

"Mmm."

"I need you to be honest. You seem to imply that Ariadne had affairs after your marriage."

"She had enough of those before we were married," he said bitterly.

"I need to know if you have any knowledge that Ariadne and Shaw had seen each other over the years—in Dublin—and since you were married."

Silence greeted this query, and James turned the car for Howth once again.

"I might as well tell you what I learned from Mrs. Shaw when I went to see her in England."

"I'd forgotten about that. It's just with my job being so abruptly—"

"Harry, Mrs. Shaw told me that her husband came over to Dublin—on an irregular basis, to be sure, but this recent trip was not his first. The second salient point"—he paused, wondering how much to reveal to Harry of what he knew himself, wanting still for Harry to speak more freely—"the second point is that apparently Shaw at least knew Ariadne's married name. With that information, obviously it would have been easy to trace her."

"Obviously. She never hid herself away, did she?"

Sarcasm, always sarcasm, thought James. Always evasive and sarcastic.

"You've some real Irish traits, you know that, Conroy?" James pulled the car into one of the many vacant parking spots along the southern pier.

"Such as?"

"Such as always answering a question with a question."

They climbed out and walked quickly, for the breeze was stiff and cold. In silence they strode down the pier, in silence passed the few fishermen and hardy strollers. The small harbour was quiet. The fishing boats had long since left on the morning tide. And on this particular work day no one had taken out a boat for pleasure.

"Always wanted to sail over there but never did," said James to break the continuing silence.

"Nor I."

"Seen it many times from the air, though. Great name, isn't it?"

"Ireland's Eye? Yes, I suppose so."

James stared at the island that lay dead ahead of them. Ireland's Eye, seen from the Hill of Howth or from a plane coming in low to land at Dublin airport, illustrated the aptness of its name. There it lay, looking out to sea speculatively, calmly, or looking back to shore, remote, contained, appraising.

"Harry, you have conveyed to me that you suspected Ariadne, but you won't admit that it was with Shaw. Perhaps that is neither here nor there. Perhaps it doesn't matter if it is true. The point is, your wife may have known you suspected her, may have known you thought she had been seeing Shaw. She must have realized you were jealous. I want you to consider this objectively. I need your particular insight, your special point of view."

"Yes, all right, Fleming." The walk, the air, the sea had seemed to calm him. He took out a pipe and, despite the strong breeze, managed to get it lighting.

"You . . . loved your wife. And she must have loved you, for she married you and stayed with you. Is it possible that Shaw could have used this love for you?"

"How so?"

"For whatever reason, Ariadne never told you about Shaw. Perhaps he knew that, and perhaps he threatened her—with blackmail."

"Well, anything is possible." He paused, saddened. "Who would have believed all this just a few weeks ago? Who would have believed the trip to Kenya was our last . . ." He trailed off.

"Allowing for some such motive, could you believe that your wife was capable of murder? Could she have arranged for Shaw's murder?"

"What? Fleming, you're mad! This is the line Molloy was following before she died. *He* suspected her. How in God's name could Ari kill Shaw when we were in Africa at the time of his death?"

"I didn't say that. I said she could have arranged for it." In the same way as you might have, Conroy, he thought, but he didn't mention this to his client. "It's just a theory, Harry, but one that might explain certain disturbing facts."

"But you must see that it involves a second person. The man who actually did the killing."

"Exactly. There could have been an accomplice."

"This is too bizarre," said Harry. They'd reached the shore end of the pier and turned again to walk its length.

"Put that aside for a minute. Somebody killed Ariadne."

"And it wasn't me," said Harry neutrally.

"But it had to be someone connected with the death of Shaw. The accomplice and blackmail theory at least covers these points. It suggests a motive, it explains how it was accomplished when you were in Africa, it gave Ariadne an unbreakable alibi, it—"

"It doesn't explain why Shaw's body was in our bed."

"No, but it might explain why Ariadne's was. If the accomplice also murdered Ariadne, then something obviously went wrong with the plan. The accomplice left Shaw in your house and bed, and did it, it would seem, to implicate Ariadne. And succeeded. The accomplice doesn't get what he wants from her, and he kills her. Or Ariadne decides that it's all gone too far and is determined to confess, to reveal to the police who murdered Shaw—"

"Even if it reveals her connection?"

"Yes. Perhaps she can no longer live with what has happened. The accomplice—to save himself—kills Ari, putting her in the bed to confuse the issue further."

"It's too daring."

"Whatever is the truth, Harry—and I will find it out— the plan from beginning to end was daring. Whoever conceived it and whoever executed it was daring."

"I have to admit that Ariadne was a creative person in her

own way. Her career, much as I disliked it, was proof of that. Yes, she could be imaginative."

And what about you, thought James bitterly as he glanced at the man who walked beside him, lost in thought. You— acquiescing so easily to the proposed idea that your wife arranged for Shaw's death. You—so dull, so limited. What is real here, he wondered desperately.

"It posits a third and entirely unknown person," James continued as they returned to the car. "Molloy wouldn't even think along these lines. But I'd like to explore it for a little bit even before I approach Madigan with my theory."

"Do what you have to do, then," said Harry. Receiving no reply, he remained silent on the much quicker return trip to his home.

James pulled the car over to the side and prepared to ask his final question.

"Harry, did you personally have any contact with Philip Shaw over the years? Or with Mrs. Shaw?"

Harry grew red, and his neck thickened. "I am assuming, Fleming, that you are asking this because of Madigan. Because you're suggesting by that question that I had something to do with Shaw's death."

James waited. At last he said simply, "Well?"

"No, of course not."

James hesitated to show his trump card, but he desperately wanted Harry to reveal himself.

"I have some information that Molloy does not have. A woman was seen disposing of Shaw's jacket at an itinerant camp."

"What woman? Are you saying it was Ari?" James was surprised that Harry immediately thought of his wife.

"If it was Ari, there are two ways to look at it. She was involved in the murder and was getting rid of evidence. Or . . ."

"Or . . ." Harry was impatient.

"Or she was concealing evidence to protect someone she knew."

"Who?"

"You tell me."

Harry gasped. "You've been leading up to this—not just today, but before. You suspect me!" Harry looked astonished, angry. "You think it was I. That I somehow had Shaw killed, and that Ari found out and tried to protect me."

James didn't answer.

"In that event, you might also suspect that I killed her to keep her quiet. Is that it?" Harry was shouting.

James looked straight ahead, uncertain how to proceed, uneasy that he had unintentionally revealed his own doubts about Harry.

"You are my client, Conroy," he said at last, calmer than he felt.

"And I bet you're sorry." Harry was bitter.

"No."

"Really." Sarcasm again.

"There's one other possibility," James said, trying to restore some semblance of orderly process. "Perhaps the woman disposing of the clothing was . . ."

"Was?" Harry was eager now.

"Was Mrs. Shaw."

Harry was silent, trying to assimilate this new and different approach to the problem.

"You've seen her! Perhaps you're right. Mrs. Shaw had a motive, too! Jealousy, revenge, hatred. You said yourself when you told me about Ari and Shaw that he'd had a lot of women, right?"

"Right," murmured James.

"So she killed Shaw somehow and then got rid of his clothes?"

"Possibly."

"So you don't suspect me, then." Was that relief or triumph, wondered James. "You think Shaw's wife did it, don't you? God, I'm exhausted, Fleming. Let me go in."

Without farewell he opened the car door and walked quickly up the road to his front steps, leaving James relieved both at his departure and at the fact that, for whatever reasons, Harry had just convinced himself that James still believed in his innocence.

It was just as well, sighed James, for he hadn't wanted Harry to become aware so soon of his own doubts about him. And James himself—at least just then—didn't have the heart to face the fact that Harry might be guilty.

James chuckled to himself as he sat in the Citroën, precariously double-parked, his eyes glued to the door of the Residents' Hall. He ignored the glares of the guard in the tiny gate lodge as he smoothed his hair.

It would be so good to see Geraldine again. Between his work on Harry's case and her schedule at the hospital there had been only time for long, comfortable telephone calls. But they had kept up with each other's lives and, James believed, had been getting to know each other. He'd been thinking of her since he'd returned to his flat to shower and change into casual light grey trousers and his newest custom-made shirt. He straightened his teal-blue tie for the tenth time and chuckled again. He felt that old feeling of anticipation that he'd had when he was younger. A date! It was a pleasant feeling.

Geraldine wrenched open the passenger door, startling him. And her kiss startled him, too.

"Well, then, off to meet the mother!" She laughed gaily. "Tell me, is this significant, James?"

James blushed as he pulled the car out into traffic and drove through the late rush hour towards his mother's home.

"Let me put it this way, Ger," he said after some hesitation. "I don't bring everyone home to meet Mother. She will certainly be curious about you. After years of unsuccessful match-making on my behalf she may well want to know how I've managed this time without her help. And by the way, I should say you look especially stunning tonight."

And so she did, in an oversize, well-cut gunmetal silk jacket beneath which showed just a hint of black lace. She'd paired it with a pencil skirt that showed off her slim figure. And with her grey suede court shoes Geraldine looked breath-takingly classy from top to toe. She'd pinned up her thick dark brown hair in a seemingly artless way, and a few curls fell around her face onto the nape of her neck.

James was thinking about the nape of her neck when she placed a cool hand on his leg.

"You're looking rather trendy yourself tonight, James," she cooed. And then she laughed with mischief as he blushed. "Go on, tell me who'll be there."

"Actually, I don't know." A bit of apprehension crept into his voice. "I haven't spoken directly with my mother for a while. She's been communicating with Maggie, my secretary, since I've been so preoccupied with Harry's case and trying to keep the rest of my work on-going."

"How is Harry?" Geraldine's voice was sombre.

"Very hard to say. I've been finding him difficult."

"I'm surprised. I always thought Harry was a bit of a teddy bear."

James groaned.

"No, seriously, a bit of a dote, easy-going, a push-over really."

"Hah!" James's bitterness surprised himself. "Easy-going. I've seen very little of that."

"Honestly, whenever we'd meet he was always affable, calm, perhaps a bit dull, but yes, easy-going."

"Well, then, what about these fights you used to overhear? You mentioned those at the pub. And what about the separate holidays, or were you exaggerating?"

"That's all true, James, as far as it went. But I thought nothing of it at the time. Honestly, they just seemed to me to be marital spats. Lord, two people living together for ten years and still getting along. I gave them credit for sticking it out."

James winced at her unself-conscious, pessimistic point of view. Ger lit up a cigarette, but he restrained himself.

"You mean sticking it out with Ariadne? That seems to coincide with Brona's view."

"Not at all. Don't pay any heed to Brona. She never liked Ariadne, thought she was a shallow snob. A bit like myself, I suppose. No, no. I meant just sticking out being married. I think it takes a lot to keep a marriage going after ten long years. If separate vacations work, why not? Whatever works, that's my philosophy."

"I take your point on that, but what about these spats you spoke of?"

"Just that—marital arguments. Did you know if you reverse two letters in the word marital it turns into martial?" She laughed. "Sure they were loud, loud enough for us to hear. And yes, they were heated. But what of it? Most people don't have tenants listening at their door, ready to spill the beans."

"Then what about the fight the evening of the party? From what you know of it, would you say it was in the same vein as the others over the years?" James knew he was leading her answers but couldn't help himself, anxious as he was to hear her speak in the affirmative.

"Listen, James, darling, that fight, I feel sure, was probably like any of the others. What has changed is that Ariadne was murdered. That fact focuses more light on the fight than it merits. Don't you see—no, you're too close to it—it was probably a fight just like any other. If she hadn't died then, that fight would have been forgotten in a matter of days by them, by Brona, by the people at Ariadne's party—who, most of all, would certainly have forgotten it if they hadn't been questioned by the police so soon after the event."

"You're very astute about people, Geraldine," James observed, and he went on to explain that Harry's barrister, Madigan, had had his investigators talk with some people who knew Ariadne quite well: women friends, and some of her colleagues at the ad agency and at the three studios she used for producing the television and radio ads for the agency. The written report concluded that there was never a breath of scandal regarding Ariadne's conduct. People had commented on her flirting, but they were quick to say that it was always clear that was all it was. They pointed out as well that, in their field of endeavour, all kinds of easy liaisons form and fade. So it was even more noteworthy that Ariadne remained, as one fella had said, "ever-faithful to the undeserving, bumptious Harry Conroy."

"Those who'd been at the party—and you're exactly on the mark, Ger—they saw the argument as just a heated exchange, a fleeting thing, and nothing more. I was relieved to read their comments." James heaved a sigh, and Ger put up a cool hand to stroke the back of his neck.

"I can feel the tension in your muscles, James. Very bad for your health, you know."

"What do you recommend?"

"One of my superior massages, perhaps followed by a hot shower." She was coquettish.

"Keep talking like that and I'll need a cold shower." They laughed conspiratorially, and James began to wonder how early they could decently leave his mother's house.

"Then let's get back to your case. You know, James, I've enjoyed being involved in it. Don't misunderstand. I'm terribly sorry for both Ariadne and Harry. But I have liked talking things over with you, enjoyed my bit of sleuthing, too." James cringed. Geraldine's attitude towards confidentiality was remarkably cavalier, he believed, for a doctor. But it was such an integral part of her gregarious nature that for the most part he hadn't taken much notice.

But now he acknowledged reluctantly to himself that he had knowingly used that attitude of Geraldine's by asking her to inquire discreetly about the details of Ariadne Conroy's medical history. And why? Ostensibly to save himself some time, but was it not also because of his own misgivings? Were his own ethics as blurred as hers, he wondered. And had they been in the past? He was hesitant suddenly to hear what she might have learned.

"Well, did you succeed in your sleuthing, as you say?" he asked her finally.

"Actually it was easy, James. I went on the premise that Mrs. Conroy'd seen one of the big names—".

"Pardon?"

"One of the big OB-GYNs." She enunciated the individual letters for him. "'Obs and gyny' we used to call it in college. There are only three, there are only ever three—I mean three top people in any one specialty. Dublin is so bloody small." She heaved a huge sigh, and he sensed again the breadth of her professional ambition. "Anyway, I knew pretty well what might have been Ariadne's problem. Not uncommon or life-threatening, mind you. But given her age and what you told me about her having perhaps rather numerous affairs before she was married, well . . . to cut a long story short, it seems—now don't take me up wrongly, I say *seems*. And please remember, James, that no one told me directly."

"I understand your discretion, Ger! What are you telling me?" James was testy.

"Right, I'm telling you that she had PID."

"More letters?"

"It's a pelvic disorder transmitted by a partner to the woman. And, well, it can often be symptomless. Often one doesn't know one's contracted it until one goes looking for something else."

"Venereal disease? What is this?" James was cross, reluctant to go further.

"No, it is not VD in the sense you imply. It affects the woman, and the sad outcome is that often she can't conceive a child when she attempts to—because of the earlier infection, because of scarring." Geraldine fell silent, realizing that although it was neutral information to her, it was more than that to James. "Just as well you didn't become a medical man," she said gently.

"Why?" James was startled by her observation.

"Too soft-hearted by far."

James was aware they'd been approaching his mother's road with its blossoming cherry trees and was only too glad to bring this conversation to a natural close.

"Here we are then, Ger." He turned and took her hand. "Thank you for getting me the information. It clears up a rather important point." And spares me from discussing the issue further with Harry, he noted to himself.

Suddenly apprehensive, he warned her: "Don't let my mother . . ." But here he realized that if there was going to be a match for his mother, Geraldine was it.

The double doors opened as if by remote control as they approached James's childhood home. His mother appeared, looking suddenly stouter than he remembered. Ruffles at her neck and wrists, an acre of white cream linen across her bosom on which nestled a magnificent and very old amethyst and gold brooch.

"Formal tonight?" murmured James as he kissed the air beside her cheek and she did the same to him.

"James, darling, how you've aged," she greeted him.

"Jesus Christ!" blurted James.

"Don't take the Lord's name in vain. And you *have* aged, James."

"Mother!" James's voice went up in a warning tone.

"Well, why wouldn't you have? It's years since you were here." She smiled enigmatically at Geraldine.

"Last month, Mother," said James, moving through the small enclosed foyer and into the front hall.

"Just so," she continued, smiling. "And this must be Benedictine, yes? May I take your wrap? Oh . . . no wrap," she observed, in a tone that conveyed that somehow Geraldine was not suitably attired.

"Mother," James cut in, "this is Geraldine!" He stressed her name.

"Ah, well, these Catholic names, one gets muddled. Geraldine, do come in and join the rest." The two women walked ahead into the drawing room at the front of the house, and James was sorry they had come.

"Now," Mrs. Fleming said brightly, "you must have a drink. Donald? Drink, please." James watched as his brother Donald unfolded his lanky frame from the low fireside chair and without a glance at them wandered into the dining room and stood lounging at the sideboard.

"People, this is Jenine, James's new friend."

James died a death. "Geraldine," he interjected loudly.

"Of course, she was another friend of James. Now sit. Drink, Donald!" she called out peremptorily.

"What type?" said Donald laconically, and James wanted to kill him.

Unabashed, Geraldine answered, "A gin and tonic, and make it quite strong, Donald."

"Sherry, surely," said Mrs. Fleming in shocked tones.

"How do you do?" said Geraldine to the man standing near her. No one was sitting, despite the valiant efforts of James's mother. Geraldine quickly made herself at home chatting to the other three invited guests, who included a friend of Mrs. Fleming's schooldays who was visiting from England and a married couple contemporary with her, the husband of which couple had taken a kindly and unwelcome interest in James since his father had died. And this was a golden opportunity for him now. James squirmed under the man's demands to know—in the politest terms—how James's firm was doing since he'd taken it into his own hands.

During this inquisition he glanced occasionally, longingly, in Geraldine's direction, only to see her being cross-examined by his mother and her dearest friend Daphne. Daffy by name and by nature, James murmured under his

ANN C. FALLON

breath. But he was relieved to hear Geraldine's merry laughter, and then as alarmed to hear its more raucous colouration.

"Excuse me," he said abruptly, startling the portly and prosperous Mr. Lonigan into enforced silence. But he was immediately entrapped by Mrs. Lonigan, who was hard pressed to tell him that her eldest son, James's peer, had recently bought one of the finest houses in Ballsbridge and was spending two weeks in the Canary Islands with dear Patty and the darling children while the house was done up. James felt his eyes rolling in his head but hoped no one would notice.

Each time he moved Mrs. Lonigan would press a small, firm hand on his arm, effectively paralyzing him as he watched, as from a great distance, Donald finally, languidly moving to his mother's side and urging, from long years of practice, that she retire to the kitchen and get the meal under way. Flushed with sherry and pleasure at having congenial company in her comfortable home, she disappeared to the kitchen, off-limits to the guests. Her disappearance was followed very shortly by the sounds of pans or pots crashing and muffled cries, but not for help.

James refilled his glass and freshened the Lonigans' drinks. Donald was looking after Daffy MacIntyre and Geraldine and seemed, to James's surprise, to be entertaining them quite well. As James seldom found his brother amusing, this new version of things surprised him.

Exasperated, James left the drawing room and passed through the dining room, where the table was most beautifully laid with pale pink linen, heavy, gleaming silverware, and a spray of early spring flowers in a low crystal bowl . . . all in readiness. He pushed open the hinged door and stuck in his head.

"Mother?"

"James, don't startle me that way."

James was dismayed to see his mother prodding a quite outrageously undercooked roast beef. The mashed potatoes

202

sat cooling in the pan on the sink, the steam taking with it whatever heat was still left. The peas, too, sat cooling, the cheese sauce for the cauliflower coagulating. His heart sank, and his appetite grumbled. He was starving and guessed that, at a quarter to nine, so were the others.

"Shoo, shoo, James!" Mrs. Fleming waved a tea towel in his direction, but he firmly took her hand and removed the carving knife. Red juice ran freely onto the platter as he removed the fork from the meat.

"I can't understand it," she said without much alarm but with a good deal of puzzlement. "Fifteen minutes a pound —that's what I always do." James recalled the numerous ruined Sunday dinners of his youth, and he shrugged.

"Did you weigh the joint?"

"Don't be silly, James. I can't bear it when you're silly." James was quietly covering the vegetables and adding milk to the cheese sauce.

"Well, I don't suppose you pre-heated the oven either."

"If I've told you once, I've told you a thousand times that's a terrible waste of gas. I can't imagine how you manage on your own. Oh, dear! Must revive—it's the heat in this kitchen," she said as she sat down and watched James slice the meat.

He quickly broiled it while he made a rather tasty gravy from the juices, red wine, and the scrapings of the pan. His mother transferred the now-hot vegetables to her lovely covered serving bowls, ladling the sauce into two unique sauce boats. James laid out the newly transformed roast on a large platter, pouring over the gravy and garnishing the plate with the parsley that grew in merry little pots on his mother's sill. In her kitchen it was more decorative than culinary.

Between them they served the meal as the guests took their seats. As James laid out the platter and sauce boats he noted the heightened voices, the animation of the conversation, and the reddened faces of guests who had quelled their hunger with a few too many cocktails. And whether it was James's skill or the gift of the red wine provided by the Lonigans or the Floating Islands made by Daffy for dessert, lavish praise was heaped on Mrs. Fleming's dinner.

They lingered over the coffee.

"Isn't it absolutely marvelous about Donald?" Mrs. Fleming held the floor.

James was mellow and curious. And so he asked, "What?" innocently enough.

"He saw his first patients today," she exclaimed. "In the surgery."

James was suddenly annoyed. He glanced at his brother across the table and realized, a little late in the day, that Donald was seated beside Geraldine, whereas he, the elder, was squashed between Mrs. Lonigan and her auntlike tenacity on his right, and Daffy in the full bloom of her wiftiness on his left. They had occupied him throughout the meal and only now, as a bit of hush fell over the table, did he sense that Geraldine and Donald had been talking rather exclusively to each other. His mother, at the head of the table, had virtually ignored Geraldine on her left in favour of Mr. Lonigan on her right and his sage but rather parabolic views on life.

"Oh, congratulations," murmured the little party sincerely.

"Yes, indeed," said James. "Perhaps a toast is in order?" He raised his glass as Donald lazily raised his eyes to meet his brother's.

"To Donald's success!" His mother had pre-empted him.

"Hear! Hear!" joined the others.

"It's a great step," said a voice James didn't recognize as Geraldine's, and he watched dismayed as she raised her own glass directly to Donald. And smiled at him.

"Tell us, Donald," James interrupted. "How has your fame spread so quickly?"

"James, you *are* being silly this evening. Hasn't your own mother told everybody she knows?" his mother answered.

Donald's eyes crinkled at the corners in his version of a smile. "Indeed, I owe a great deal to Mother. She has shown great faith in me from the very start of my medical career. And ever since. And now even more so. She has—let's be frank amongst friends—financed this endeavour. It's a red-letter day, and I would like to raise my glass to her in gratitude for her faith in me. Sometimes only a cliché can express what is so very true. But without her I would not be where I am today."

Appropriately serious now, the little group raised their glasses and drained their wine. Mrs. Fleming's eyes were bright, possibly with tears.

But Geraldine's were brighter. "I'd like to add something if I may," she said. "I don't know Donald well. We've only met briefly over the years at medical things, you know." She looked down demurely, briefly. "But I do know of Donald through his reputation. He's a bit of a legend with us younger medical students. And I would like to add that although he's going out on his own, he's attached to the Adelaide Hospital, still working under Mr. Ryan. And I'm not the only one who's heard it said that Donald may be in line one day—not so far off, either, in our terms—to becoming a consultant." She held Donald's eyes and raised her own glass.

"Hear, hear," said the little group. But what was it that James saw in her eyes, heard in her voice: admiration or ambition? Or both? He shook his head.

They left the table and, as is the way after food and wine, they stretched themselves. Mr. Lonigan unbuttoned his suit jacket and hauled his trousers up to his waist, patting his belly.

"Great meal, Vivienne," he said. "Don't know how you've done it over the years. Always a marvelous meal." He clapped James heartily on the back. "Isn't that right, my boy?"

James nodded speechlessly.

"Now, people, how about a rubber of bridge?"

Daffy fluttered to his side, nodding with pleasure and then dismay. "We can't make up two tables unless someone plays the dummy."

"Now, Daffy, these young people aren't going to play bridge with us old fogies," Mr. Lonigan's heartiness was burgeoning. James thought fleetingly of his own father—serious, quiet, but kindly, like the friend who survived him in this life.

"You are exactly right!" chimed in Mrs. Fleming. "So thoughtful, as always. Donald, Donald. It's your night—of course, I didn't plan it this way. Completely forgot the two events coincided, but so nice to celebrate with old friends. And new."

James's antennae went up as it always did when his mother spoke in bullet points.

"Donald," she carried on. "So nice for you to celebrate with a medical friend. Now, I would suggest—but of course dancing is so different nowadays—but when Mr. Fleming and I would celebrate we always included a bit of tripping the light fantastic." She moved towards the hallway, carrying all behind her. "Donald! James! Come, come." She called her sons the way other people might call their pets. She handed them their coats.

"Now, Geraldine, your wrap. Yes, so nice . . ." her voice trailed behind her from the enclosed porch as she opened the outer door. "So nice to be with medical people like yourself, Donald dear. I know Geraldine will be terribly interested in your patients. The first of many, I trust." She stepped back to let the three of them pass, willy-nilly, shooed out the door, away from the grown-ups, like kindergarten children before the principal teacher.

"And so nice, too," she called as she started to close the door on them, "that you can go to the dance in James's unacceptably expensive German car."

"French, Mother, it's French!" James shouted to her in

vain as the door shut behind them with the solid clunk of
finality peculiar to a good, heavy mahogany door.

James drove slowly home, tired and preoccupied. They
had, after a few tries, got admitted to one of the clubs on
Leeson Street. Tiny and dark, with very loud music, the
small nightclub had kept their conversation to a minimum.
Donald, however, had livened up—for Donald—and he'd
taken James's gesture of ordering a bottle of champagne
with good grace.

But it wasn't the champagne that brought that twinkle to
his eye, or to Geraldine's. The pair of them had hit it off, and
it was obvious—at least to James. He wasn't even sure
Geraldine realized it. She hadn't flirted, but it was their
conversation—the pool of acquaintances from college,
from the hospitals, the shared gossip and jokes. And, too,
the shared concern that they brought to their practice of
medicine.

He'd felt left out, but they hadn't excluded him. Donald
had had the sense to take a taxi home, and Geraldine was as
vivacious as ever as James drove her back to the hospital
residence. And despite her affectionate good-night kiss, that
bit of magic, that spark between them he had sensed earlier
in the evening, was gone. Maybe not, though, he hoped. She
loved merriment, she loved excitement. Perhaps it had only
been the circumstances of the evening.

Tiredly he parked the car and entered his flat. He glanced
at his mail desultorily and then checked his answering
machine. The evening felt flat now—the ragged end of a
very long and confusing day. Restlessly he moved around
the sitting room, something nagging at the corners of his
mind, something to do with Geraldine.

He showered, and as he let the water pound on the back of
his neck he tried to recall what it was that she'd said in
passing, that had triggered the beginning of a train of
thought. It wasn't the information about Ariadne's medical
condition. Although that had clarified an important issue. It

was the fighting, the fighting between Harry and Ariadne! And how did they know, how did Geraldine and Brona know, all those years? Creeping up the stairs, muffling their girlish laughter, pressing an ear to the door, the door at the top of the stairs.

In all of his focus on who had committed the murders, and why, he had neglected to look at the how. He remembered Madigan's cautionary words—physical detail. Concentrating on detail, he realized almost with a sense of relief, had provided the key in his previous cases. Perhaps this time, too, it would be the small details that would help him.

But despite his resolve he found himself trying to pinpoint his unease about Geraldine. Why the flirting, why so friendly with him at their first meeting despite his early rebuff? Almost imperceptibly she'd become enmeshed in this case. Was her enthusiasm now suspect? Or was he suspicious of her now, he pondered sleepily, because she'd found his own brother so bloody compatible!

Chapter Twelve

"Listen, Harry, I appreciate this."

"Don't thank me, Fleming. It's my life you're trying to salvage here."

Harry was looking and acting a bit more energetic that midday, James noted. He, too, had wakened that morning with a greater sense of purpose, with a sense that it was in his power to resolve some of the complexities of Ariadne's case—for that's how he defined it to himself.

"So you don't have the impression the police concentrated on this fact?" asked James.

"No, but Fleming, I was pretty distracted, and since Ariadne—a lot of it is a big blur."

"And since Ariadne's death Molloy has been satisfied, apparently, with his case against you. In successfully prosecuting you he may feel the case regarding Shaw can in the process be resolved, if not solved. Tell me again what you remember."

"They searched the house. They searched Brona's flat. They questioned us both about the communicating door. I

209

explained, as did Ari, that we always left it bolted on our side. Since we moved in. Brona, as you know, was already installed. She kept it locked from her side as well. There was never a reason for either party to open the door. It gave us and Brona the sense of being entirely separate. Molloy and the investigators who were taking the samples of the carpet and so on seemed to accept that."

"They didn't make much of it?"

"No."

"And they didn't make much of the fact that the body was moved here to your house. Molloy did not address that issue at the time—sufficiently to my mind, at least. When I phoned him today all he would admit to was that they were working on it. That could mean anything. We don't know where Shaw was killed, and we don't know how the body was got into your house!"

"I see you're harking back to the accomplice theory." Harry grew tense.

"What I'm thinking is that the fact that Shaw's body was carried into this house and up to your room indicates that more than one person was involved. I need to have another look around, Harry."

"Fine. I'm going out."

James looked questioningly at him.

"I've decided to go into the office . . . a couple of hours each day. It just seemed the way to go. If I'm innocent— which I am—then I don't see why I should be forced away from what is in the end my whole life."

James shrugged.

"No, what I mean, Fleming, is please carry on. Here, this is Ariadne's key. I have my own." He took the key off the ring in the drawer in the hallstand quite mechanically.

"How many other keys are there?"

"To my certain knowledge there are only these two. The police are ahead of you there, Fleming. Here, you can see they're of the same vintage."

James examined the key, which was in fact extremely old.

A heavy key with complex teeth. Harry's was the same. Not a key that could be easily duplicated. James groaned inwardly, foreseeing a lot of time being expended in checking all the locksmiths and key makers in the greater Dublin area. With nothing to say that the key had been duplicated at all, let alone in Dublin itself.

James now examined the lock. It, too, was very old.

"It's ironic, James," added Harry with a note of sadness. "Before we went to Kenya Ariadne had asked me to have an alarm system installed. I did have them come. They explained how all the doors and windows would be independently wired. And among other things, they explained that this lock would not be sufficient for their purposes. A new lock would have to be fitted. There wasn't enough time for them to do the job before we left. She was cross with me, I remember, coming home in the taxi. Thought the house would have been stripped bare when we arrived. Instead—"

"Instead, whoever entered your home left something behind!"

"Yes," said Harry, and then he left. James watched as he walked down the road and turned into the alley that led to the mews at the rear.

He continued to examine the lock of the front door and then closed it behind him. He walked around the first floor, uneasy to be alone in the house. Eventually he moved to the rear of the main hall and stepped down two steps onto a small landing. Directly ahead of him was a small room, what once would have been the box room in the original house, and which had been made into a very large closet. To his left was the opening of the stairwell for the stairs that led to the floor below, to what would have been the kitchen and staff quarters. A door had been fitted into the top of the stairwell and a false wall placed above that. The door that faced him was of long standing, but obviously not original to the house. Its style was simple, a plain door fitted into a very solid doorframe. The hinges, like the door, could have been thirty years old, entirely intact and unmarked. There was a

single large dead bolt made of what James guessed to be a
lead compound. It, too, was discoloured but unscratched.
He slipped the bolt and then tried the knob, but it didn't
turn freely. The snib on the other side was obviously
engaged. All was exactly as Harry had said.

James stepped out onto the granite porch and closed the
door behind him, pocketing the heavy key. He noted the old
iron boot scraper first, embedded in the granite. The hand
rails, too, were granite, and in good order, having been
repaired at some date in the 150-year history of the house.
He looked more closely at the lines of mortar that joined the
large blocks in the stairs, his eyes following them down to
the rectangle on which he stood. And there, virtually under
his feet, was the round metal ring sunk level with the surface
of the stone. He quickly bent down and examined the ring
closely, sliding his fingers beneath it. It stood up freely on its
hinge. So well made that years of rain and use had not
ruined or rusted it. His excitement grew. He stood up, eager
to pursue his idea. He ran lightly down the steps and along
the short run of wrought-iron black fencing to Brona's gate,
and then down to her door. He rang the small bell with
impatience.

"Who is it?"

"Brona, it's James Fleming."

The door opened, and Brona stepped back into the
shadows. "Come in, James."

"I'm delighted you're home, Brona, and I'm terribly sorry
to disturb you." He ducked his head to enter the low
doorway. Brona shut the door, and they stepped into the
kitchen.

"You seem excited, James," observed Brona dryly.

"Yes, I am, actually. I was upstairs just now, and I had an
idea. Tell me, Brona, when the police were here after Shaw's
death—how thoroughly did they search your flat?"

"Quite thoroughly, I think. I was present, of course, and
they were asking questions. They checked the door and

windows and the stairs to the next floor. It's not a big flat, as you know."

"How about the coal cellar?"

"I don't have a coal cellar. I've always had the gas fire there, built into the wall where the original fireplace was. The other fireplaces are gone. Before my time."

Without comment he turned back into the small hall and quickly found the light switch. The naked bulb fixed to the wall lit up. James looked up into the triangular space above his head in the oddly shaped gable-roofed room.

"Do you see, Brona? This was the coal cellar. There would have been a wooden box, actually, up to this height." His hand showed her a ridge on two walls and running to the jamb of the door. "It would have been fitted just here." He put off the light and looked up at the ceiling yet again. He crowed.

"Look! Do you see daylight?"

Above their heads was the faint outline of the rectangle that James had spotted from the outside.

"But what is it we're seeing?" asked Brona, intrigued.

"That's a granite hatch, Brona. I spotted it just now upstairs. The ring is still in good order. Because these houses are terraced with no access on either side, these hatches were designed to facilitate coal deliveries. The hatch was opened, the bags of coal were tipped, and the coal fell into the wooden box, which would have been here, directly below. When your former landlord put in the gas fires all over the house—"

"The Conroys still have working fireplaces in some of their rooms," interrupted Brona.

James rushed on. "Then when the former owners converted this ground floor into a flat they must have had their coal delivered at the rear."

"And so do the Conroys, James. I've seen the coal left in the mews at the back. And sometimes Harry would bring in one of those carrypacks of the peat briquettes." She looked up. "I was the first tenant in this flat, James. This hatch hasn't seen coal for over seven years."

"But that's not my point. I think I've discovered how Shaw's body was brought into this house. The police established that it wasn't taken in through the back, because the grass and clay of the garden were not disturbed. Nor were the windows and sills marked in any way. The front door was not disturbed either—and we know that there were only two keys, both in the Conroys' possession."

James and Brona returned to the kitchen, but he was too excited by his newfound knowledge to sit. He paced about the room. "Likewise, your door was not interfered with."

"And I have the only key," added Brona.

"Do you see? I believe that the body could have entered the house through the hatch and been lowered down into your hall. Perhaps the police forensic team could check the granite edges of the hatch to determine how recently it was moved."

But as he spoke he realized it was unlikely they would find any evidence. He considered also how unlikely it was that the killers had not worn gloves to lift the ring. As he mentally pictured these men, these conspirators, he realized how daring it would have been to deliver the body to the front of the house. Yet the whole murder, as he'd said before, was amazingly daring.

"They would have had to do it at night," he said aloud.

"Do what?" said Brona, putting the kettle on to boil.

He sat down uninvited, preoccupied with his scenario. "Whoever delivered his body—they'd have to do it under cover of darkness. They couldn't have taken the chance of doing it in broad daylight."

"But on what night?" Brona said gently.

"Oh, God, I don't know! The police say he could have been dead ten days."

Without being asked Brona fetched her desk diary from her bedroom and looked at the entries.

"I'm sorry, James. You see, the police had asked me, as I

think you yourself did, if I were at home on those evenings. And I'm afraid I was, and I know that I was—this has been an intense period of study for me. So it couldn't have been done at night, thank goodness! It's been bad enough thinking of what was going on upstairs when I was down here." Her voice grew strident.

James didn't notice as his enthusiasm rapidly deflated.

"Obviously, then, it wasn't done at night." And he realized that he'd been foolish. To have done what he proposed meant that the killers needed to know both that the Conroys were absent and Brona was absent. And even allowing for the fact they just might have delivered the body during the day—disguised as coal men, perhaps—it was still too risky. And if they had, they still met the same obstacle he kept coming up against—the locked communicating door.

He became aware of Brona's eyes on him and accepted her offer of a cup of coffee.

"I hope I'm not keeping you," he said rather sheepishly.

"Well, I will have to get going, but I'll enjoy my cup of coffee nonetheless." She sat down at the long wooden table. "Biscuits?"

"No, thanks. Listen, Brona, obviously my theory has some loopholes. But I do still believe the body came through this flat."

Brona shivered. "Please, James. I have to live here. I've succeeded in putting the whole business out of my mind, and you are reviving it. It's most unwelcome."

"Sorry, I'm sorry. But surely the more quickly this case is resolved, the more quickly you can return to a sense of security and peace of mind, yes?"

"It doesn't matter now as much as it would have. I'll be leaving here soon in any case. Once I've left the College and taken up a post."

James was startled. He'd pictured her there always, ensconced in her cozy flat with her cats and her manuscripts, her books and her bicycle.

"I hadn't realized," he said lamely.

"Why would you?" she responded, and he thought he detected some annoyance.

"I remember now . . . Harry did mention something about your giving him notice."

"Yes, just lately."

"Then you'll be returning your keys."

"Just the one, to my door. Of course, if he wants the padlock and key for the chain on the gate, he can have it. I don't expect I'll be needing a chain and padlock." She laughed. "At least I hope not. I hope I'll be getting a proper flat."

"I see." James sipped his coffee. "By the way, did you ever have a key to the front door upstairs?"

"No, there was no need. When I moved in here Mr. Callahan was rather ill. They were an elderly couple, you see. They'd spent two years, I think, gradually having the house remodelled, putting in a good kitchen upstairs and creating this flat down here. The house had got too big and empty for them with all their children gone. And poor Mrs. Callahan, her legs were bad and she didn't need to be climbing up and down all these flights of stairs. It's really a very big house." She sipped her coffee and added more brown sugar. It was as though the size of the house finally pressed in on James. He was suddenly aware of all the empty rooms on the three floors above their heads.

"A fine house," he said at last.

"Oh, absolutely!" said Brona with enthusiasm. "A wonderful house."

"You know it well, I take it?" asked James.

"Oh, yes. I was only here a short time when Mr. Callahan became ill, poor thing. I got to know them both, especially Mrs. C., as I called her. She was a little dote, a small, round woman with a full head of white hair that she'd wear pinned up at the back. She had round, plump arms, and they always seemed to be covered with a fine dusting of flour. She loved to bake. Used to make me lovely treats." She smiled a happy inward smile. "We became great friends. It made my coming to Dublin from Monaghan so much less strange, so much less lonely. Where was I going . . . you'd asked me a question?" She stopped abruptly.

"The key?" James said, putting down his empty cup.

"Oh, yes." She absent-mindedly refilled his cup. "No, I didn't have need of a key. You see, then we kept the door not only unlocked, but open. I would run up and down to Mrs. C., and when she needed me she'd come to the head of the stairs and call me."

"Need you?"

"Yes, when Mr. Callahan was dying she'd often call me. And then . . . when she too grew ill I'd check on her, or she'd call out. It was all very sad."

"But you stayed on after they died?"

"Oh, yes. The location, as you know, is great. Five minutes on the bike into College. Mrs. C. had let the flat to me unfurnished, so under the law I'd acquired the right to stay if I wanted, and without a significant increase in my rent. The house was sold at auction. And I went with the house, in a manner of speaking." She laughed. "But then things changed with the Conroys."

"That's natural, I think. I've seen a lot of these sales—on account of my particular work, you know—and often it doesn't work out for the sitting tenant. Despite the financial arrangements," added James.

"Oh, yes. Oh, dear, yes. I didn't expect to be running up and down to them!" She stressed the last word. "We all wanted our privacy. And of course, she re-decorated." Brona paused, disdain clear in her voice. "I much preferred the old house—more character. Mrs. Callahan had some lovely old things, but it wasn't just that. The house was a home then, cozy, safe, filled with the past. Lovely, really . . ." Her voice diminished.

"Then what about Geraldine?" James suddenly shifted tack.

Brona stiffened and got up, removing the coffee things. "I

was, briefly, rather lonely. I did rather miss Mrs. C. I'd put up a notice on the board at front gate at College, and Geraldine replied. And it was fun sharing in those days for a while." She splashed water into the basin. It was a gesture, James had no doubt.

"Let me help you," he said, taking the linen tea towel off the little rod like a familiar friend and not an intrusive solicitor. He had realized too late that his mention of Geraldine had annoyed her.

"If you insist."

"I do," he said in his most charming tone. "Tell me, if you are planning to move so shortly, then you must be nearly finished your work, am I right?"

"Yes, indeed." She sighed. "My deadline is rapidly getting closer. And of course that means that I must be in a position to hand in to the examining committee my completed dissertation." She drew breath. "It's virtually finished, but now I'm in a bit of a panic, actually. There's one final small but important piece of documentation I have to attend to. It may be quite minor, and yet if I want this thesis to be completely definitive, I have to see the document with my own eyes."

James was intrigued. Any mystery, no matter how small, always captured his imagination. "What is it?"

"Well, it makes a good story, actually. At one point earlier in my research I wrote to various magazines, journals, and so on. A brief letter requesting that anyone in Ireland who had documents, letters, and so on pertaining to O'Suillebhean would contact me."

"I've seen that type of letter all right. They always struck me as rather romantic, rather nineteenth century in intent and in method."

"Yes, indeed. Often, as with someone obscure, it's merely a shot in the dark. I did this some years ago. I got a bit of a response, but nothing surfaced of any real importance. People were eager to contribute, or eager to be somehow included in my project, or to receive recognition themselves.

They wrote to say they had first editions, but those were all available to me in the various libraries. In fact, I had already purchased a number of them at Greene's of Clare Street. But just lately a man, a Mr. Thomas Aherne, wrote to me to say that he'd only recently seen my letter in an old copy of a now-defunct literary magazine. He'd bought it at a church sale—you know the thing, a jumble sale. I answered his letter, which was in rather scrawled penmanship. I'm assuming he's an elderly man. He does strike me as a bit eccentric. Apparently he's a book collector of sorts. I'm still not sure of how he describes himself. Perhaps it's a hobby and not a profession. He's not on the phone, so how could he conduct business? Anyway, he claims to have a notebook of O'Suillebhean's, which apparently his mother owned before him, with some poems in draft form."

"How exciting."

"I'm glad you appreciate that fact. It *is* exciting, but disturbing, too. Until I see the notebook and gauge its authenticity I'm really rather in the dark. You see, if they are major poems that have been unavailable in published form, it's a huge discovery, but such a find would put back my thesis perhaps a year or more." She sighed deeply.

"And you've already been working for six years."

"Yes. Not all that time on the thesis, but yes, years of work that I finally saw drawing to a close. I would like to get on with my—"

"Could you p'rhaps ignore this old man and his claims? He may be more than eccentric, he could be mistaken."

"Senile?"

"Perhaps. It's possible." James's mind was actively conjuring up a picture of Aherne. "I meet these people in my particular line of work. Elderly, living alone, with terribly faulty memories when it comes to hard facts. Brona, as you said yourself, your writing the letter of request was a shot in the dark. And it was mere chance that he bought the old magazine when he did and then proceeded to read it when he did."

Yet as he spoke he knew that his own nature would never allow him to overlook or ignore such a possibility as now faced Brona. He was a believer in coincidence, or fate—like all the Irish. Was he playing the devil's advocate with her just now, he wondered, and if so, why?

"No, James." She was talking through his cogitation. "I can't say I'm even tempted to do such a thing. I love my subject too much. And I am a scholar in this field. We all of us together have to keep that sacred bond with one another. We all of us must act honourably in our academic pursuits. There is no official body to oversee such things, James. It is a noble and tacit agreement. We must put truth ahead of our own comfort and ease. As O'Suillebhean did himself! I must be true to my subject! Perhaps"—she paused, looking at him, challenging him—"perhaps you see this as a trivial issue." She sucked in her breath, turning away to put the crockery in its place.

It was the longest and most passionate conversation James had had with her, and he answered her quickly. "Oh, no, don't take me up wrongly. I was just rambling, thinking perhaps that you could finish up your dissertation and then at some future date verify this old man's claims, verify the document. Think of it, Brona—what if his letter had come a few months later?"

"Even if I were the only one to know about this, which I am at the moment, James, I would still know it. When I present my dissertation I want it to be as complete, as perfect as is humanly possible. No, it's a question, unfortunately, of leaving no stone unturned. Certainly you of all people can sympathize with that intellectual position."

James laughed as her tone lightened. "Indeed, we share that philosophy at least. Tell me, when are you going?"

"That's the crux of the problem." Brona moved to the table and began packing up her satchel and checking through her handbag, signalling that their conversation was at an end. "The village in Connemara is virtually inaccessible by public transportation. I've been trying to work out a route."

"Surely to save time you could rent a car," he interrupted, annoyed as he had been at other times by her wittiness.

"I don't have such disposable income as you might imagine," she said sharply, an accusation in her tone against the materialist she saw in James.

"Look, believe it or not, trains are my hobby. Let me see if I can work out a route for you." Quickly she got her maps and train schedules, and for some silent minutes James made notations. In the end he sighed, throwing his pencil onto the map on the table.

"It can be done, Brona, but it's going to take you time. You'd need to spread your visit over two days. You'd need to spend a night, because you can't make your connections in a single day." He looked at her sympathetically.

She swept the wisps of brown hair away from her face in irritation. "Oh, Lord, and time is so precious." She slumped down into her chair, worried and pensive.

James considered for a moment, but only for a moment, what he was about to do. He saw before him someone who held the highest standards up for herself, someone who didn't shirk what she saw as her particular responsibility, someone who'd been lonely—as he had sometimes been. Perhaps it was the beneficent presence of Mrs. Callahan in what was her old kitchen, but within the time it took to vaguely feel these things he heard himself offering to drive Brona to Connemara.

Her answer was to look at him quizzically.

He barrelled on, explaining that they'd be passing through a town en route where he could take care of some legal business, matters which he'd lately put on the long finger and which were now nagging at him. What he didn't mention was that there was a steam engine in that part of the country, in private hands, that he'd been wanting an excuse to see. He heard himself validating his offer to Brona's peculiar silence. If he'd expected gratitude he was misled. But she accepted, and they made arrangements to meet early the next morning.

A strange girl, James thought to himself as he drove in the direction of his office. And a strange morning altogether. He'd gone from the high of what he'd thought a breakthrough only to see it evaporate under the mildest scrutiny.

As he contemplated the pile of work on his desk and avoided the critical comments of Maggie he grew near despair. He'd devoted a disproportionate amount of time to this case, and his other work was mounting. And now he'd committed himself to this wild goose chase with Brona. His mind wandered as he worked on the will before him, a document for one of his most active clients, the heiress Mrs. O'Boyle. It had been an impulse, and he could be impulsive when it came to women. He smiled fleetingly. It had been odd to think that Brona was jealous of him and Geraldine. He hoped there was something to be jealous of. But he banished such thoughts as guilt drove him to do some effective work for the body of clients that kept him and his staff in bread and butter.

The late afternoon meeting with Bill Carey went off well. Carey's caseload was well under control. He did fine work, mused James. Perhaps he needn't hire a junior after all—he'd save money. And it wasn't as though they were knocking down his door.

Darkness was falling over the street outside, and traffic had long since quietened when he finally bid Maggie and Carey and the others a pleasant good night as they left. He could feel their relief that the senior partner was actually staying behind to do some work. Maggie had made this quite plain, as was her way. His absence from the office had been noted, obliquely, by the others. His absence was having, he realized with chagrin, a deleterious effect. And suddenly the responsibility of his position made him uneasy. He poured out a mineral water and sipped slowly, his mouth dry with anxiety. The train trip in Peru he'd planned for so long was receding yet again.

But despite his staff, he thought ruefully, he would not be working tonight on writing an airtight will for the plump and prosperous Mrs. O'Boyle. No, the time had come for a complete review of Ariadne's case. Case. What case? He sat at his desk and methodically placed a few sheets of very blank paper on its surface. Notes. Like details, notes had worked to his benefit before. He hoped they would do so again. And he began to write.

At eleven o'clock that same night James leaned back in his well-worn leather chair and stretched his arms over his head. He had come at last to his strongest conclusion—where the logic of emotion and the logic of necessity seemed to coalesce. He had posited to himself the scenario that Mrs. Shaw had approached Harry with information concerning Ariadne and Shaw: presumably that they were lovers still.

God! It was so frustrating. The two principals were dead; there was neither proof they were having an on-going affair nor proof they were not. And they could never tell, lying now in their graves. As they had once lain in the same bed as young lovers in England, and as they'd lain in the same bed in death.

He shivered at the image, graven on his memory, of Ariadne's body lying on her bed, her white face composed in death. And the image, so similar, of Shaw's body lying on Ariadne's bed. Was it their deaths that were lying to him now? Had he, like everyone else, let his imagination be captured and his judgment blurred by the two bodies lying in death on the same bed? No—the link was inescapably there.

Fatigue was creeping into his bones, and the residual heat of the building was now seeping out of the office into the night air. He tried to shake off his mood by pouring a large brandy from the drinks cupboard in the conference room, and he drank it down with a splash of ginger ale.

Philip Shaw and Ariadne. He pondered the connection: Mrs. Shaw had an unfaithful husband, Harry an unfaithful wife—whether he could verify that or not, Harry believed it. And Mrs. Shaw had been in Dublin, had seen Ariadne. Ariadne had been afraid, afraid of her, of this James was convinced. And Ariadne had called him. The phone call—he would regret forever not returning that call, for it was that which had held the key.

Mrs. Shaw, responsible for Shaw's death, would have demanded—emotional logic would demand—that Ariadne die, too. And was that the answer, as Molloy had so justifiably acted upon—that Harry had indeed killed Ariadne?

Discouraged beyond words, he put his notes aside and finished his brandy. He threw himself down on the brown leather couch in his outer office and huddled in a blanket he kept in his own closet for just this purpose.

Too late, he thought, too late to drive, to read, even to think. And he had a long day of driving ahead of him with the inscrutable and sometimes insufferable Brona O'Connell. The sleep of exhaustion came quickly this night.

James and Brona made a very early start the next day and were well on their way before the morning rush hour clogged the roads of suburban Dublin. The highway before them was clear, the morning fine, and James found himself enjoying the drive more than he'd expected. They reached Athlone by ten, and he swiftly completed the filing of the probate papers on the Morrissey will.

His conscience now completely clear, he sped on the road that led them further west into the margins of Connemara. The scene gradually changed from one of lush early growth to the barren rocks of the west, but nonetheless the colours were rich and unique, muted as in an old tapestry. The lichen-covered rocks, the grayness of the granite, the undulating fields that grew rocks as other fields grew grain filled the land with a lonely beauty. Unique flora stretched for miles to the right, and frequently he stopped the car as either he or Brona caught a scenic view that merited a pause in their headlong passage to see Mr. Aherne.

At one crossroads marked only by a mound of rocks and the foundations of a ruined cottage they stopped to watch some donkeys grazing. James lowered his window, and one of the donkeys, not the least shy of man, wandered over and stuck its oversized gray head in the window to nuzzle James's shoulder. The beast studied them with large, sad, knowing eyes.

"At this rate," said James, "we'll never reach Ballinaderg!" They laughed together. "But the trip will still have been worth it." He started up the car. "Tell me—it's a bit late to ask, but I assume you did telegraph Aherne?"

"Of course, and he sent one in response. Brief. He said he'd be at home all day today."

"Great." He checked his map and the time. "Actually, we've made excellent time. Good thing we're both morning people, as they say. When we get to Ballinaderg let's stop for some luncheon. It's seems a very long time since my meager breakfast."

"All right, it will put off the evil hour for a few more minutes," said Brona.

James looked at her quickly. His own mood had been so good that morning he hadn't really noticed how pale Brona was, and how wan.

"Are you very worried about this interview with Aherne, Brona?" he asked sympathetically as they drove slowly through the small village at last. But Brona didn't answer.

"Look, here's a place worth trying!" James had pulled the car off the road onto a track. Nestled into some enormous hedges was a small thatched-roofed cottage.

"What is it?" she asked brusquely.

"A pub! A real country pub. See, you can just make out the license over the door."

They entered through the low door and allowed their eyes to adjust to the dimness. James persuaded Brona to come further in and to sit on one of the low wooden stools at the hearth.

After just a few moments a large, friendly woman with a red and weather-worn face came out from the back room. She pleasantly accepted James's order and within minutes returned with two large plates on which she'd placed some generous slices of Limerick ham, its edging of pure white fat glistening in the low light. James's mouth watered as he saw the thick slices of fresh, crusty white bread, the mound of creamy butter, and the small jar of hot English mustard. They bent over their lunch with gusto, and Brona was persuaded to join James in drinking a pint of most excellent stout. Although their backs ached from the low stools it suddenly didn't seem to matter as time and intention were put on hold. The pub itself was timeless, and they were caught for a while in its magic. Even the arrival of some local farmers only added to the comfort of the scene as they ate and talked and smoked in virtual silence—the silence of the west of Ireland.

They watched together in companionable silence as the rough-cut peat slumbered in its embers, the pungent wild scent wafting around the room and drifting with the plume of smoke up through the hole cut in the ceiling. James spoke at last.

"Perhaps you could tell me again what you are expecting from this visit with Aherne. If you don't mind my saying so, you seem a little apprehensive."

Brona sighed, admitting she had been tense, admitting at last she was nervous of the interview ahead and what it might mean to her in terms of additional work.

"You see, after I talked to you yesterday I went in to College, and I was told by the secretary that the date has been set for my oral defense."

"Which is?"

"Next Thursday, a week from tomorrow. I was quite alarmed, even though I'd been expecting it. The chairman, you see, has been away, but he returns on Monday. My advisor, Professor Kennedy, had mentioned this date previously, and I had agreed to it. Term is officially drawing to a close. In fact, exam period has begun."

"But I was under the impression you were still actively writing," said James.

"Oh, no, I've been revising. A great deal of my work these last weeks has been checking and re-checking my bibliography. Reading my notes, returning to some material I haven't looked at in perhaps over a year. Fortunately, I am using a service, and the woman preparing my manuscript is well versed in this kind of work. With her word processor it is much easier than previously to add in new material, new entries, new footnotes. The thesis is virtually ready. I have proof-read large portions of it, and it reads and looks well."

"Is there a but in there, Brona?"

"Two of them, actually." She sighed. "One is my own reluctance to let it out of my hands after so many years, to finally let someone see it. My dissertation advisor seems well pleased. He's read it all in draft form, of course. But he's not been very supportive. O'Suillebhean never really interested him to the same extent he interested me."

"And the other concern?"

"Well, it's this interview. If what Mr. Aherne has in his possession means the introduction of major new material, it will be exciting, but it won't allow me to finish the thesis and present it to the committee in time. The latest I can hand it in would be Monday. That's the day the extern reader arrives from Belfast, Kennedy said. He acknowledged that I had to see Aherne, of course, but also hoped I would not need to request an extension—not a sympathetic man, really. Of course, I'd rather not be placed in that position. I do believe things have a natural span, and my work on O'Suillebhean is drawing to a natural close. I want to get on with my career."

James had urged her to take a brandy and port for her nerves, but she shrugged his suggestion aside, drumming her long fingers on the table as he finished his stout. James, now aware of her anxiety, left the table and asked the landlady if she knew of a Mr. Aherne. He was pleased she was able to give him quite specific directions to Aherne's remote cottage.

As James drove Brona explained that Aherne claimed to have in his possession poems written by O'Suillebhean to Aherne's own mother. They were written in his own hand, or so Mr. Aherne had said in his letter.

"Then this could be a real discovery for you," exclaimed James.

"Indeed, I am anxious to determine how important these poems might be to O'Suillebhean's entire corpus, how substantial they are. But if what Aherne says is true, at least their provenance is clear."

She was twisting her fingers in her lap, looking anxiously ahead, silent, straining like James to spot the nearly indistinguishable break in the high hedgerow that would be the turning to Aherne's. They saw it together, and James turned the car slowly into the opening, wincing as the hawthorne brushed against the pristine paint of his car.

"What do you think?" he said half to himself.

"God knows. I saw no post box or house name."

"Look, there's a house!" Inexplicable excitement thrilled James. He was looking forward to meeting the mysterious Mr. Aherne.

James pulled to the left of a long, low, rambling structure that dated back to the last century. Together they got out of the car and slowly approached the house, James commenting aloud on the fact that parts of it were roofed with ancient thatch, others with slate—an amalgam of local building materials and the varying styles of successive generations. Three doors at different points on the front of the house presented a choice. All were tightly closed, windowless. The seven or eight windows were built small and deeply set, some leaded, some quite modern. The sun was shining full on the front of the white-washed house, and the reflected light made James squint. Some Rhode Island Reds followed by two fat geese suddenly whooshed around the far side of the house, pecking and scattering as a large tabby cat stood up from the suntrap of one of the steps and stretched lazily, studying James as he did so.

The house was in good order, and James was relieved. It was a welcoming, picturesque scene. He strode with confidence to the door and lifted the brass lion's head, letting it fall heavily three times. He waited, then let it fall again. The door was heavy and the thud satisfying. Nothing. Brona moved away to the next door, set into a portion of the house older than the part that jutted out at the front. He followed her. Here two small windows set on either side of the door gave the impression of two eyes and a big nose. He smiled to himself. This door was slatted, less heavy and solid. He let the old horseshoe that had been fitted on a hinge fall against the wood. It clattered. He was beginning to feel like a character in the story of the Three Bears. He turned to Brona, about to speak, when the door opened suddenly and he found that they were being inspected by an old man, rather hunched, with a full head of white hair and half-glasses resting on the bulbous tip of his nose. His clear light blue eyes peered at James.

"Yes?" said the tremulous voice. The tabby had come to inspect James, too, and was twining around his legs, leaving orange-gold hairs on his impeccable navy trousers.

"My name is James Fleming. And this is Miss Brona O'Connell. I think you received a wire from her yesterday?"

The old man, so much shorter than he, looked up at him almost blankly.

"I'm sorry, but are you Mr. Aherne?" Brona spoke up clearly, commandingly.

"Who . . . who's there?" The old man squinted into the sun.

"This is Miss O'Connell," repeated James as she moved forward.

"Oh, yes, yes, but of course. Indeed, I am Thomas Aherne." He extended his hand to Brona formally. "You

229

must be the O'Suillebhean scholar. Please do come this way, both of you." He bustled into the small hallway and led them—rather energetically, thought James—through low-ceilinged rooms that led into other small, crowded rooms, thence through an ancient hallway to a more modern room. It was very bright in this room, sun streaming in the windows, but Aherne left the two standing lamps burning despite this.

The room was large and cluttered, with stacks of books on the floor, piles of books on the eight or nine chairs, towers of papers and manuscripts on the various tables. The floor was littered with papers of every kind. The walls were lined with shelves, jammed with books and magazines. A large electric typewriter sat on an old dining table, it, too, covered with sheaves of papers, and loose reams of paper covered the floor around the desk chair that stood nearby. But the higgledy-piggledy nature of the room was nonetheless appealing. There were all the signs of activity and great endeavor, to what end was less apparent. However, a large rolltop desk stood, more organized, in the corner, with envelopes, stamps, and neat stacks of what seemed to be ledger books. James quickly noted a large pile of correspondence, active he assumed, some of the letters with foreign stamps on them. Wire baskets and old rattan baskets filled with new padded mailing envelopes sat in a place of safety in the cold fireplace. Rolls of brown paper and neat balls of twine lay at the ready on the stone hearth beside a small weighing scales. Yes, thought James, there was order and system here, more than was apparent at first glance, but it was certainly peculiar to Mr. Aherne. James smiled, responding as always to what was intriguing in the nature of man.

Mr. Aherne went directly to two fireside chairs and cleared them. He drew his own desk chair across the floor, scoring the papers beneath it in the process. Brona reflexively went to move them, but he waved her away.

"Sit, sit, we don't have much time. I have a great deal of work to get through today."

"Thank you," said Brona simply. James moved slightly back from the two of them, aware that his presence might be intrusive, perhaps unwelcome to both, but he was reluctant to leave this interesting scene. Brona took out her notebook.

"Mr. Aherne, you wrote to me recently describing a notebook or book in O'Suillebhean's handwriting that you have in your possession. You mentioned that this was a book of poems that O'Suillebhean had given to your own mother." Brona spoke earnestly.

"Did I?" Aherne looked startled.

"Yes, I have the letter here." Although Brona was equally startled at his response, she calmly produced the letter from her bag.

He examined it. "Seems I did." He passed a hand over his eyes. "Can't recall why I wrote to you." Brona looked uneasy.

"I see," she said quickly, "that you have a great collection of books, Mr. Aherne. Is your interest in Irish works only?"

"Ah, my dear, of course. That is all there is for me." He waved his arm and then leapt up. "Come, come." He led them, James keeping a discreet distance, through three other connecting rooms. It resembled a public library, thought James, an old rural lending library with its hundreds of volumes. The man was rambling on about the collection, and Brona was drawing him gently back to her subject.

"It was a long drive to reach you," she said at last in a soft voice.

"My dear, my dear, I'm forgetting my manners. Do come and sit down." Brona walked quickly ahead of them back to the sunny room, where she sat again. The old man drew up his chair and with their knees almost touching began to talk compulsively, as one who's been lonely for compatible company.

"I see you are a book lover like meself," he said earnestly.

231

"My business has very much fallen off in these latter years. Can't understand it. I do believe, don't you, it's a general decline in literacy. There seems no interest taken now in our great writers of the past. It's all Yeats, Yeats and more Yeats. And he not even an Irish speaker. Hyde had him tagged, I can tell you! And that father of his—the cause of all the trouble in that family—with his wayward life. And Joyce. I'm always getting letters for Joyce books and Yeats books—wouldn't give such volumes house room, I can tell you."

James shifted in his chair and realized the man had forgotten his presence, having found his audience in Brona's pale oval face and large deep-set eyes. James had never realized before how arresting were her features. He watched her as she began to speak lovingly about Irish literature and O'Suillebhean's contribution to it.

"Aha! O'Suillebhean, is it? Is that why you've come?" the man exclaimed, as though starting the conversation entirely anew. James began to pity the extent of Aherne's mental confusion. "Aye, but shouldn't I have known it from your eyes?"

Brona smiled demurely. "O'Suillebhean and his work are my whole life, you see, Mr. Aherne. For years now he has been my life. That's why I've come—to see the book O'Suillebhean gave to your mother."

Aherne's eyes were briefly vacant and then focussed again, his voice soft. "She was so young to die, she seemed so young."

"Your mother?" said Brona again, her voice like a whisper.

"O'Suillebhean loved her, you see, and it changed her whole life." Aherne's conversation was disjointed. "Here, I'll show you." He took up an album from the floor, the leather worn by much handling, and he began to show Brona the snapshots of his mother.

James realized then that the portraits and photos he'd seen scattered here and there throughout the rooms of the house were all representations of Mrs. Aherne at every age, many of her late years. She had lived to a great age, and now her son was of a great age, too. The span of years that these two lives, mother and son, represented reached back to the late nineteenth century. Mrs. Aherne could indeed have known O'Suillebhean. And her son, the man now speaking to Brona, was in a sense a living connection with the poet.

James strained to hear as Aherne murmured on to Brona.

"And he courted her, you see. They had been in love, perhaps might have wed. Oh, she was young, a mere innocent girleen in her virginity. His poems to her all tell that. She was all her life so pure. . . ."

"I've no doubt," assented Brona. "They were pure and simple times . . . I know. . . ." Her voice was soft, lulling, intense.

"A whole sheaf of them he wrote to her, put them in a book and gave it to her. She had told me of her book, but she'd kept it hidden, hidden for years, had never let me see it. She knew all the poems by heart and would recite them to me—in the Irish and others in English. I finally found the book itself amongst her things after she . . . after she was gone."

"Who else had she told—about O'Suillebhean? Your father, perhaps?" Brona pressed on, sweetly insistent.

"No, that man, with his money, no, he never let her talk about O'Suillebhean or poetry or any fine thing. And so she lived, as you see, here, with her books and dreams. When I was a lad she would read to me for hours—in the summer in the pasture, away from the man. In the winter in the old house." Aherne indicated the smaller rooms with a wave of his hand, not taking his eyes off Brona. "By the light of the fire she would read to me when the man put out her candles. We had each other. When I grew I read to her, he never liked that. He never liked us reading together. He wanted me to go on the land, but she wouldn't permit it. He was a cold man, I tell you, and his words with her were rough."

"Not everyone can know the beauty and power of the word, Mr. Aherne."

"When he was gone . . ."

"When your father died?" Brona was so gentle.

"Yes, when the man was gone we were all right then. We had our books, and we got more books, and then when she, too, was gone . . ." Aherne's voice broke ever so slightly. "Ah, so sweet and lovely she was. I . . . I kept on at the books. . . ." Aherne's voice faded, and Brona rested her hand on his hand for a moment.

James wondered about Aherne's father. A rougher, perhaps older country man with no time or inclination for books, for poetry, for dreams. How excluded he must have felt, mused James, by the mother and son. He must have died a disappointed man, to know that the labour of his back—his land and the family home—would fall to this son, unmarried, who loved not the land nor woman, but only his mother's dreams. And so the farmer's drudgery had served only to allow this strange son to carry on his life in isolation, in the uncertain trade of second-hand bookselling in the absolute back of beyond.

"O'Suillebhean loved her?" Brona stated it as fact, feeding into Aherne's memory or fantasy, James didn't know which.

"The love of his life. She was his inspiration. Here! You can see for yourself." He stood up, and the action seemed to bring him into the present. "You, what's your name?" He addressed James.

"Fleming, James Fleming. I'm a solicitor." He saw Brona shaking her head behind the old man's back.

"A lawyer, is it? And who are you when you're at home?" He whirled on Brona, rudeness in his manner, aggression in his voice.

"A scholar, as you know, Mr. Aherne." Her voice was level, her demeanor unperturbed. "Someone who wishes all the world to know and respect O'Suillebhean's work—as we do."

"A sneak, a snoop. Scholar, bah!" The old man was

234

trembling. At this Brona showed some sign of anxiety. "No, no, no," he said to himself, moving over to the window, looking out blankly.

Brona glanced at James.

She stood up and spoke in an ordinary tone. "Mr. Aherne, I feel rather faint. And my friend here, James, he very kindly brought me. I don't drive, you see." She gestured helplessly with her long white hands as he turned to face her. "And now the excitement of our conversation, the wonderful things you've been able to tell me . . . Could I perhaps make myself a cup of tea?" she appealed to him.

"Manners, manners. My dear, my dear." The repetition of his earlier word was unsettling, disturbing, thought James, as though he'd learned the phrase by rote as a child. Or from being closeted with an unhappy, sensitive mother, James thought with asperity.

"Come, I will make it, and you will lay the tea things, just as she did." His voice fell. "She'd pale skin, much like yours. He loved her paleness. He wrote of it, you see."

"I'd love to see," murmured Brona as she followed him out to the kitchen. James waited impatiently, poking around the room, hoping now to locate this manuscript, this book of which the eccentric old man had spoken so obsessively. He passed many of the papers through his hands, filled with crabbed handwriting on yellowing sheets, with spidery scrawls on fresher, whiter paper. Hundreds of thousands of words; Aherne's thoughts on Irish literature of every type and sort, of every era and time. Some was intelligible, even intelligent, but much was not—vituperative and disjointed or melancholy and mournful. He despaired for Brona and for himself.

But within moments James heard their steps on the wooden flooring, and he quickly returned to his seat, as if a Greek chorus observing the action. He accepted a cup of tea from Aherne as Brona played mother, pouring the tea and passing the cream and sugar. The silver tea service was of antique value, thought James, Irish silver with a gorgeous patina. He sat back as Brona relentlessly led Aherne to her purpose.

"I love O'Suillebhean," she said simply. Aherne nodded, staring at her face. "I want the rest of the country, the rest of the world to know the beauty that you and I know. I've worked for years towards this end." She had abandoned, thought James, the attempt to deal with her reality and instead was dealing with his.

"If my work succeeds, I could have . . . access to promoting knowledge of the man and his work." She was seeking a different way to describe her situation.

"You love him, yes, but not as she did."

"No, no, no," said the gentle voice. "That was unique. You were so fortunate to have known her. To have known him through her. I can only know him through his work, but I have his picture always before me, above my typewriter and —"

"You *are* one of them," Aherne shrieked. "Do you think you can trick me again? Am I a fool to be robbed blind twice? To see her name dragged through mud, her inviolate self spotted and stained? I won't allow it. I trusted him. Do you come from him, to get her book? It is my treasure, it is my life." He crossed his hands over his chest.

"Who?" said Brona, now visibly alarmed. "I come only out of love for O'Suillebhean." She said the same again in Irish, or so James guessed. The man relaxed his arms.

"A Yank, no, you're not a Yank. He thought he'd learned the Irish, but he hadn't. I should have been more suspicious, more careful. But he knew so much, and it had been so long since I'd heard O'Suillebhean spoken of."

"Who, when?" Brona stumbled and recovered. "Who offended your mother?"

"The Yank, and not long after she was gone. I was longing . . ." He stopped. "I'd seen his letter. He'd written to an Irish-language paper. It was the first anniversary of her death, the very day I saw his letter. It seemed like a sign."

James felt he was losing the thread of their conversation, slight as it was. The mother had died twenty years ago. Aherne was speaking vividly of an event two decades before.

"I answered the letter—a request much like yours, Miss O'Connell—and the young man came here. He knew O'Suillebhean's poetry very well, I thought. We spoke long . . . I . . ." He rubbed his eyes and sat down heavily.

"You showed him your mother's book." Brona leaned forward, gently touching the veined hand that trembled on his knee.

"And do you know"—his voice shook—"that treacherous American, that lying Yank said that my dear mother and O'Suillebhean were lovers. In print, in print," he shrieked, "for all the world to see!"

Brona patted his hand. "Mr. Aherne, I know." Her voice was calm and sonorous, deep, lulling. "I know they were not. O'Suillebhean was as pure as the corporal body can be." Aherne looked into her face. "Your mother was a girleen," she said, echoing his word, "O'Suillebhean gone from us tragically at the early age of twenty-four. I know what they experienced was the purest love of the soul and of two minds that saw the world, corporal and spiritual, in the same way. How could some hard-nosed Yank know anything of all that purity? You, you are a true scholar. You know what is thought of American literary scholarship. Only we Irish can truly know the Irish heart, the Irish soul." The sonorous, mellifluous voice paused. James found himself waiting, watching as though an observer at a play. "If you grant me the great privilege, the grace"—she slightly stressed the word—"of letting me see your mother's notebook, I would only use that great privilege to help the world to come to know O'Suillebhean's poetry. I am not dealing with his life, with his private personal life, but with his great work. I will have the chance to make that work known. You would be making an important contribution to scholarship, to the cause of Irish poetry, to further enhance our knowledge about O'Suillebhean. I know now that I would never believe my own work was complete without at least being able to see, to read these precious poems. In fact, Mr. Aherne, wouldn't it be wrong of you, perhaps selfish of you, not to share them with the world, this precious gift of your mother's book? And you can share that gift through helping me in my work. I assure you, I will never betray you or your mother's memory."

Aherne had been watching Brona's earnest face, her pleading eyes, and at last, as she finished her speech, he smiled. Without further commotion the old man went to a leather-bound steamer trunk in the corner, removed the book, and handed it to Brona. "I do trust you," he said simply.

James could see it was a cloth-bound book with lined pages now yellow but in good condition. He watched as Brona exclaimed, handling it gently, as though it were a holy relic. She leafed through the pages silently, unobtrusively making notes in her own notebook. The room was very quiet as Aherne returned to his own work table to write, as though they were a little family comfortable together. The slanting rays of the sun caught James on the back through the tiny window, and he found himself dozing.

After perhaps half an hour Brona quietly closed the book, wrapping it again in the crackling tissue paper, the only noise in the room. She walked over to Aherne, immersed in his work, handing him the bundle. She stood almost impatiently as he returned the precious keepsake to its home in the trunk.

"Thank you for seeing me today and for the great favour of your conversation," she said simply as she shook hands. "My friend and I have a long drive back to Dublin, and we must be going."

After the suppressed emotion of the last two hours Brona's tone was businesslike, almost abrupt, but still formal. Aherne responded by seeing them to the door, preoccupied, speaking of his own writing, an essay on

Mangan. James was tempted to mention Brona's cats but
thought the better of it.

With a sigh of relief he pulled the car out of the front yard
and retraced their winding route back to the main Dublin
road.

Brona had been silent all this time, and James could wait
no longer.

"Well, Brona, was it significant?" He realized that he
wanted the trip, the visit with Aherne, the machinations of
the last few hours to have achieved something.

"Significant?" she mused, considering. "Let me say this,
the notebook was certainly worth seeing." Her tone was one
of recital, of a rehearsal perhaps for her oral defense. James
was irritated but kept quiet. "My judgment is that the few
poems he copied into the book to give to Mrs. Aherne, or
Miss Ronan as she was then, were very early work—
juvenilia, as we call it. Some of O'Suillebhean's constant
themes were there, but in very unsophisticated form. I
would date them as being written in his late teens, not later
than his twentieth year. He had written an inscription to
Aherne's mother all right. I imagine they were friends, but I
didn't detect that she had been a source of inspiration.
Despite what Aherne was misremembering, the poems were
not personal to her. Either she had an exaggerated sense of
her own importance or her son Aherne did and still does.
It's unlikely some insignificant country girl could have
served as a source of inspiration for a genius such as
O'Suillebhean." Brona's tone was dismissive, belittling.

"Much the same was said of Fanny Brawn and Keats, if I
remember rightly," snapped James, but Brona only
shrugged.

"And so what you were saying to Aherne just now—about
his sainted mother's love for O'Suillebhean being incorpo-
real, that they shared a common imaginative life—"

"Was rubbish." Brona finished his sentence. "I needed to
see that manuscript, James, and I wasn't about to leave

239

without doing so. I copied down the few truly significant lines. It will only be necessary for me to include perhaps a paragraph or two in the early section of my thesis and insert the titles and rough dates in my chronology and bibliography." She sighed, apparently with relief.

"Then the trip was worth it?" James was insistent.

"Yes, certainly. I've covered the ground. I will mention Aherne's assistance, such as it was, on the acknowledgment page."

"And that's it?"

"I'm afraid so, yes. He's just a deluded, foolish old man. He imagined his mother had played an important role in O'Suillebhean's life, probably imagined that gave him some self-importance, riding into history—literary history—on O'Suillebhean's coattails, so to speak. Aherne's pathetic."

James was shocked at her callousness and the coldness of her tone, and he let the matter drop. He had pitied Aherne. It had struck him that the old man had had only one friend, his mother. And since her death his only link to her was his own life of books and dreams, and the treasure of her having known O'Suillebhean. He had thought Brona would have shared those feelings, and as a result perhaps empathized with the old man. He sighed. He was sorry to have been a part of what now seemed like some horrible intrusion into a lonely old man's private life. He was sorry he had sat and listened as Aherne had spoken of what to him had been a blissful boyhood.

They were approaching Castlebar when James pulled over to consult the map. It was another half hour before they reached his destination, but it was time well spent, for here indeed was a sight worth seeing, albeit housed in a barn. It was a Belpaire-boilered three-cylinder compound. And the restoration work, though far from complete, was certainly impressive. And inspiring.

Even James's irritation with Brona dissipated, and he coaxed her out of the car and around to the back of the barn.

"I don't understand it, James," she said finally.

"What, what don't you understand? I can explain anything."

"No, it's not that I want to know about this . . . this engine. To me it's just a machine. I don't quite understand your enthusiasm."

"But you must appreciate its age," said James, warming to the subject. "Surely you can see its power, its beautiful lines. Look at that workmanship." He lovingly stroked the copperwork, the brass fittings. He leapt up onto the footplate, pointing out the engine's features.

"Don't you see," he called to Brona, who remained on the ground, "it has both beauty and function. Look at the skill this represents, the combined skill of so many men. Look, can't you just imagine this engine doing Trojan work year after year, pulling goods, hauling cars full of travellers safely to their destinations all over Ireland?"

"I'll tell you, it merely reminds me of that English clergyman's books about that silly little train called Toby or Tommy or something." James shrugged as he stepped down, realizing he didn't have a convert to his particular cause.

Before he bid his farewell to both the wonderful steam engine and its owner he asked the man to take their photograph, with Brona beside the front buffer. James had already taken quite a few with the Polaroid camera he kept at the ready for just such occasions. More fodder for his own bulging albums, he mused as he put them carefully into his briefcase back in the car, and with no one but himself to enjoy them.

He hadn't really expected her to be interested in his enthusiasm, as he had been in hers. But he'd expected common courtesy, and he hadn't even got that. He mentally kicked himself as he pulled away from the kerb outside Brona's flat and Conroy's house. Barely a word of thanks for his driving her to see Aherne. Barely a word, in fact, on the whole ride home as she sat silently reading her copious notes in the waning light of what had been a glorious spring day.

Ah, Brona, he said aloud to the empty car, you used me,

and I let you. I was a means to an end, just as poor old Aherne was. A user, he mused silently, so single-minded you can only consider your own obsession—your work, your subject. Her conduct of the interview with Aherne had depressed him, and somewhere on the margins of his tired mind something nagged at him, too. If only she'd feigned interest in the steam engine he would have forgiven her much.

— *Chapter Thirteen* —

James watched the door of the Residents' Hall in the dropping twilight. Fatigue battled with excitement as he waited for Geraldine to come out. It had been a hectic week, but . . . but what, he wondered. A successful week?

What he had felt that morning after he'd phoned her was relief. He had feared she'd be on duty, and she was, but she willingly arranged a swap and called him back to say she'd be free to meet him that evening. There was a tap of red fingernails on the side window, and he jumped.

"Hello, wake up in there!" Geraldine flashed a great smile, white teeth, red lips.

"Sorry, sorry!" James sheepishly got out and opened the passenger door. "You're looking well, Ger," he said admiringly.

"I wasn't sure you'd recognize me. It's been a week at least."

"I know, Ger. I am sorry, and it was a bloody awful week, too, but . . ."

"But?"

"It's behind me now," he mumbled.

"Well, despite all that, I believe this is a great idea, James. I'd say you're being very thoughtful. Truth to tell, it would never have occurred to me."

"Please, Ger."

"No, you're very good."

"As good as Donald?" James's tone was lighter than his heart.

"Oh . . . I see. Did Donald tell you? Actually, it wasn't a date, more of a coincidence. We were both going to a drug company reception. You know that kind of thing—free food, free drink, free samples. And then a crowd of us went on to a pub."

"Listen, Ger, you don't have to explain."

James tried to assimilate this bit of news—Donald hadn't told him anything. He hadn't even clapped eyes on James since the dinner party. Few people had. James had been busy fishing, and sadly he had caught something.

At last Ger spoke, her tone rather colorless. "By the way, I brought along a bottle of wine."

"Oh, I don't know, Geraldine. I imagine Brona will be very nervous tonight."

"That's exactly why I brought it. A glass or two would relax her. It would relax me, anyway."

He laughed. "Let's see how it goes." He parked at the kerb, and they descended the steps to Brona's flat.

"You were so right not to phone ahead. She'd never have agreed to us coming by tonight."

James shrugged as he pressed the bell. "That's the point, Ger. Remember! Be persuasive when she answers the door." At which point the door did open a crack.

"Who's there?" called Brona's voice, as pale and weak as her appearance. "Oh, God, Geraldine!"

"Hello, pet. Yes, it is I, and James, too. We've come to cheer you up."

"Oh, Lord, I don't think so. Really . . . I've a great deal left to do." Brona did not widen the door, blocking their entrance with her body.

"Nonsense! Rubbish!" said Geraldine. "You are as ready now as you will be tomorrow. Right now you want to clear your mind, rest it."

"You don't understand, Ger, you've never understood." Brona was vexed.

"Don't be a twit, Brona. I've taken plenty of oral exams, as you well know."

"Ger," hushed James, hearing the irritation in Brona's voice.

"Brona, darling, we are not going away, so you might as well let us in. The sooner you do, the sooner we'll go, if you want us to. Honestly, pet, we've just come to supply moral support and lift some of that anxiety. Right, James?"

James murmured and moved towards the door.

"Just a few minutes, then," said Brona reluctantly, ushering them in.

James was startled to see the state of the kitchen, once so orderly. A thick typed manuscript was at one end of the table, sitting neatly apart, its pages stacked in two almost equal piles. He glanced over the page on the top; it was obviously Brona's thesis. As Brona hung up Geraldine's coat he quickly flipped through the pages. Numerous notes were handwritten in the margins. Other manuscripts, texts, and old books of poetry littered the table. He sighed yet again at the sight of so much effort.

And he jumped as Geraldine swept over to the table and plunked down her bottle of wine.

"Careful, Ger. For heaven's sake," snapped Brona excitedly. She was heavily dressed in casual clothes—blue jeans and a flecked woollen pullover—and for the first time James noticed that the small flat was cold. And he noticed that her long brown hair was loosely tied up from her face. She looked both fit and vulnerable, like a young girl ready for a day's tramp out on the fields of Monaghan.

"Careful, Ger," he said again. But Geraldine took no notice, rooting around in the kitchen drawer for a corkscrew, familiar as she was with the flat, at home there. When she found it she opened the wine and then turned and bent to put a few fifty-pence pieces into the meter that ran the gas fire. Brona sagged into a chair.

"Well, I don't know about the wine," said Brona, relaxing ever so slightly, "but I am grateful for the coins. You see, I'd run out, and I didn't want to leave to go to the shop for change. But I was beginning to get chilled to the bone. I still have a great deal to do, and the warmth is very welcome." She smiled wanly to herself.

"Brona, darling, this is the worst possible thing you can do to yourself," Ger said brightly. "Tell us, what time is this annoying oral exam?"

"It's at eleven tomorrow morning." Brona glanced at her watch. "And it's eight now. Oh, God." She sighed and unconsciously rubbed her midriff.

"Butterflies?" said James.

"More like bats," said Brona.

"That is my point exactly. You've got yourself into a state. What possible good can this do." Ger tapped the table and then swept some of the books and papers into a heap as Brona started to exclaim.

"Here, let me quiz you, then. A few minutes' solid revision will put your mind at rest." Ger picked up one of the stacks of papers, scanning it.

"You still don't understand after all these years." Brona's voice cracked as though she might cry, but with frustration. "There are no dates here, no lists of pharmaceuticals, no chemicals from the periodic table. There are no famous theories from even more famous physicians to regurgitate."

Geraldine looked startled. "Brona, it's a viva like any other. I'll ask you a few questions and—"

"And what? If you could form the questions, how would you understand my answers? How would you know if I were right or wrong?"

"You'll know, though," she said.

"These issues are insubstantial things, Ger. Not neatly quantifiable. Some of your vivas—oh, I remember—took about twenty minutes. In and out. And off you'd go to the pub to celebrate once again with your medical friends. I could be at this oral for hours. Hours, do you understand? With four people, perhaps more, interrogating me. And not just about O'Suillebhean, but on the whole field of nineteenth-century Irish literature—in Irish and in English. Now, tell me"—her face flushed a sickly red—"how can you ask me any questions?"

Geraldine shrugged, suddenly unhappy. "Brona, I do wish you well, you know. It can't be all that different," she said, irritated at last by Brona's attitude of dismissal.

"Oh, yes, it can." She stood up as James quietly handed her a small glass of red wine.

"Drink a little of this," he said, so softly it silenced both women. He took a glass and handed one to Geraldine.

"This time Brona's right," he said quietly as they sat down. The mood had changed as a little warmth permeated the room.

"You see, Geraldine, I've been learning a little about this process. I'll explain if I may."

Brona nodded, surprised but smiling now, as at someone who understood.

"You see, some years ago, when Brona finished the coursework required for the doctoral program, she needed to choose a subject for her doctoral thesis, a subject worthy of extensive upper-level graduate work. For years Brona had studied Irish literature, both in English and in Irish, following perhaps in the footsteps of her famous uncle." Brona looked startled but nodded.

Geraldine poured more wine. "Go on, James," she said softly.

"In the course of her reading she came across a nineteenth-century Irish poet, a poor young man who had lived in the west of Ireland, near the village of Ballinaderg. He died tragically young from tuberculosis—"

"Possibly brucellosis," Brona added quickly.

"She began to do her preliminary research and realized

that she'd found her subject. A poet whose life, whose poetry, whose philosophy interested her, intrigued her—perhaps she even identified with him in some way."

"Yes, yes, that sounds like Brona." Geraldine laughed. "You know, James, I was a part of Brona's life during some of this."

"That's true, Ger," said Brona bitterly, "but you never paid any attention."

"Please, I'm just summarizing," said James seriously. "What perhaps you missed, Ger, was how important Brona's choice of subject was to her. She eschewed tackling one of the major writers in her field. She came to believe that O'Suillebhean and his work were as worthy as any of the, let's say, better-known literary figures. She found that he'd been neglected during his short life, isolated as he was by his illness, his lack of contact with the developing Irish literary movement in Dublin. And she was going to remedy this neglect, bringing his life and work to light."

"That rings true! I've heard Brona speak of him often, too often!" Ger laughed merrily.

James continued addressing Geraldine. "Brona had chosen someone whom the world of scholarship had overlooked. Thus her research, her work, her interpretation, her conclusions had all the advantages of being fresh, new, in the nature of a valuable contribution to the field. Her advisor approved her choice but, as she has told me, was not really very interested."

"You're right, he sees it still as merely a means to an end."

"Nonetheless, Brona believes in her subject. And Ger, she has spent the last three years in particular pursuing her goal. Weaving it out of her own substance, much as a spider weaves its silk from its own belly, spinning its web from its own substance."

"Quite an image, James," remarked Brona.

"Patient reading, scrupulous documentation, piecing together this young man's life and biography, coming to terms with his poetry and his prose, what letters survived, what mention other writers made of him, and so on. Years, years of work coming to one single, final, and irrevocable conclusion, Geraldine. Tomorrow"—James paused briefly— "tomorrow Brona goes in to meet a committee, a group of people who will demand that she defend that work, that scholarship, its value, its very validity."

Brona was nodding. He thought fleetingly there were tears in her bright eyes.

"Who can know what Brona has sacrificed all these years? Perhaps you know a bit of that, Ger. This was not an easy route to choose. Her subject wasn't popular. Even if it had been, she had to work in isolation. There was no group of students sharing the work. No, it was hours spent in the various libraries alone, reading, writing, taking notes, tracking down perhaps the meaning of a single word, the accurate spelling of a single word. There was no crowd of like-minded people to go with to the pub at the end of the day, sharing anecdotes, exchanging information."

"Oh, Brona, I never saw it this way."

"I know that," said Brona.

"But I used to drag her out, James, with me—"

"Yes, and I daresay you were kind, Ger," said James.

"Yes, she meant well," added Brona.

"But you take my point, Ger. Brona's been working alone. And I imagine there were other sacrifices, too. She had to live prudently, carefully. Even her bike was old and heavy. Yes, she sacrificed much these last few years for her almost intangible goal. And, as I say, she worked alone."

He looked neutrally at Brona, who shrugged. Geraldine poured out more wine. James stood up to stretch, smiling briefly as Brona's three cats padded in single file into the room and lay before the electric fire glowing red in the wall.

"Everything depends on her defense tomorrow, Ger. The committee has now read copies of that massive manuscript you see there on the table. They've prepared their questions on her dissertation and on her knowledge of both her poet and her field. She gets one chance to defend years of work.

But if she passes this gruelling ordeal she'll not only be free, she'll be accepted into that indefinable body of scholars, that world-wide elite group of persons who have achieved the Ph.D. in their field. To achieve that goal for herself has been her lifelong dream. She will acquire status, respect, acknowledgment of those peers wherever she might go. She will at last hold in her hand—metaphorically speaking—the key to the ivory tower. Tomorrow is the most important day of Brona's life—in her terms."

Though clearly impressed, Ger could not resist one final try.

"Still, James, last-minute swotting won't change anything." But she was poking fun at herself this time, and Brona smiled.

"No, it won't help." James did not lighten his mood or his tone. "Reading over her manuscript—who's to say what would help? I'm not sure if anything would now. You see, Ger, this poet O'Suillebhean was obscure, was lost for decades to the literary world, but along the way, years ago, someone came across his work. Don't you think, Brona, that it was amazing that somebody so far removed from the scene, thousands of miles away from this little island of ours, stumbled across him? Who would have thought an American without Irish connections at all would have found O'Suillebhean, would have chosen him out of all the hundreds of subjects to write about?"

James turned to face Brona as she leapt to her feet.

"Your extern reader, Professor Shaw, knew about him, though, didn't he, Brona?" Brona had been staring at James and now spoke out.

"Of course not," she said loudly to the quiet room.

"How do you know, Brona, since you never knew who your extern reader was to be?" he asked quietly. "You've said time and again that a candidate never knows the extern reader beforehand, that that reader's objectivity is central to the procedure."

"I never knew who the extern reader was! I only knew

which members of the English Department at the College would be on my committee. My proposal and my summary were sent on to a reader. I never had contact with anyone outside of the College!" Brona's voice was rising.

"What's the matter? James? Brona? What's going on?" Geraldine was now also standing, looking agog at her two friends, James pale and tense, Brona flushed and wild-eyed.

They stared at each other.

"What's wrong? For God's sake, is it this American? What has he to do with this?"

"Haven't you been listening, Ger?" Brona swung on her. "No, even after he explained it to you, you still don't see it, do you? Well, let me explain, then!" She was hoarse.

"By all means," said James coldly. "Explain it then, Brona."

"Oh, God, it's all so . . . unfair." She slumped down in her seat, the cats prowling around her, alarmed by the raised voices. She stroked them intently. "You see, Ger, twenty years ago some American student from some godforsaken little college . . . some American man chose O'Suillebhean as the subject of his doctoral dissertation—which he completed."

"That's it?" cried Ger. "Why are you all so upset? Sacred Heart, I thought something was terribly wrong here. There are hundreds of books on—well, on Yeats. They're all over town. And Joyce. And—"

"Shut up, won't you?" Brona threw her head in her hands.

"Geraldine," said James, "it does make a difference to Brona. Perhaps she should tell you."

Brona looked pleadingly at James, but he turned towards the window.

"No one knows this but you, James," she said at last.

"*You* know it, Brona," he said simply, not facing her.

"Oh, God . . ."

"Brona, tell me, what is it? What has happened?"

"It was so horrible, Ger. It was so horrible," Brona said at last to her old friend.

"I was here one night, working. I'd been at the College all day. My head was aching from the work I'd been doing. I'd been translating some of O'Suillebhean's Irish poetry into English for one of the addenda I was including with the thesis. I felt all along that I could publish my translations one day, if not my entire thesis. My head was full of this particular poem. . . ."

Geraldine sat down as Brona's voice took on a dreamy narrative quality.

"The poem was one that concerned a vision of the world as seemingly a great barren desert place, but then as it moved into his true vision the poet begins to see it peopled with spirits—not disembodied souls, but the spirits of truth, of love. This was a loving vision of the world, not modern and alien as Eliot or Yeats with their vortexes and voids. . . ." She sighed again.

"A world almost as I had known as a girl in Monaghan. I was so immersed in it that I barely heard the telephone ring. A man's voice came on the phone, very distinguished, very English. He said his name was Philip Shaw, that he was a professor of English at Leston University in England.

"I thought for a moment that perhaps I'd applied there for a post—I've written to so many colleges. I waited, and he said that he was in Dublin, had just disembarked from the ferry. I was so puzzled I didn't know why he was telling me this. He mentioned then that he was over in Dublin to see a publisher and would be calling in at the College also. I said could I help him, and he said no, it was the other way around. He then identified himself as my extern reader. I was so shocked I didn't know what to say. He said he'd been invited to sit on my dissertation committee and had received my proposal and the summary of my work, and that it was imperative he see me. I gave him the address and waited anxiously.

"When I opened the door I was even more shocked. It was well after ten o'clock, and he'd still got his bags with him. I was frightened then, for a minute. I felt it was stupid to let him in. The Conroys were in Africa, and the house seemed so completely empty, so large, so empty. . . ."

"Go on . . . what happened then?" Ger had drawn her chair closer to Brona. It was as though she could see and hear it all through Brona's eyes and ears.

Shaw placed his bags in the small hallway and strode quickly into the kitchen, taking the room in at a glance.

"Poverty row, is it, my love?" he said abruptly, turning to Brona and handing her his scarf and tossing his overcoat on the chair.

"Pardon me, Professor Shaw?" said Brona, startled.

"You are obviously not a girl of independent means, are you?"

"No, I'm not," said Brona, squaring her shoulders at the slight.

"I'm thirsty, Miss O'Connell. Let's have some of this famous Irish hospitality." He smiled, taking the edge off his very British accent.

"I'm sorry," said Brona, and she put the kettle on to boil.

"Tea? Nothing stronger? How about a drop of the *uisce bar?*" His imitation of an Irish accent irritated her.

"No, I'm sorry, Professor Shaw, but I do not keep whiskey in the house. To get to the point, your call made me very curious."

"Ah, I see, very professional—straight to the point. Too bad, but I'm afraid you won't like what I have to say."

"Go on."

"This O'Suillebhean character, I suppose he would have been all right in his way—for a subject of a thesis. Probably thought you'd made a real find, am I right?"

She nodded, blushing.

"It's all right. You know, I've done the same thing for years. Grist for my mill. Finding someone obscure, neglected, writing up an essay, an article, perhaps controversial. I've published hundreds of such items. As I say, such subjects are grist for the academic mill. Churning them out, but then what are we scholars to do?" He flashed a knowing smile, stroking his greying beard as he did so.

"But the mills of the gods grind slowly, and . . ." He challenged her, his tone changing.

"But they grind exceedingly fine," said Brona, finishing the quote.

"I'm afraid you've got caught up in that grinding, my girl." He patronized her, and it alarmed her.

"Milk and sugar?" she asked, trying to quell her rising panic.

"Thought you wouldn't be found out? Did you lift the whole idea—tell me, I am curious—or did you find out after you'd begun writing?" He stirred his tea.

"Excuse me?"

"Drake's dissertation on O'Suillebhean. Did you read it first and then make your choice, or did you find it out later?"

"I know of no such Drake," Brona answered but her voice was filled with panic.

"Should I believe you?"

"Whatever you are trying to say, please say it." Brona had remained standing.

"When I received your proposal from the English Department here I did what I normally do. I checked in the library for any previously published works on your subject. In so doing I of course routinely checked in the volumes of the Dissertation Abstracts published in the States. And there for the world to see was a summary of Drake's dissertation on your little Irish poet. I sent for a copy, and although it was granted a degree by a very small university, the dissertation showed good scholarship. He covered all the ground . . . but *you* know."

"I *don't* know," cried Brona, horrified. She watched wide-eyed as he retrieved his briefcase in the hall and withdrew a bound manuscript. He tossed it triumphantly on the table in front of Brona.

"He covered the ground pretty thoroughly," said Shaw, for the first time speaking in a more professional tone. "His writing style is leaden, but the facts are there—the biography, chronology—and he patiently analyzed every scrap of that poor boy's work."

Brona stared at the table, silent, her tea untouched.

"You seem shocked by my information."

"I am."

"Do you mean to say that you were unaware of this previous work?" His scoffing tone returned.

"Yes."

He loosened his tie. "Well," he said at last, "I can say two things to you. One is that all the work you've done has already been done. O'Suillebhean hardly merits an additional work of this type. He's too unimportant." Shaw watched as Brona flushed. "And secondly"—he went on regardless—"if, as you say, you were unaware of the existence of this work by Drake—and I'm not entirely sure about that—then your own scholarship was terribly, terribly faulty."

"Oh, my God, how can you say that?" she nearly cried. "I've spent three years of my life doing this research—"

"But you have nothing to add to what has already been done. You may well have written about it in a better style, perhaps you have even brought to bear on it some of that Irish soul—Drake had no soul—but that won't make a significant enough difference." He poured his own second cup of tea as Brona sat trembling on the edge of her chair.

"You must believe me. I knew nothing of this man Drake's work. It just didn't occur to me to look at the American abstracts. I did check the few published articles, but Drake's work must not have been published. I would have seen some reference to it. Oh, my God!"

Shaw watched as she cast her mind over the hours and months and years of reading. "No," she said. "I never saw a reference to Drake."

"Possibly not. Not only is Drake obscure, but your subject is also obscure. Nonetheless, it was your responsibility. You can hardly think that regurgitating something already done

—and so long ago, twenty years ago—merits the award of a doctoral degree." His tone was harsh.

"But I did all the work in good faith. I swear to you, all of the work is my own. I never took an idea, I never stole anyone else's work. This isn't plagiarism. I would never do such a thing!"

"What else does it look like? Plagiarizing his central idea, if not his exact words. Lord, you wouldn't even have had to have read O'Suillebhean's work in the original unless—"

"Stop, stop!" Brona covered her ears with her hands, then stood up and paced the room. "I tell you," she said more calmly, "I am not dishonest. I did not plagiarize, I didn't steal Drake's ideas, or anyone else's. This dissertation is entirely my own. For God's sake, it's been my life . . ." She waved her hands as if showing him the flat and indicating how she'd lived all this time.

"If—and I still say if—that is all true, then I feel very sorry for you. You've lost three years of your life."

"Stop it," she cried.

"If it is true, you have only yourself to blame. And I think that's always so much harder, don't you, when people bring a tragedy on themselves?" He lit a cigarette without asking her if he could smoke. She waved her hands, her anger rising.

"Stop saying 'if.' I tell you I did not know."

"Then your scholarship was at fault. If *I* could check it out in matter of weeks? Come on! You had three years to check it out. Either way, do you honestly think that you deserve to be granted the highest of academic degrees? Do you think a scholar, as you describe yourself, who missed such a basic piece of information should be granted a degree of this nature? And if you stole Drake's idea, stole the work of another, do you think I can let you be granted that degree? Either way . . ."

"Either way I . . . oh, dear God."

"That's correct. Either way you cannot receive your degree. At your dissertation defense I will announce my conclusion. It will embarrass them sorely, I imagine. Your own advisor should have caught this fatal flaw, Miss O'Connell." He ceased, watching her carefully.

She didn't speak, sitting entirely defeated, devastated by his evaluation of her as not merely a less-than-adequate scholar, but as someone who had plagiarized.

When Shaw spoke again his voice was softer, cajoling. "Miss O'Connell, I am inclined to believe that you had no knowledge of Drake's work, that you did not intentionally steal or attempt to get your degree by fraud."

When she didn't look at him he continued, again speaking softly. "I have been a teacher for years, and I've dealt with many young students, serious young women such as yourself."

She looked up, curiosity and anxiety mingled in her expression. "Yes?"

"Do you have anything to drink? I'm chilled from the ferry."

"I'll get you some wine." She got up and walked listlessly to the press as he drew his chair nearer the fire, facing it, to warm himself. She heard him speaking as from a great distance as she found the wine and hunted for the corkscrew.

"Of course," he continued, "I've sat on committees here before, and occasionally in England I've had some Irish girls in my courses. Always so innocent. There was one in particular I remember—her name was Ariadne. Such an unusual name that it stuck with me, that and her naïveté. That gave novelty to our love-making . . . before she became tiresome."

Brona was frozen in the act of opening the wine. "Ariadne?" she said finally when she could control her voice. "It *is* unusual. I know of one Ariadne, but she is in advertising here."

"Yes, no doubt that is she. Strange you'd know of her, but then Ireland is such a small town, don't you think?"

He smiled at her sardonically as she handed him his wine

with a trembling hand, rage and disgust briefly clouding her brain.

He sipped it slowly.

"You were saying?" she prompted. The trembling had stopped.

"Yes, I think we can come to a private arrangement. I think it is possible to keep this between ourselves, but in order for me to do this I would need a show of good faith on your part."

"Yes," she said hesitantly, her grim suspicion confirmed.

His eyes surveyed her appraisingly, offensively, as she stood near the fire. "I think I could teach you a lot of things you don't know. And who knows, you might like it. That's happened in my experience." His short laugh was both vain and lewd. "I'd expect you to be a good student, of course, Miss O'Connell, and work hard over the next few days— and nights—at learning your new skills. I like my girls to graduate with honours." He laughed again. "Please, you don't have to answer immediately." Shaw's voice was already full of the assumption Brona would readily agree. "Think about it, by all means, and consider"—he paused— "what is hanging in the balance." He sipped his wine contentedly and stared at the glowing red bars.

"Can you imagine!" Brona shrieked at Geraldine. "He was going to betray his profession, his calling as a teacher. He was going to betray the trust that exists between student and teacher, between scholar and peer, betray all the others who have gone before. Sell out his own ethics and theirs— and for what? For what? For sex!

"And I suddenly saw that but for one oversight all my work, all that I'd sacrificed, would be like dust, like ashes in my mouth—for the rest of my life! There was no turning back, I tell you.

"This loathsome creature had crawled in here and dirtied everything I believed in, had dirtied my work, and in the end thought he would bring me down, thought he would have me, as he had all the others before me, thought that I was like that slut Ariadne." Brona's voice was hoarse.

"I saw it all immediately. He thought I was getting a drink. Me! I walked behind him and saw his head bent, his shoulders slouched, warming his filthy self at my own fire! I picked up the statue Daddy had given me years ago." She looked steadily at Geraldine now. "You remember it, Ger? The Apostle John standing on a marble base?" Ger nodded, transfixed and white.

"I took it and smashed it down on the back of his filthy skull. And it was over. The whole horrible episode was over."

"Oh, my God," murmured Geraldine as she crossed herself. "Oh, Brona . . ."

Brona sat down and leaned her elbows on her manuscript without seeing it.

"And all this time you've watched us running around, here in your flat and upstairs. And all this time you've answered the police and me and whoever else asked . . . as coolly, as cold as death?" James was bitter, but he was deliberately goading her.

"Indeed. It was even amusing sometimes. The newspaper reports of Shaw's suicide, on the ferry? You remember, James. I found that quite amusing. But you were even more so."

"Then tell us how you did it. For that was your real triumph, wasn't it? Deceiving us, all of us."

"I gave it a lot of thought, James."

"As is your way," he said, playing her game, but speaking the truth, too.

"I was lucky in one essential thing. The Conroys were away. Once I established for myself that I could leave Shaw's filthy body in their house, the rest fell into place."

"But Brona, how could you possibly have managed to do all this yourself?" cried Geraldine. "You?"

"You never knew me, Ger. You . . . I'll tell you, and perhaps at last you will see how resourceful—"

"How strong?" added James.

"Indeed . . . how strong I am. I planned to move the body upstairs, as I said. But I could not have any traces of it here. First I stripped the body completely and washed all the blood away. Fortunately there hadn't been much, a little from his nose and ears and the back of his head." Brona's voice was toneless, her eyes seeing again what she was reciting.

"I placed the body in one of those large polyethylene bags people use for trash. I thought that was fitting at the time. Then I dragged the body to the foot of the stairs." She laughed suddenly, looking at James.

"You were so funny that day, James, when you came in here with your great discovery of the coal hatch. I pitied you then."

"Did you?" said James, but his tone was detached.

"I slept a little that night, but when I awoke it was not yet light. I took the key Mrs. Callahan had given me—yes, James, you were on the right track then."

"More than that, Brona. The estate agents who handled the sale of this house to the Conroys verified that there had been three original keys. You see, I can do research, too."

"When, when was that?" she snapped.

"Last Friday, I think it was," he said casually.

"Well, then, you know the rest." She stopped abruptly.

"What? What is the rest?" cried Geraldine.

"The Conroys had been gone barely a week when Brona took her key to the front door and entered their house. She was thus able to unlock, from their side, the door at the top of the stairs here. The door you used to eavesdrop at."

Geraldine's eyes fell before his, and she sat down at the table. James moved restlessly about the room, disturbing the cats.

"Then she returned down here and unlocked the door from this side. She proceeded to drag the body up this flight of stairs, and then up the much longer flight of stairs to the Conroys' bedroom. It must have been a hell of a task. I would not have thought she was capable of it until I lifted her bike from her hands the other day. Brona's strong . . . and hatred made her stronger."

Brona nodded, listening without looking at either Ger or James.

"And the fact that she had so much time, under no pressure, undisturbed by the Conroys—yes, that, too, was significant. She put the body in the Conroys' bed. . . ."

"And what a beautiful irony, don't you agree, James? That filthy Shaw had no idea that he was sitting in the ground floor of his old lover's house. No idea that her bed would be his own deathbed. I thought of it as I was dragging the body up the stairs. Shaw naked in her bed! To think! It would have been enough for them to find any corpse in their precious house, but to think that it was Shaw's. Oh, I set the cat amongst the pigeons, didn't I? You have to admit that, at least. They thought they were so safe, so secure. Harry and Ari—oh, how 'cute'. They were so superior. Gloating over their silly, meaningless careers, their house, their *things*. After I laid him in the bed I walked about the room. More of their possessions. That's when I saw the golf trophy, with the marble base, so like the Apostle John." Brona's voice faded momentarily.

"And to think that Shaw and Ariadne had been lovers! It was bound to come out when the police investigated. With one blow I'd struck at Shaw, and at them and their self-satisfied marriage. I nearly burst for want of someone to tell when I found out from Harry that morning the police had arrived."

"You were laughing at us, Brona."

"No, no, no. It was much more than that. Such feelings were petty. No, I was bursting with pride—it was wonderful, you see. You—all of you—overlooked me as a suspect. And why? Because you underestimated me. You've all underestimated me, all my life."

Her voice was starting to crack with tears, but she composed herself. "It was a wonderful feeling. But worrying, too. I had lost almost forty-eight hours over Shaw. I had to hoover the whole route his body had taken, and then I had to wash the floors. I went over it and over it so no physical clues would be left. And then there were the clothes and the luggage. The ferry trip, the campsites . . . so time-consuming! I lost so much time, so much valuable writing time. . . ."

Geraldine, moved to see her friend seemingly bewildered, went and sat beside her, leaning her arm across the back of her chair as Brona sat bolt upright, rigid and controlled.

"I think, Brona," James said at last, "that I can actually understand why you killed Shaw." The eyes of the two women flicked over at his face.

"Once I suspected you I was persuaded of some academic motive. I put the pieces together all right. Funny enough, it was the visit to Connemara, to Aherne, that did it."

"Yes, I assumed so. The word you used, 'funny,' is apt, because I had no idea that Aherne had had any contact with the American, Drake, whom Shaw had told me about. Yet again one of those coincidences one meets in life," said Brona. "Perhaps that was the largest irony of all—that I brought with me a witness to what I had already killed to conceal."

"Then it did strike you that I was a potential witness to this information that you were only just assimilating?" said James, genuinely curious.

"It did then, and later . . . but I didn't believe you'd be quick enough to pick up on it," she said simply, dismissively.

"I see." James paused, thinking. "What I want to acknowledge here, among ourselves, was that it was only now, when I heard you speak so passionately about Shaw, about your work and how he sullied it . . . well, I can see that it was in a sense a crime of passion. You were defending your cub, your baby, for your thesis was like your child—the only one you were likely to conceive and bear. This man was assaulting your child, your very life, your integrity, all you stood for, all you believed in. And you struck him down in a terrible rage."

Brona nodded, and Geraldine with her.

"But why, for God's sake, why did you strike down Ariadne Conroy?" His voice was ice cold, his own rage and distaste barely controlled. "Why take the life of another? Shaw, perhaps: a bizarre set of circumstances that brought your world crumbling down. You were fighting to save it. But why Ariadne?"

Brona's high peals of laughter split the air.

"Oh, God, how typical! How bloody typical. That's who you're really concerned about, isn't it? Not Shaw, not me, not even your client Harry. No, Ariadne Conroy. You were no different than all the other men."

"Ariadne Conroy was my client, Brona," James almost shouted. "She was about to be charged with a crime that you committed!"

"I know, it was so beautiful. The wonderful irony, the beautiful coincidence. And I had used to believe that only in fiction did such beautiful composition of events take place. And here I was proved wrong. How trite to say that truth was stranger than fiction, but it was. It is."

"Answer me, Brona. I will know."

"Oh, this is funny, too, James. Of course, it happened after that party and the fight I overheard, the one you kept on at me about, thinking you were ever so subtle." Her eyes laughed at him. "In the pub, that first night? You thought you were being the artful sleuth, leading me, asking me key questions. And you, too, Geraldine. Putting in your bits here and there, and as usual flirting with James, as with anyone else in trousers." Geraldine went white to the lips, her lipstick garish against her pallor.

"Stop it," she murmured, but Brona didn't hear her.

"Of course I'll tell you, James. It will be a lesson to you. After the now-famous party and the quarrel Ariadne hung about the house. Harry was out a good deal. I was always aware of their patterns, and I knew something was up. I was working at home on that Monday afternoon, typing my secondary bibliography. . . ." She stopped suddenly, flipping through the manuscript at her elbow, preoccupied in checking some alphabetized listing. James grew cold, and not with rage this time.

"Where was I? Oh, yes, she could probably hear me typing. I heard a loud knocking on the door at the top of the stairs. That was good, don't you think? I went up the stairs and unlocked the door on my side. Ariadne was standing there smirking.

" 'So that's how you did it,' she said immediately. I admit I was taken aback. I went down the stairs, and she followed. Ariadne had figured it out long before any of you men: you, Harry, the police. She was clever. And she had the advantage, of course, of knowing that she hadn't killed Shaw. The rest of you let that get in the way of your thinking. She knew that Shaw was a professor of literature, and she knew I was a literature student. That was the first connection she'd made. She guessed the connection was an academic one. But of course she couldn't know what it was, so she made—for her—the logical assumption that I was sleeping with Shaw to get a job in England, either at his college or at some other college where he had connections." She laughed mirthlessly.

"That was typical, too—of Ariadne, I mean. That she would think of sleeping with men to get ahead. She didn't even ask me the details. Just stood there accusing me. Said I had killed Shaw to prevent him from exposing me somehow. It was despicable, really, to have her accusing me in my own home. For a moment I wanted to tell her how wrong she was, that I'd killed Shaw, but for such very different reasons. But she wouldn't have understood. A woman like that couldn't understand me or my life, my beliefs. No more than you, Ger." She suddenly swung around, inches from Geraldine's stricken face. "You are just like her, you always were, with your flirtations, your men, your lovers. What would you know? You're more like her than . . . ach!"

Brona jumped up as though her words were disgusting in

her mouth. "All women are like you, Geraldine. And all men like Harry! Fools, fools, trailing after such women. Or else"—she paused dramatically, looking at James, and lowered her voice with hatred—"or else they are like you, James Fleming, the real traitors, because men like you betray the gifts of the mind, of the intellect, twist them, use them, abuse them, and finally pervert them!"

James was shaking, but he did not respond. The table was between them. Geraldine held her hands to her face.

"It was quick," Brona said at last. "Is that what you want to hear, James? And it was easy. I had denied everything, of course, but I was so demure she was taken by surprise. As a consequence she said she'd give me a little time to consider going to the police, or even to you. Yes, she said that. She said she'd already telephoned you, but that you were away. And then she left. I think she knew better, but she let sentiment get in her way.

"That evening I watched as Harry went out around seven, all dickied up. I knew it would be one of those long client things he goes to. I waited and then went up and let myself in very quietly at the front door. The whole house was lit up, lights in every room. And I could hear voices and music, almost like a radio, only the same thing over and over. It was fun going around her precious house, touching her beautiful ornaments, her silly trophies. I put yet another one of those trophies in my pocket, and eventually I followed the sounds and went to her door upstairs. She was engrossed in listening to some tapes of a radio or television commercial. She was very startled to see me, alarmed that I'd let myself in. I lied and said she'd left the door unbolted on her side. She asked me if I had reconsidered, and I said yes, but it was a terrible burden. I couldn't get his death off my mind. I asked her if we could talk a little. She agreed. I spoke a little about my work. She couldn't seem to focus on that." Brona's smile was bitter. "Then I lured her—I suppose that's the correct word—into the bedroom with a promise to tell her why I'd put Shaw in her bed. That was her key question. Well, it was for all of you, wasn't it? Her own bed!" Suddenly Brona's tone was exultant. "What symmetry, what poetic justice!"

"Oh, God," James barely murmured.

"We were standing at the bed. I asked her if she would just draw down the covers. Oh, she was so indulgent, almost chatting that it would soon be over, that I'd feel better when I'd confessed. Confessed? What a religious word from someone so secular!" She paused as though struck by some new insight.

"And then you struck her with . . ." James prompted.

"Yes, with the golf trophy. One blow. Again so little blood. And then I simply laid her out on the bed she'd so neatly turned down. Of course, it was only the box spring, you know. The mattress was gone. She'd covered it with a set of sheets. And then I covered her. Laid her out, isn't that what the Catholics do?" She looked archly at Geraldine.

"And you hid the trophy?"

"It was still early, James. I guessed Harry wouldn't be back. I looked for a good—incriminating—place. You see, they were so predictable in their habits. A box of trophies in the attic. Four short steps . . ."

"Why no fingerprints?"

"Oh, I had my handkerchief. I learned a lot when the police investigated my flat, James. I'm a quick study, as they used to say in the old novels." She laughed. "But don't you secretly admire the symmetry of it, James? Using the trophy to kill Ariadne. Didn't that mirror so beautifully my earlier theft of the golf trophy from her room? Tell me—I don't know for certain—don't the police still believe Shaw was killed with that missing golf trophy? And not with poor Daddy's St. John the Apostle? One of the patron saints of writers and students, right, Geraldine? Poor Daddy—with his leanings towards the other side." She shook her head.

James was hanging on to detail, trivial detail, as his mind swirled. "You mean to tell me that after you'd killed Shaw and placed his body in the bed, you actually considered what in the Conroy's house resembled the murder weapon you in fact used?" His voice was rising to a shriek, and he saw Geraldine's face suddenly looking at him, suddenly frightened at his loss of control.

Brona didn't seem to notice, and she answered mildly, "Yes. You forget, James, how methodical, how orderly are my habits of mind. They never desert me.

"Tell me, James. Don't you think that the parallelism of the two bodies in the same bed has all the qualities of the internal structure of an ode? You seem to know your Keats very well."

James was galvanized by her detached, conversational tone and was propelled by it into rational thought. He paused for but a moment.

"That's it, Brona," he said levelly, firmly. "It's over, it's all over. You are too intelligent not to understand that."

Brona looked at him suddenly, leaning against the sink, her eyes alight with intelligent, possibly rational curiosity.

"Isn't it better this way?" asked James.

"What way, James?"

He was startled by her challenging tone.

He repeated, "Isn't it better now that you've spoken of these . . . events? You are relieved of your responsibilities." He trod carefully. "You won't have to go into an assemblage of your peers and—well, dissemble."

"You mean lie, don't you, James?"

"Yes, lie. There have been enough lies!" He wanted to shout.

Brona shrugged, moving towards the table to sit down.

The room was suddenly very quiet, the tension at last dissipating. The cats moved towards her, sensing that relief, and they curled around her legs. Mangan climbed onto her lap, and she stroked her affectionately, almost sadly.

"Ger," James said softly, "perhaps you could make us all some tea, some very strong tea."

ANN C. FALLON

Geraldine stood up stiffly and walked to the sink, where she filled the kettle, staring straight before her. James gauged his next move carefully.

"If you'll excuse me a moment," he said without explanation. Neither Brona nor Geraldine glanced at him as he moved to the rear hall as if to go to the phone, but with two light bounds he was at the top of the interior stairs. Swiftly he turned the snib on the connecting door and waited as it slowly opened to reveal Molloy, with Harry crowding behind him. James and Molloy read each other's faces in mute understanding. Molloy put his hand gently on Harry's chest, pushing his astonished face away as he quietly shut the door behind him and followed James down the stairs on catlike feet.

James paused as he re-entered the kitchen, struck by Brona's aspect, her hands limply in her lap, her face abstracted and forlorn. And yet he hardened his heart, aware as he was of Harry alone upstairs, aware as he was of the empty rooms upstairs where Ariadne had formed and shaped her life, had dreamt her dreams, had felt joy and sadness, had at last felt that deadening pain across the back of her head. Had she known? Was there a fleeting second, as the life breathed from her body, that she knew she was dying, that all the potential was over, the task left undone? And had she known her death had come at the hand of Brona? He looked again at those limp hands and shivered into action.

"Brona?" he said sharply. "I think you have met Chief Inspector Molloy."

"No, actually. I only talked to his various underlings," said Brona bitterly as Molloy circled the far end of the table, inevitably warming the backs of his legs at the small gas fire. "I wasn't important enough to merit his personal attention." She looked at him boldly.

"Miss O'Connell," said Molloy, ignoring her comments, "James Fleming informed me this morning of his suspicions concerning you. He has just now indicated to me that you

268

confirmed those terrible suspicions. I think it would be advisable"—the mild voice was firm—"if you come with me now. I have a ban garda waiting to accompany you in my car."

"But my tea." Suddenly Brona's voice was childlike.

"As her friend and as her doctor," Geraldine interjected with authority, "I would like Miss O'Connell to drink this tea. It's very sweet and will raise her blood sugar to—"

She stopped as Molloy turned to face her, his pale blue eyes almost blank. "As you say, Doctor—"

"Keohane," she supplied.

Suddenly James exploded. "Tea, is it, Geraldine?" His voice was scornful. "We're to sit here drinking tea?" He swung on Molloy, who raised his eyebrows slightly. "I see, I see." Sarcasm emphasized his words. "Aren't we all very civilized now, aren't we bloody civilized?" He drew in his breath with a hiss. "Let me see." He started to saunter, bowing to each in turn. "Why, we have the medical profession represented. And, of course, the ultimate representative of the people, the self-effacing civil servant whose only goal is to restore order and balance when the world is out of joint. Get the reference, Brona? Sorry! Miss O'Connell. You! You are the emblem of the arts—nay, the humanities —all that humanity has struggled to grub up from our miserable existence over the centuries and place above us. And not only that—my, don't we contain multitudes! Not only that, but, my dear Brona, you also represent the teaching profession. Making the world and academia free from the likes of Philip Shaw. And wait, wait! Through you, don't we have religion represented, too? The mild clergyman's daughter, off-spring of the church.

"And then, of course, there's myself, embodying the law. Now surely you can see how the law orders and governs intercourse amongst people, providing all the commonly agreed-upon routes for dealing with one another.

"And here we are, aren't we? All friends together, congenial, about to drink bloody tea—"

"Fleming!" Molloy's voice was lost.

"No, I refuse to act in this charade. This act that's been going on so long. It wasn't enough that you killed Ariadne, brutally, coldly, planning it all here in your *den!* You know what really gets me in this whole thing—what gets me? That you went to her funeral. That you stood in that church, that you stood at her grave, that you shook hands with Harry with the same hand that deprived him of his wife, his own life, as it were. And then you sat and chatted in my car all the way back to town. . . ." James broke off, breathless.

"What bothers you most, James?" Brona said, her eyes hard and her tone scathing. "I think it's your own ego that's screaming here. That you didn't see through me, hmm? That you drove Ariadne's murderer home from her grave and flirted with her—yes, flirted with her, in your insufferable arrogance, right here in what you call my den." She looked calm and smug, and he wanted to strike her.

Geraldine brought the tea to the table without looking at James.

"No, I tell you, no!" He was glowering at Brona.

"Oh, shush, James," said Geraldine, still not looking at him.

"Has no one been listening? We're all acting here. Now you in the role of kind friend. My God."

"You strip away the conventions you've just enumerated, Fleming, and you'll have chaos. I should know." Molloy carefully lit his pipe, sitting back, leaving his tea untouched.

"Are you participant or audience?" said James, turning on him.

"Audience, no doubt."

"Indeed," interrupted Brona. "Always on the sidelines, aren't you? As James said, representing ordered society. What society? There is no such thing as civilized society. Merely, but importantly, there are the fragments of blazing insight, flashing brilliance in the centuries of mediocre intellectual darkness. Like O'Suillebhean in the west of

Ireland, in the dark, ignorant countryside. Flashing light and beauty . . ."

"Like you, I suppose," murmured James.

"Yes, I illuminated the darkness." She tapped her manuscript. "But no one has recognized it."

"Now we have blasphemy," said Molloy suddenly, "I'll listen to this no more." He stood up.

"A voice from the sidelines of life," said Brona, "at last. Sitting in judgment of what you don't know and will never understand."

"Get your things, Miss O'Connell."

"No, not yet!" exclaimed Geraldine piteously. Her sudden movement startled the cats, and they scampered and fled. Brona jumped up from her chair.

"No, no, come back, my darlings. Please . . ." She stood, her hands hanging limp by her sides, as if her cats' flight had driven home her own reality.

"Who'll look after them, I wonder?" she said rhetorically. She picked up her bulky manuscript and placed it slowly in her satchel as Geraldine helped her with her coat and scarf, for the night without was wild and wet.

Geraldine arranged the scarf around her friend's face, but Brona flicked her head away. "I trusted you, Ger."

Geraldine blushed a deep, sickly red.

Molloy moved to Brona's side as they walked to the small hallway. "My man will be down directly." He looked at James. "I'll expect you momentarily at headquarters so that your statements can be taken down tonight."

Brona turned, hesitating, glancing around her kitchen as though for the last time.

"James," she said. "Surely my plight would make an interesting case to add to your roster." The eyes were mocking, but the voice was serious. James started.

"Not in this life, Brona. Not in this life."

Suddenly they were gone, and as suddenly a palpable emptiness filled the room. Then a car door slammed, an engine engaged, footsteps approached down the stairs and through the open door.

"I'll be securing the premises now, sir," said the uniformed garda.

"Right. Right," said James as he and Geraldine gathered their coats and belongings. They stepped out into the raw night in silence and trod slowly up the stairs to the wet pavement.

They drove the short distance in silence and in silence separated, each to a different room to give their sworn statements. And each with a different grief relived those few hours just past.

The sense of unreality was overpowering as James and Geraldine walked slowly down the fluorescent-illuminated corridors of the central police station. They didn't speak, they didn't touch, their bodies tied in knots of fatigue, their muscles responding only to the desire to be gone, out of this alien place.

James felt nothing except the intellectual realization that after their statements had been taken Molloy had told him the charges against Harry Conroy would be dropped.

An ironic smile curled James's lips. Harry, Harry. He hadn't thought of Harry Conroy in days. But now his duty to this client was done. His client was free. His client who had in these last hours had perhaps had a drink, read the paper, even gone to bed. It had never been Harry. It was Ariadne who had been cleared this night.

The cold fresh air of a bitter Dublin dawn woke him up. And Geraldine, too. She shook herself visibly and turned to look at James. He didn't look at her.

"Shall I call for a cab?" she asked.

"No, please, let me drive you."

They walked despondently to the car, but the air and the streaks of red in the east lighting up the sky and turning as always the tops of Dublin's municipal buildings a pale shade of green, wakened James's spirit.

They paused at the car, both acknowledging what was unspoken between them.

"Why?" he said, not looking at her directly.

"I've been asking myself that, James."

"Why were you so sympathetic to her, Ger, when you had grasped what she had done?" he repeated coldly.

"Why? Why? Because she was my friend, James. For years and years."

"And so you pet her like a sick child!" He was incredulous.

"Yes, because right then she seemed more the victim. Christ! I shared years of my life with her! We . . . oh, you wouldn't understand. A man couldn't understand."

"I'm sick of this!" James exploded. "I am sick of women telling me what I can or cannot understand. You were forgiving her, Ger, after all she had done!"

"And *you* used me!" said Geraldine, her voice low and intense.

"Is this about you now?" he demanded.

"You used me, James. And you did it knowingly. You tricked me into going with you, you tricked me into thinking"—her voice broke with tears—"into thinking that you were—oh God, so kind, so thoughtful. 'Let's cheer Brona up!'" Her voice was sarcastic now, and bitter. "And I trusted you. And she trusted me! James, she never would have let you into that flat if I hadn't been with you. You knew that, and you used me to get to her. Oh, my God, would this night ever have happened if I hadn't gone with you?" She began to cry.

James felt desperate. He hadn't felt this way in a long time. Desperate to be understood, and no one was listening.

"Geraldine," he said at last, sternly, not touching her, "let me drive you back."

"No." She shrugged but didn't leave.

He was grateful for that much.

"Geraldine, she killed two people. One of them you knew fairly well—you lived in her house, for God's sake!"

"Oh, God, I don't know. Brona seemed so bereft. It was as though—she hadn't done it, any of it. Does that make sense?"

"Yes," James said after a long pause. "I've had that feeling before. Perhaps it's when your heart cannot accept what the mind is telling you is true . . ."

"That's it, that's it." Ger almost cried, this time with relief. "It's like when one of my patients has died. At just that point I know he's gone, but I don't accept it. I work on. I've seen the others do it, too."

"The other doctors?"

She nodded, seeking in her handbag for a tissue. He watched her abstractedly, thinking suddenly of his brother Donald, and of how he didn't really know him. Or anyone, for that matter. Fatigue pulled at his body.

"Perhaps, Ger," he said with less anger, "perhaps that's how Brona felt when Shaw killed her dissertation. Her heart could not accept what her intellect—more acute than most—so immediately grasped."

Geraldine nodded, and they got into the car at last. He ran the engine, and warm air flooded the interior.

"Perhaps she was truly brilliant."

"In ways I believe she was." But he didn't say in what ways.

"Molloy was so horrible when he described her as a cold-blooded, calculating killer."

"I'm sorry, Ger." James patted her hand, knowing it would be the last time he ever touched her.

She moved her hand away. "She's sick. Oh, God! I'm a doctor, and I didn't see the sickness when I should have."

"You weren't a doctor with her, Ger, but a friend."

Suddenly there was nothing more to say. They had arrived at the Residents' Hall at the hospital.

"You'd better go in, Ger," James forced himself to say. "Good night."

"Good bye, James." And she was gone.

* * *

"But what was the first thing you did, Fleming, after your expedition to Connemara?" Matt was leaning across the table of James's favourite pub.

"You mean after I'd realized that Brona's story of her thesis being original didn't fit with Aherne's mention of the American?"

"Go on. I am completely befuddled, and not by the drink." Matt laughed, and James did, too, relaxing at last.

"Well, then, first I decided to clarify this issue of the American scholar Aherne had mentioned. I contacted the reference librarian at the National Library with the details I had. It took him two days, but he confirmed that a doctoral dissertation had been written by an American, Drake by name, some twenty years ago. When I had that information it spurred me on. I knew that Brona's dissertation defense was now less than a week away. I moved quickly and learned from the chairman of the English Department at College—who had returned on the Monday, as Brona had foretold—that Philip Shaw would have been the original extern reader on Brona's thesis. Since I told him I was defending Harry Conroy, he didn't question my interest."

"Why didn't you approach Brona directly?" Matt queried.

James paused, slightly embarrassed. "Two reasons, I think, Matt. One was that on the one hand I had respected her and her work, even admired her commitment. I have never believed in anything intangible in the way she did. Secondly, I think after the trip to Connemara I had also become uneasy about her. She was so utilitarian and manipulative with Aherne. Her coldness struck me as ruthless. I suppose I didn't want to show my hand too soon. I wanted to be completely sure, or as sure as I could be."

"You were right. The way you describe it, your theory was just that—a theory," said Matt seriously.

"True, Matt. But then I tried to look at the whole issue from the point of view of Brona as the key player.

"Firstly, it struck me that Brona could have had a

key—the third key—to the front door. She could therefore have had access to the upstairs. That communicating door had nagged me from the very start. How had the body been brought into Ariadne's house? I confirmed from the estate agents that she had had a key—in the past, at least. Of course, it was obvious that she would know when the Conroys were absent. Their absence was crucial to the disposal of Shaw's body in their house."

Matt was dissatisfied. "You seemed to put the case together little piece by little piece."

"You might say that. But I was only patiently working through an idea. And this idea was as vague as some of my others. I decided to look at the next level of questions I hadn't been able to answer."

"The woman at the itinerant camp?"

"Yes. I asked myself—why not Brona, instead of Ariadne or Mrs. Shaw? That solicitous attitude the fortune teller had described fit! She'd helped her father as a clergyman's daughter, handing out charity to the poor of the parish, things like that. She'd have been fully aware of itinerant camps. Perhaps it was in her nature not to throw away good clothes!"

Matt considered for a moment. "Or she was afraid to leave them in the trash to be collected, or worse, picked over by passers-by. What if Shaw's belongings had been found in the Conroys' own bins!" Matt was ever the more realistic of the two.

"Indeed. On the strength of this particular suspicion I brought the photo we'd had taken when we'd stopped to see the steam engine in Castlebar. But none of them could say for certain it was Brona, and none could say for certain it wasn't, either."

"A bit of real detective work there, James, but what about Shaw's manufactured suicide?"

"That issue was very troubling. I'd got it in my mind that Mrs. Shaw could have done it from the Holyhead side, but of course it followed that it could be done in a single day-trip from the Dublin side. I knew Brona had the time to do it, but no proof, of course. I only know now, from her own lips, that she actually did it. She wanted to throw off suspicion. Or so she said."

"Had she got nervous—worried, perhaps?" asked Matt.

"Hard to say. She's so calculating, you see. Listen, this is a girl who looks like a cameo, as though butter wouldn't melt in her mouth. Here, let's order again."

They sat in silence as their pints were delivered.

"I think that she'd got caught up in the ruse. She often spoke about the value and power of the imagination, how only people with imagination were truly alive, truly intelligent. She had also a high opinion of her own intellect. She might well have seen her trip on the ferry as equivalent to a creative act. The trips to the campsites, the trip on the ferry—they were perhaps part of an intricate design, a challenging mental puzzle she was creating. And remember, Matt, at no time was she in real jeopardy of being discovered. She could move with total anonymity and confidence. She did admit on the night I confronted her that she'd enjoyed reading in the papers about Shaw's supposed suicide and had scoffed at the police."

"Then was she also scoffing at you when she let you go to Aherne's with her?"

"That's the irony, Matt. She kept speaking of irony, but that one was the most transcendent of all. She went to see Aherne in all innocence. Even after she'd killed Shaw she didn't or couldn't bring herself to read Drake's dissertation. She went on as before."

"Ah, James! But that's completely logical, both emotionally and intellectually. She killed Shaw and with him killed this unwanted knowledge. She was back to where she was before Shaw had ever spoken with her." Matt grew animated. "It was as though the whole episode never happened."

"I think that's it exactly. Well done, Watson."

"Right, Sherlock," teased Matt.

"To get back to the point"—he smiled—"when Aherne mentioned the American she never missed a beat, never drew attention to it or to her own reaction to this news. She must have hoped I wouldn't notice, or if I did, that it would mean nothing to me."

"And she was almost right!"

"Yes. It was only that night, when I was labouring hopelessly over my notes, that it came back to me, more as an idle question about Brona's personality. It arose as I was reviewing my thoughts on Shaw, puzzling at why he'd come to Dublin, trying to find a reason other than to see Ariadne. I realized that two others in this group of victims and the people surrounding them indeed had something in common! I posited that Brona and Shaw might be connected through their common occupation, both of them being academics, both of them connected with the College here in Dublin, both of them in Dublin at the same time.

"That was when I contacted the librarian, and after that the chairman. When I found that Shaw was to be the extern reader I had the connection between them at last! I spoke to an old friend in another department of College—you'd remember McWhirter—and he explained to me that under the circumstances I described—hypothetically, of course—a candidate's thesis would not be accepted by the examining committee. This meant, of course, that a degree would not be granted.

"And that was it, Matt! It was an awful moment, but I had the motive at last, the reason for Brona to have killed Shaw—because he knew about Drake's earlier work, and because he was in a position to use that information to prevent her from getting her degree."

"And so you figured Shaw had approached Brona. Trying his luck, do you think?"

"It's hard to say. Perhaps he was genuine when he went to speak to Brona. But the remark he made to his wife—that he was going to see an Irish girl when he was in Dublin—leads me to believe that he had something in mind." James heaved a deep sigh. "Shaw's decision, however inchoate, cost him his life. If he'd even waited and spoken to the chairman, or drawn the attention of the committee to the problem with Brona's dissertation either before or at the oral defense, I imagine the whole matter would have been handled internally in the Department. Ach! If he had only abided by the ethics that govern such discourse—do you realize, Matt, he'd be alive, Ariadne would be alive, Harry's world would not have been destroyed, and even Brona might have weathered the terrible blow to her career. Now . . ." James sagged, depression overwhelming him.

"Go on, please, James."

"When I realized she could have killed Shaw—had a valid reason, in her terms, to kill him—then I knew it had to follow that it was also she who had murdered Ariadne. I guessed that Ariadne had stumbled on the truth. The day she called it was to tell me her suspicions, of that I became certain. If only . . ."

"If only you'd rung her back, is that it?"

"Yes. If I'd phoned her back, she'd have told me. I could have approached Brona myself, or Molloy directly with the information."

Matt didn't attempt to tell James not to reproach himself. "I think I understand," he said. "It will be a burden to bear."

"No Job's comforter, then? No telling me things could be worse?" James asked quietly.

"No. It is as you've said. You'll have to live with it."

Their suddenly heavy silence was broken by the arrival of a number of skinny, dirty boys laden with the afternoon newspapers.

"Papuhs!" they shouted in a caterwauling tone. "Thirty-five pence, papuhs!" They moved quickly among the patrons, hawking their wares, swiftly making change with grimy hands. Matt called one over and bought a copy, opening it and glancing indifferently at the headlines of that day.

"Oh, Lord!" he exclaimed, handing the paper to James to see.

James shrugged, half smiling at Matt's reaction.

The headlines shouted in bold typeface: "Double Murder Suspect Charged."

Matt was shaking his head. "Yet another of your infamous cases to hit the papers, I see. How do you stand the notoriety, Fleming?" Matt laughed.

James shrugged. "I don't, Matt. I suppose as a lawyer I have to expect that I'll come into contact with these kinds of events. But it wasn't what I chose, what I wanted when I became a solicitor. Dry and dusty paperwork . . ."

"Safe, secure?"

"Exactly. A desk job. Giving me time to pursue my other interests, like my train travels, like my constantly postponed trip to Peru."

"And yet you've been drawn into, let's say, some very serious situations any number of times. I hardly think it's mere coincidence."

"I've been pondering that myself, Matt. It's been worrying me a bit."

"The thing is, you might consider that there's something in you that attracts you to these—what should I say?— dramatic puzzles."

"Yes," said James slowly. He plucked at the threads of his thick pullover.

"Yes, but . . ."

"But I wonder why. And when I find myself in the situation I dread its outcome. I despair of what has happened, and I despair of what it reveals about other people, their lives, their choices. And I am shocked about what it reveals about myself."

Matt snorted. "And you're still too caught up in that mad poor girl and her convoluted thinking, James. It's over. Let it go."

"In other words, case closed, Matt?" James seemed tired and forlorn. "Indeed it is, and in more ways than one."

"Geraldine, you mean?" asked Matt.

"Right, first time."

"Stands to reason, man. Brona, and all this case represents for you personally, would always stand between you." He stopped, reflecting. "She was true to her name, wasn't she, then?"

"I wondered about its meaning in Irish, Matt. You seem to know it."

"Indeed and I do, James." Matt signalled the barman for another round of stout. "Brona is the Irish for sorrow, Fleming. The Irish for sorrow."

MALICE

DOMESTIC

Anthologies of Original Traditional Mystery Stories

1

Presented by the acclaimed Elizabeth Peters.
Featuring Carolyn G. Hart, Charlotte and Aaron Elkins,
Valerie Frankel, Sharyn McCumb, Charlotte Maclead
and many others!

2

**Presented by bestselling author Mary Higgins
Clark.** Featuring Gary Alexander, Amanda Cross,
Sally Gunning, Margaret Maron, Sharon Shankman
and many more!

And Coming in May 1994

3

**Presented by Agatha Award winner
Nancy Pickard**

616-01

**Available from
Pocket Books**

POCKET
B O O K S